DESTINY

THE FRACTURED KINGDOM

DESTINY

M.L. FERGUS

tundra

Tundra Books, an imprint of Tundra Book Group,
a division of Penguin Random House of Canada Ltd.,
320 Front Street West, Suite 1400, Toronto, Ontario, M5V 3B6, Canada
penguinrandomhouse.ca

Published simultaneously in the United States of America by Tundra Books
of Northern New York, an imprint of Tundra Book Group,
a division of Penguin Random House of Canada Ltd.,
P.O. Box 2040, Plattsburgh, NY 12901, USA

Tundra with colophon is a registered trademark of Penguin Random House Canada Ltd.

The authorized representative in the EU for product safety and compliance is
Penguin Random House Ireland, Morrison Chambers, 32 Nassau Street,
Dublin D02 YH68, Ireland, https://eu-contact.penguin.ie

*Publisher's note: This book is a work of fiction. Names, characters, places and incidents
either are the product of the author's imagination or are used fictitiously, and any
resemblance to actual persons living or dead, events, or locales is entirely coincidental.*

Library and Archives Canada Cataloguing in Publication

Title: Destiny / M.L. Fergus.
Other titles: Tomorrow's kingdom
Names: Fergus, Maureen, author.
Description: Series statement: Fractured kingdom ; 3 |
Substantially revised edition of: Tomorrow's kingdom.
Identifiers: Canadiana (print) 20240514882 | Canadiana (ebook) 20240522133 |
ISBN 9781774886113 (softcover) | ISBN 9781774886120 (EPUB)
Subjects: LCGFT: Fantasy fiction. | LCGFT: Novels.
Classification: LCC PS8611.E735 T64 2025 | DDC jC813/.6—dc23

Library of Congress Control Number: 2024950484

Edited by Lynne Missen (original) and Margot Blankier (updated)
Cover designed by Sophie Paas-Lang
Cover art: Christos Georghiou / Adobe Stock
Typeset by Daniella Zanchetta
The text was set in Adobe Caslon Pro.

Printed in Canada

1 2 3 4 5   29 28 27 26 25

In celebration of second chances.

You are about to enter a dark and dangerous kingdom. Over the course of your journey, you will encounter or hear mention of sexual situations as well as the abuse, kidnap, murder, enslavement, imprisonment, brutal torture, illness, death and grief of people of all ages. The mistreatment and death of animals are also a part of this harsh world. Readers who may be sensitive to these elements, please take note before joining the adventure.

One

"WHAT IN THE NAME of the gods was Persephone thinking going to face Mordesius alone?" demanded Azriel, his blue eyes blazing in the dimness of the harbor shed.

Heart heavy with the secret knowledge that Persephone was not truly alone, Rachel leaned her head against Zdeno's homespun-clad shoulder and said, "You know what she was thinking, Azriel. She was thinking of the terrible things Mordesius would do to you if he but had the chance."

"And what of the terrible things he will do to her?" hissed Azriel, his powerful hands clenching into fists. "Tell me, Rachel: What, exactly, do you imagine Mordesius will do to Persephone when he discovers that she lied about having found the healing Pool of Genezing?"

"We must stay positive," faltered Rachel as a thousand images—all of them hideous—flitted through her mind. "We have to believe that until the Methusian king is come, the Fates will keep—"

The sudden sound of raised voices and many boots clattering over cobblestone some distance down the harbor front caused Rachel to freeze mid-sentence, but it was the look that passed between Azriel and Zdeno that turned her blood to ice.

"What is it?" she whispered fearfully. "You don't think the commotion out there has something to do with us, do you?"

Instead of answering, Zdeno kissed her hard on the mouth. It was the first time he'd ever done such a bold thing, and Rachel refused to think on why he should dare to do so now. Instead, she touched her trembling fingertips to her lips and pressed so close to him that she could feel his compact body coiling with tension. Together, they watched Azriel draw his sword, ease open the door of the shed and peer in the direction of the approaching danger.

The next instant, the handsome Methusian's head turned as suddenly as if it had been yanked around by an invisible string. Bellowing Persephone's name, he flung the shed door wide and dashed out into the street like a man possessed.

"Azriel, what are you doing?" screamed Rachel as she bolted to her feet. "Zdeno, *what is he doing?*"

"Stay back," ordered Zdeno, who was already halfway to the door with his deadly slingshot loaded and whirling above his head.

But Rachel would not stay back, could not stay back! Driven forward by her terror, she reached the doorway just in time to see Azriel cut down the first two snarling New Men who rushed him. He ducked and skewered a third; a fourth would have cleaved his head in two if Zdeno had not scored a direct hit. As the soldier's head snapped back from the force of the stone that had slammed into his forehead, his sword flew out of his hand. Snatching it out of midair, Azriel speared him with it. Then he bounded forward to attack the rest of the charging soldiers. With a blade in each hand, Azriel cut, thrust and parried with preternatural speed while terrified onlookers ran shrieking for cover, and Zdeno did what damage he could without leaving Rachel unprotected.

In a matter of seconds, the street was strewn with black-clad bodies, and Azriel was running for the docks with a bloody sword in each hand and a look of savage determination on his face. He'd not gone ten steps, however, before a seemingly endless horde of New Men began pouring into the far end of the harbor front.

One look was evidently enough for Zdeno: resolutely turning his back on the husband of the princess he'd once sworn to protect, he grabbed Rachel's hand and tried to drag her away. Though half-mad with fear, she resisted. Bracing her heels as best she could against the slippery red street, she screamed Azriel's name.

He checked briefly at the sound of her voice, then again at the sight of the many soldiers who were rapidly closing in on him. For one heart-stopping moment, Rachel thought he was going to turn and fight even though any fool could see that to do so would mean certain death.

But Azriel did not turn and fight.

Instead, he shouted Persephone's name in a voice so anguished that it made the hairs on the back of Rachel's neck stand on end.

Then he turned and ran.

TWO

IGNORING THE URGE to drift back down into the seductive depths of sleep, Persephone fought her way to the surface of consciousness. The sound of Azriel shouting her name seemed to echo in the fetid darkness in which she lay with her hands bound behind her back, but whether it was real or only a dream, she could not say. Her normally sharp senses felt as dull as a cheap blade.

Without moving or opening her eyes, Persephone struggled to remember what had happened to her and to figure out where she was. At first, her efforts produced no clear answers, only called up a series of random images that began dissolving almost as soon as they appeared. Finn standing on an overturned milk pail delivering a fiery harangue to a deaf horse . . . Azriel standing at the edge of a hot spring wearing nothing but his boots and his breeches . . . Fireflies trapped in colored glass jars . . . Wet sand beneath her bare back . . .

A vision of Mordesius reverently clutching a tiny, carved box that contained the so-called proof that she'd found the healing pool melted into a vision of him standing at the threshold of the royal bedchamber, his dark eyes glowing with pleasure as he beckoned her to come forward and see what lay beyond.

Finn.

The truth about the moments before everything went black came back to Persephone in a sickening rush. The sight of her beautiful twin gasping out his last labored breaths; the promise she'd made to fight for the throne that was hers by right of birth. The way she'd eluded Mordesius by escaping through the secret passageway behind the hanging tapestry; the sound of her heart thudding against her rib cage as she quelled the urge to run away and instead turned toward the harbor where Azriel, Rachel and Zdeno were hiding.

Because I desperately needed the shelter of Azriel's embrace, and because even if I could have run away from everything else, there was one thing I could not have run away from no matter how hard or how far I ran, she recalled with a flutter of panic.

Shoving the thought aside, Persephone had just started to replay the memory of being grabbed from behind and having a pungent-smelling cloth pressed over her face when she felt something sink its sharp little teeth into the tender flesh at the back of her ankle. Gasping aloud, she kicked out violently, then tucked her legs up to her chest and rolled to her knees. The instant she did so, the plank floor seemed to tilt beneath her. Thrown off-balance and unable to use her hands to break her fall, she hit the floor like a sack of potatoes and gouged her forehead on the corner of a wooden pallet in the bargain.

I see you still have the grace and poise of a natural dancer, Persephone, said a gently mocking voice in her head.

In spite of everything, Persephone found herself smiling at the memory of the pirate grin that had accompanied those words.

Then she remembered why she'd rolled to her knees in the first place.

Scrambling up into a sitting position, she tossed her wild, dark hair out of her eyes and strained for a glimpse of the thing that had bitten her. As she did so, she felt something warm dribble down her forehead.

Blood.

Drawn by the sight and smell of it, the rat warily crept out of the shadows, dragging its long skinny tail behind it. Persephone lashed out with her feet and snarled threats in a bid to scare the creature off, but her efforts only seemed to excite it. Beady eyes gleaming, it continued toward her. As if inspired by its boldness, other rats—a veritable army of other rats—began creeping out of the shadows as well.

Persephone staggered to her feet. Taking care to stay low and well-balanced, she gave the nearest rat a kick that sent it sailing back into the shadows. The meaty thud with which it landed attracted the attention of half a dozen other rats. While they excitedly scuttled after their fallen comrade, Persephone looked around for the highest spot she'd be able to reach with her hands tied behind her back. Almost at once, she spied two large wooden crates haphazardly stacked against the nearest wall. Pausing for just long enough to send another rat sailing, she staggered toward them and jumped onto the jutting corner of the bottom crate. Jerking her hands up behind her and bending at the waist so that her heaving chest was pressed against the slatted lid of the top crate, she then wriggled, rolled and flopped her way on top of it.

Even before she'd fully recovered from the wave of dizziness caused by her exertions, Persephone set about taking stock of her circumstances. She could not say what had happened or how much time had passed since she'd been rendered unconscious down on the docks. However, the sound of waves splashing, sails snapping and boots stomping overhead told her that she'd somehow ended up in the hold of a ship. That was why the floor had tilted beneath her when she'd first rolled to her knees, and why it continued to rise and fall enough to set her already-queasy stomach churning. It was also why it was cold, damp and so dark that she'd have been as good as blind if not for the slivers of light that bled through those cracks in the hull that sat high enough above the waterline to have gone unnoticed and untarred.

Maneuvering around so that she could press her eye against one of these cracks, Persephone's relief upon seeing that the docks were yet within hailing distance turned to dread when she realized that they were littered with bodies and swarming with New Men.

Breathing hard, she strained to determine if Azriel, Rachel or Zdeno were among the fallen, but it was no use. The swiftly moving ship had already carried her too far away to make out such details. And though it had not yet carried her too far away to be heard, she knew that screaming Azriel's name would be both foolish and dangerous. For if he was still in hiding, the sound of her scream would almost certainly drive him to do something reckless, and if he was dead or gone, he wouldn't hear it anyway.

Persephone's captors, on the other hand, *would* hear her scream, and upon hearing it, they would know that she was awake. She'd thus lose the element of surprise, and since this was one of the very few advantages she had at the moment, she did not intend to give it away.

And so she knelt, still and silent, watching as she was taken farther and farther away from . . . everything.

When she could no longer hear even the faintest sounds from shore and could no longer see the docks for the ghostly mists that had drifted in from the sea, she turned away from the crack in the hull. After noting that her dagger was gone, she spent a few minutes futilely straining against the ropes that bound her wrists and then a few minutes more searching the wall behind her for a nail or sharp edge she could use to saw through the ropes. When she found none, she sat back on her heels to consider what to do next. As she did so, one of the larger rats on the floor below ambled over to the wooden pallet upon which she'd earlier gouged her forehead. Laboriously hauling his greasy bulk up onto the corner of the pallet, he began delicately licking at the blood she'd left behind. The sight did not make Persephone feel any sicker than she already felt; on the contrary, it made her wonder how long it would be before her captors came down to feed and water her. She hoped it wouldn't be long. She was beginning to feel thirsty, and though the mere thought of food was enough to turn her stomach, she knew she needed to eat to keep up her strength. She had no idea what lay ahead, but a lifetime of hard experience had taught her that it was always best to assume that the unknown was a place of deprivation and hardship, where an extra mouthful of food today could mean the difference between life and death tomorrow.

Easing herself onto her backside, Persephone drew her legs up to her chest in an attempt to ward off the chill that seemed to be deepening with each passing moment. A fleeting image of a lovely claw-footed bathtub filled to the brim with hot, perfumed water seemed more like a dream than a memory. Resting her chin on her knees, she shivered in the gathering gloom and tried not to notice the way the small swell of her belly pressed against her thighs. She could not afford to think about that now, just as she could not afford to think about Azriel or about Finn or about the impossible promise she'd made to fight for the throne of Glyndoria.

All she could afford to think about was surviving to see another day.

Persephone felt an unexpected pang of regret as she realized how quickly she'd stopped thinking like a princess and started thinking like an enslaved girl again. Not that she'd ever really thought like either, but she'd started to get used to the idea that—

Eeeeeeeek.

The sudden squeal of rusty hinges wiped all thought from Persephone's mind and set her heart pounding.

Silently scrambling up into a crouch and pressing her back against the hull, she watched the heavy hatch slowly being heaved open.

A moment later, two pairs of black boots appeared at the top step of the ladder leading down into the hold.

Whoever her captors were, they were coming.

Three

WHEN AZRIEL RAN from the horde of New Men at the harbor front, Rachel and Zdeno ran, too.

Indeed, Zdeno ran so swiftly that Rachel was nearly yanked off her feet trying to keep up with him. The head start they had on the soldiers was desperately small, but Zdeno made remarkable use of it. As she flew along, clutching his calloused hand for dear life, Rachel could not help but recall his heartrending tales of a childhood spent being chased through the streets of Parthania by those who despised him for the unusually shaped wine-colored birthmark he bore on one cheek.

Clearly, he'd learned a few tricks along the way.

With the sure-footedness of someone who knew exactly where he was going, he led her and Azriel through alehouses with back windows big enough to dive through, into pleasure-houses with rear exits discreet enough to slip through, down alleys that seemed to lead nowhere, up staircases that appeared as if by magic, over rooftops pitched just gently enough to safely traverse and through nondescript doors that, bizarrely, opened directly onto other streets. And though he did it all at such a pace and for so long that even *his* breathing eventually grew labored, he never wavered, never slowed, never let them get cornered.

For her part, Rachel was so focused on trying to keep up that it wasn't until they staggered into the farthest corner of a neglected graveyard that she realized that the sounds and sights of pursuit had faded to nothingness.

Zdeno had done it.

He'd saved them from death—or worse.

Reckless with relief, Rachel backed him up against the crumbling wall of the nearby crypt and kissed him soundly to express her profound gratitude.

Then she turned to Azriel and said, "What happened back there, Azriel? Why did you run out of the shed like that? What did you see?"

"I saw Persephone grabbed and taken aboard a ship," he replied savagely. "I saw the crew of the ship throw off the ropes, kick aside the gangplank and hoist the mainsail."

"Oh, *no!*" cried Rachel.

"Oh, yes. I saw it all, and I—did—nothing," said Azriel, spitting out the words as though they disgusted him.

"That is not true," said Zdeno, who was still looking rather dazed from Rachel's kiss. "You single-handedly cut down at least a dozen soldiers."

"And then I abandoned her!"

"You didn't abandon her," protested Rachel, sick at the thought of how much more harshly he'd be judging himself if he knew what she knew. "You only ran when you saw that to stay was to die."

As if on cue, the great brass bells of the imperial palace began to toll. The last time they'd done so was seventeen years past, and Rachel felt a chill at the tidings they dolefully proclaimed. Namely, that poor King Finnius was dead and that as his only living relative, Persephone had just become a player—or a pawn—in the dangerous battle for the throne that was sure to follow.

After the bells stopped tolling, there was a moment of stunned silence.

Then Zdeno put his right hand over his heart and went down on one knee. "The king is dead," he said in a voice strained with grief. "Long live the queen, and long live her husband, the prince consort."

Azriel looked almost angry at these words, but all he said was, "I was a fool to run—a fool and a coward." His swords having been tossed aside during their flight from the soldiers, he pulled the knife from his belt and announced, "I'm going back for her. Now, before it's too late."

"It's already too late," said Zdeno gently. "Forgive me, my prince, but you said yourself that whoever took the queen set sail."

"I'm no prince and I never said the ship set sail," snapped Azriel. "I said that the ship's crew had raised the mainsail. The ship may yet be in the harbor."

"And if it is?" said Rachel. "What then? The harbor is teeming with soldiers, Azriel. You just slaughtered their comrades in broad daylight! Do you honestly imagine that, armed with that tiny knife and injured as you are, you'll be able to slip past every last one of them, commandeer a ship and give chase without attracting attention?"

Azriel glared at the dark-haired girl who so resembled his kidnapped wife.

Rachel ignored his glare in much the same way as Persephone might have done. "I'm not saying that we should give her up for lost, Azriel," she said. "I'm only saying that we need to think before we act."

"But if her brother, the king, is truly dead—"

"Then the need for us to proceed with caution and wisdom is all the greater."

"But I made a vow—"

"To protect her with your life," snapped Rachel, her own fear for Persephone rearing up without warning, "not to make her an eighteen-year-old widow by embarking upon a foolhardy suicide mission that has absolutely no chance of seeing her rescued!"

At Rachel's uncharacteristically sharp tone, Azriel's broad shoulders sagged and the wild look in his eyes slowly turned to one of bleakest despair.

"You're right," he murmured, wincing as he palpated a particularly long cut on his arm. "We need to proceed with caution and wisdom.

We need to figure out who took her and where they've taken her, and then we need to come up with a plan to rescue her. And we need to do so quickly, for I fear she is much weakened by the mysterious illness that has plagued her over these last weeks."

"Illness?" said Rachel, hoping she sounded perplexed.

Eyes crinkling in a painful parody of amusement, Azriel said, "Do not attempt to play the fool, Rachel. You're not very good at it, and it doesn't become you, anyway. You know exactly what I'm talking about."

Rachel opened her mouth to dispute this but closed it again at once. Because the truth was that she *did* know what he was talking about. It was him who didn't know what he was talking about. And though she didn't like the thought of telling Persephone's secret, and though she didn't like to give Azriel more cause to judge himself harshly, she liked even less the idea of letting him torture himself with thoughts that on top of everything else, his beloved wife was slowly succumbing to some mysterious illness.

And so, offering up a quick prayer to the gods that she was doing the right thing, Rachel took a deep breath and said, "Persephone isn't ill, Azriel."

"Don't lie to me," he flared, jabbing his finger at her with such vehemence that Zdeno calmly but deliberately reached out and pushed his hand aside. "There's been something wrong with her ever since we left the Island of Ru and maybe even before that. I didn't say anything because I knew she'd only deny it, but I have eyes, Rachel. I know what I saw! The unnatural exhaustion, the nausea, the bloating . . . I've been half-sick myself with worry. And now she's gone and who knows how she's being treated and—"

"Persephone isn't ill, Azriel," repeated Rachel, who cringed only slightly before adding, "she's pregnant."

Four

FROM HER SPOT high upon the crates, Persephone held her breath as she watched the two pairs of black boots descend into the rat-infested hold.

To her surprise, she recognized the men who wore the boots. They were the same New Men who'd delivered a battered Azriel to her palace chambers following the dreadful feast held in celebration of the execution of poor Lord Pembleton's son. On that long-ago night, Persephone had sent the two of them scurrying with a frosty bearing and the threat of the Regent's displeasure. She highly doubted that such tactics would work this time, particularly given that Mordesius had almost certainly given the order to have her kidnapped.

As she was trying to figure out what tactics *would* work, the New Man who looked like a Latin tutor lifted the grimy lantern in his hand higher.

"Where is she?" he asked in a voice that sounded more puzzled than alarmed.

"Don't know," muttered the other one, snatching the lantern from him. The wiry chest hair that spilled from the open collar of his limp, pit-stained shirt looked like a bushy black beard that had mistakenly attached itself to his chest instead of his face.

"We left her on the floor, right there by those crates," reminded Tutor, pointing to the crates upon which Persephone was crouched.

"I know where we left her!" exploded Hairy, rounding on him. "I also know that I said we ought to bind her wrists and ankles and gag her. *You* said binding her wrists would be sufficient. *You* said she'd not regain consciousness until we were well underway."

"I didn't say she'd not regain consciousness," corrected Tutor mildly. "I said I didn't think she'd regain consciousness. And I never said that binding her wrists would be sufficient. I said that I saw no need to bind her ankles because there was nowhere for her to run and that I was reluctant to gag her for fear that if she were to start retching, she'd choke to death on her own vomit."

A pleasant notion, thought Persephone, grimacing.

"Ye gods, I shudder to think what will happen to us if she has escaped," whined Hairy.

Smiling so benignly it was easy to forget that he'd sworn an oath to kidnap and butcher on command, Tutor said, "She cannot possibly have escaped. There is no way out of the hold but one, and we've had two guards posted there since the moment we carried her down here. If she's not where we left her, she must be hiding somewhere."

Visibly relieved by this logic, Hairy undertook a thorough exploration of the hold. He looked behind every barrel, bale and crate. He looked into every nook and cranny. Then he happened to look up and see Persephone perched on top of the crate like an avenging angel about to deliver a message from unhappy gods.

After letting out a yelp of surprise, he demanded to know how she'd gotten up there.

"I flew," she replied, striving to sound scornful in spite of her madly beating heart.

"You did not fly," retorted Hairy.

"I did, too," insisted Persephone, who could think of nothing cleverer to say.

Looking a little nonplussed, Hairy turned to his comrade as though seeking his opinion.

"I'm almost certain she didn't fly," said Tutor in a low voice.

"Oh, for gods' sakes, I know she didn't fly," snarled Hairy, shoving the lantern at him. Turning back to Persephone, he jammed his hairy hands on his hips and said, "We've orders to take you aft."

"So?" said Persephone, lifting her chin.

Hairy scowled. "So you must come down from there at once."

Persephone was about to tell him "no" when, without warning, a monstrous rogue wave smashed against the ship's starboard side, causing the ship to list so sharply that Hairy and Tutor were thrown backward. All over the hold, cargo went tumbling. Though the crate beneath Persephone didn't crash to the floor, it did lurch sickeningly, pitching her forward. She braced herself for a hard landing.

Instead, she had the dubious luck to land directly on top of Hairy.

Gagging at the reek of the bushy chest hair in which she suddenly found her face buried, Persephone rolled off the flailing New Man at once. Staggering to her feet as best she could with her wrists yet bound, she made a dash for the open hatch. She had no idea what she'd do if she made it up the ladder, but if life had taught her to assume that the unknown was a place of deprivation and hardship, it had also taught her that if one was quick, resourceful and just the tiniest bit lucky, solutions often presented themselves.

Unfortunately, before she'd gone three steps, the Tutor managed to grab hold of one of her biceps with his free hand. Instead of struggling against his grip as most girls would have done, Persephone drove her body backward in the hope that the unexpected impact would throw him off-balance, thus giving her a chance to shake free of him. Her plan half worked. He was thrown off-balance enough to come within a hair's breadth of smashing the lantern against a rather flammable-looking wooden barrel, but not enough to loosen his grip on her arm.

"Let go of me," she grunted, as Hairy lumbered to his feet and took hold of her other arm.

They did not let go of her. Instead, they dragged her up out of the ship's hold. Mercifully, they did not immediately drag her off to face Mordesius as she'd feared they would. Nor did they fling her overboard, a treatment she'd received on a prior sea voyage and had not cared for in the least.

Instead, they hustled her across the deck, through an archway and down six steep stairs. At the bottom of the stairs, Tutor flung open a door, and Hairy produced a nasty-looking blade. Jerking Persephone around, he used it to slice through the ropes that bound her wrists. Then he shoved her into the lantern-lit cabin, slamming and locking the door behind her.

Persephone warily surveyed her new accommodations. The cabin was tiny but the air was fresh on account of the open window. The bedsheets looked coarse but reasonably clean. The table was small and heavily scarred, but it was set with an empty mug, a jug of drink and a platter heaping with meat and bread.

Striding over to the window, Persephone grabbed the splintery sill and peered out. A twilight horizon empty of anything but water and sky informed her that however loud she might scream now, there was no one to hear her, and that even if she somehow managed to escape, there was nowhere to go.

Mutinously thinking that this was probably the reason they'd let her out of the hold, Persephone sat down on the edge of the narrow bunk, poured herself a mug of ale and drank deeply of it. Then, mindful of the need to keep up her strength, she picked up a piece of meat and gingerly placed it in her mouth. Unfortunately, the meat turned out to be mostly fat and gristle, and after chewing it for several minutes, Persephone's already-queasy stomach gurgled and turned over.

Hastily spitting out the meat, Persephone felt a familiar flutter of panic as it suddenly occurred to her that it wouldn't be long before her belly was gurgling for a different reason altogether. After all, most babies started moving in the fourth month, and it had been about three since she and Azriel had made love on the beach on the Island of Ru.

Though Persephone tingled every time she recalled the feel of Azriel's bare skin against hers, she fiercely regretted the consequences of what they'd done. When she'd missed her monthly courses the first time, she'd put it down to inclement weather, eating too much fish and the strain of trying to find the healing pool before Mordesius murdered Finn and took over the kingdom. When she'd missed them for the second time, she'd known the real reason for it, of course, but had stubbornly refused to acknowledge it. She was not a girl who'd grown up caring for a boisterous gaggle of younger siblings and yearning for the day she'd have babies of her own. She was a girl who'd grown up knowing all the hardships and terrors it was possible for an overworked, underfed, orphaned, enslaved child to know, one who'd grown up yearning for nothing but freedom and a destiny that belonged to none but her.

On the night the Methusians decided she might be the girl in the dead Seer's sketch of the one destined to set their prophesied king upon his throne, Persephone had seen her dream of freedom without entanglements put at considerable risk. But that risk was nothing compared to the risk posed by a baby. For what was a baby but a lifelong entanglement—a crying, hungry set of fetters?

Unhappily, the knowledge that Azriel would likely be thrilled by the prospect of becoming a father brought Persephone no comfort at all. On the contrary, it made her feel guilty, just as Rachel had made her feel guilty when she'd hinted that Persephone was being irresponsible venturing into the dangerous Valley of Gorg while pregnant. If Azriel hadn't been right there, Persephone would have shouted at Rachel that if the baby was meant to be, the Fates would keep her safe no matter what. It was a foolish notion but one that Persephone had clung to, reasoning that if she came to harm and lost the baby as a result, she'd be able to console herself with the thought that the Fates had never intended it to be born in the first place.

It wasn't that she'd wanted to harm the baby, it was more that she'd wanted the whole situation to just . . . go away.

As she tore into the hunk of dark bread, Persephone shuddered as she recalled stories of girls so desperate to make their situations "go away" that they'd hurled themselves down staircases or drunk potions of unknown provenance or even risked death at the hands of some cackling back-alley hag armed with a filthy scalpel.

Certain that things would be different if it were powerful men who found themselves in such impossible situations, Persephone irritably crammed down the rest of the bread. Then she shoved the platter to one side and pulled from her pocket the rusty key, scrap of lace, rat tail and auburn curl that she carried with her always. Together with the silver necklace that had belonged to her mother and the ruby ring that bore the seal of the Erok royal family, these were her most prized possessions.

Setting all else on the table, she closed her fingers around the keepsake curl. Back when she'd cut it from Azriel's head, she'd believed that she'd never see the handsome rascal again or even know if he lived or died. The possibility that this might yet come to pass was so unbearable that she turned her thoughts to others she had loved. But, of course, she found no comfort there, either. She hadn't seen Cookie in years. Faust had met a hideous end. She had no idea if she'd ever again see Ivan, Fleet or Cur. At best, Rachel was a fugitive on the run.

And Finn was dead.

The Methusians had considered him one of their own, and if Persephone had found the mythical healing pool, he might have lived to prove himself that which they believed him to be: the prophesied Methusian king come to end the persecution of their clan and set things to right for all people. But she had not found the pool, and so he'd only lived long enough to extract from her a reluctant promise to fight for the throne that was hers by right of birth.

Captive and alone but for the child who so troubled her thoughts, Persephone knew she had scant hope of fulfilling her deathbed promise to Finn.

Yet scant hope was not no hope.

And though the Fates had often played their tricks on her, she'd overcome seemingly insurmountable odds before.

Perhaps she would do so again.

Five

AZRIEL SAGGED AGAINST the wall of the crumbling crypt, his eyes wide with shock.

"Pregnant!" he all but bellowed.

Her eyes never leaving his face, Rachel nodded anxiously, while Zdeno calmly gestured for him to keep his voice down.

Wildly, Azriel scanned earth and sky as though in search of the answer to some unuttered question. Then his eyes drifted back to Rachel. "So you're saying . . . you're saying that Persephone is going to have a *baby*?" he spluttered.

Concerned though she was for him, Rachel could not help smiling just a little. "Yes, Azriel," she said. "That is what being pregnant means."

"And you're sure about this?" he pressed, grabbing Rachel by the shoulders and giving her a little shake. "Persephone told you that she was with child—told you but did not tell me?"

Rachel felt Zdeno tense when Azriel grabbed hold of her, so she threw him a quick, reassuring smile to let him know that she was fine. Then she looked back at Azriel and said, "You needn't fret that she told me but not you because she didn't tell me anything. She didn't have to. I know a pregnant girl when I see one, Azriel. Besides, the queen nearly bit my head off when I mentioned it. Why would she do that unless she was pregnant and not ready to talk about it?"

Abruptly letting go of Rachel, Azriel flung his hands up. "I don't even know what you mean when you say 'not ready to talk about it,'" he said harshly, but not harshly enough to mask his bewilderment, frustration, hurt and fear. "What is there to talk about? And why would she not have been ready to do so?"

"There are many things to talk about," replied Rachel, wondering if Azriel was being deliberately obtuse. "As for why she might not have been ready to do so, try to recall that her platter has been rather full of late, what with searching for a mythical healing pool, surviving any number of near-death experiences and trying to save her brother's life. Moreover, even at the best of times, these situations can sometimes be . . . complicated."

At these words, Azriel's breathing got deeper and slower, and he seemed to grow larger, fiercer and wilder. "Persephone is my wedded wife, Rachel. She carries my child and I made a solemn vow to protect them both. There is nothing complicated about *that*," he said, the intensity of his feelings coming off him in waves. "The only complication I see is that my pregnant wife has been kidnapped by unknown villains for unknown reasons to meet an unknown fate in an unknown destination!"

Stricken by the grim, almost hopeless picture he painted and unable to think of a single word of comfort to offer in response, Rachel stared at the ground and said nothing at all.

After a few moments of heavy silence, Zdeno cleared his throat and said, "So, I've been thinking that if we're going to save the queen, the first thing we need to do is get out of Parthania."

"Get out of Parthania?" echoed Rachel, feeling a rush of gratitude that he should speak so matter-of-factly of rescuing Persephone. "But isn't this the best place to start looking for answers?"

"It is," said Azriel, who likewise seemed to have been jerked back from the precipice of despair. "But though we are safe enough at the moment, you can be sure that Mordesius's soldiers are not going to stop looking for us."

"The longer we remain in the city," added Zdeno, "the greater the danger to us and therefore to the queen, for we are the only ones who know she has been kidnapped and is in need of rescuing."

Rachel did not really like the sound of any of that. Nevertheless, she tried to appear unconcerned as she said, "So, how are we going to get out of the city if the soldiers are going to be looking for us, Zdeno? Between my resemblance to the queen and your birthmark, we'll be easy to spot." Pausing to give the large, wine-colored birthmark on his face a kiss to reassure him that she didn't find it ugly, only noticeable, she added, "Swathing our heads in leper bandages won't work because you can be sure that the New Men will be on the lookout for anyone who seems to be hiding his or her face."

"Well, uh, the Council will have to lay the king to rest, and they'll have to do it soon," said Zdeno, who was still blushing furiously from Rachel's kiss. "People will throng to Parthania for the funeral procession, and as soon as the streets are too crowded for Mordesius's soldiers to properly look for anyone, we'll slip through the city gates unnoticed."

"And then?" said Rachel hopefully.

"And then we'll make for my clan's hidden camp," said Azriel. "Cairn, Tiny and Fayla are as brave and clever as they come. Together with them, we'll come up with a plan to find and rescue Persephone and the child."

Rachel smiled weakly, wondering if she was the only one who'd noticed that after fleeing Parthania, the next step in their plan was to "come up with a plan."

Before she could begin to worry in earnest about this, Azriel seized her by the arms so suddenly that she let out a startled squeak and Zdeno nearly attacked him.

"Do you know what I just realized, Rachel?" exclaimed Azriel. "Persephone may not have told me about the child, but after escaping Mordesius, she did not run as she once would have done. She was coming back to me!"

"Yes," said Rachel, smiling in spite of the discomfort of his fingers digging into her flesh.

"She loves me," declared Azriel, sounding triumphant and defiant. "And I'm going to save her—her and the baby."

Though Rachel really did not see how he was going to be able to do so, the fearful orphan girl who'd ever longed to do something important with her life barely hesitated.

"I know you will, Azriel," she said fervently as she reached up to peel his fingers off her arms. "I know you will."

Six

"CAREFUL, FOOL!" snarled Mordesius as one of the many servants assigned to cart his belongings down to the palace courtyard stumbled beneath the weight of a particularly heavy crate. "That crate contains a set of priceless crystal goblets that I mean to give to my royal bride when I am reunited with her five days hence. Do you want to see them shattered to bits before my journey is even begun? Are you *trying* to ruin my wedding?"

"No, Your Grace, of course not!" spluttered the brawny red-headed wretch, his green eyes wide with horror. "I wish you a most joyous wedding and . . . and a long and happy union with Queen Persephone!"

The only thing Mordesius despised more than servants who failed to act like pieces of furniture to be used, smashed or replaced as he saw fit was servants who dared to flaunt their strong bodies and straight limbs in front of him. He stared at this particular servant with eyes that glittered so malevolently that a sheen of sweat appeared upon the young man's broad, freckled forehead.

Mordesius could smell the stench of his fear from across the room.

"See that the crate is safely stowed in one of the wagons," Mordesius said softly, his badly scarred hands clenching into fists. "Pretend that your life depends upon those goblets arriving at their destination intact."

The terrified young man leapt to obey so quickly that he bashed the crate into the doorframe twice before finally managing to make his escape.

Mordesius chuckled at the knowledge that, in truth, the crate contained nothing but rocks, and that it would be painstakingly loaded onto the back of a wagon that would follow an empty carriage going nowhere at all. Shuffling into his bedchamber, he eased his aching body down onto a cushioned chair by an open trunk full of women's undergarments. As he did so, he marveled yet again at how dramatically the world had changed since that terrible moment three days past when he'd entered the king's bedchamber to discover that the royal fool was dead and that his rightful heir, the new queen, was gone. How providential that one of the New Men in the palace courtyard had recognized the queen in spite of her grubby clothes! How fortunate that he'd had the wits to quietly follow her through the watchtower passageway and out into the street instead of trying to abduct her in plain view of the palace! How remarkable that the queen had proceeded down to the common harbor and past the waiting ship, all of her own accord! Though her despicable Methusian husband had somehow escaped capture that day, all in all, things had worked out better than Mordesius could have hoped.

The king was dead. Mordesius was in possession of the queen. She swore she'd discovered the location of the healing pool, and the dewy sprig he'd transferred to the locket that now lay against his thin chest suggested that she'd spoken the truth.

The game was almost over, and Mordesius had won.

Wishing he could see the expression on the face of that high-and-mighty bastard Lord Bartok when he realized that he'd lost because he'd been outsmarted, Mordesius reached into the trunk and pulled out a pair of ivory-colored silk underpants trimmed with lace. As he rubbed them against his cheek, he idly wondered how Queen Persephone was being treated. He hoped she was being treated well, as befitted her station as uncrowned monarch of the realm and future mother of his half-royal sons. He also hoped she was being treated wretchedly, as befitted her base character and as payback for having played him for a fool on more than one occasion.

The knowledge that she was both a royal personage and a lying whore made Mordesius want to groan aloud. He resisted the urge to indulge in fantasies of their impending reunion, however, for he had much to do. He needed to see to the final details of that afternoon's royal funeral and to ensure that all was in readiness for the secret journey he'd be making thereafter. He needed to finish sifting through the pilfered belongings of the queen's dead mother to find those bits of fragrant silk he most longed to see hugging his bride-to-be's curves on their wedding night. He needed to meet with Murdock to ensure that he understood what was expected of him while he presided over the court in the days to come and also to whet his appetite for the vast and bloody assignment that would follow.

And Mordesius needed—nay, he wanted—to visit the one he'd neglected of late. The one with whom he could chat so companionably; the one he could trust with his secrets as he could trust no other.

There was much he was looking forward to telling her.

Seven

"SO YOU'RE CERTAIN THAT you're not with child?" Lord Bartok asked his only daughter.

Little Lady Aurelia shifted uncomfortably, the voluminous skirts of her shimmering black mourning gown whispering as she did so.

"Yes, Father," she replied in a voice that bore no resemblance to the chirping one she normally spoke with. "My courses came yesterday as . . . as I knew they would."

"As you knew they would," echoed Lord Bartok coolly.

Aurelia swallowed hard. "Yes, Father," she murmured, casting a darting glance at her bleary-eyed brother, Atticus.

He was slouched in a cushioned armchair beside her father at the far end of the table; she, herself, was standing.

"I told you before, Father," she continued haltingly. "The king was unable to . . . that is to say, he never managed to . . . I was never properly bedded."

Lord Bartok's lips thinned. "You are the most useless thing," he said in conversational tones. "I arranged everything. Everything. I approached the king. I orchestrated your secret marriage to him. I outsmarted that insufferable upstart Mordesius. All you had to do was lie on your back and get the king to climb on top of you, and you couldn't even manage that."

Aurelia flushed at the baldness of his words. "I tried, Father. I swear I did!" she protested, clutching at her skirts with her bony little hands. "I kissed him ever so passionately. I . . . I promised things that would have made a whore blush. But the king was ill and tired all the time! And though he was ever courteous to me, he never seemed desirous of me. Indeed, I would not be surprised if he was a man who did not feel desire for women at all!"

"He was hot enough for Lady Bothwell," reminded Atticus, "until he discovered that the bitch was his own sister, that is. Perhaps you should have behaved more like a bitch, Aurelia—or more like a sister."

He followed up this clever bit of advice by ostentatiously ogling Aurelia's chest while running his pink tongue along his fleshy lips. He then laughed shrilly and poured himself another goblet of wine.

Lord Bartok eyed his son askance, wondering for the thousandth time how it was that he'd been cursed with an heir who was such a wastrel. Then, shifting his pale blue eyes to his daughter once more, he said, "Are any of your servants aware that you've begun your monthly bleeding?"

"No, Father," said Aurelia with an eagerness that suggested she was relieved to have gotten something right. "I kept knowledge of it from them, just as you instructed."

"Good," said Lord Bartok.

"Shall I continue to pretend to be with child, then?" asked Aurelia, still brimming with eagerness. "Shall I begin padding my bodice and skirts? When the time comes, do you mean to find an infant I can claim to have birthed?"

Wordlessly, Lord Bartok shook his head. Then he turned to his son and said, "Atticus, you will see Aurelia serviced."

Atticus choked on his mouthful of wine. "Serviced?" he gasped as he clumsily wiped wine from his chin with his pudgy white fingers.

"If we can get her with child in the next few weeks, we'll be able to pass the infant off as the dead king's child," explained Lord Bartok. "With luck it will be born early and a boy."

"And you would have *me* service her?" asked Atticus, smiling slightly as he licked the last of the wine from his fingers.

Lord Bartok cocked his head to one side and stroked his trim, silvery beard as he considered the possibility. At length he shook his head and said, "No. You will arrange to have her serviced by a trusted servant who resembles the dead king."

"Even trusted servants talk," warned Atticus.

"Dead servants don't talk, trusted or no," said Lord Bartok. "As soon as Aurelia's monthly time has passed, you will see to it that the chosen servant lies with her as often as he can manage for three weeks, and thereafter you will see that he lies with the dirt and the worms."

"But—"

"That is my decision, Atticus."

Scowling, the drunken young lord snatched up the wine jug and splashed some into his goblet. "Very well," he muttered. "I will arrange matters as you've instructed, Father, but if we are found out—"

"If we are found out, I will be branded a traitor and a whore!" burst Aurelia, who could hold her tongue no longer.

"And if we are not found out, I will be the grandfather of and Lord Regent to the next king of Glyndoria," said Lord Bartok with quiet satisfaction. "I deem that reward well worth the risk."

"But what of the cost?" said Aurelia, her small hands clenched into even smaller fists.

"The cost?" frowned Lord Bartok, not understanding.

"The cost to me!" she cried. "Father, please! My skin crawls at the thought of some lowborn lackey's dirty, work-worn hands upon me. I could not bear to have one peel off his disgusting rags and crawl into my bed. I swear to you, I could not!"

"You can and will do your duty to me and this family by lying with whomever you are ordered to lie with," said Lord Bartok, who was not the least moved by the impassioned pleas of his girl child.

"If you cannot bear to have the man crawl into your bed, crawl into his. But see it done, for you are no use to me if you do not."

Lady Aurelia blanched at this. "That . . . that is not true, Father," she said, her lower lip trembling. "I could yet be of use to you. I am young, comely and well dowered. You could yet make another marriage for me."

Lord Bartok shook his head. "You are used goods, and unless we can get you with child immediately, there will be rumors of barrenness. Besides, in the whole of the realm there is no noble family as great as ours. Unless we are marrying royalty, we are marrying beneath ourselves."

"Then I'm never to marry again—ever?"

"Bear a son who can be called king and you shall have whatever your heart desires."

At these words, Lord Bartok's daughter went very still. "Whatever my heart desires?" she asked, touching her index finger to her still-trembling lip.

Lord Bartok nodded and watched his daughter's face as she considered all the many, many things that her little heart desired.

"Would you give me a king's ransom in jewels, a new gown for every day of the year and an estate of my very own?" she asked tentatively.

"Yes," replied her father without hesitation.

Aurelia made no sound, but her lip stopped trembling and her bright eyes got brighter. Hands fluttering as though unable to decide what to reach for next, she said, "Would you see banished, beaten or imprisoned all those who displease me? Would you find an excuse to execute the innocent, if I so desired it?"

"Yes," replied Lord Bartok.

This time, Aurelia could not contain a burble of amazed laughter. Looking as though she finally understood the power she held in her tiny hands and the full extent of what she stood to gain by cooperating, she cocked her head to one side, bent at the waist like a bird about to pluck a juicy worm from the earth and said, "Would you make me your heir over Atticus?"

Her brother gave a cry of outrage. "Don't be absurd!" he spluttered. "You are the younger and nothing but a girl, besides! Father would never—"

"Yes," said Lord Bartok, his eyes never leaving his daughter's face.

Aurelia shrieked loudly before quickly clapping her hands over her mouth. Almost immediately, she snatched her hands away again so that she could stick her tongue out at her blustering, red-faced brother. Fairly hopping with excitement, she turned toward her father and said, "If you will give me all these things and also promise that I'll not have to truly mother the half-lowborn bastard I bear, I will do my duty to you and this family. So long as Atticus sees the base creature bathed and scented before delivering him to my bed, I will endure what I must to get myself with child as soon as may be."

"Excellent," murmured Lord Bartok. "You are a good girl, Aurelia."

Flushing with pleasure, Lady Aurelia dipped him a curtsey and chirped, "Thank you, Father."

After favoring his daughter with a wintry smile, Lord Bartok dismissed her that she might finish readying herself for her dead husband's funeral.

As soon as she'd flitted from the room, Atticus sprang to his feet, pounded his soft fist upon the table and bellowed, "Father, this is an outrage! You cannot possibly mean to make Aurelia your heir!"

"Of course I don't mean to make Aurelia my heir," said Lord Bartok calmly. "Don't *you* be absurd, Atticus. We needed your sister's cooperation, and now we have it. When are you going to learn the way of things? Sit down and stop behaving like a commoner."

Atticus didn't seem to know whether to look relieved, nonplussed or insulted. "But . . . but what will happen when Aurelia discovers that you have lied to her?" he asked as he plopped back down into his seat.

"Nothing will happen," said Lord Bartok, taking a small sip from the finely wrought silver goblet before him. "As Aurelia, herself, pointed out, if the court was to learn of her actions, she would be branded a traitor and a whore. And with the servant who studded her dead, there will be no one's word but hers that you or I had any part of the scheme."

"She will not be best pleased," said Atticus doubtfully.

"She will keep her displeasure to herself or be ruined," said Lord Bartok with an elegant wave of his hand. "I am not worried about what problems your sister may cause. It is the new queen who worries me."

"Let me get my hands on her, and she'll never worry you again, Father," growled Atticus, fingering the dent in his skull that had been inflicted by the queen's broken-down horse on the night her true identity was revealed. "I owe the bitch a debt that I mean to repay in full—and then some."

"Stop being melodramatic," said Lord Bartok. "How in the world would our cause be furthered by your murdering the dead king's named heir?"

"It would pave the path to the throne for Aurelia's bastard child," said Atticus, stifling a hiccup.

Lord Bartok pursed his lips ever so slightly. "That is true, but only if Aurelia can get herself with child, carry it to term and deliver it alive," he said. "What if she cannot?"

"Well . . . well . . . ," began Atticus. When he could think of nothing further to say, he shrugged and reached for the wine jug, presumably in the hope that another drink would help him come up with a suitable response.

Lord Bartok deftly moved the jug beyond his son's reach. "If Aurelia fails in her task—an outcome I rather expect, frankly, since she hardly has the look of a female built for breeding—there will be no one of the Bartok bloodline who could challenge the queen's right to rule."

"Give me an army, and I could challenge it," boasted Atticus.

Wordlessly, Lord Bartok reached out and slapped his son hard across the side of his dented head. "Don't be an imbecile," he said, ignoring Atticus's high-pitched yelps of protest and pain. "This family does not commit treason openly, and when we finally sit upon the throne of Glyndoria, I will not suffer whispers that we stole it. Besides, the upstart might have something to say about you trying to fight your way to the throne, and I do not have an army to rival the size of his."

"Not even if you take into account the men and horses of those great lords who've secretly promised you their support?" asked Atticus, who was still rubbing his head.

"'Secret' support isn't worth the paper it's written on, Atticus."

The petulant young lord's mouth fell open in amazement. "The great lords put their support in *writing*?" he asked incredulously.

Lord Bartok stared at his son. "No, Atticus," he finally said. "That is my very point. They have *not* put their support in writing. They have openly declared their support for the queen, but they have not openly declared their support for me. They fear Mordesius, and until they are certain I will triumph over him, they dare not openly move against him."

"But how are you to triumph if they will not help you do so?" whined Atticus.

"I intend to make it impossible for them to continue to withhold military support without appearing cowards and traitors to their own kind," replied Lord Bartok.

Predictably, Atticus did not press for details of the plan. Instead, in a tone that betrayed his smug pleasure at having detected the fatal flaw in his illustrious father's reasoning, he said, "Even if your plan works and you manage to defeat the upstart's army with the help of the great lords, Father, it will get us no closer to the throne. As you've already pointed out, they have openly declared for the queen. With Mordesius out of the picture, I hardly think they're going to be seized by a sudden desire to anoint and crown you in her stead."

"I agree," said Lord Bartok dryly. "That is why I'm going to do something far cleverer than continue to challenge her right to rule."

"What are you going to do?" asked Atticus, his eyes drifting past his father to the wine jug.

"I am going to support her right to rule."

"SUPPORT IT?" screeched Atticus, his watery gaze snapping back to his father's expressionless face. "But . . . but you said that the upstart has the queen!" he spluttered. "You said that he means to marry her and get sons upon her! If you fail to defeat him and she is anointed, he will be prince consort. Or even king, should she choose to give him a crown of his own. Either way, his lowborn brats will sit upon the throne after him. How in the name of the gods will supporting *that* further our cause?"

Lord Bartok closed his eyes, pinched the bridge of his highborn nose and breathed deeply in an effort to keep from slapping his son again. "Atticus," he said slowly, "do you remember what I said to Aurelia when she proposed that I make another marriage for her?"

"You said that she was used goods and probably barren in the bargain," snickered Atticus.

"Yes," agreed Lord Bartok. "But I also said that in the whole of the realm there was no noble family as great as ours and that unless we were marrying royalty, we were marrying beneath ourselves."

He looked at his son expectantly. Atticus's gaze had just begun to drift back to the wine jug when he realized what his father was saying.

"You mean to steal the queen away from the upstart, don't you?" he blurted, sitting bolt upright in his chair. "You mean to . . . wait, do you mean to marry her to me?"

Lord Bartok chuckled softly. "No, Atticus, if need be, I mean to marry her to me," he said. "I'd sooner rule through Aurelia's bastard than have to contend with a royal wife who may wish to have a say in the running of the kingdom, but I intend to keep my options open. That is why, while I continue to push the nobility to rise against Mordesius, you are going to liberate the queen from his clutches. After you have done so, you will deliver her to my country estate, there to reside as my honored guest until we determine if Aurelia has succeeded or failed in the task she has been set."

"And if she has succeeded?" asked Atticus, who'd resumed slouching.

"After the upstart's army has been annihilated, I will command the most powerful fighting force in the realm in addition to possessing the dead king's sister and his so-called son," replied Lord Bartok. "When I present these facts to my fellow noblemen, I am confident they'll agree that my grandson should be anointed king, I should be declared his regent and the dethroned queen should remain my honored guest until the end of her days."

"And if Aurelia has failed?"

Lord Bartok shrugged. "I will marry the queen to whom the great lords and I have already declared our support. In doing so, I will become prince consort, but only until such time as I am able to demonstrate to my new bride that it is in her best interests to give me a crown of my own, that I might be called king."

"You are old enough to be the queen's grandfather," said Atticus with the slightest of sneers. "What will you do if she does not care to marry you?"

Lord Bartok tilted his head slightly in acknowledgment of this possibility. "She will be made to speak her vows—at knifepoint, if necessary. She will then be bedded before witnesses that she may never claim that we are not truly man and wife."

Smirking at the thought of the one who'd dented his head brought so low, Atticus said, "So, my men and I are to follow the royal carriage when it sets out upon the morrow, then?"

"No," said Lord Bartok with a chuckle. "The upstart thinks he can outsmart me, but he is an arrogant, lowborn fool. To be sure,

I will send men to follow the carriage—but only so that his spies do not suspect that I know it's nothing but a ruse."

"A ruse?" said Atticus in bewilderment.

"I have it on excellent authority that instead of setting out by carriage tomorrow, late this night the upstart will board a ship bound for northern waters," said Lord Bartok. "Though I have not been able to determine its final destination, it will undoubtedly follow in the path of the ship that carried away the queen three days past. Prior to this afternoon's funeral, you will make arrangements to have Aurelia serviced. Immediately after the funeral, you and your chosen men will board a ship of your own, this one hidden in a cove just beyond the mouth of the royal harbor. When the upstart's ship sets sail this night, yours will follow it at a distance that ensures you are undetectable to all but the keenest eye. Where his ship docks, so, too, shall yours. If he thereafter travels overland, buy horses and follow him to his final destination, wherever that may be. There, you will surely find the queen being held captive. Do what you must to rescue her. If you can kill the upstart while you're at it, so much the better, but remember that securing possession of the queen is your main objective."

"I will, Father," said Atticus even as a vaguely calculating look flitted across his soft-featured face.

Lord Bartok considered his son for a long moment. Then he said, "Atticus, do not get into your head the idea that you ought to wed and bed the queen yourself."

Looking as guilty as a child caught filching sweetmeats, the young nobleman wildly cast about for something clever to say, but all he could manage to come up with was a blustering "Father, I would never!"

"I'm glad to hear it," said Lord Bartok calmly, "because if you did, I would do far, far worse than disinherit you."

At these words, Atticus's wine-reddened face got considerably redder. "For gods' sakes, Father, I know—"

"Good," said Lord Bartok. "Go, now. Prepare for your journey, then dress for the funeral. And when you take your place in the procession this afternoon, Atticus, remember to look sad. The dead king was your beloved brother-in-law, after all."

Eight

AS ZDENO HAD PREDICTED, people thronged to Parthania from the surrounding countryside to pay their final respects to the king. From their hiding place, Rachel could hear the noise of the restless crowds that had packed the streets along the funeral procession route.

"Is it almost time to go?" she asked Zdeno nervously as she smeared her already grimy face with yet another handful of camouflaging dirt.

"Almost," he replied, carefully smoothing a final layer of pale clay over his birthmark before leaning forward to give her a kiss on the mouth.

Rachel smiled, grateful to have had these past three days with him, even if they had been spent hiding out in a crumbling crypt. While it was true that he'd scared her half to death on that first night by promising that no one would come looking for them on account of the flesh-eating nightwalkers who were rumored to inhabit the graveyard, it was also true that he'd bravely declared that no earthbound demon in existence would be able to feast on her while *he* was around. He'd then single-handedly transferred the crypt's dusty corpses to another resting place before hurrying off to steal bandages, candles, food and drink enough to last them for several days. Not only that, but upon his return, he'd insisted upon taking over the task of sponging clean the wounds on Azriel's arms, chest and abdomen. Despite the fact that he was even gentler than she had been, Azriel had groaned and grimaced and gnashed his teeth so agonizingly that Rachel had feared his wounds must be far worse than they looked. But by the next morning, he'd seemed none the worse for wear. And now, as they prepared to make their escape from the city, he looked as fit as ever and a thousand times fiercer, the thought of his kidnapped wife and their unborn child ever upon his mind.

"So it is agreed?" said Azriel as he tucked his auburn curls beneath the filthy piece of linen he'd found under the sugarberry bushes that grew behind the crypt. "If one or two of us fall or are captured this day, whoever escapes will find my clan and tell them what has happened to Persephone?"

"It is agreed," said Rachel, even though she quailed at the prospect of carrying on alone.

"It is agreed," said Zdeno shortly.

"Good," said Azriel, his blue eyes glowing from beneath his makeshift scarf. "Let's go."

Zdeno's prediction that the streets would be so crowded that Mordesius's soldiers would find it impossible to properly look for anyone turned out to be exactly right. Unfortunately, his prediction that they'd be able to slip through the gates unnoticed fell alarmingly short of the mark.

"We're going to need to create a diversion," said Azriel as he stared at the half-dozen New Men who stood, sword in hand, scrutinizing anyone who ventured anywhere near the gates.

"What kind of diversion?" asked Rachel unhappily.

Before Azriel could answer, the funeral procession came into view at the far end of the street. Leading the way was Mordesius himself. Rachel shivered when she caught sight of him. Dressed as he was in a hooded robe of black velvet and astride an enormous black stallion, he did not look like a mourner at all.

He looked like Death.

Directly behind him was a wheeled platform drawn by six white horses. The platform was covered with a flowing purple cloth so long that it swept the cobblestone street. Centered upon the cloth was a silver-handled coffin crafted from polished ebony and heaped with white lilies. Surrounding the platform were black-clad, poleax-wielding New Men whose job it clearly was to keep people away. Even so, every few seconds someone dressed in low-born rags or worse darted out of the crowd to call a blessing on the dead king, touch his coffin or to toss a garland of wildflowers atop the lilies.

Rachel had not really known King Finnius, but seeing how well the common people had loved him, and knowing how well Persephone had loved him, she felt her eyes begin to sting.

Before she could shed even a single tear, however, there came such a piercing screech from three feet above her head that she instinctively ducked. Squinting skyward, she was amazed to see Ivan, the hawk that had followed Persephone so far and so well. He had a plump hare clutched in his talons, and even though she knew it was impossible, it seemed to Rachel that as he swooped around, he was staring right at her.

"What is he doing?" she whispered agitatedly as Zdeno sidled closer and the people around them looked up and pointed.

"I think he thinks you're her, Rachel," muttered Azriel through his teeth as he scowled at his feathered nemesis. "And I think he means to give you a little gift."

Rachel's knees turned to water at the thought of the dangerous attention Ivan's generosity would surely attract. But if the hawk had meant to give her the hare, he sadly misjudged the trajectory it would take when he released it. Because instead of landing anywhere near Rachel, it landed directly on top of the coffin, scattering the white lilies and homemade garlands, and setting the nearby New Men shouting in alarm. Yanking hard on the reins, the furious former regent wheeled his horse about to see what was going on.

As he did so, Ivan flew straight at him.

Ducking, Mordesius glared up at the creature that had dared to attack him only to find himself treated to a close-up view of that same creature releasing a large splatter of droppings as it cruised by. Fortunately for Mordesius, only a few in the crowd actually saw him suffer this indignity, the rest being riveted by the pandemonium that had been caused by the scattered lilies. For even before the first one had hit the cobblestones, a dozen quick-thinking lowborns had run forward, eager to get their hands on a memento of the day. Alarmed when they realized that they'd be left empty-handed if they didn't act fast, hundreds of other lowborns had immediately stampeded toward the fallen flowers. Unfortunately, there were only an armful of lilies, and many of those had been trampled underfoot in the initial rush. People got angry. The New Men bellowed and lashed out, but they were hopelessly outnumbered. Shoving matches were breaking out now, and fistfights, too. Those who cared nothing for the lilies but were glad of an excuse to vent their discontent with life were jumping into the fray; those too fearful of reprisals to do so were pressing forward in their eagerness to see what was happening. Several people near the front fell, screaming as they went down. The crowd surged ahead, forcing the New Men guarding the king's coffin to scramble on top of the platform to avoid being crushed. Outraged that Mordesius's hated soldiers would dare to desecrate their beloved king's funeral bier by treading upon the purple cloth of royalty with their filthy boots, the people nearest the platform grabbed for the soldiers' legs. The platform began to rock dangerously as the mob tried to topple the soldiers while at the same time avoiding their wildly swinging poleaxes.

Just when it seemed that the poor king's coffin would be dumped onto the street, Mordesius unsteadily stood up in his stirrups.

Splatter still dripping from his face, he jabbed his finger in the direction of the half-dozen New Men guarding the city gates and screamed, *"Don't just stand there, you useless imbeciles—go help them!"*

His face half shadowed by the makeshift scarf, Azriel turned toward Rachel and smiled for the first time in three days.

Nine

BLISSFULLY UNAWARE that he'd made possible the escape of the man he hated more than any other in the realm, Mordesius saw the funeral procession concluded, the king entombed and the low-born rabble-rousers rounded up and punished.

Hours later, he descended into the vast labyrinth of fetid tunnels that lay beneath the palace. Setting a flickering torch in the rusted wall bracket of one particularly stifling dungeon cell, he called out, "Have you missed me?"

The woman whose chains were shackled to the weeping wall at the back of the cell said nothing, only stared unblinking into the shadows.

Undeterred by her lack of response, Mordesius shuffled over to examine her more closely. The one the king had called Moira was now so thin that she could only truly be thought of as a cow if she were a cow in a land of terrible famine. Her ragged shift hung in rotting tatters that left precious little to the imagination. Her hair was falling out in clumps, her nails were torn, she was caked in her own filth, and her skin was covered with oozing sores and festering rat bites.

"You look a little peaked," frowned Mordesius. "Have you been eating your greens?"

Lifting up the hem of his fur-trimmed velvet robe, he used the toe of his crumpled left foot to nudge a silver platter heaped with fresh grass and clover closer to her. It was a little jest he'd thought up months ago, and though he'd been compelled to add regular rations of moldy bread to keep her from starving to death before he'd finished having his fun with her, he'd left standing orders that she should receive fresh "cow fodder" on a daily basis.

When the dead king's nursemaid failed to respond to his question about eating her greens, Mordesius sat down in the armchair he'd had placed just beyond her reach. Leaning back and sighing loudly to show how comfortable the chair was, Mordesius said, "I lied when I said you looked a little peaked. In truth, you look disgusting, and you smell worse. But I didn't come here to give you a lecture about your personal hygiene. I'm afraid I have some tragic news. The king—"

"Is dead," rasped the nursemaid, her colorless eyes flicking toward him. "I know. I heard."

Mordesius felt a hot stab of disappointment at her reaction. Or, rather, at her lack thereof. "What do you mean 'you heard'?" he snapped. "Who could you possibly have heard it from?"

The cow shrugged her bony shoulders.

Mordesius eyed her malevolently, wondering if he ought to beat the answer out of her. Deciding he did not wish to give her the satisfaction of thinking that he truly cared what she heard from whom, he hastened on to impart the second bit of information he'd been looking forward to sharing with her.

"I wish I could tell you that he died an easy death, but he did not."

The nursemaid said nothing for a long moment. Then she cleared her throat and said, "You smothered him, then?"

"The gods smothered him—drowned him in his own stinking juices," replied Mordesius, wrinkling his nose to emphasize how nauseating the king's bloody phlegm had smelled by the end. "And do you know what else? Aside from informing me that he was content to let you die in agony if it meant furthering his own pathetic little plans to defeat me, the king never once mentioned you.

Not in casual conversation, not during his fever dreams, not even as he gasped out his final, tortured breaths."

The cow did not seem the least bothered by the revelation that she'd been sacrificed and forgotten. On the contrary, she actually seemed to glow at the knowledge that her beloved king had fought the enemy of his people to the very end.

"His Majesty was kind and brave," she said with quiet satisfaction. "I hope he was given a proper state funeral."

"He was, but only because the great lords insisted upon it," replied Mordesius, his mood darkening dangerously. "If it had been up to me alone, I'd have dumped the fool's naked corpse onto the slag heap and been done with it."

"And what of His Majesty's twin?" asked the nursemaid, her chains clinking softly as she shifted upon her bed of rotting straw. "Does she yet wander the kingdom seeking the healing pool, or did the poor thing return empty-handed only to watch her brother die?"

At the mention of the healing pool, Mordesius's dark mood vanished and his spirits soared. Clutching the locket that contained the miraculous leafy sprig that showed no signs of wilting, he said, "The queen returned to watch her brother die, but she did not return empty-handed."

"Perhaps not empty-handed, but not with a map to any healing pool," guessed the cow.

"Oh?" said Mordesius, striving to sound nonchalant. "What makes you so sure?"

"Besides the fact that your body is yet twisted and scarred from the burns that nearly killed you? The queen loved her brother," said the nursemaid. "If she and her Methusian lover had found a pool of waters with the power to cure his cursèd cough, His Majesty would be alive today."

Mordesius's dark eyes bulged with outrage.

"How many times do I have to tell you that the cockroach is not . . . the queen's . . . *lover!*" he shrieked, kicking out at the silver platter so hard that it overturned with a clatter, scattering grass and clover across the muck and slime.

Startled, the cow jumped; in the shadows, unseen things scuttled about, squeaking in distress. Pushing himself to his feet so violently that he wrenched a muscle in his back, Mordesius snatched the cow's own crochet needle from the pocket of his robe and started toward her. She turned her head and shrank against the wall, but it was no use. With the aid of a nearby bar of iron, Mordesius knocked her over. Then, grunting with exertion, he knelt heavily upon her bleeding temple and pressed the crochet needle against her fluttering eyelid.

"And even if the queen has defiled herself with the cockroach," he hissed, his guts twisting with the hateful knowledge that she almost certainly had, "it matters not because she will soon be mine, and he will be dead."

The cow started to struggle. "What do you—?"

Her words were cut short by a hideous, high-pitched scream from a nearby corridor.

"Do not be alarmed," soothed Mordesius. "It is only the sound of General Murdock delivering instruction to a certain redheaded imbecile on the subject of what happens to servants who fail to take proper care of the belongings of their betters." He paused to grind his knee harder into the side of her head. "Between you and me, I confess that I once doubted Murdock's loyalty and had thoughts toward destroying him, but that is all behind me now—for the moment, at least. Now, what were you asking?"

"I was asking . . . I was asking what you meant when you said that the queen will soon be yours," stammered the cow, panting with pain.

"I meant that within the hour I shall board a ship that will take me to her," explained Mordesius. "On the very day of our joyful reunion, she shall take me as her wedded husband in a union so ironclad that even the great Lord Bartok will not be able to tear it asunder."

"And . . . and if she will not take you?"

"As you, yourself, have come to learn, obedience can come easily or with great difficulty," murmured Mordesius, applying so much pressure to the crochet needle that he could feel the eyeball beneath getting ready to pop. "The queen will take me, one way or another. And then she will *take* me, and she will do so with vigor and enthusiasm, or I will know the reason why."

"I pray the gods help her," murmured the cow as a single tear squeezed out from under her eyelid.

Mordesius laughed loudly. Then he leaned very close and whispered, "Save your prayers for yourself."

Later that same night, while the rest of the palace's inhabitants slumbered, Murdock rowed Mordesius out to a nondescript vessel that had quietly sailed into the royal harbor less than an hour earlier.

As the rowboat came alongside the hull, Mordesius stood, grabbed the rope ladder that the soldiers had let down and awkwardly began to climb. By the time he reached the top, he'd almost slipped twice, and he was trembling so hard that one of the soldiers had to drag him over the deck rail by the back of his robe. Tight-lipped with rage and humiliation, Mordesius said not a word but lurched after the captain to the cabin that had been prepared in anticipation of his arrival. It was stuffy and small and not nearly as sumptuously appointed as the living quarters to which Mordesius had become accustomed.

"Will there be anything else, Your Gr—"

Mordesius closed the cabin door in the captain's face. Exhaling heavily, he let his head droop and gave his aching neck a useless massage. After a moment, he shuffled over to the tiny window. As he pulled open the shutters, he heard the captain quietly calling out the orders that would see the ship on its way.

Mordesius felt the cool breeze upon his hot face; he watched the starlight play upon the rippling water of the open sea.

Absently lifting his hand to the locket about his neck, he decided he would not think about how he'd just been dragged over the deck rail like a sack of bad potatoes. Nor would he think about the nursemaid's haunting assertion that if the current queen had truly discovered the healing pool, the dead king would yet be alive.

Instead, he'd think about the woman he'd shortly take as his bride. He'd recall how she'd made him feel in those first heady days after he'd found her hiding in the alley pretending to be the intrepid Lady Bothwell—how she'd tantalized him by flaunting her unusual appetites and treating him as a man like any other. He'd remember the sight of her being forced to the floor at his feet and the way her breasts had heaved as she'd struggled and begged, even if it was for the life of the cockroach. He'd savor the memory of her promising that she'd do *anything*, and he'd indulge himself in imagining that she'd willingly do anything and more, once she could be made to see how much the two of them actually had in common and how great they could be together.

Most of all, he'd believe that Queen Persephone had found the healing Pool of Genezing and that the only reason she'd not saved her brother, the king, was that she'd returned to Parthania too late to do so. He'd believe that the royal fool who'd thought to thwart him had thus died in agony, knowing that if he could've clung to this world for just a few days more, the long life of health and happiness he'd ever dreamt of would have been his.

For the sake of his beautiful bride-to-be, Mordesius hoped this last part was true.

For if it was not, not even the gods themselves would be able to save her from his wrath.

Ten

AFTER SEVEN DAYS on stormy seas, the ship on which Persephone was sailing finally dropped anchor in a deserted cove.

Flinging open the door of the small cabin in which she'd been imprisoned, Hairy ordered Persephone to follow him. When she refused to comply until he told her where they were going, he shoved her face-first onto the bunk and sat on her while he bound her flailing hands and kicking feet. Then, ignoring her threats and insults, he carried her up the steep stairs to the ship's deck, tied a rope around her and lowered her down to Tutor's waiting arms. By the time Tutor had gotten her safely stowed in the bow of the small rowboat, Hairy had made his way down the slippery rope ladder that hung from the ship's rail. Throwing off the rope that tethered the rowboat to the ship, he seized the oars and rowed through the choppy water until they slid up onto a sandy beach. Tutor immediately reached for Persephone, and when she tried to bite his hand, he slapped her hard across the side of the head.

"You shall pay dearly for that someday," she vowed in a voice that she hoped was dripping with menace.

In response, Tutor dragged her out of the rowboat by the scruff of her neck. Whistling cheerfully, he hauled her over to a waiting carriage, dumped her inside and slammed the door. Thus consigned to the gloom, Persephone felt the carriage lean sharply to the side as the two New Men climbed up onto the driver's seat.

And then, with the crack of a whip, they were off.

The road along which they traveled was so badly rutted that Persephone bounced painfully hard upon the carriage floor and had to clench her teeth to keep them from rattling. She was soon longing for the moment they'd stop for the night, but they didn't stop. Instead, they galloped onward through the gathering darkness and the ever-deepening chill. Cold, hungry, thirsty, fearful of what Mordesius had planned for her and haunted by the lonely sound of the wind that never stopped blowing, Persephone slept fitfully. Sometimes she dreamt. Mostly these were nightmares—flashing images of a tiny blue baby with translucent hands, of auburn curls sodden with blood, of blue eyes that stared unseeing at the screaming black carrion birds that circled overhead.

Once, though, she dreamt that Azriel was not dead but as alive as he could be and lying on his side right behind her. The dream was so real that Persephone could feel the weight of his strong arm holding her close, could feel his warm breath tickling the back of her neck. With a soft sigh, she felt the tension and apprehension begin to leach out of her, felt herself responding to his nearness.

Safe, she thought as she rolled over and tilted her head for a kiss. *We're*—

The coach hit a particularly large rut then, jarring her awake.

She didn't sleep again after that. Instead, she lay awake in the cold darkness, trying not to think at all. After what seemed like an eternity of doing so, an almost imperceptible thinning of the darkness beyond the coach's one tiny window heralded the arrival of a new day.

Still the coach raced on.

Mile after dreary mile, hour after exhausting hour, all through that second day they traveled, stopping only once, briefly, to allow Persephone to eat, drink and (mercifully!) tend to the call of nature.

Nigh about dusk that day, just when Persephone had begun to wonder if Hairy and Tutor meant to drive her around until her teeth rattled right out of her head, an agitated voice from somewhere up ahead shouted for them to halt and state their business. The coach slowed, and Tutor called out that they'd come to deliver a package of royal sweetmeats. Sounding considerably more agitated than before, the voice bade them enter at once. The whip cracked and the coach started forward again. A moment later, it passed beneath a gate that must have been ponderous judging from the way it creaked and groaned as it was cranked up.

As it crashed shut behind them and the sound of hooves on cobblestones filled her ears, Persephone's already pounding heart began to pound harder. Suddenly deciding that she didn't want to face her unknown fate lying down, she flopped and wriggled her way into a sitting position. Maneuvering herself as far from the door of the coach as she could, she pressed her back against the wall and pulled her knees up to her chest.

If I am quick, resourceful and just the tiniest bit lucky, a solution will present itself, she reminded herself as the coach clattered to a halt. *I just need to be patient and wait for it to do so.*

The next instant the door was flung open. Grabbing Persephone by the legs, Hairy yanked her forward so roughly that her skirt rode up. Gripping her naked thigh hard to keep her from squirming, he cut the rope that bound her ankles. Then he hauled her out of the carriage and into the deserted courtyard.

So much for a solution presenting itself, she thought grimly as she beheld the sprawling castle that rose up before her. Built in the shadow of a barren mountain at the very edge of a high cliff, it was constructed of blackest stone. Except for along the cliff edge, it was protected by a wall so thick that a brace of oxen could have pulled a wagon along the top if it hadn't been for the iron spikes set every few feet. Several of these spikes were topped with heads that appeared to have been dipped in tar to slow the process of decay; the rest stood empty and waiting against a backdrop of low clouds scudding across a stormy sky.

The shiver that swept through Persephone at that moment had nothing to do with the cold.

"He . . . he's here, isn't he?" she asked, fighting to sound brave.

"No," replied Hairy as the massive iron door at the top of the granite steps slowly and silently swung open as if by its own accord. "But he will be. Soon."

Eleven

BACK IN PARTHANIA, General Murdock was doing his best to adjust to his temporary role as ruler of the city.

"I'm sorry, Lord Bartok, but I cannot permit you or anyone else to leave the imperial capital at this time," he said for the umpteenth time. "As I have already told you, His Grace Mordesius ordered me to keep the city gates shut until he returns with the queen."

"And as I have already told *you*, your orders mean nothing to me," replied Lord Bartok, casting a sweeping look around the Council table at his fellow noblemen. "Mordesius's right to power died with my royal son-in-law's final breath. Who is he to think that he can tell the great lords of this realm what they can and cannot do? Who are you to think that you can do so?"

"I think I am the man who commands the thousands of soldiers who patrol the city and guard the gates," replied General Murdock as he reached up to give his long, thin nose a scratch.

Lord Bartok's eyes narrowed imperceptibly but all he said was, "There are rumors of an outbreak of the Great Sickness in the city. My daughter Aurelia carries the king's son in her belly; if she were to fall sick and the child were to be lost, the realm would surely suffer."

Recalling Mordesius's command that he at least *attempt* to be diplomatic in his dealings with the nobility, General Murdock refrained from asking Lord Bartok why the royal midwives had not yet been called upon to confirm the so-called pregnancy. Instead, he said, "Such a loss would be a tragedy for you and yours, of course, my lord. However, you must understand that it would not be an event of consequence for the realm. The late king named his sister, Persephone, as his successor, and your fellow lords have publicly declared for her."

"Some have privately declared to me their belief that if the king had been aware that his wife was pregnant, he'd have set his unborn child before his sister," said Lord Bartok.

"But he did not set his unborn child before his sister," said General Murdock as he carefully smoothed a stray strand of thin, colorless hair back from his sloping brow, "and so the princess is queen, and my Lord Mordesius shall be prince consort—or king."

"We shall see," muttered Lord Bartok with a shrug.

At these words, General Murdock gave the greatest of the great lords the same calm, blank-eyed stare that had preceded death for so many. "Careful, my lord," he said softly.

Lord Bartok held his stare without flinching. "I only meant that many things can happen between the death of a king and the anointing of his successor."

"Indeed," said General Murdock, smelling liver.

The late evening Council meeting did not last long after that.

As he moved through the torch-lit palace corridors toward his next appointment, General Murdock kept to the shadows as much as possible to avoid the unwelcome feel of eyes upon him. He thought about how much more difficult it was to be a man of words than it was to be a man of action, and about how much riskier it was.

Coming to a halt before the door of a storage closet not far from the chambers assigned to the more distinguished members of court, General Murdock checked to make sure no one was watching, then opened the door and slipped inside. Navigating across the closet easily in spite of the darkness, he crept behind a stack of old barrels, slid aside a loose piece of paneling and stepped into the low passageway beyond. The passageway smelled of worms and mice, was dark as pitch and so narrow in places that he was forced to turn sideways to carry on, but none of this bothered General Murdock in the least.

Indeed, the passageway was the kind of place in which he'd always felt most at home.

At length, he arrived at the location of his next appointment. Pressing his beady eye against the pinprick hole in the wall, he watched the dead king's birdlike little widow flit about her chambers issuing orders to the harried servants who were helping her prepare for bed.

General Murdock had watched Lady Aurelia often of late. He did not believe that she was with child but he did believe that her lord father was up to something and that she had a part to play in it. As he pondered what that part might be, he watched her stand still for long enough to allow her maids to undress her.

General Murdock felt no stirrings of desire at the sight of the young noblewoman's naked body because he was not a man to feel stirrings. He was not a man to feel desire either, except perhaps for the desire to fulfill his duty.

Duty.

For General Murdock, it ever came back to duty.

As he listened to Lady Aurelia dismiss her maids, General Murdock frowned at the memory of how the men under his command had recently failed in their duty to capture the queen's husband. He did not like to think what Mordesius would have done if he'd not been able to assure him that the Methusian was doomed anyway. Years of hunting Methusians had taught General Murdock that in times of danger, they always returned to the safety of their hidden nests. Unfortunately for this particular Methusian, his nest was no longer hidden or safe. General Murdock had discovered it while tracking the queen during her quest for the healing pool. Its secret location had almost died with him when he'd suffered a ghastly belly wound in the Great Forest, but he'd somehow managed to survive, and prior to returning to Parthania a fortnight past, he'd sent a dozen highly trained soldiers to slaughter every man, woman and child in the camp.

Watching Lady Aurelia now as she turned from side to side before her full-length mirror, cupping her small breasts in her hands and examining her childlike body from every possible angle, General Murdock thought about what he *hadn't* told Mordesius. Namely, that the report confirming the destruction of the nest had not arrived in Parthania at the expected hour. Indeed, it had not arrived in Parthania at all. Though it was only a few days late, General Murdock was beginning to think—

A knock at the door of Lady Aurelia's outer chamber interrupted his thoughts. Intrigued as to who could be calling upon an unmarried noblewoman so late at night, General Murdock watched as Lady Aurelia wrapped a black satin dressing gown tightly around her tiny body and hurried into the adjoining chamber to answer the door. A moment later, she strode back into General Murdock's field of vision. Behind her trailed a tall, dark-haired young man dressed in faded Bartok colors. Stopping abruptly, Lord Bartok's daughter whirled around, stepped toward the young man and took a deep sniff. The expression on her face informed General Murdock—and, no doubt, the young man—that she did not find his scent pleasing. Nevertheless, with a toss of her golden curls, she threw off the dressing gown and climbed between the sheets of her big bed. Lying flat on her back as stiff as a wooden doll, she deliberately turned her face to the opposite wall. The young man hesitated for only a moment before slowly removing his own clothes and climbing in after her.

As he impassively watched the young man set to work, General Murdock felt pleased to have discovered what part Lady Aurelia was obviously meant to play in her lord father's plans. Setting aside the question of what to do with this information, he turned his thoughts back to the overdue report from the Methusian nest. Though the most likely explanation was that the messenger carrying the report had been delayed or waylaid, General Murdock decided to dispatch another battalion of soldiers to the nest immediately.

He did not wish to give Mordesius cause to question his loyalty, and besides, if all went according to plan, His Grace would shortly return to Parthania with a royal bride.

And General Murdock could imagine no wedding gift his master would find so welcome as the headless corpse of the Methusian who'd once dared to call himself husband to the queen.

Twelve

PERSEPHONE WASN'T SURE what she'd expected to find waiting for her inside the forbidding black castle. A pair of rusted manacles dangling above a belching pot full of bubbling oil and deep-fried body parts, perhaps, or a rack upon which Mordesius would stretch her until her limbs popped from their sockets and her body was broken beyond repair.

Whatever Persephone had expected, it certainly wasn't *this*.

"Are you sure this is where you're supposed to take me?" she asked dubiously.

The one-footed ancient who'd laboriously ushered her up the winding staircase to the top of the turret silently nodded, so Persephone hesitated for only a second more before stepping through the open door.

The round chamber was as cozy and welcoming as it could be. The rug in the center of the room was at least an inch thick, snowy white and so soft that it could only have been made from the wool of the Panoraki's beloved mountain sheep. From the high, beamed ceiling hung a five-tiered circular candelabra crammed with so many candles that the room was bright and the sweet scent of beeswax hung heavy in the air. To Persephone's immediate right was a crescent-shaped table. Most regrettably, it was not loaded down with platters of food. Instead, upon its gleaming surface sat the amethyst pendant

Mordesius had given her a lifetime ago, two crystal goblets and a heavy crystal decanter filled with red wine. About ten paces past the table were the room's only windows. Each was as tall as a man and made of heavy glass decorated with crisscrossing strips of black. From where she stood, the only thing Persephone could see when she looked out the windows was the vast, windswept plain at the bottom of the cliff upon which the castle had been built.

Promising herself that the moment she was alone she'd open a window and check the outside wall of the turret for handholds, Persephone turned her attention to the left side of the chamber. Next to a generously pillowed canopy bed hung with gauzy white curtains was a privacy screen. It was also white, save for the delicate design of swirls and teardrops painted upon it in blackest ink. Draped over the screen was a gown of royal purple that shimmered in the light of the fire that crackled in the nearby hearth. On the floor before the fire sat a sturdy wooden tub lined with a white sheet and filled to the brim with steaming water; beside the tub stood three serving women of indeterminate age. One held a silver comb and matching hairbrush, another held several sponges, a washcloth and a drying sheet, and the third clutched a basket of jars and vials that undoubtedly contained soaps, creams, oils and perfumes.

Abruptly realizing that there could be only one reason Mordesius wanted her bathed and scented, Persephone was struck by a wave of nausea so violent that she was nearly sick on the spot. All at once, she didn't know if she had the strength to continue fighting in the hope that, against all odds, things would work out in the end. Though she wasn't even sure what a happy ending would look like, she could not help recalling the pretty little thatch-roofed cottage Azriel had once described to her. The one with the yard full of scratching chickens, the pond stocked with fish and the oak tree with the swing hung from a low branch so that on warm summer days Azriel could push her—and later, their babies.

I no longer seek a destiny that belongs to none but me, thought Persephone as her throat tightened and her eyes began to sting, *and yet that is exactly the destiny I fear I shall have, for I am in a place where no one will ever find me, and no one but me shall feel Mordesius's cold hands upon their skin, and no one but me shall have to endure—*

Steady, m'lady, came Azriel's whispered voice in her head.

At the sound of it, Persephone's heart turned over. Closing her eyes, she saw him gazing up at her as he'd done on that fateful night they'd first entered Parthania. She'd been dressed as a highborn lady; he'd been dressed as her servant. She saw his beautiful auburn curls being ruffled by the warm wind; she saw the calm, expectant expression on his handsome face. It told her that he had no doubt she was brave and strong and clever enough to do what had to be done; it said that he was just waiting for her to get on with it.

Without thinking, Persephone straightened her back and lifted her chin. As she opened her eyes, she reminded herself that a warm bath and a glass of strong wine beat dangling by her wrists from a pair of rusted manacles any day. And though it would seem that Mordesius intended to ravish her, he wasn't ravishing her now, and many things could happen between now and that future moment when he sought to place his hands upon her.

Turning to the old man, Persephone said, "I know you are Mordesius's servant, but I am your queen and I need your help."

When the old man said nothing, only gaped at her, Persephone strode across the chamber to where the three women stood. Recalling the kindness and great bravery that had been shown by Martha, Neeka, Anya and Reeta, the servants who'd tended her when she'd played at being Lady Bothwell, Persephone smiled encouragingly at the women who stood ready to tend to her now.

Then she glanced down and her smile froze on her lips when she noticed that, just like the old man, each of the women was missing most of one foot.

"What happened to your feet?" blurted Persephone.

Two of the women just looked at her. The third opened her mouth to reveal a gruesomely amputated tongue before pantomiming having her foot chopped off and her tongue snipped out.

So that no matter what Mordesius does to them, they cannot run and they cannot cry out, thought Persephone with a shudder.

Thinking that she couldn't imagine anything worse, Persephone looked away only to see that half-hidden behind the privacy screen, on the floor beside a chair heaped with women's undergarments, were a pair of impossibly high-heeled purple slippers, a pile of cut rope and a riding crop.

Refusing to dwell on the possibility that whatever Mordesius had planned for her might actually be worse than having her tongue snipped out, Persephone considered the possibility of using the riding crop to try to fight her way past the guard at the bottom of the spiral staircase. Deciding that she'd never get past him without a blade, she turned to the old man and said, "Can you fetch me something to eat? I'm partial to large hunks of meat carved thin before my eyes."

Blinking at the oddness of her request, the old man pointed first to the tub, then to the dress, then to the closed door. Then he pantomimed shoving food into his mouth.

"You'll bring me food once I'm bathed and dressed?" asked Persephone.

The old man shook his head and jabbed his finger more insistently at the door.

"I'm to dine elsewhere once I'm bathed and dressed?" said Persephone.

The old man nodded enthusiastically.

"With Mordesius," she guessed.

The old man nodded again, though less enthusiastically this time, as though he wasn't entirely sure he was supposed to be telling her all this.

Persephone folded her arms across her chest. "And what happens if I refuse to bathe and dress?" she said. "What happens if I refuse to dine with him?"

The old man pointed first to himself, then to the three trembling women. Then he drew his finger across his throat.

"You'll all be *killed*?" exclaimed Persephone, letting her arms fall to her sides.

The old man nodded and then pantomimed ripping off his own head and jamming it down onto a spike.

Persephone hesitated, but only briefly. A show of defiance was not worth four lives, and besides, if she refused to cooperate, Mordesius was unlikely to respond by sending up a juicy haunch of beef and a nice sharp carving knife. More likely, he'd send up Hairy to strip her, bathe her, dress her and drag her down to dinner.

Or else he'd leave her to starve.

And so Persephone dismissed the old man, called for wine and set to work preparing for an evening with her enemy.

Thirteen

ELSEWHERE IN THE black stone castle, Mordesius sat in one of two red-velvet-covered armchairs set before a blazing fire.

Shifting in his seat, he fingered the locket that held the dewy sprig the queen had given him, and he thought about how she would be forced this night to reveal the location of the healing pool. After a moment, he noticed a particle of dust on the furred hem of his long purple robe. Grunting softly with the effort, he leaned over and brushed it off. When he sat back up, he carefully smoothed and patted down his thick, glossy hair. He crossed his left leg over his right leg. He crossed his right leg over his left leg. He crossed his left leg over his right leg again.

Then, feeling unaccountably agitated, he pushed himself to his feet and slouched over to the dining table. Though it was long enough to seat forty comfortably, this would be the first evening ever on which it would seat more than one. As usual, he would sit at the head of the table.

On this occasion, the queen would sit at his right hand. On future occasions, when they dined in private as man and wife, she would sit at her proper place at the far end of the table. When they dined in the Great Hall at the imperial palace in Parthania, she would sit beside him on a throne he was determined would be no grander than his own as king.

For tonight, however, Mordesius felt that a more intimate seating arrangement was called for.

After carefully examining the place settings to ensure that all was to his satisfaction, he lurched back over to the armchair and sat down. Taking a deep breath to expand slightly his thin chest, he straightened his back, squared his uneven shoulders and held his head as high as he possibly could. After only a few moments, however, his neck began to ache so badly that he slouched over again and let his head droop. It would not serve to look as though he was trying too hard, and besides, he was already feeling depleted and needed to ensure that when the time came, he'd have the strength and vigor to make her his own, body and soul.

A soft rustling sound across the room caught Mordesius's attention. Looking over, he inhaled sharply at the sight of Queen Persephone framed in the arched entranceway of the dining hall. That she did not look surprised to see him did not surprise him at all; that she was bathed, dressed and coiffed did. Knowing that she had a defiant streak in her a mile long, he'd rather expected her to balk at the idea of doing his bidding. Perhaps grief and terror had finally broken her; then again, perhaps she'd found out what would happen to her servants if she failed to do his bidding and shared the dead king's weakness when it came to protecting useless lives.

Scowling slightly at the thought, Mordesius let his gaze travel upward to the hair that had reportedly been a wild mess when she'd been dragged from the coach earlier that day and which had since been brushed to a glossy shine, twisted, curled and neatly pinned atop her head. Dropping his gaze, he noted with pleasure that she was wearing the gown that he had chosen for her from among her dead mother's things. Shimmering royal purple with real gold stitching, it had generous skirts and cloth-of-gold underskirts pinned in cunning swoops and frills. The sleeves were snug as a second skin from shoulder to elbow, then flared so dramatically that they hung far below the exquisitely shaped forearms over which they were draped.

As for the bodice, it was cut low and set with diamonds. That the gown seemed to fit a bit tight across the chest surprised Mordesius but it did not disappoint him in the least. Indeed, he let his gaze linger upon the queen's bosom for even longer than he normally would have before letting it wander downward. Though he could not see her feet, he knew she must be wearing the high-heeled slippers he'd set out for her. However, it was impossible to say which of the silken undergarments she was wearing—or, indeed, if she was wearing any at all. The possibility that she might not be caused Mordesius's breath to quicken. He did not really believe she'd be so lewd as to appear before him naked beneath her gown but he could not be sure. Though she'd been born a princess, she'd been raised in the gutter. Anything was—

"Aren't you going to offer me a glass of wine?" she asked.

For a moment, Mordesius was too startled to reply. He'd hoped that the queen would sound terrified and broken; he'd thought she might sound strained and desperate. He'd expected her to sound belligerent and hostile.

The one thing he hadn't even considered was that she would sound composed and . . . and civil.

"Wine?" she repeated now as she absently fingered the amethyst pendant that lay against the hollow of her throat—the pendant that *he* had given her.

"What? Oh, yes," blurted Mordesius, feeling flustered.

Jerking his head around so fast that his spindly neck screamed with pain, he snarled for wine. Instantly, one of the liveried servants who'd been standing in the shadows by the wall hobbled over to the long dining table. Filling two goblets from the decanter that had been set out earlier, he carried them over to where Mordesius sat. Mordesius hardly noticed his presence, so transfixed was he by the sight of the queen gliding toward him. Brushing past him and around the servant, she swung her hips gently to settle her skirts and then gracefully sank down onto the cushioned seat of the second armchair. Leaning forward so that her breasts seemed in imminent danger of spilling out of the bodice altogether, she reached for a goblet of wine.

"Thank you," she murmured, favoring the servant with a small smile.

Luckily for him, the wretch knew better than to smile back at her. Ducking his head, he silently handed the second goblet to Mordesius. Then, after bowing deeply, he backed away until he was once again swallowed up by the shadows.

Mordesius watched him go in order to buy time to compose himself. He'd dreamt of this moment for weeks. Indeed, he'd rehearsed what he was going to say and do a thousand times! But now that the moment was finally here, it wasn't unfolding at all as he'd anticipated. Regardless of the reason, the fact remained that the queen had dressed at his behest in the clothes and jewels that he had selected for her. And instead of having to be dragged down here by her hair and tied to a chair that afforded her an excellent view of the severed heads of her murdered servants, she'd come down quietly of her own accord and was now sitting so near to him that Mordesius could feel his chest tightening at the scent of her perfumed skin.

Of course, he knew that she was a lying whore and that he should not be fooled by her tricks. Indeed, he was *not* fooled by her tricks. It was just that he could not entirely forget that when she'd been Lady Bothwell, she'd fluttered her eyelashes at him and flushed at his touch. And he could not entirely believe that it had all been an act. And he could not entirely help hoping that a lifetime spent wallowing in the gutter had made her sufficiently pragmatic that once she understood that she had no choice in the matter of their marriage that she'd reconcile herself to it, or even embrace it. And why shouldn't she? He was rich and powerful and handsome, and as soon as she revealed to him the whereabouts of the healing pool, he'd have the body of a god and prowess enough to make even a nubile young queen forget any other man she'd ever known.

"Why have you brought me here?" she asked now, taking a small sip of wine.

Mordesius watched the movement of her throat as she swallowed. Then, slowly lifting his gaze, he looked deep into her beautiful violet eyes and said, "You know why."

She did not say anything, but she did not look away either.

Mordesius's dark heart sang.

"Your Majesty," he said, grunting slightly as he shifted to the edge of his seat. "I heard how you were dragged out of the coach upon your arrival at the castle earlier, and I want to assure you that the beast who dared to put his filthy hand upon your naked thigh has been suitably punished."

The queen did not say anything in response to this either, but her cheeks flushed charmingly, and her mouth fell open just enough for Mordesius to see her little pink tongue.

She could be feeling anything right now, thought Mordesius exultantly. *After all, she has always been a woman of strange appetites!*

As this exciting thought crossed his mind, hobbling servants began silently filing into the room. Each carried a platter or dish of some kind, and the sight of them made Mordesius's blood boil even though it was he who'd ordered supper served as soon as the queen arrived in the dining hall. Indeed, he'd informed the steward that he'd snip off something a good deal more precious to him than his tongue if he did not see it done. At the time, moving the evening along had seemed a sensible idea, for Mordesius had been exhausted from the ordeal of having made in four days the same journey that the queen had made in seven.

Now, however, Mordesius did not wish to move the evening along. The sight of the queen sitting so obediently before him, the intoxicating scent of her, the way she swallowed his wine and held his gaze—these things had caused his exhaustion to vanish. Now he wanted every minute of the evening to last forever. He wanted to broach the subject of marriage as a lover might—by candlelight, over a fine meal and a goblet of good wine—and these idiot servants were ruining everything! Opening his mouth, he was about to bark at them to get out when he happened to notice that the queen was staring fixedly at one of the juicy roasts that was just waiting to be carved.

Mordesius's furious expression immediately melted into one of oozing solicitousness.

"I ordered supper brought at once because I knew you'd be famished," he said.

The queen tore her gaze away from the roast with apparent difficulty. "I am famished," she said. Looking from one servant to the next, she said, "Tell me, will we be dining alone or will your servants be hovering over us the entire time, listening to our every word?"

Mordesius smiled. "My servants dare not hover, and though they may hear what we say, I can assure you they'll never speak of it."

"Because you have cut out their tongues," said the queen.

"Yes," said Mordesius, his smile fading at the tiny edge in her voice.

The queen offered no further comment, but the fact that she'd commented at all instantly put Mordesius on his guard. It reminded him that although she was a beautiful woman who'd always treated him as though he was a man like any another, she was also a deceitful woman who'd often played him for a fool. A woman who'd laughed in his face when he'd caught her in the arms of a eunuch slave who'd later been revealed to be neither eunuch nor slave . . .

All at once, Mordesius did not care to ease into the subject of marriage.

All at once, he just wanted it done.

Fixing his dark eyes upon the queen, he said, "As it happens, Your Majesty, there is one in the room whose tongue I've not yet cut out." Seeing her blanch, he smiled thinly and added, "I mean one besides you."

"Oh?" she said guardedly. "And who is that?"

"The cleric who shall momentarily perform our marriage ceremony," replied Mordesius with a wave toward the far corner of the hall where the hard-faced cleric and his fully functioning tongue were waiting.

At these words, the crystal goblet slipped from the queen's hand and shattered upon the hearth. Her jaw dropped halfway to her knees, and she looked like what she'd been for most of her life: an ignorant, uncultured, ill-mannered nobody.

Promising himself that as her lord husband, he would do whatever it took to train her out of such detestable lowborn displays of emotion, Mordesius said, "Uniting us in matrimony is the reason I brought you here, Your Majesty. Surely you're clever enough to have figured that out?"

The queen shook her head so violently that she lost a few hairpins. "You tried to get Finn to name you his heir so that you could . . . could kill him and take the throne," she stammered as the unpinned curls tumbled down to frame her face. "I guess I just assumed that . . . that—"

"I wanted the same from you?" Mordesius might have been amused if his insides hadn't felt like they were turning to ice at the horrified look on her face. "Why should I go to all that trouble only to suffer the great lords forever trying to tear me down for my low birth and the weakness of my claim? Why should I content myself with fathering half-noble sons when I can father half-royal ones?"

At the mention of him fathering sons, the queen clutched her belly and looked as though she might faint—or vomit.

Mordesius nearly hit her.

After she recovered, she lifted her chin and said, "What you propose is impossible, for I already have a husband."

Though Mordesius knew this, hearing her speak the words inflamed him almost beyond endurance. "General Murdock told me about your so-called wedding," he hissed through clenched teeth. "However, there is not a single great lord in the realm who would consider it valid, for it was not a real wedding fit for an Erok queen."

"It matters not what the great lords or anyone else might think," she said as she lifted that chin of hers a little higher. "The simple fact is that I have already been wedded and bedded."

The sudden mental image of his future wife lying naked in the arms of the despicable Methusian made Mordesius want to rip someone apart with his bare hands, but he only snarled, "Well, then I am especially pleased to be able to inform you that when General Murdock's men catch your dear husband—"

"*When* General Murdock's men catch him?" The queen inhaled sharply and pressed her hands against her chest. "You mean Azriel escaped capture? He is still alive?"

Cursing himself for having given her this bit of information—this bit of *hope*—Mordesius snapped, "If he is, he won't be for long. General Murdock has dispatched soldiers to slaughter every last cockroach they find scuttling about the nest hidden behind the waterfall."

"No," whispered the white-faced queen, swaying in her seat.

"Yes," mocked Mordesius. "Chances are that in his cowardly flight to safety, your beloved will end up running straight into the already bloodied arms of the General's men. If he doesn't, I intend to offer a thousand gold pieces to whomever brings me him *or* his head. As it is a vast fortune by anyone's standards, I expect that half the realm will soon be out hunting him."

"Please, Your Grace—"

"Oh, so it's 'Your Grace' now, is it?" sneered Mordesius. "Spare me your false displays of respect, Your Majesty. And spare me, too, your heartfelt pleas that you would 'do anything' to save the life of the cockroach. His life is forfeit, as are the lives of every other cockroach and clansman in the realm."

"What do you mean?" she asked, clutching the arms of her chair so tightly that the bones of her hands stood out.

Mordesius stared at her hands, imagining how exquisitely good it would feel to kiss them . . . and break them. "Oh, did I forget to mention that after being crowned king, my first order of business shall be to eliminate all the lesser clans of Glyndoria?" he said airily. "I've always hated the Methusians, but I never gave serious consideration to wiping out the other clans until after you managed to visit each of them and emerge unscathed. I began to wonder why it should be so when you are the sister of the king in whose name untold legions of their kin had been slaughtered or enslaved. I began to wonder if, against all odds, you'd somehow managed to win them over."

"No, I swear—"

"Swear all you like," interrupted Mordesius with a shrug of one uneven shoulder. "I'll not have the clans uniting behind you and against me. As soon as I return to Parthania, General Murdock will lead my army from mountain to valley to sea putting to sword every last clansman he can find." Lifting his wine goblet, Mordesius idly swirled the contents and took a sip before dropping his voice a notch and adding, "Between you and me, Your Majesty, I'd initially toyed with the idea of allowing a handful of Gorgishmen to choose between death and a lifetime of slavery in the Mines of Torodania, but I've since decided against it. They cling like fleas to the memory of those long-ago days when they were lords of the mines. Why risk even the remote possibility that they will one day attempt to retake their precious mines? Lowborn Eroks breed like rabbits—I'll put their surplus infants to work in the deepest, most treacherous shafts. Though they'll die alone, hungry, frightened and in cold darkness, perhaps they'll take some comfort from the knowledge that their short lives weren't a complete waste."

"You are a monster," whispered the queen.

Though Mordesius had been deliberately provoking her, he flinched at her words. "Perhaps," he muttered as he beckoned the cleric to them, "but I am about to become your monster."

As the cleric strode forward to stand before them, the queen shrank back in her chair. "No, please—you can't truly mean to do this!" she blurted. "Everyone knows that a woman cannot wed another while her husband yet lives!"

At the desperation in her voice, Mordesius felt a powerful stirring in his loins. "Even if the cockroach yet lives, as I already told you, Your Majesty, no one who matters would consider your union to be a valid one," he said. Rising to his feet, he indicated to the cleric that he should drag the queen to hers. "The marriage ceremony between us will proceed at once, and then we shall retire to your bedchamber where I shall do my utmost to get a son upon you this very night."

"Wait!" cried the queen as she struggled to free herself from the cleric's grasping hands. "What if you knew that it would be no use? What if you knew you'd never be able to get a child upon me?"

This time, Mordesius did hit her—as hard as he could, right across her pretty face. When she didn't cry out, he hit her again. "Are you suggesting that I am incapable of—"

"I am not suggesting anything," she burst, her eyes flashing. "I am telling you that I am already with child!"

Mordesius was so surprised that instead of hitting her a third time, he just blinked at her. The queen looked almost as surprised as he felt. It was as if she'd spoken in the heat of the moment and was now having serious second thoughts about having done so.

As well she should, thought Mordesius, for though he knew her for a lying whore, the ripeness of her body, the glow of her skin and the fear in her eyes told him that she was not lying now. Worse, it told him that the unborn child was thriving, and that the queen already felt something for it. The thought filled Mordesius with a rage so terrible that he nearly shrieked for the cleric to knock her to the ground and kick her until her traitorous womb expelled its vile contents. Indeed, the only thing that held him back was the knowledge that if it didn't kill the mother, such treatment often destroyed the womb, and he was going to need both to get the half-royal sons he desired.

So instead of shrieking, Mordesius took a deep, calming breath, fixed his dark eyes upon the queen and softly said, "Though the news of your pregnancy does not find me best pleased, I suppose I ought to be grateful for the proof of your fertility. How far along are you, Your Majesty?"

Swallowing hard, the queen pressed her free hand against her belly and tried to step back but the cleric swiftly moved to block her way. "Y-Your Grace," she faltered as the cleric shoved her forward so hard that she stumbled on the hem of her gown. "I . . . I know things aren't going to work out exactly as you'd hoped they would, but I am sure we can come to some sort of arrangement that—"

"How—far—along?" repeated Mordesius, even more softly than before.

"About three months."

"Hmm," breathed Mordesius, placing his cold hand over top of her warm one. The queen shuddered at his touch, but did not pull away her shielding hand. "Too late for some remedies," he murmured as he began to lightly stroke her fingers, "but not too late for others."

The stricken look on the queen's face told him that she knew exactly what he meant to do. "No!" she gasped as she began to struggle anew. "Please, I'll do—"

"Anything?" suggested Mordesius. "Yes, I know you will. Because as soon as we've rid ourselves of your little problem, you will become my wedded wife, and queen or no, I shall demand absolute obedience from you in all things." Turning to the cleric, he said, "Do you know of a hag skilled enough to cut out the little cockroach without killing or ruining her?"

The cleric shook his head. "I don't, Your Grace," he said.

Out of the corner of his eye, Mordesius saw his beautiful bride-to-be heave a sigh of relief—a sigh that was cut short when the cleric added, "But I know someone who does."

Fourteen

STUPID, STUPID, STUPID! thought Persephone as the cleric hustled her from the dining hall. *How could I have been so stupid?*

If only she'd stuck to her plan to play to Mordesius's lust as she'd done on that long-ago night when he'd discovered her standing ankle-deep in alley muck! Once she'd drawn him in, her intention had been to nudge him into dismissing the servants and then bash him over the head with the fireplace poker. Or, if she could get her hands on a carving knife, to slit him from bow to stern. She hadn't quite worked out how she was going to explain the blood and brain splatters on her gown to the various New Men she'd encounter as she thereafter fled the castle grounds, nor how she was going to convince them to give her a horse and raise the gate, but she'd been confident that she'd think of something.

Her first mistake, of course, had been commenting on the servants' missing tongues, because it was something no highborn woman in the realm would have noticed, let alone commented on. But that mistake was nothing compared to the one she'd made when she'd told Mordesius about the baby. Her desperate hope had been that perhaps if he knew she was already with child it would give him pause—and give her time to come up with another plan.

But it had not given him pause. And now she was being forced back to the turret chamber from which there was but a single perilous route of escape, there to stay until they came with the hag who would rip the baby from her womb.

As the cleric continued to hurry her along, a fierceness the likes of which she'd never felt before unexpectedly reared up inside of Persephone. Instead of being afraid *of* the baby, she was suddenly afraid *for* him; though she could not yet feel him in her belly, she suddenly felt him in her heart.

And just like that, the girl who'd once wanted the whole situation to just "go away" became a mother who would risk anything to save the life of her unborn child.

"She's to return to her chambers," announced the cleric as they arrived at the bottom of the spiral staircase where Tutor was standing guard.

"Alone?" said Tutor in surprise.

"Aye, alone," replied the cleric, leering at Persephone in a way that made her wonder what the gods thought of people who drove their knees into holy men's crotches. "Seems the little queen here has got herself in the family way, and His Grace wants it taken care of before the wedding."

"By 'taken care of' he means killed," Persephone could not help saying.

"I know what he means," said Tutor as unconcernedly as if they were speaking of killing a chicken for the stewpot.

He'll pay for that, too, vowed Persephone, recalling how she'd promised him he'd pay for slapping her.

The cleric turned and hurried away then, presumably to seek out the one who knew the hag. After he'd gone, Tutor stepped to one side and, laying one hand upon the hilt of his sheathed sword, used the other to gesture toward the winding staircase.

Persephone stared at him, her face determinedly impassive in spite of the fact that her mind was racing. She didn't think she'd be able to outrun him in her high-heeled shoes and she knew she'd never be able to beat him in a fight, but there had to be some way to keep from being trapped in—

"You can climb up by yourself," said Tutor, "or I can throw you over my shoulder and carry you up."

With a jolt, Persephone realized that Tutor's own words had just shown her the way. Looking down so that he'd not see the sudden fire in her eyes, Persephone wordlessly gathered up her beautiful skirts, swished past him and, wobbling slightly on her high heels, began to climb. When she was two-thirds of the way up, she silently slipped off her left shoe, set the heel against the edge of one of the stairs and leaned until the heel snapped. Then she slipped the shoe back on, carefully arranged herself in a sprawled position upon the stairs and gave a loud shriek.

An instant later, Tutor was crouched beside her, sword in hand.

"What is it?" he demanded in alarm as he scanned for danger. "What happened?"

"I broke a heel!" gasped Persephone. Clutching at her ankle, she moaned and rocked back and forth in what she hoped was a convincing display of unutterable agony.

Looking visibly relieved, Tutor sheathed his sword, jammed his hands on his hips and said, "Can you walk?"

"I . . . I think so," panted Persephone. Biting her lower lip, she gingerly attempted to push herself to her feet several times before scowling up at Tutor and snapping, "Well, don't just stand there. Give me your arm!"

Smiling slightly, Tutor did as he was bid. As they began climbing, Persephone clutched Tutor's right arm as though it were the last piece of flotsam in a storm-tossed sea.

"Mordesius said that your hairy friend was punished for his beastly behavior toward me," she grunted as she laboriously dragged herself up onto the landing at the top of the stairs.

"He wasn't my friend," said Tutor.

"Nor mine," Persephone said as they stepped up to the chamber door. Still clutching Tutor's arm with her left hand, she casually held her right hand out in readiness as she said, "Still, you must've felt something when you learned that he'd been punished."

"Not really," shrugged Tutor, pushing open the door and stepping into the deserted chamber. "In fact, I was the one who beheaded him."

Though she'd already made up her mind to do whatever she had to in order to save her baby, Tutor's heartless words made Persephone feel a good deal better about stepping into the chamber after him, snatching up the heavy crystal wine decanter from the half-moon table and smashing it down on the back of his head with all her strength.

Unfortunately, the sigh of relief Persephone heaved upon seeing Tutor crumple to the ground was cut short when she heard a distant shout of alarm. The blast of the hunting horn that followed lasted no more than a few seconds, but by the time it was over, the castle was alive with the sound of doors opening and slamming and many men running.

Not knowing what was going on but guessing that it wouldn't be long before someone came looking for her, Persephone looked toward the chamber windows. If a climber was especially strong and lucky, she just might be able to descend the outer wall of the turret without slipping and plummeting to her death on the jagged rocks far below.

Persephone's breath came faster. She was desperate to escape and save her baby, but was she desperate enough to try that?

Fifteen

A QUARTER OF AN HOUR after the hunting horn sounded, the door of the cramped closet in which Mordesius had been stuffed for his own safety opened without warning.

Lifting his hand to shield his eyes from the flickering light of the torches that lined the corridor, Mordesius squinted up at the man who'd recently been promoted to commander of castle security—the man whose head would shortly adorn a wall spike as punishment for allowing the castle defenses to be breached.

"Well?" snapped Mordesius, biting back a groan as he staggered to his feet and shuffled out of the closet. "Is it over?"

The brawny young commander nearly tripped over his own feet in his haste to get out of Mordesius's way. "The intruders have been overpowered, Your Grace," he replied with a weak but ingratiating smile.

Pursing his lips at the fool's eagerness to please, Mordesius demanded to know if any of the intruders yet lived.

"One," said the commander. He hesitated before adding, "It is . . . well, it is Lord Atticus, Your Grace."

"Lord Atticus?" exclaimed Mordesius. "Bartok's son?"

The commander nodded and said, "He was apprehended in an alcove off the main corridor leading to the kitchens."

"What in the name of the gods was he doing there?"

Fidgeting in a way that made Mordesius want to slap him, the commander replied, "My soldiers say that after getting separated from those of his men who'd managed to fight their way into the castle, he somehow got turned around."

"It would appear that my ruse with the empty carriage didn't fool Bartok, after all," mused Mordesius. Then, careless of the throbbing pain in his neck, he threw back his head and let out a bark of laughter that echoed up and down the corridor. "Oh, how *furious* Bartok is going to be when he learns that his plan to rescue the queen has failed! How utterly *horrified* he is going to be when he realizes that in addition to retaining possession of the queen, I have now taken possession of his only son and heir!"

The commander said nothing in response to these exclamations of delight, and it wasn't until the last echoes of laughter had faded that Mordesius noticed the expression of pure dread upon the man's face.

"What is it?" he snarled, his own happy countenance vanishing at once.

The commander swallowed hard. "I . . . I—"

"*What is it?*" bellowed Mordesius, raking his fingernails down the fool's cheek.

The not-so-eager-now commander cringed. "Your Grace," he practically whimpered, "the queen is gone."

Mordesius gaped at him. "What do you mean she's gone?" he spluttered. "A moment ago, you told me that the intruders had been overpowered! You said that only one yet lived! Are you telling me now that one escaped with the queen?"

"No!" cried the commander, who did not even seem to notice the rivulets of blood running down his face. "No, Your Grace, no, I swear to you, *no*! The very instant the hunting horn sounded, I raced to the tower chamber to see to the queen's safety and security. It would not have been possible for one of the intruders to get to her before I did!"

"WELL, SOMEONE GOT TO HER, YOU BABBLING MORON!" shrieked Mordesius, raking his fingernails down the commander's other cheek. "What does the soldier who was supposed to be guarding her have to say for himself?"

"He's gone, too, Your Grace," whimpered the commander, wringing his hands like some old woman. "But I cannot believe he had anything to do with the queen's disappearance. I know the man personally. He's not one of those conscripted wretches whose loyalty must ever be suspect. He was a volunteer—a career soldier enriched and raised far above his lowborn station by the opportunity to serve in your army. I swear he'd sooner cut off his own nose than fail to carry out an order!"

"We'll see about that when we find the deserting bastard," snarled Mordesius. "In the meantime, I want every man, woman and child in this castle searching for him and the queen. No one sleeps until they are found, do you understand me? Do you? If Bartok's lackeys didn't get to them then they must be around here somewhere."

"Y-yes, Your Grace," faltered the commander. "Only . . ."

"Only what?" demanded Mordesius, disgusted by the overpowering stench of the fool's terror.

"When I entered the queen's chamber, I noticed that the windows were open and . . . and that there was a pair of high-heeled shoes lying on the floor nearby," said the commander, his voice barely more than a whisper. "Your Grace, I fear she may have tried to escape by climbing down the outside of the turret."

Mordesius's cold heart went into freefall as he suddenly realized that he should have anticipated something like this. No one knew better than he that the gutter-reared queen was as reckless as she was fearless. Faced with the choice of seeing the little cockroach cut from her womb or risking her own life to save them both, he knew what choice she would make.

"Proceed with searching the castle and grounds tonight," barked Mordesius. "At first light, you will look to the rocks at the bottom of the cliff."

"And what shall I do with Lord Atticus, Your Grace?" asked the commander, his relieved expression betraying his hope that being issued orders to carry out upon the morrow meant that he had a future, after all.

"Put him somewhere dark and cold," said Mordesius, hating the fool for daring to have hope at a time like this. "I'll deal with him tomorrow. And then I'll deal with you."

Exhausted though he was from the long, hard journey north, the draining events of the evening and the pain that never gave him a moment's respite, Mordesius did not sleep at all that night.

Instead, he returned to his bedchamber, dismissed his body servants, wrapped himself in a thick blanket and settled into a comfortable armchair by the fire. Hour after hour he stared into the flames. He wracked his brains for another explanation for the open tower windows, the discarded shoes and the disappearance of the queen. He tried not to picture her crouched on the windowsill, her dark hair and skirts whipping around her, her violet eyes fixed on the ground so far below. He tried not to imagine how her heart would have hammered in her chest as she'd slid onto her belly and edged backward over the sill, her bare feet scrabbling for a toehold. He tried not to think about how desperately she'd have clung to the damp bricks of the turret, and how insistently the wind would have tugged at her body. How surprised she'd have been when the inevitable finally happened, and how graceful she'd have looked as she'd fallen.

He tried not to believe that, having forgotten to ask the queen the location of the healing pool, the locket around his neck might be as close as he ever came to finding it.

Most of all, however, Mordesius tried not to think that the tightness in his chest might mean that he felt something besides rage and disappointment at the prospect of the death of the beautiful, bold, brazen young woman who'd never caused him anything but trouble.

Sixteen

FOR PERSEPHONE, the quarter of an hour after the hunting horn sounded passed like this:

For half a heartbeat she just stood at the threshold of the turret chamber clutching the handle of the shattered decanter, listening to the ragged sound of her own breathing and looking toward the windows through which she might escape if she was strong and lucky enough not to slip and plummet to her death.

Then, abruptly deciding that she'd probably used up her luck knocking Tutor unconscious with one blow, she tossed the decanter handle to one side and shut the door of the chamber. Taking care to avoid the shards of shattered crystal, she dropped to her knees beside Tutor, rolled him onto his back and pressed her ear against his chest. When she heard the steady beat of his heart, she sat back on her heels and considered her options. Though the idea of finishing him with his own sword strongly appealed to her, she reluctantly settled upon a less permanent way of ensuring that he could not interfere with her escape.

Hurrying over to the chair behind the privacy screen, she snatched up three pairs of silken panties and several lengths of rope. As she did so, it occurred to her that half a dozen snowy petticoats, a voluminous gown and high-heeled dancing slippers were not exactly an ideal escape ensemble. Before she could even begin to curse the fact that the servants had taken away the grubby lowborn garments she'd been wearing when she arrived, however, she noticed that Tutor was not much bigger than she was.

And that he was suddenly looking just a tad overdressed.

It took Persephone longer than she would have liked to strip the unconscious New Man, and she was nearly knocked over by the stink when she tugged off his boots, but at last she had him down to his badly stained underpants. Too revolted by the prospect of seeing him completely naked to give in to the urge to yank off his underpants and stuff them down his throat, she settled for tying his hands behind his back, binding his ankles together and using the panties to stop his mouth.

Slipping behind the privacy screen, she hurriedly wriggled out of her own clothes and pulled on Tutor's smelly black breeches, shirt, doublet and boots. None of them fit well, but none of them fit so poorly (she hoped!) as to be conspicuous. To her delight, she found her own little dagger in the inside pocket of the doublet. Giving it a small but noisy kiss, she slipped it into the scabbard at her thigh through a conveniently located rip in the outer seam of the breeches. Shoving the bit of lace, the rat tail, the key and the curl into the pocket of the doublet, she then tossed aside the amethyst necklace, put back on her own silver one and began yanking hairpins out of her updo as fast as she could. Lock after wavy lock of dark hair tumbled down until she had a glossy mass rippling halfway down her back. Though she knew that such hair was rather likely to tip people off to the fact that she was not actually a soldier—or even a man, for that matter—instead of cutting it, she plaited it into a messy braid, turned up the collar of her doublet and tucked the braid down the back of it.

Whatever path lies before me, I shall not walk it bald, she thought fiercely as she stepped out from behind the privacy screen to make her final preparations.

Using the beautiful purple gown, she mopped up as much of the wine and blood as she could. When she was done, she crammed a pillow into the bodice of the gown, tucked her creation under one arm, grabbed the damaged high-heeled shoes and strode across the chamber. Dropping the shoes, she flung open the windows and expertly ran her hand along the outer wall of the turret. A grim smile came to her lips when she discovered that, as she'd hoped, the stones jutted out from the mortar just far enough to entice an especially daring and desperate prisoner to attempt to climb to freedom.

"Godspeed and good luck," she sang to the crudely fashioned dummy as she heaved it out the window.

It won't fool them for long, she thought as she turned away without closing the windows, *but it might fool them for long enough.*

Returning for the final time to where Tutor yet lay unmoving, Persephone swept the shards of crystal under the snowy carpet, which, mercifully, had not been stained by his blood. Then, deciding that she had no need for Tutor's heavy sword, she tossed it onto his chest, grabbed him by the wrists and dragged him over to the bed. Panting with exertion, she sat down and used her booted feet to unceremoniously shove him beneath it. If he awoke and started moaning or thrashing about, he'd be found at once by whoever was in the chamber, of course, but until then, Mordesius's soldiers would have no idea that they should be looking for her dressed as one of them.

With Tutor safely stowed, Persephone jumped to her feet and hurried over to the chamber door. Easing it open, she ran down the winding staircase. As she hit the bottom step, the door at the end of the corridor to her right burst open and a dozen black-clad New Men came charging toward her.

Instinctively throwing herself against the right wall of the stairwell so that at least one of her flanks would be protected, Persephone was about to draw her dagger when she realized that the soldiers were not running at her but past her. Unable to believe her good luck, she held her breath and averted her face. And when the last of them had swept past her, she jumped off the step and fell in behind them. She'd have felt safer by far slipping away unseen and unnoticed, but with the castle in an uproar that was simply no longer an option.

The soldiers Persephone was following moved swiftly toward the front of the castle, collecting every soldier they met along the way with the exception of one who was running hard in the direction of the turret chamber. As they drew closer to the entrance hall, the sound of fighting grew louder and more distinct. Not wanting to get caught up in a melee with nothing but a dagger to defend herself and not at all confident that her disguise would stand up to any real scrutiny, Persephone surreptitiously ducked into a shadowed alcove to plan her next move. From her hiding spot, she watched as the soldiers drew their swords and plunged into the entrance hall. A moment of even fiercer fighting was followed by a high-pitched shriek and the sight of several rumpled, blood-splattered men not dressed in black staggering through the archway and into the corridor. Persephone gasped when she glimpsed the face of the one in the lead, for she'd have known those fleshy lips and bloodshot eyes anywhere.

Lord Atticus.

Persephone drew even farther back into the shadows. Whatever reason Lord Bartok's son had for being here—and she could well believe the reason had something to do with her—she knew that to throw herself upon his mercies might very well be to jump from the frying pan into the fire.

So instead of calling upon him to do his duty and save his rightful queen, Persephone watched silently as he and his companions dashed off down the corridor. Seconds later, the soldiers in the entrance hall managed to hack their way through the men Lord Atticus had presumably left to hold the archway. Wild-eyed and panting with blood lust, they took off after the intruders.

When the last of them had rounded the corner at the far end of the corridor, Persephone cautiously stepped out of the shadows.

Making her way over to the archway, she peered into the entrance hall. It was in complete disarray. Curtains and tapestries had been torn down, tables and pedestals had been knocked over, priceless vases and busts had been smashed to bits. The polished floor was littered with the wounded, dying and dead; the air was filled with the terrible sounds and smells of them. The great iron door was ajar; a body lay face down across the threshold, a bloodied hunting horn at its side.

Persephone didn't hesitate but headed straight for the open door. As she lifted the torch from the nearest wall bracket and stepped over the body that lay across the threshold, an angry, rasping voice behind her demanded to know where she thought she was going. She didn't answer or look back but instead plunged forward into the darkness.

Descending the gleaming granite steps into a soup of fog so thick that even with the torch she could barely see past her own nose, Persephone cautiously struck out across the cobblestone courtyard in the direction of the high castle wall. She recalled how impenetrable it had looked but she could not believe that even Lord Atticus would be fool enough to invade Mordesius's stronghold without some means of escape.

At least, she hoped he wouldn't be fool enough, for she was counting on his means of escape to be hers as well.

By the time her outstretched hand touched the damp castle wall, the sound of calmly shouted orders from within the castle told Persephone that the New Men were over the initial shock of the unexpected assault and were rapidly getting organized. Forcing down her panic at the knowledge that her disappearance would surely be discovered any moment, Persephone turned and, keeping a guiding hand on the wall, stumbled toward the gate. She didn't really believe it would be open, but she couldn't think how else Lord Atticus and his companions might have gotten into the courtyard.

Without warning, her fingertips brushed against something that moved beneath her touch. Badly startled, she snatched her hand away from the wall a split second before her mind registered what she'd just touched:

It was the end of a dangling rope.

Suddenly, she understood exactly how the buffoon had gotten in—and how he'd planned to get out.

Quickly (but reluctantly) snuffing out the torch, Persephone grasped the rope with both hands, took a deep breath and started to climb. Her arms began to tire almost immediately but she refused to acknowledge the burn. Hand over hand, higher and higher she climbed until she emerged out of the fog into the gloom of the night. Feeling a burst of energy at the sight of the top of the wall, she tucked the rope firmly between her booted feet, thrust herself upward . . .

And nearly suffered an apoplexy when she found herself nose to nose with Hairy's decapitated head.

Stifling a scream, Persephone jerked her own head back. Even as she did so, however, she knew that there was nowhere to go but onward or down—and down with a mighty thump, if the violent trembling in her arms was any indication. So, without giving herself time to reconsider, she flung herself forward, grasped the gory base of the iron pike just above the rope's grappling hook and heaved herself onto the top of the wall. Then, taking care not to look at Hairy's sagging gray face and ragged neck stump, she scrambled to her knees, hauled up the rope and tossed it over the other side of the wall that she might use it to climb down. The instant she did so, an unseen horse whickered softly and someone below anxiously whispered,

"Atticus? Is that you, Atticus?"

Persephone held her breath, cursing herself for not having considered that Lord Atticus might have left someone behind to watch over the horses that he and his surviving companions would need to make good their escape.

"Atticus?" came the voice again.

Persephone knew she'd have to deal with the whisperer one way or another. Doubting her ability to talk sense into any friend of

Lord Atticus's and unwilling to risk a knife fight in the foggy darkness against an assailant of unknown size and strength, she decided that her best bet would be to try to distract him.

Mouthing a silent apology to Hairy even though he really didn't deserve one after the shabby way he'd treated her, she gingerly grasped his cold, clammy ears, tugged his head off the iron pike and dropped it over the spot from which the voice had issued.

The horrified shriek that followed the squashy thud told her she'd scored a perfect bull's-eye. Sliding to the ground so fast she got rope burns on her hands, Persephone chirruped softly. The face of a curious horse immediately loomed before her in the fog. A heartbeat later she was in the saddle on her way.

She'd done it.

Her baby was safe and she was free.

All that was left to do was to find Azriel, prevent the slaughter of the clans, save the kingdom and take the throne.

Seventeen

AS PERSEPHONE WAS BEGINNING her desperate flight toward the Methusian camp, many miles away Azriel, Rachel and Zdeno were nearing the end of theirs.

"Please stop looking at me like that," said Azriel with exaggerated patience. "I've already told you a thousand times that I don't know where she is."

This unwelcome news was met with moody silence.

"How about another bit of intestine?" said Azriel, using a stick to lift up a pale, skinny piece about six inches long. "I understand that such treats are best served warm from the torn belly of a fresh—and, ideally, still squirming—victim. However, I can assure you that the piece I offer is just as slimy and disgusting a morsel as you could hope for."

In an agony of temptation, Ivan took several agitated steps to one side of the rock on which he was perched, then several steps to the other. Then, without warning, he launched himself forward in a blur of brown feathers, snagged the piece of intestine with his talons and flew so low over the startled Methusian's head that the dangling tail of the "morsel" dragged through his crown of auburn curls.

As Rachel listened to Azriel huff in disgust and watched Ivan disappear into the darkness beyond the campfire's light, she smiled and snuggled deeper into Zdeno's arms. The hawk had joined up with them about a mile outside Parthania. Since then, Azriel had been making a supreme effort to find common ground with the creature.

He claimed it was repayment for the vital part Ivan had played in helping them to escape the city, but Rachel suspected it had more to do with a long-ago promise she knew he'd made to Persephone that he'd take care of her animals if anything should happen to her. At the time, she'd shown her gratitude by being willful, uncooperative and reckless, thwarting him at every turn and generally making his life as difficult as possible. Yet Rachel did not have to wonder what Azriel would have given to return to those days, because she saw the answer every time she looked at him.

And the answer was: everything.

"Tomorrow, I'll let the horses go," he said now as he tossed the last of the grouse entrails onto the fire.

"Why?" asked Rachel.

"The tracks left by hooves are easier to follow than those left by feet," explained Zdeno as he tenderly brushed a lock of hair behind her ear. "We're less than a day from the Methusian camp and on the off chance that the man we stole the horses from—"

"Borrowed the horses from," interjected Azriel.

"Either way," said Zdeno diplomatically, "if the horses' owner has somehow managed to pick up our trail, we'd not want to make it easy for him to follow us the rest of the way. Though I could probably catch and kill him before he told anyone the location of the camp, I'd rather not have to do so."

"And if the man did somehow get away, the clan would be in such danger that no one would have time to waste helping us find Persephone," added Azriel. "As devoted as Cairn is to the idea of the coming Methusian king, even she would not set the lives of the entire clan behind the life of one girl who may or may not be the key to the prophecy."

"No," said Rachel, shivering as much at the distant sound of a wolf howl as at the memory of how ruthless the Methusian leader, Cairn, could be. "No, I don't imagine she would."

Eighteen

SHORTLY AFTER DAWN on the day following the disappearance of the queen, the commander of the black castle had spotted the bloody body at the base of the cliff, and Mordesius had been devastated.

By mid-morning, the soldier lowered down the side of the turret to retrieve the body had discovered that it was a fake, and Mordesius had been elated *and* furious.

By early afternoon, the rope hanging from the castle wall and the New Man lying under the bed had both been found, and Mordesius had come to the conclusion that the queen had engineered her own escape and played him for a fool—again.

And by late evening, trackers had been dispatched to hunt down and bring back the queen, and Bartok's wastrel son had pissed himself.

Again.

Disgusted though he was by Lord Atticus's utter lack of courage, dignity and self-control, Mordesius smiled inwardly at the sight of the dark, spreading stain at the crotch of the hysterical noble worm's vomit-splattered breeches. Having spent the previous night and most of the day in a damp, windowless cell in the soldiers' barracks without food, drink or a blanket, Bartok's heir looked like death warmed over. His skin was pasty, his close-set eyes were bloodshot and the spasms that intermittently wracked his soft body suggested to Mordesius that he was suffering badly from a lack of wine. Indeed, he'd probably have long ago toppled over if he'd not been tightly lashed to the straight-backed chair in which he currently sat.

The New Man who had failed so spectacularly in his duty to guard the queen was likewise lashed to a straight-backed chair, one that was positioned directly in front of Lord Atticus. The incompetent soldier was yet clad in nothing but his underwear and in Mordesius's considered opinion, he was not long for this world.

Well, four hours of relentless interrogation could do that to a person.

Even before giving the soldier the opportunity to prove his loyalty by cutting off his own nose, Mordesius had believed the man to be ignorant of the queen's whereabouts. Unfortunately for him, that was irrelevant. What was relevant was that he deserved to be brutally punished for allowing himself to be overpowered by the unarmed pregnant woman who was the key to all of Mordesius's great plans. That his punishment was serving to impress upon Lord Atticus just what would happen to him if he failed to cooperate was merely a happy bonus.

"Wine," snapped Mordesius to no one in particular.

A bleary-eyed servant immediately hobbled over with a jewel-encrusted silver goblet filled nearly to the brim. Leaning closer to the dying New Man, Mordesius used his thumb and index finger to pluck the nose from the palm of the man's badly shaking hand. Then, shuffling around so that his noble guest had an unobstructed view, he dropped the severed nose into the goblet, causing a small measure of wine to slosh over the sides.

"Care for a drink, my lord?" Mordesius asked politely as he held the goblet out to Lord Atticus.

Small, close-set eyes bulging in horror, Lord Atticus alternated between squealing and grunting as he frantically shook his head and strained against his bindings.

Gratified by this further evidence that he had the noble worm exactly where he wanted him, Mordesius ordered the nearest soldier to remove his gag.

"P-p-please—" stuttered Lord Atticus, the instant the gag was removed.

"Please, you'd like a sip of wine?" asked Mordesius, affecting surprise.

"No!" shrieked Lord Atticus, bucking and twisting with renewed vigor. "Please, get away from me! Please, let me go!" He moaned loudly. "By the gods, this is a nightmare!"

"No, my lord, that is a nightmare," said Mordesius softly, pointing to the battered, burnt, nose-less thing strapped to the other chair. "This"—he used his free hand to gesture between himself and Bartok's blubbering spawn—"is a conversation between two civilized men. One that need not end in unpleasantness, I might add."

At these words, Lord Atticus's thrashing gradually subsided. Taking a deep, shuddering breath, he panted, "My . . . my father will pay any ransom you demand."

Smiling broadly at the uncertainty in the young lord's voice, Mordesius said, "I do not think he would. And even if he would, I am not interested in money. And even if I were, I wouldn't know where to begin setting the price on the head of a nobleman who behaved like a common brigand."

Provoked into momentarily forgetting the rather precarious position in which he found himself, Lord Atticus's watery eyes bulged again, this time with indignation. "Do not compare me to some low-born piece of refuse," he huffed, puffing out his soft chest. "I am a lord of impeccable breeding, one day to be the greatest nobleman in all the realm!"

"And yet instead of announcing yourself at my gate, you slunk over my castle wall in the dead of night, murdered my soldiers in cold blood and raced toward my kitchens to . . . what? Abduct my cook? Raid my larder?"

Lord Atticus's pasty face went blotchy with embarrassment. "I didn't mean to make my way to your kitchens," he muttered.

"No?" said Mordesius, his dark eyes glittering. "What did you mean to do?"

When the future "greatest nobleman in all the realm" mashed his fleshy lips together to show that he had no intention of replying, Mordesius slowly and deliberately turned his head and stared at the fireplace poker, the tip of which was nestled deep within the glowing embers of the fire. Then, just as slowly and deliberately, he turned his head back around, fixed his gaze upon the reluctant young lord and hissed, "Answer me."

Though still firmly tied to the chair, Lord Atticus yelped and jerked as though he'd just been jabbed with the business end of the poker. Then, his words running together in his haste to spit them out, he cried, "Imeanttorescuethequeen!"

"Who set you to this evil, treasonous task?" barked Mordesius, who already knew the answer. "What did he hope to accomplish by it? And are you quite sure that kidnapping my beloved betrothed was the only thing you meant to do?"

Eyes bulging—again—Bartok's terrified idiot heir opened and closed his mouth several times, but nothing came out.

Ignoring the death rattle of the dying New Man, Mordesius shuffled closer to Lord Atticus. As he did so, he casually lowered the wine goblet and gave it a vigorous swirl so that the young nobleman had a good view of the nose.

"Are you sure you didn't also mean to cause me mischief, my lord?" asked Mordesius softly. "Are you sure you didn't mean to murder me in cold blood, just as you murdered my soldiers?"

Though the accusation pushed Lord Atticus to the brink of tears, he did not deny it. Instead, he squeezed his eyes shut and moaned, "Why are you torturing me like this? If you do not want money, for gods' sakes, tell me: What do you want?"

Amazed and disgusted that the spoiled young lord could indulge himself in feeling "tortured" when the results of real torture sat not three feet away from him, Mordesius said, "I want information, and I want cooperation."

Lord Atticus stopped moaning and reluctantly opened his puffy eyes. "What kind of information?" he muttered, more petulant than wary. "What kind of cooperation?"

"The kind that will allow me to outmaneuver that pack of noble worms that wriggle around to your father's tune," replied Mordesius serenely as he gave the goblet in his hand another swirl. "The kind that will see your father destroyed utterly."

The young lord gaped up at Mordesius like some goggle-eyed bottom-feeder. "See my father destroyed?" he said, speaking as slowly as if he were trying to decipher words spoken in a foreign tongue. "What do you mean? Do you mean . . . do you mean that you want me to betray my father? You want me to help you ruin him?"

"Yes, my lord," said Mordesius, who actually had a more permanent form of destruction in mind. "That is exactly what I mean."

At these words, a violent spasm ran through Lord Atticus's wine-thirsty body. Mordesius idly wondered if the boy was going to vomit again.

"P-please," whined the panting nobleman after the worst of the attack had passed. "You don't understand what you're asking. My father—he's not like other fathers. He'll never forgive me if I betray him." Then, as though the thought had only just occurred to him, a look of utter horror settled upon his face and he screeched, "Never mind forgiving me. He will kill me if I betray him! He will actually kill me!"

"And I will 'actually' kill you if you do not betray him," said Mordesius, resisting the urge to laugh aloud at the nobleman's histrionics. "But first—"

He casually waved his hand in the direction of the now silent and still (but still nose-less) New Man.

Lord Atticus hung his head and sobbed freely.

Mordesius let him sob. He knew the worm was going to agree to his terms because he was a coward and weakling, and he would do anything to save his pathetic noble hide. Moreover, he was too thick-headed to realize that he would not actually be saving his hide, only delaying the skinning process.

At length, Lord Atticus's sobs ebbed. Raising his head, he sniffled loudly and said, "If . . . if I cooperate and do all that you ask of me, what will I get in return? Besides my life, I mean?"

Mordesius laughed at this very Bartok-esque question. Then he took a long, slow drink of wine from the goblet in his hand, wiped his mouth with his sleeve, leaned very close to the piss-scented young lord and whispered, "You will get the chance to keep your nose."

Nineteen

FOUR DAYS LATER, Lord Bartok stood in his imperial palace chambers fingering the parchment in his hands. Though the broken wax seal bore the imprint of Atticus's ring and though it was written in Atticus's atrociously sloppy hand, Lord Bartok questioned its authenticity. For one thing, though it contained spelling errors, it contained too few to have been written by Atticus alone. For another thing, it was too clever by half. Since when did Atticus offer suggestions that were even remotely insightful? And when was the last time he referred to the queen as anything other than "the bitch"? His gaze dropping to the parchment once more, Lord Bartok read the most telling passage for the umpteenth time:

> . . . the queen is in my safekeaping and the upstart is dead at last, murdured in his own bed. As I am weery to the bone and also wounded, I will be delayed in delivering her (the queen) two you. Meantime, I beg you to stay where you are. Do nothing to raise the suspishuns of General Murdock for I think he will not react well to the death of his master . . .

No, it didn't sound at all like Atticus, except perhaps for the part about being weary and wounded, for the boy had ever been the most infernal complainer.

What it sounded like was someone talking through Atticus.

And Lord Bartok knew who that someone must be as surely as he knew that his only living son was now a walking dead man.

Deliberately setting the parchment down on his desk, Lord Bartok rested his elbows upon the table and touched his lips to his gracefully clasped hands.

When he'd sent Atticus after the upstart, he'd known that something like this might happen, of course. Yet what choice had he had? It simply would not have done to allow his own flesh and blood to loll about guzzling wine like a common sot while lesser men undertook the rescue of a queen. Theirs was the greatest noble family in the kingdom and had been since before the beginning of recorded history. It was each Bartok man's responsibility to bring the family more land, more riches and more glory than the Bartok men who'd come before him had done.

Unfortunately, time and again Atticus had demonstrated that he not only lacked the ability and temperament required to improve upon anything that had been done by those who'd come before him, but also that he was in full possession of every single quality required to drag a family into utter ruin.

The specter of his noble descendants scratching a living out of the dirt or bending the knee to some jumped-up New Man was the stuff of nightmares for Lord Bartok. By sending Atticus to rescue the queen, he'd given his son a chance to banish those nightmares, either by finally proving himself worthy or by signing his own death warrant.

Lord Bartok frowned now, his pale eyes like chips of ice beneath his silvery brows.

Though the knowledge that Atticus had done the latter caused Lord Bartok the father a measure of genuine grief, Lord Bartok the patriarch saw it for what it was: an opportunity to start over. After all, he was not so old that he could not father more sons—sons who would hopefully be better suited to their elevated positions in this world.

And though the royal woman upon whom he sought to father them was, at present, most likely warming the bed of the lowborn upstart who'd forced her into marriage, with some shrewd maneuvering, she'd soon be a widow free to marry him and warm his bed.

Whether she liked it or not.

Twenty

LORD BARTOK MAY HAVE been comforted if he'd known that at that particular moment, Persephone was not warming anyone's bed. Rather, she was standing with her back pressed against the wall of a barn, her dagger clutched tight in one sweaty palm. Across the nearby yard, all was still and silent in the thatch-roofed cottage where the unsuspecting farmer and his wife slumbered.

In the four days since her dramatic escape from Mordesius's black stone castle, Persephone had done everything she could to elude trackers, and she'd eaten almost nothing at all. To her intense disappointment, the panniers slung across the haunches of her stolen horse had contained no food or hunting weapons, only a ridiculous feathered cap, a riding crop and an empty silver flask. Unable to hunt and too wary (and proud) to beg, she'd thus been forced to rely on foraging. The first day she'd found a sugarberry bush and a handful of mushrooms. The second day she'd found nothing; the third she'd come across a stunted stalk that boasted three scraggly ears of wild corn. Yesterday she'd passed by an orchard, and even though the apples had been small, green and bitter she'd forced herself to eat half a dozen of them. She'd gotten a stomachache for her trouble and it had hardly made a difference, anyway. Her body was crying out for sustenance, real sustenance. Her last meal had been on the evening before the ship had dropped anchor in the deserted cove; she could feel herself weakening and her ribs were beginning to protrude.

Fearing for the life of the baby if she did not eat soon, she'd decided to take a page from Azriel's book and "borrow" what she and the baby needed to survive.

Adjusting her grip on the dagger, Persephone slipped through the open barn door. The moist animal smell inside evoked powerful memories of the owner's barn where she'd laid her head for five years' worth of nights, but Persephone paid these memories no mind. Instead, she hurriedly tiptoed past the slumbering goats, geese, cows and sow. Coming to a halt before the chicken coop at the far end of the barn, she slowly eased open the wire door, leaned over and lifted one of the chickens off her roost so gently that the creature did little more than cluck softly in her sleep.

Relieved that it had been so easy, Persephone choked down a burble of near-hysterical laughter at the thought that Azriel was no longer the only chicken thief in the family. Then she turned . . .

And froze at the sight of the now-wide-awake sow glaring up at her from between the boards of its stall, looking quite as ill-tempered as the owner's sow had ever looked.

Without warning, it began to squeal.

Loudly.

"Reeeee," it squealed. "*Reeeee!*"

"Shush," whispered Persephone frantically. "Shush!"

But the sow would not shush. Indeed, in addition to squealing, it began to snort and charge around in small, frenzied circles as though to demonstrate how it planned to trample her if it but got the chance. Thoroughly alarmed by the cacophony, the chicken tucked under Persephone's arm began clucking at the top of its lungs. Its clucking awoke the rest of the chickens and also the cow, goats and geese.

Given that the racket the animals were making could easily have awoken the dead, Persephone knew she had only minutes before the farmer came running.

Turned out she had less than that.

For she was barely halfway to the open barn door when the silhouette of a large bearded man holding a shovel suddenly loomed at the threshold, blocking her escape.

"Who's there?" boomed the farmer.

As if in reply, the chicken tucked under Persephone's arm squawked for all it was worth.

Alas, for the chicken, it was too late.

For Persephone had already skidded to a halt and spun back around. Bolting to the far end of the barn, she leapt clear over the fence of the sow stall, past the startled sow and across the sty. Dropping to her knees, she wrung the noisy chicken's neck with one deft twist and then wriggled through the sow-sized opening that allowed the creature access to its outdoor pen. At that moment, having evidently recovered from the shock of seeing her dash past, the outraged sow gave a mighty squeal and came charging after her.

But it was too late for the sow, too, because by the time it burst out of the barn with mischief on its tiny mind, Persephone and the dead chicken had escaped into the night.

Persephone did not stop running until she got back to the spot by the stream where she'd tethered the beautiful chestnut mare whom she'd named Flight. She was trembling with exertion and nerves and so hungry that she truly thought she could have eaten the chicken raw, possibly without gutting or even plucking it. Yet she forced herself to be patient. Giving Flight a pat on the nose to let her know that all was well, Persephone walked a short distance downstream to a place where the ground was clear enough to safely start a campfire. After building one out of the driest wood she could find to minimize the smoke it produced and driving two forked branches into the ground so that she'd have something to hang the spit on, she quickly dressed and spit the chicken and set it over the fire to roast.

As she sat on her haunches turning the spit and feeling the heat of the fire upon her face, it occurred to Persephone that the last time she'd turned meat on a spit had been the evening Azriel had shown up at the owner's farm intent upon purchasing her. She smiled into the flames as she recalled how fine he'd looked in his "borrowed" doublet. And later, how undignified he'd looked trying to scramble up onto his "borrowed" horse before Cur removed a chunk from his well-muscled backside.

Then her smile faded. She knew that if Azriel, Rachel and Zdeno were still alive, there was nowhere for them to go but to the Methusian camp to which soldiers had already been dispatched on a mission of blood. Trying to reach the camp before the soldiers did was the reason Persephone had pressed onward at such a grueling pace in spite of her exhaustion, hunger and fear for the baby. If only she'd had the presence of mind to ask Mordesius when the soldiers had been dispatched, she'd know if there was any hope that—

SNAP.

She was on her feet with her dagger in hand in an instant, but by the time she'd spun around to face the threat it was too late.

Like her, the three dirty, rank-smelling New Men were all dressed in black doublets, breeches and boots. Unlike her, each wielded a rather large sword instead of a rather small dagger. In fact, the tallest of the three had the cold tip of his sword pressed firmly against the tender hollow at the base of Persephone's throat.

"Drop your blade," he ordered tersely.

When she hesitated, he applied a little more pressure to the sword.

Reluctantly, she dropped her blade.

"We saw your fire and smelt your bird," he said, his eyes straying from her to the fat roast chicken that sizzled above the flames. "You alone?"

"Well . . ."

"You a deserter?"

Persephone felt a leap of hope—and dread. That the three New Men did not appear to have any inkling that she was the runaway queen was a tremendous relief. At the same time, their belief that she was a deserter from Mordesius's army was a significant concern, for although she did not know exactly what happened to deserters, she'd heard enough rumors to know that it was agonizing, gruesome and fatal.

"Of course I'm not a deserter," she blurted gruffly. "I'm, uh, on a mission."

The shortest of the three New Men looked her up and down and then narrowed his eyes in suspicion. "What kinda mission?" he demanded.

Heart hammering hard, Persephone folded her arms across her chest. "A secret one," she said, even more gruffly than before. "So, you know, you'd better shove off before—"

"Liar," hissed the tall man.

Persephone stopped breathing. But instead of doing something rash, for the first time since being confronted she really looked at the three New Men—at their unkempt hair and beards, at their torn, filthy clothes, at the agitated looks in their eyes. And then she took a chance:

"You're right. I am a liar," she said. "I'm a liar *and* a deserter."

The short New Man immediately heaved a great sigh, the medium-sized one cracked a rotten-toothed grin and the tall one took his sword from her throat.

"Thank the gods!" he declared hoarsely, taking a step backward. "We thought maybe you were part of a tracking party sent to hunt us down. As it happens, we three are deserters, too, from the training camp north of Syon. Been on the run so long I can't hardly remember the last time we ate fresh meat."

He addressed this last comment directly to the roast chicken. Though Persephone knew that sharing her supper was a small price to pay for not having been dragged back to Mordesius or stabbed in the throat, her heart nevertheless sank.

"Well, since we're all in the same boat, you're welcome to share my fire," she offered, trying not to sound as grudging as she felt. "And my chicken, too, of course."

"Much obliged," said the tall man, licking his lips. Slinging the pack from his shoulder, he said, "We've cheese and bread enough to share, but a man needs meat, after all."

"He certainly does," agreed Persephone, her excitement at the prospect of adding cheese and bread to her meal withering at the sight of the filthy lumps of green-tinged gray and brown the man dug up from the bottom of his pack.

Turning away before her recently settled belly rebelled, Persephone lifted the spit off the forked branches, retrieved her dagger, sat down on the trunk of a fallen tree and set to work dividing up the steaming chicken.

After shoving into her mouth a piece of meat so tender, juicy, fragrant and delicious that she almost started to cry, Persephone unenthusiastically handed the rotten-toothed man his share.

"So, why'd you desert?" she asked.

"Never wanted to join the army in the first place, did we?" he replied, cramming so much meat into his mouth that juice ran down his chin, making his already filthy beard shine wetly. "But we was given a choice: join up or else."

"Or else what?" asked Persephone, surreptitiously shoving another piece of meat into her mouth before passing a fat drumstick to the short man and most of a succulent breast to the tall one.

"What do you mean 'or else what?'" said the short man irritably, snatching the drumstick from her without a word of thanks.

"You know good and well 'or else what.' Or else get beat to death in front of your own wife and children!"

"Or else get shipped to some northern outpost to build bridges for the realm until you're crushed, starved or hacked to death by some screaming clansman," added the tall man.

"Oh," murmured Persephone, who'd never given much thought to the fact that not all New Men joined the army out of choice. With the vague notion that this information could be useful at some point down the road, she filed it away. Then she sheathed her dagger and, clutching the chicken carcass protectively in one greasy hand, she reverently sank her teeth into the second drumstick. Closing her eyes, she tore off mouthful after mouthful of meat, swallowing so fast she hardly had time to chew. With each bite she swore she could feel herself *and* the baby getting stronger and—

". . . headed?"

"Huh?" blurted Persephone, coming out of her roast-chicken-induced trance so fast that she forgot to use her gruff voice.

The tall man gave her a puzzled look. "I asked where you were headed," he repeated.

"Oh. Uh, nowhere in particular," she lied hurriedly as she inwardly cursed herself for her carelessness. "You three?"

"To my village in the west to seek out someone who knows where the General sent my family," replied the rotten-toothed New Man at once.

"Not me," said the short one in a hard voice. "I'm off to join one of them outlaw gangs what goes about making trouble for Mordesius. I heard there's a fearsome one what lives in the Great Forest."

"There is, but they'll kill you dressed like that," commented Persephone, grimacing as she recalled the treatment that Robert and his band of pitchfork-wielding bandits had afforded the last batch of New Men they'd caught tromping through their forest.

"I guess I don't need advice from an untried boy like you," grunted the short man, sucking at a piece of chicken caught between his teeth.

"And I guess I don't need to share my fire and chicken with a hunted arsehole like you," retorted Persephone before she could stop herself.

The rotten-toothed man chortled appreciatively at this, but the short man just grunted again.

"Him's the only one really believes we're being hunted," he muttered, jerking his chin toward the tall man. "I say there's too many of us slipping away these days for the General to give proper chase to any of us."

"Why are there so many of you . . . us . . . slipping away?" asked Persephone as she painstakingly stripped the last bits of meat from the chicken carcass.

"Why'd you think?" asked the perpetually irritated short man. "The king is dead, his heir, the queen, ain't nowhere to be found, Mordesius's quit the capital, the gates has been shut, the common folk is getting restless, and there's rumors that the great lords is set to rebel. Bad times is coming, they is, and thems of us what never wanted to join the New Man army in the first place is none too keen to be around when they do. We gots a funny feeling, see, that if it comes to war, us'll end up in the vanguard, our blood and guts greasing the way for them what joined up of their own accord." He paused to regard Persephone with eyes that were once again narrowed in suspicion. "How long you been on the run that you don't know all this?"

Before she could answer, Flight whickered softly in the darkness some twenty paces off.

"Someone's coming!" cried the tall man softly.

All three New Men snatched up their swords and jumped to their feet.

"No one is coming," said Persephone calmly as she flung the chicken carcass into the nearby stream. "That's just my horse."

"You got a horse?" exclaimed the rotten-toothed man, rounding on her.

Though he mostly sounded surprised, there was an undercurrent of speculation in his voice that immediately put Persephone on her guard. It reminded her that although the three men were reluctant lowborn conscripts who almost certainly had tragic pasts, they were bigger than she, better armed than she and three to her one—well, one and a half. It also reminded her that although they appeared to believe she was a deserter, if she were in their smelly boots, she might think it safer to slit her throat and steal her horse than to run the risk that she was not what she seemed.

And that is why she casually got to her feet, wiped her greasy hands on her breeches and gruffly said, "Not only have I got a horse, but in the pannier across his back I've a full flask of fine spirits. I had intended to save it for medicinal purposes but after supping with you three, I find I've had a change of heart. Life for such as us is hard and short, and a man needs drink as well as meat, after all. So if you're of a mind to partake of my drink this night, I'm of a mind to share it with you."

When the three New Men endorsed her suggestion quite as heartily as she'd anticipated they would, Persephone strode purposefully into the darkness toward the place she'd left Flight. Upon reaching the mare, she silently unwound the reins from the branch to which she'd been tethered, climbed up into the saddle, laid her cheek against the horse's warm neck and urged her into a gallop.

It didn't take long for the three thirsty New Men to figure out what had happened, and as Persephone listened to their fading exclamations of dismay and felt the wind against her sweaty face, she made the decision not to stop again until she reached the Methusian camp.

Fulfilling her promise to Finn, warning the clans, saving the realm—everything hinged on reaching the camp before the soldiers did. Or at least upon reaching it before Azriel reached it, that she might prevent him from walking into a death trap.

For if she was not able to do at least that, she'd be utterly alone in the world—again.

And quite apart from the fact that she simply could no longer bear the thought of a life without the handsome rascal with whom she'd fallen hopelessly, desperately in love, alone was no position for a powerless, pregnant queen with an impossible destiny to find herself in.

Twenty-One

AS A FIRST STEP in his plan to destroy Mordesius and take the queen to his own bed, Lord Bartok invited half a dozen of his most influential peers down to the palace archery butts under the auspices of passing the idle midday hours with a private tourney dedicated to the memory of his recently deceased royal son-in-law.

Under normal circumstances, the ladies of the court would have trailed after them—twirling their parasols and swishing their skirts, gossiping and giggling, clapping their white-gloved hands and vying for the privilege of awarding trinkets to winners. With the young king barely cold in his tomb, however, the only thing any of them seemed to be vying for these days was who could put on the finest show of grief for the benefit of anyone who might be watching. This made the butts an excellent place for important men to speak without fear of being bothered by women or being overheard by the rats in the castle walls.

That is why Lord Bartok did not bother to lower his voice when he said, "Mordesius has kidnapped my son."

The other great lords gaped at him, thunderstruck. Indeed, tall, skinny Lord Tweedsmuir was so startled that he loosed the arrow nocked in his drawn bow without bothering to take aim. The arrow came within a hair's breadth of piercing the heart of a gardener trimming the leafy tail of a topiary mermaid in a distant garden.

"Atticus kidnapped by His Grace!" exclaimed Lord Tweedsmuir in his reedy voice. "How can you be sure, my lord?"

"Yesterday I received a note—"

"A ransom note?" asked Lord Tweedsmuir's dandified nineteen-year-old brother-in-law with an eagerness that Lord Bartok found in poor taste.

"No, not a ransom note," he said thinly. "A note written in Atticus's own hand, but with words he would never use and advice he would never give."

"That is not necessarily evidence of mischief, my lord," offered Lord Tweedsmuir by way of comfort.

"And yet I am certain that Mordesius has my son and means him far worse than mere mischief."

Lord Belmont, who was too ponderous to participate but too sociable to be left out, was lounging on a nearby couch being tended to by a deaf servant who had nothing but a stump where her tongue should have been. Having simply watched and listened up to that point, Lord Belmont now asked what evidence Lord Bartok had to support his accusations against the former regent.

"I sent Atticus on a mission to rescue Queen Persephone," shrugged Lord Bartok.

Grunting and digging his elbows into the back of the couch, Lord Belmont heaved himself into a more-or-less upright position. "You did this thing without informing the rest of the Council?" he rumbled.

"You openly declared your support for Mordesius," reminded Lord Bartok, taking care to ensure that his words sounded like an accusation.

"We openly declared our support for the named successor of the dead King Finnius," corrected Lord Belmont indignantly, wheezing slightly as he reached up to adjust one of his gigantic shoulder pads.

"And when that lowborn upstart lurched into the Council chamber and announced that he and the queen were to marry, you—just—sat—there," said Lord Bartok, biting off each word. "Even though you knew there was no possible way that the queen had willingly agreed to marry him."

Twitching the sleeve of his forest-green doublet, Lord Tweedsmuir's young brother-in-law sucked in his cheeks and muttered, "As I recall, Lord Bartok, you just sat there as well—"

"*And then, by the gods, I sacrificed my only son and heir in a desperate attempt to save her!*" thundered Lord Bartok.

Though the stump-tongued servant didn't even blink, the far-off gardener glanced over in their direction.

"Quietly, my lord, please!" begged Lord Tweedsmuir, flapping his hands like an overexcited bat. "Remember that we are trapped in a city crawling with armed New Men!"

Lord Bartok sneered and swatted the air in front of his face to show what he thought of this.

Selecting a large sweetmeat from the silver bowl being presented to him by the servant, Lord Belmont crammed it into his mouth. "You accuse us fairly, Lord Bartok," he admitted as he chewed the sticky treat. "I only regret that you did not come to us before you sent Atticus to rescue the queen."

"I am coming to you now."

"Coming to us now?" grunted Lord Belmont's second cousin, a squat, beetle-browed nobleman who looked more like a blacksmith than a duke.

"I am going to challenge the upstart on the battlefield," explained Lord Bartok.

After a short, shocked silence, Lord Belmont's second cousin responded with all the crude bluntness of a blacksmith born and bred, saying, "That would be suicide! Your army hasn't strength enough to defeat Mordesius's army."

"I know," said Lord Bartok. "Unless I am able to call upon considerably more men and horses, my army will be utterly destroyed." He let his words hang in the air for a moment before continuing. "But I can no longer ignore the fact that some things are worth dying for, my lords. Honor. Justice. Chivalry. I cannot sit idly by and allow that low creature to make a mockery of all we hold sacred by murdering my noble son and violating the queen night after night." His eyes burning with fervor, Lord Bartok said, "My lords, do you not think it is time that we of high birth stopped trembling before those of vile birth? Do you not think it is time that we came together to set things to rights for men like us, men who've suffered too long beneath the rule of a *nobody*? Join with me, my lords! Together, let us rescue the queen, save my son, vanquish the upstart and send his despicable New Men back to the gutters where they belong!"

For a long moment, the noblemen all fidgeted and cast furtive glances at one another. All except Lord Belmont, that is. He busied himself selecting another sweetmeat.

Eventually, his reedy voice sounding higher and thinner than ever, Lord Tweedsmuir said, "My lord, you . . . you are speaking of war."

"Yes," agreed Lord Bartok, a trifle impatiently. "I am speaking of war."

Having never worn his gleaming suit of armor outside the tiltyard, Lord Tweedsmuir's brother-in-law glowed at the prospect of adventure and battle glory.

Lord Belmont frowned. "Why would we not simply mount another attack on Mordesius's stronghold?"

"Because I do not know where it is," replied Lord Bartok. "Atticus followed the upstart to his lair, and the note I received made no mention of its location and was delivered anonymously. Attacking his army is the only way to draw him out. He will not stand by and see it destroyed because without it, he is nothing."

"You may be right," admitted Lord Belmont. "Even so, my lord, you are asking a great deal."

"And offering a great deal in return," said Lord Bartok, who needed Belmont's support above all others.

The lounging lord shrugged one massive shoulder. "I and my noble brethren will need some time to consider—"

"There is no time," interrupted Lord Bartok flatly. "Our queen is in the clutches of a monster, and my only son is in imminent danger. That is why, though I well know it may be the end of me, I intend to move against Mordesius's army as soon as may be. You can join with me or not as you see fit, but mark me, my lords: if you fail to support me now and my army is annihilated, you will never have the strength to rid yourselves of the upstart. You will be forced to stand by and watch as he comes out of his hiding hole, plants his bony backside on the throne of Glyndoria and crowns himself king, and then you will spend the rest of your days bending the knee to him—or, if you are blessed with long life, to the half-lowborn brat who comes after him."

The vision was so unspeakable that the great lords shuddered and gasped.

When he'd sufficiently recovered from the horror of what could be, Lord Tweedsmuir said, "Lord Bartok, even if we agree to support your cause, and even if we can persuade other lords to do the same, there may be noblemen who do not care for the idea of sending thousands to their deaths in a war to save your son and set things to rights for us few, even if we do mean to rescue the queen in the bargain."

"When we are victorious, those of noble blood who failed to support our cause will be stripped of titles, land and money," said Lord Bartok tightly.

"If our ruling monarch says it shall be so," said Lord Belmont pointedly. Heaving himself even farther forward on the couch, he said, "Pray tell, my lord, who shall that ruling monarch be?"

Lord Bartok made a great show of hesitating. Then, sighing heavily, he laid his hand over his heart and said, "While I truly believe that my son-in-law, the king, would have named his unborn child heir if he'd known that Aurelia was pregnant, as has been pointed out to me by some, he did not know. And so, my lords, since I would not have us divided on such a vital issue, I . . . I hereby declare myself content to abide by the dead king's expressed wishes."

Lord Belmont raised his unkempt eyebrows so high that his forehead wrinkled impressively. "Upon your honor, Lord Bartok, you swear to see Queen Persephone crowned and anointed whether your daughter is safely delivered of a royal child or not?" he asked in surprise.

"Provided that the upstart is dead so that he cannot claim the title of king, I do so swear, yes," said Lord Bartok, consoling himself with the thought that the lie would only be exposed in the unlikely event that Aurelia managed to do her duty and that it was for the greater good of the Bartok dynasty in any event.

Lord Belmont smiled and stuck out his hand. "Then I pledge my sworn swords to your cause, Lord Bartok. And I pray that we soon find a way to overcome the soldiers who hold the city, for unless we do, I fear that any attack we might launch upon the former regent will come too late to prevent him getting the poor queen with child and murdering your son."

Wrapping his own elegant hand firmly around the enormous lord's sticky fingers, Lord Bartok smiled and said, "I think we will not need your prayers, Lord Belmont. For you see, I have a plan."

Much later that night, there came a tentative knock at the door of Lord Bartok's private chambers. Setting his pen down next to the inkwell, he sprinkled the parchment before him with sand to dry the ink, then set it to one side. With a nod, he indicated to his man-servant that he was to admit the visitor.

By the time the door closed behind the departing servant, Lord Bartok's daughter, Aurelia, had come to a nervous halt before him. It did not occur to him to greet her with a pleasantry, to tell her of the fate that had befallen her brother or even to offer her a chair. Instead, he examined her body carefully for signs that it was beginning to ripen. When he saw none, he frowned slightly. Then, without preamble, he explained what he wanted her to do.

Her pale face was paler still by the time he'd finished. "You . . . you would have me invite *another* disgusting commoner into my bedchamber?" she stammered in the voice of one struggling for control.

"Yes, Aurelia," he said impassively.

She stared at him without speaking for a moment. Then tears welled in her bright eyes and her lower lip began to tremble. She opened her mouth to speak but Lord Bartok cut her off before she had the chance to utter a single word.

"In spite of the fact that you are a girl and the younger, I have agreed to make you my heir over Atticus, Aurelia," he reminded her. "I did not grant that privilege to you that you might shirk your duty to this family."

Aurelia flinched as though struck and a wild look flashed in her eyes.

Boldly taking a step forward, she slapped her hands down onto his desk—right on top of his papers!—and hissed, "You know perfectly well that you've no cause to accuse me of shirking my duty, Father, for you are the one who ordered me to suffer through my duty each and every night!"

Lord Bartok stared at his daughter's hands until she removed them. Then he looked up at her and calmly said, "You struck a bargain, Aurelia. Do not complain to me now that you do not care for its terms. And remember that attempting to do your duty is not what matters. Succeeding is what matters. Can you tell me for a certainty that the stable boy has impregnated you with a bastard you are going to be able to carry to term and deliver alive?"

Color suffused the girl's face. "No," she mumbled, stifling a small cough. "But—"

"But nothing," interrupted Lord Bartok, returning to his papers. "You will play your part in this, Aurelia, and that is final."

Face pinched with displeasure, Lady Aurelia watched him scratching away at his latest letter. Then she dipped him a stiff curtsey and left the chamber without another word.

Twenty-Two

LATER THAT SAME DAY, in a far less sumptuous chamber within the imperial palace, General Murdock daintily slurped a raw oyster from its half shell. Tipping his small head back, he let it slide, unchewed, down his throat. As it joined its slimy brethren in his belly, the distant sound of a shouting mob floated in through the open window. The sound swelled as the mob drew nearer, reached a crescendo as it swept through the street on the far side of the palace wall and then faded again as the street veered away from the palace and the mob melted back into the noisy city.

After a moment's hesitation, General Murdock sighed and reached for another oyster. That his New Men had not been able to prevent a mob from forming was a troubling reminder that in spite of his best efforts, his grip on the city was growing more tenuous with each passing day.

General Murdock had expected those of noble birth to take exception to being trapped in the city against their will, of course, and he'd expected the merchant class to complain that the inability to trade with those outside the city walls was bad for business. He'd even expected the working poor to protest the abuses of the soldiers who invaded their narrow, crowded streets with intent to cause mischief.

What he'd not expected was that instead of cowering in the shadows hoping not to be noticed, the lowborns who'd thus far escaped deportation from Parthania would start making trouble. It had begun with the disturbance they'd caused during the king's funeral procession almost a fortnight earlier and had gotten progressively worse from there. They were untrained and poorly armed, but they were also angry and suddenly, recklessly brave. It was as though they'd finally been pushed over the edge by the death of their king, the absence of their uncrowned queen and the omnipresent hordes of hated New Men who'd ever caused them so much suffering; it was as though they'd finally realized that they had nothing but their lives to lose—or give. And the more aggressively General Murdock and his soldiers tried to subdue them, the more defiant they became.

Like a snowball in the sun, the fear that had kept them in check all these years seemed to be slowly, inexorably melting away.

More concerning still were the reports of sabotage and revolt that had begun to trickle in from all corners of the realm. In the seaside village of Syon, a New Man had been beaten to death on the quay when he'd threatened to deport a pair of urchins to the Mines of Torodania. To the west, someone had set fire to a half-built bridge at a lowborn work camp. On the northern frontier, a hundred head of woolly sheep stolen from the Panoraki had mysteriously escaped from their pens in the dead of night.

Taken in isolation, these were minor incidents.

Taken altogether, they spoke of a kingdom creeping toward chaos.

The previous day, General Murdock had been in the midst of crafting a carefully worded letter explaining all this to Mordesius and requesting permission to begin executing children en masse to bring the Parthanian lowborns to heel when he'd received a coded communiqué from His Grace. It had contained no information, only an order to kill Lord Bartok and Lady Aurelia as soon as may be. If possible, he was to make their deaths appear accidental; if not, he was to make their deaths appear the random acts of a madman.

Since Mordesius had always insisted that he wished to show the world that he need not kill Lord Bartok to triumph over him, the order had come as a surprise to General Murdock, though admittedly a most welcome one. He'd long believed that the Bartoks posed an unacceptable risk to His Grace's ambitions; having been finally granted leave to eliminate this risk was a considerable relief.

Unfortunately, since Lord Bartok and his daughter did nothing together and went nowhere together, General Murdock knew it would be impossible to stage a single accident that would kill them both. Taking a small nibble from the wedge of smelly cheese he'd selected from the artfully arranged tray of exotic cheeses that had been served alongside the oysters, he permitted himself a small smile.

Though he was a military man who always executed his orders to the best of his ability, there were some orders he enjoyed executing more than others, and eliminating Lord Bartok and his daughter in a manner that would convince people that it was the work of a madman was going to be one of these. All that remained was to find the perfect opportunity to—

A knock at the door interrupted General Murdock's thoughts and his dinner. Frowning slightly, he lifted the white linen napkin off of his lap, dabbed at the corners of his mouth and then nodded to the attendant that he should open the door.

A servant in Bartok livery stepped into the room. In his hand, he held a folded piece of parchment.

Pursing his thin lips, General Murdock wondered what the doomed Lord Bartok wanted now. Then he read the note, and his eyes seemed to protrude a little farther out of his narrow face.

The note was not from whom he'd expected it to be, and the message it contained was similarly unexpected.

Unexpected—but most convenient.

Much later that night, General Murdock quietly rapped on the unattended door of one of the finest suites in the castle. Almost immediately, the door swung open to reveal Lady Aurelia dressed in the same black satin dressing gown she wore each night when she received the servant who studded her. Like a frightened little bird, she poked her head into the torch-lit corridor. She cast one jerky glance to the left and one to the right. Then, apparently satisfied that there was no one lurking about, she hopped back and nervously gestured to General Murdock that he should step inside.

Wordlessly, he did as she bid. By the time he'd closed the door and turned around to face her, she'd flitted halfway across the room, which appeared to be deserted but for the two of them.

Laying a hand at the gaping collar of her peignoir, Lady Aurelia cleared her throat several times as though in an effort to remove a persistent tickle. Then she said, "Thank you for coming, General."

If General Murdock had been the sort of man to feel awkward, uncomfortable or even desirous, he might have felt one of those things at that moment. But of course, he was not the sort of man to feel any of those things, and so all he felt was the slight weight of the sharpened straight razor he was carrying in the front pocket of his perfectly tailored black doublet.

"I was pleased to answer your summons, my lady," he said, taking a step toward her. "However, I must confess that it surprised me, for it is rather . . . unusual for a woman of your station to invite a man of my station to her chambers, let alone to receive him at night and in the complete absence of attendants."

"I know," said Lady Aurelia with a toss of her honey-blond curls. "And I'd not have sent for you or received you in such an unseemly manner if I was not in desperate need of your help."

General Murdock nodded, pleased that she'd confirmed that they were alone. Though he could easily have disposed of a few terrified female attendants, and though doing so in a frenzied manner would certainly have heightened the impression that Lady Aurelia's murder was a random act of madness, their presence would have compli-cated the mission, and a military man always avoided complications when he could.

"I understand completely," he murmured now. Casually slipping his hand into the pocket of his doublet, General Murdock closed his fingers around the handle of the straight razor and took another step toward the little noblewoman. "Tell me, how can I be of assistance?"

Instead of answering, Lady Aurelia abruptly fluttered over to a chair near the fire, flung herself down and began to weep.

Hand still in his pocket, General Murdock started toward her. "There, there," he said, repeating words he'd heard other men say to other teary-eyed women.

"Forgive me my womanly weakness, General," said Lady Aurelia with a dainty sniffle. "I just . . . I didn't know who else to turn to. My father is so powerful, so frightening . . ."

Leaning forward so far that General Murdock could have seen her breasts if he'd been inclined to drop his gaze, she dropped her voice a notch and added, "You cannot imagine the wicked things he has made me do, nor the unspeakable thing he would have me do now."

"What wicked things has he made you do?" asked General Murdock, who already knew at least part of the answer and thought it prudent to learn the rest of it before he silenced Lady Aurelia forever. "What unspeakable thing would he have you do now?"

The noblewoman opened her mouth, but instead of replying, she bolted to her tiny bare feet, fixed her bright eyes upon something behind him and gasped, "What was that?"

"What was what?" asked General Murdock, looking around.

"Out in the corridor!" whispered Lady Aurelia frantically. "I heard a noise!"

Lifting his long, thin nose as though he might be able to smell the threat, even if he could not hear it, General Murdock said, "I heard nothing—"

"Come quickly, General, please!" interrupted Lady Aurelia in a panicked whisper as she flew across the room and flung open the door of her bedchamber. "You must hide under the bed at once, for if that is my lord father out there and he finds you in here, I swear to you that he will kill you and beat me to within an inch of my life!"

His eyes gleaming in the firelight, General Murdock hesitated for just a moment before adjusting his grip on the straight razor in his pocket and starting after Lady Aurelia. Though he was quite sure that she was having hysterics over nothing, and even more sure that her lord father would never in a thousand years be able to kill him, the bedchamber was as convenient a place as any to take her apart. As long as—

He saw them hiding in the shadows the instant he stepped into the bedchamber. Unfortunately for General Murdock, it was an instant too late, for although he managed to slit two throats, slash one face and bite off the lobe of one ear, in the end there were simply too many attackers to fight off.

When the Bartok lackeys disguised as New Men lieutenants had finished binding General Murdock's arms behind his back and beating him for the injuries he'd inflicted upon their number, Lady Aurelia flounced over to the place on the floor where he was lying.

Jamming her bony hands upon her hips, she thrust her pointy chin at him and said, "As it happens, General, the thing my lord father wanted me to do now was to lure you into my bedchamber that his men might capture you. And upon reflection, I must confess that I didn't really find the act unspeakable at all."

After calling for reinforcements to make absolutely sure there was no way their captive could escape, Bartok's men gagged General Murdock, put a sack over his bleeding head and took him away.

As he was being led through the palace corridors, down the stairs, out into the back courtyard and across the lawn to the place he knew so well, General Murdock could tell that he was walking past dozens of New Men on guard duty. He could hear them murmuring amongst themselves; he could feel them staring as he went by. He guessed that the more observant among them recognized his fine clothing and distinctive body type and were uneasily wondering if the man beneath the sack was him.

He did not wonder why these observant men did not accost the ones dragging him away, however. Time and again General Murdock had made brutal examples of men who'd dared to question their orders or to question the decisions and actions of their superiors.

Clearly, the lesson he'd sought to teach had been so well learned that the men no longer dared to question even those superiors they clearly recognized as Bartok men in disguise.

Upon reaching the outer building that housed the entrance to the dungeon, one of the Bartok men dismissed the New Men on duty, who hesitated only until the Bartok man added that the order had come directly from General Murdock himself. After that, the New Men fairly tripped over themselves in their haste to obey.

It was gratifying, in a way.

After the guards departed, General Murdock was shoved, slipping and tripping, down the winding staircase to the dungeon far below. There, the sack, gag and ropes were removed. He was roughly stripped of his black doublet and forced to don the rags of a corpse. He was then beaten again before being led deeper through the maze of tunnels to the threshold of a cell for which he'd ever had an especial affinity. It was large, low ceilinged and stifling hot on account of the fire that never stopped burning. To General Murdock's right hung the narrow, rusty cage that until recently had housed the Gorgish ambassador; to his left lay the dusty, blond skeleton of the Marinese ambassador. Directly ahead of him were a butcher block and several trays of interrogation implements. And beyond all these things was the little cage where Methusian infants used to be kept prior to being brought forth by His Grace, who tirelessly sought to harness the healing power of their blood.

Wordlessly, Bartok's lackeys dragged General Murdock over to the wall to which the Panoraki ambassador had been shackled for so many years. As they shoved him to the ground, half a dozen startled rats fled from their hiding spots in the filthy straw. With something vaguely resembling envy, General Murdock watched them scuttle into the farthest, darkest corners of the hot cell, their long, skinny tails lashing behind them.

By the time the last of them had taken refuge from the light, General Murdock had been clapped in wrist irons and chained to the wall, and Lord Bartok himself had entered the cell to stand before him.

"You once said you thought you could tell me what to do because you were the man who commanded the soldiers who patrolled the city and guarded its gates," said Lord Bartok. Spreading his elegant hands wide, he shrugged and said, "It would appear that you are no longer that man."

General Murdock said nothing, only stared up at Lord Bartok with the eye that wasn't swollen shut.

"It would also appear that without your soldiers to protect you, you are easy prey," said Lord Bartok.

General Murdock did not correct him. He did not point out that he'd maimed or killed four of Lord Bartok's men before being subdued. He did not tell him that he'd not resisted thereafter because he'd been disarmed and so hopelessly outnumbered that resistance could only have resulted in further harm to himself; he did not explain that a military man knew better than to fight when defeat was a certainty.

He did not warn that a military man bided his time.

"Your New Man army is like a great snake that wrapped its fat coils around this city," Lord Bartok was saying now. "By imprisoning you, I have cut off the head of the snake."

"Why imprison me?" asked General Murdock, who would never have left an enemy as dangerous as he alive.

"Why imprison you instead of killing you, you mean?" said Lord Bartok. He wrinkled his nose in distaste. "Unlike you, Murdock, I am a civilized man, not an animal."

General Murdock would have liked to say that he was not an animal either—that he enjoyed the finer things in life just as Lord Bartok himself did. However, he knew that the great lord would feel provoked by such a comment, and at present, he could see no advantage to be gained by provoking him.

"Besides," continued Lord Bartok, "I may yet have use for you—alive."

General Murdock nodded, for he could see the sense in this. "And how do you propose to control my New Men?" he asked.

"I am going to give out that you've been stricken by the Great Sickness and that you've asked me to assume command of the army during your convalescence."

"My soldiers will never believe you."

"And yet, as you have already seen, they will do as commanded," said Lord Bartok with quiet satisfaction. "The city gates shall shortly be opened. By sunrise tomorrow most of my fellow noblemen will be headed to their various estates. There, they will call upon all loyal, able-bodied men to take up arms. And when they have assembled, we shall march upon your unsuspecting army, rescue the queen from your despicable lowborn master and crush him and his ambitions once and for all."

With that, Lord Bartok and his men left the cell.

As he listened to the sound of them locking the heavy door behind them, General Murdock closed his good eye and sighed softly. If he'd not been a military man, he might have allowed himself to despair. But he *was* a military man and so he forced himself to think. Clearly, he needed to escape the dungeon quickly so that he could take back control of the city. And if it was too late to do that, he needed to reach the main force of his army in time to lead them into war and protect the life of the master whom he'd served for so long.

At the thought of Mordesius, General Murdock shifted uneasily. He knew that as furious as His Grace was going to be when he found out that the first contingent of soldiers sent to destroy the Methusian nest had failed to report back on schedule, this was nothing compared to how he was going to feel when he learned that control of the imperial capital had fallen into Bartok's hands. At best, Mordesius would accuse General Murdock of incompetence; at worst, he'd suspect him of disloyalty.

Either way, General Murdock knew he had a dangerous uphill battle ahead of him when it came to regaining his master's trust.

Yet it was a battle he would willingly wage because a military man honored his oath of loyalty.

Even unto death.

Twenty-Three

DEATH WAS THE FURTHEST thing from Rachel's mind the next day as she, Zdeno and Azriel prepared to slip behind the waterfall that hid the entrance to the Methusian camp.

A hot meal with all the fixings: this was the thing that was on Rachel's mind.

Licking her lips in anticipation, she watched as Zdeno took two steps down the crumbling path that led to the ledge at the bottom of the waterfall where Azriel was already waiting.

Suddenly, Zdeno turned, stretched his calloused hand back toward her and called, "Take my hand!"

Rachel smiled and did as he bid. The path was not especially treacherous, and she was confident she'd have been able to manage the dozen steps to the bottom without falling to her death, but she liked the feel of his strong hand holding hers. Moreover, she liked that he liked to take care of her. Though she'd not exactly felt jealous watching Azriel fall in love with Persephone—and she with him—it was a truly lovely thing to be cherished by a man who had eyes for none but her and who acted as though she was more beautiful than the stars, more fragile than blown glass and more precious than a bucketful of jewels. And though Zdeno may not have been considered handsome by many, Rachel had come to think of him as very handsome indeed. Oh, perhaps not handsome in the way that Azriel was handsome, for he was just *ridiculously* handsome, but handsome in a way that made Rachel's heart beat a little faster whenever she looked at him.

"Are you all right?" Zdeno asked anxiously when they reached the ledge.

"Yes," she said, smiling again as she reached up to brush the speckles of mist off his messy brown hair.

Zdeno grabbed her hand and kissed her fingertips. She, in turn, kissed him on the lips. Looking as he always did after she kissed him—which is to say, like a man about to burst into flight—Zdeno grinned and clutched her hand tighter.

Eyeing the two of them with a mixture of impatience and yearning, Azriel gestured for them to follow him and then ducked behind the pounding sheets of water. After she and Zdeno had done the same, Rachel stepped up to the mouth of the tunnel that led to the Methusian camp. Closing her eyes, she breathed deeply of the cool, piney breeze that blew through it. She was so looking forward to a real meal, a safe place to sleep and to hearing what ideas Cairn and the others had for finding and rescuing—

"Listen!" hissed Azriel, freezing.

Rachel listened so hard that she could almost feel her ears quivering with exertion. "What is it? What do you hear?" she whispered in a panicky voice. "I don't hear anything!"

"Neither do I," said Zdeno grimly as he took out and loaded his slingshot. "And neither does he."

The hair on the back of Rachel's neck rose when she realized what Zdeno was saying.

Azriel wasn't worried because he'd heard something threatening. He was worried because where he should have been able to hear chattering voices, clattering cooking pots, laughing children and barking dogs, he heard only silence.

Suddenly, mingled with the cool, piney smell, Rachel smelled something else:

Smoke.

"Azriel, wait!" she cried.

But Azriel would not wait. And though Zdeno made a grab for her, Rachel would not wait either. Terrified though she was by the thought of what they might find at the other end of the tunnel, she plunged into the darkness after the wild-eyed Methusian. Hands held out in front to prevent her from bashing into the tunnel walls, she stumbled along just ahead of Zdeno who kept urgently whispering for her to stop. It wasn't until she got far enough through the tunnel that she could begin to see what lay beyond it that she finally did as he asked. Indeed, she stopped so suddenly that Zdeno barreled right into the back of her.

For there, sprawled upon the ground before them, lay the battered, blood-spattered body of a giant, flame-haired Methusian.

Twenty-Four

WHEN PERSEPHONE GUESSED she was about half a day's hike to the Methusian camp, she said goodbye to Flight.

"It's nothing personal," she assured the mare as she lifted off the saddle and panniers and removed the bit and bridle. "You've been a dear and loyal friend, and I truly could not have made it this far without you. However, we cannot be certain that we've not been followed by New Men or by Lord Atticus, and I cannot take the chance that your hoofprints might lead either of them to the secret entrance beneath the falls. Then, too, there is the matter of an old friend whom I left behind at the Methusian camp some months ago. His name is Fleet and he has a heart as big as the moon, but I'm afraid that he is inordinately fond of me, and I do not think he'd take kindly at all to the sight of you in my company."

Flight snorted and tossed her head as if to show what she thought of moon-hearted jealous types. Then she nuzzled Persephone one last time, rolled in the dirt to thoroughly rid herself of the feel of the saddle, whinnied loudly and galloped away.

Relieved that Flight did not appear distraught at their parting, Persephone started walking. As she did so, excitement and anxiety began waging a battle for supremacy inside of her. One minute her spirits soared with the certainty that she'd shortly be hurling herself into Azriel's arms; the next, her spirits were crushed beneath the dread conviction that Mordesius's soldiers had gotten to the Methusian camp first and that Azriel and the others were all dead.

By the time she reached the crumbling dirt path that led to the stone ledge at the base of the falls, Persephone was wrung out by her wild emotional swings. Pausing for just long enough to cut an armful of sugarberry branches so that she'd have a reunion gift for Fleet, she hurried down the path and slipped behind the falls.

It was then that anxiety abruptly triumphed over excitement—and was joined by its bosom companions, terror and despair.

Dropping the sugarberry branches from hands shaking so hard she could barely unsheathe her dagger, Persephone told herself that the deathly quiet from the other end of the tunnel wasn't *necessarily* cause for alarm and that the sickly-sweet smell in the air wasn't *necessarily* burning flesh. Except that she knew the quiet *was* cause for alarm and the smell *was* burning flesh. And knowing these things, she knew she ought to turn and flee while she still had the chance.

But she couldn't do it.

Not without knowing whether there were any in the Methusian camp who might yet be saved, and not until she'd seen for herself if Azriel was among the dead.

Persephone made her way through the tunnel swiftly and silently. The sight that greeted her as she neared the far end was even worse than she'd imagined. Except for the hut in which she and Azriel had spent their first night together, every hut in the camp had been reduced to a charred ruin. The clearing where her beautiful wedding had taken place was a mess of overturned tables, smashed cooking pots, rotting food and discarded personal possessions. Hard and soft surfaces alike were marked with rust-colored splatters and smears too numerous to count.

After a moment of staring, numb with shock and horror, Persephone realized that she couldn't see a single body, living or dead.

She took a cautious step forward, and then another, and another, until she was standing a pace away from the threshold of the tunnel. When she still couldn't see anybody or any bodies, she covered her mouth with her sleeve to keep from breathing in the greasy, black smoke, adjusted her grip on her dagger and stepped out of the tunnel.

She was grabbed from behind so fast that she was yanked clear off her feet before she realized what was happening. Unfortunately, by the time she did realize what was happening, her attacker already had one arm clamped across her chest to trap her arms and the other tucked firmly under her chin.

And judging by the way he was squeezing with that arm, he clearly meant to choke the life out of her, break her neck or both.

Strangely, Persephone did not feel frightened as she squirmed and struggled for air. Instead, she felt furious that she and the baby had survived so much and come so far only to meet their ends at the hands of a brute too cowardly to face her in a fair fight. She was so furious, in fact, that, even as she began to see the black spots that spelled the end, she somehow found the strength to give her attacker a vicious heel stomp.

The startled grunt of pain that issued from her attacker's mouth was followed by a most welcome release of the pressure on her throat and a momentary loosening of the arm across her chest.

Gagging and wheezing, Persephone saw her chance. Tucking in her chin so that her attacker could not resume strangling her, she was about to drive her dagger backward into his belly when she heard him inhale sharply.

Something about the sound made her hesitate.

And then she was once again being pulled closer than close. This time, however, it was done with infinite tenderness, and it was accompanied by the feel of warm lips pressed against her ear and by the sound of someone raggedly whispering her name over and over in a voice so choked with emotion that it sounded like a prayer.

No, not someone.

Azriel.

Dizzy with shock and relief, Persephone sagged against him, unable to believe what her senses were telling her. As the dagger slipped from her fingers, she closed her eyes and reveled in the strength of him, hardly daring to breathe for fear that she would awaken to discover that it had all been a dream.

After what seemed like an eternity, she swallowed past the lump in her throat and whispered,

"Is it you, Azriel? Is it really you?"

"It is really me—and by the gods, it is really you," he replied, sounding as dangerously close to tears as she felt.

Turning in his arms, she wrapped her arms around him and pressed her head against his chest that she might drink in the sound of his beating heart. The calmness that washed over her as she listened to it was so intoxicating that she almost felt drunk by the time she finally leaned back to look up at him. Her heart clenched at how careworn he appeared, and at the way he was desperately searching her face for the answer to a question he could not seem to find the words to ask.

"I'm fine, Azriel," she said gently. "Though it is true that I endured mistreatment and hardship during our weeks apart, the important thing is that I endured."

When he only nodded and bit his lip, she knew.

Or rather, she knew that *he* knew.

Offering him the barest hint of a smile, she said, "Did you figure it out for yourself or did Rachel tell you?"

"Tell me about what?" asked Azriel, who seemed to have stopped breathing.

"Tell you about this," she said in a hushed voice as she guided one of his hands down to the small swell of her belly. "We're going to have a baby, husband, and though I've yet to feel him move, I am certain it is a boy and that he thrives."

His handsome face lighting up as dazzlingly as a summer sun bursting from behind storm clouds, Azriel gaped at her, then kissed her, then gaped at her some more.

"Boy or girl, it matters not to me, wife, so long as it's healthy. We're going to have a baby!"

Persephone laughed as he gave a whoop of joy and dropped to his knees before her. Pushing up the hem of her doublet, he alternated between raining kisses upon her bare belly and offering fatherly advice to the child within. Persephone buried her fingers in his auburn curls and laughed again, caught up in his enthusiasm.

It was such a perfect moment that she would have given much to see it last forever. It wasn't long, however, before a gust of wind sent several tendrils of greasy smoke lurching into her line of vision. They reminded her that she and Azriel were not standing in their own little world but in the midst of devastation—and that she had yet to see any sign that anyone but Azriel had survived it.

Her happiness all but extinguished by the thought, Persephone reluctantly pulled him to his feet and said, "Tell me, Azriel. What happened here?"

Azriel led her over to one of the few tables that hadn't been overturned. After they'd settled onto the bench beside the table, he said, "When Rachel, Zdeno and I arrived two days past, everyone was gone."

"Gone?" Persephone felt a chill as she cast a darting glance at the large pile of charred bodies on the other side of the clearing. "What do you mean 'gone'?"

"I mean escaped," clarified Azriel.

Persephone stared at him. "That is the most wonderful news, of course, but how on earth did everyone escape *this*?" she asked, gesturing to the bloody battlefield around her.

"They didn't," he said. "When I said 'everyone,' I meant everyone who survived the initial attack, which was not everyone at all. We . . . we found Tiny at the entrance of the tunnel. Judging by the pair of crutches we found nearby, he'd not yet recovered from the broken legs he suffered during the avalanche." Azriel paused before continuing in a gruff voice. "Even so, the big man still managed to slice open half a dozen New Men before they finally took him down."

Persephone did not hesitate but immediately climbed onto Azriel's lap and wrapped her arms around him. "I'm so sorry," she murmured.

"I'm sorry, too," he said. "For the death of your brother, I mean."

Persephone nodded, her throat tightening up as it always did when she thought of poor Finn. Then, not wanting to dwell upon this most painful subject—and feeling this was not the time to share that she'd promised her dying twin that she'd fight for the throne—she deftly steered the conversation back to its earlier course. "Was Tiny the only one lost in the attack, then?"

"No." Azriel shook his head. "There were five others. Three men, one woman and a child."

"A child?" said Persephone faintly, thinking of the two Methusian children she'd known best—one, a jolly, lisping toddler and the other, a brave and stoic little orphan. "It . . . it wasn't Sabian or Mateo, was it?"

Azriel shook his head.

Persephone nodded, relieved and not relieved, for who could take comfort in the death of any child?

"Six dead is six too many, and yet it seems extraordinarily lucky that more were not lost, given the number of New Men who took part in the attack," she said, gesturing toward the pile of bodies, which she now understood must belong to dead soldiers.

"Luck had nothing to do with it," said Azriel. "Tangled 'round the legs of two of the butchered New Men we found pieces of string with small weights at each end."

Persephone stared at him, puzzled, before brightening with sudden understanding. "That sounds like the device Big Ben used to take you down during our quest for the healing pool!" she exclaimed.

Looking a little miffed that she'd recalled with such enthusiasm the memory of him being soundly bested by the surly dwarf, Azriel said, "It was, indeed, the same device. That evidence, along with the discovery of a familiar trinket and the fact that several of the dead soldiers had pitchfork holes in their backs convinced me that the lowborn bandit Robert and his men somehow took part in the fight."

"What trinket did you discover?" asked Persephone, intrigued.

Azriel reached into his pocket and withdrew a charm bracelet, one of three gifts Finn had given her the day she'd set off in search of the healing pool. She'd later given the bracelet to Robert to seal her promise to him that she'd do what she could to set to rights the wrongs done to the lowborns of the realm.

"I found the bracelet on Tiny's forehead," explained Azriel, handing it to her. "Robert must have put it there so we'd know where to look for Cairn and the other survivors. Within minutes of finding it, Zdeno and Rachel headed into the Great Forest to seek them out and enlist their help coming up with a plan to rescue you."

"Why didn't you go with them?" asked Persephone.

"As the only Methusian of us three, it was my responsibility to bury my dead and burn the bodies of their murderers," said Azriel. "I finished the task less than an hour ago."

"Then let us leave this place of grief at once," she said gently.

Azriel shook his head. "It's too late to safely venture into the forest tonight," he said. "Besides, before we go anywhere, I intend to see my pregnant wife well fed, rightly rested, suitably clothed and properly bedded."

Hungry and exhausted though she was, at the mention of the last item on his "to do" list, Persephone flushed and her breath quickened. "Fed, rested, clothed and bedded—in that order?" she inquired.

Azriel flashed his wickedest pirate smile. "No," he purred as he drew her closer. "Not in that order, wife. Not in that order at all."

By the time the sun had set and twilight had begun creeping over the land, Azriel had only managed to accomplish one of the tasks he'd set for himself, though it was Persephone's considered opinion that he'd performed it very well indeed.

Intent upon accomplishing a second task, Azriel slid from the bed where they'd spent their awkward first night together as husband and wife. From the tangle of sheets in which she was lying, content beyond measure, Persephone yawned and feebly protested that she really ought to help him prepare supper. Silencing her protests with a long, deep kiss, Azriel bundled her into a heavy quilt, carried her outside and set her down beside the firepit behind the hut. A moment later, he had a blazing fire going, and a surprisingly short time after that, supper was served.

The bounty would have been enough to make Persephone weep if she'd not been so intent upon filling her belly. In addition to juicy pieces of roast venison cut from the young deer Azriel had brought down the previous day, there was all manner of food salvaged from the camp stores, from ladlefuls of thick pottage, boiled eggs and sausages smothered in syrup, to wedges of cheese and hunks of week-old bread that didn't have a speck of green on them.

"I want you to know that I'll never forgive myself for almost having killed you," Azriel said for the thousandth time as he refilled her platter and handed it to her.

"Really, you must stop fretting about that," said Persephone, using a piece of meat to gesture dismissively. "I almost killed you, too, and you don't see me fretting about it, do you?"

"No, as a matter of fact, I don't," said Azriel disapprovingly.

Persephone laughed and flicked a cheese rind in his direction.

"By the way," said Azriel, ducking the rind. "That infernal hawk of yours found us in Parthania."

"Ivan found you?" cried Persephone, thrilled to know for a certainty that at least one of her animal friends was alive and well.

"He did," confirmed Azriel, looking considerably less thrilled than she. "He followed us almost the entire way here, and even though he behaved quite as rudely and disrespectfully as he's ever behaved toward me, I did my best to honor my promise to take care of him."

Setting down her platter, Persephone clutched the quilt around her with one hand while she awkwardly leaned over and gave Azriel a kiss. He responded by kissing her passionately and suggesting something she might want to do if she was truly grateful. With a scandalized squeak, she wriggled away from him, picked up her platter and resumed eating.

"Speaking of honoring promises," said Azriel. "I wish to state for the record that I was not best pleased when you snuck away to face Mordesius on your own after you'd promised me that we'd face him together."

"I didn't mean to lie to you. Or rather, I did mean to lie to you, but I did not *want* to lie to you," said Persephone, who was determined to always tell him the truth from now on. "It's just . . . you gave me no choice, Azriel. Mordesius would've killed you if you'd accompanied me to the palace that day, I know he would have, and I simply could not allow that to happen. The important thing to remember is that—"

"You were coming back to me," said Azriel.

"Yes," said Persephone.

Azriel's eyes glowed like blue flames at this, but all he said was, "Be that as it may, pregnant or not, it would serve you right if I up and gave you a good, sound spanking."

"A spanking?" said Persephone, grinning as she recalled how he'd made the very same threat on that long-ago night she'd caught him trying to steal a chicken from the owner's barn. "That is the most absurd thing I've ever heard in my life," she said now, repeating the same words she'd said then—but saying them in an altogether more teasing, provocative manner. "You—wouldn't—dare."

"Oh, wouldn't I?" growled Azriel, pouncing so suddenly that she almost shrieked.

"Well," she said breathlessly as he eased her onto her back and began kissing her neck, "maybe you would, at that."

Twenty-Five

SHORTLY BEFORE DAWN next morning, Persephone awoke to the sight of Azriel standing at the end of the bed holding up a full-skirted, fawn-colored gown.

"Good morning to you, wife," he murmured, his eyes roving over her in the most delicious fashion.

"Good morning to you, husband," she replied with a sleepy smile. "That is a lovely gown you have there, though I must tell you I'm not sure it'll fit you across the shoulders."

"The gown is not for me, Persephone, it is for you, as are the cloak and boots," declared Azriel, gesturing toward the pile of items laid across the foot of the bed. "Last night after you fell asleep, I removed your treasures from the pocket of the disgusting uniform you'd been wearing and burnt the hateful thing to a cinder. While I, personally, would like nothing better than to see you traipsing through the Great Forest wearing nothing but the scabbard at your thigh, the silver necklace around your neck, the ruby ring upon your finger and that pretty smile, I thought perhaps that you might prefer—"

His words were cut short by the faint but unmistakable sound of dozens of male voices in the tunnel beneath the falls.

Jumping to her feet, Persephone unsheathed her dagger from its scabbard (she'd worn both to bed) and tossed it to one side. Grabbing the gown out of Azriel's hands, she threw it on, shoved her treasures into the skirt pocket, pulled on the fringed doeskin boots, swung the cloak over her shoulders and snatched up her dagger. She then pushed her hair back from her face, looked up at Azriel and breathlessly announced that she was ready to go.

"Why do I feel as though you're not going to be content to spend the next five months sitting in a rocking chair knitting baby booties?" asked Azriel dryly.

"Probably because I'm not," she replied, thinking of the dangerous fight for the throne that lay ahead.

Grimacing slightly at her response, Azriel shouldered a bulging pack, grabbed her free hand and led her outside.

Because the hut was set farther back in the woods, Persephone and Azriel managed to slip away without being spotted by the soldiers who'd no doubt come in search of their comrades.

As they made their way into the gloom of the Great Forest, Azriel set a slightly less grueling pace than he normally did when they were traveling with a purpose. Partly this was due to his concern for his pregnant wife and partly this was because he needed to be sure that they were following the correct trail. Since Robert's gang and the fleeing Methusians had been too many to travel without leaving a discernible trail, they'd done the next best thing: they'd left *many* discernible trails, so many that only a masterful tracker would be able to deduce the direction in which they'd actually gone. And even then, only if he was lucky.

Several times throughout the day, Persephone tried to tell Azriel about the promise she'd made to Finn, but each time, her courage failed. That he'd made no mention of her claim to the throne made her feel like he was purposely avoiding the subject. Moreover, he'd only just found her again after having lost her, and now he knew about the baby. She dreaded seeing the look in his eyes when she told him that she had no choice but to throw herself back into danger and that worse than this, she had to do it now, before the baby was born, because the realm could not wait five months for a new ruler, and Mordesius *would* not wait. The former regent's plan to gain the throne by marrying her had failed, but Persephone had no doubt that he had a backup plan, that it almost certainly involved bloodshed and that the blood he would seek to shed above all others was hers.

Leaving talk of such dark things to the future for just a little longer seemed like a kindness.

Long before night fell that evening, Azriel stopped beside an ancient tree with a hollow trunk large enough to comfortably sleep two. As he bustled about collecting firewood, he repeatedly informed Persephone that she was to abandon any secret plans she might harbor to drag him inside the tree and have her way with him.

"I'm serious," he said as he paused to languorously run his hands from his well-muscled chest to his flat belly. "I've much to do at present and later, I'll be spending the night protecting you and our child from the beasts of the forest."

"I understand," said Persephone solemnly.

"I mean it," warned Azriel, stretching in a manner that just happened to show off his sinewy arms and powerful legs to their best advantage.

"I believe you," smiled Persephone.

Scowling slightly at the fact that she did not appear to harbor any secret plans to have her way with him, Azriel laid his cloak on the ground near the crackling fire so that she'd have somewhere dry to sit. Then, with a rather long-suffering sigh, he set about getting supper. Since the only small game they'd seen that day had been the occasional scrawny brown bird swooping through the leafy canopy high above, there was no fresh meat. Still, the meal was a good one, for the previous evening Azriel had had the forethought to fill his pack with enough food to feed several armies.

"I do not intend that you and our child shall ever want for food again," he announced as he settled himself behind Persephone so that she'd have something comfortable to lean against. Briefly leaving off stroking her hair, he planted a lingering kiss on the sensitive spot behind her ear and said, "I do not intend that either of you shall ever again want for anything."

Persephone gave a shiver of pleasure at his kiss and at the feel of his broad chest pressed against her back. "What a clever husband you are," she sighed contentedly as she resumed licking honey off her fingers.

Azriel chuckled. "Perhaps it will be you who pushes me on the swing hung from the low branch of the oak tree by our little thatch-roofed cottage."

"Perhaps, but only if you promise to feed the chickens," she said.

"Very well, but I draw the line at tending the garden," said Azriel, his breath warm against the back of her neck. Wrapping one arm across her chest to hug her closer still, he gently slid his free hand down to rest against her belly before continuing. "What a life we shall have together, you and I, with pigs enough to keep us in bacon and sausages all winter and grain enough to make our bread and beer. Sturdy homespun shirts, a warm bed, music and laughter, and the knowledge that it will all be there tomorrow, and for a thousand tomorrows thereafter."

"That would be nice," murmured Persephone, smiling at the inexpressibly seductive picture he painted. Then her smile faded as she realized that now was the time to tell Azriel that such a life would not be possible, even supposing that she did manage to survive the fight for the throne. "It would be nice," she repeated, more hesitantly this time. "Only—"

She got no farther than this before she inhaled sharply and sat bolt upright.

Azriel was on his feet with sword in hand before she'd finished gasping. "What is it?" he demanded harshly, his gaze sweeping the darkness. "What's wrong?"

"Shh!" said Persephone, flapping her hand at him. Cocking her head to one side, she concentrated very hard. Then she exclaimed, "There it is again!"

"There what is again?" cried Azriel, who was almost hopping with agitation.

"The baby," she breathed, beaming up at him. "I've felt him move at last!"

For a moment, Azriel just gaped at her, looking nearly as dazed as the Panoraki Ghengor had looked after taking the dull edge of a battle-ax to the side of the head. Then, letting the sword slip from his hand, he fell to his knees. Using his arm for support, Persephone pulled herself up so that she was kneeling beside him. Reaching for his hand, she pressed it firmly against her belly, held her breath and waited for it to come again, that ping that felt exactly like the stamp of a tiny foot or the punch of a tiny fist.

It came again almost at once.

"There!" cried Persephone. "Did you feel that?"

Azriel shook his head.

Determined that he should share in the wonder of the moment, Persephone pressed his hand more firmly against her belly.

The ping came again and again and again.

"Did you feel that . . . or that . . . or that?" she asked eagerly.

"No!" said Azriel with mounting frustration. "I can't feel anything. Are you sure—"

"I'm sure," she said.

Feeling at once calmer and more excited than she'd ever felt in her life, Persephone sat back on her heels and let her gaze drift from the fire to the velvety darkness of the forest around her.

Then she gasped again.

"What is it?" asked Azriel, his gaze never leaving her face. "Is it the baby? Did you feel him move again?"

"I did, but it is not that," she replied in a low voice. "It is, uh, that."

Without lifting her hand, she raised her index finger and pointed at the pair of yellow eyes that glittered in the darkness just beyond the firelight. Judging from their size and spacing, they unquestionably belonged to a beast large and fierce enough to tear a grown man to pieces.

And they were unblinkingly fixed upon her.

Moving smoothly and slowly to avoid provoking an attack, Azriel picked up his bow. Rising to his feet, he pulled an arrow from the quiver on his back, nocked it and took aim.

The beast snarled wetly.

At the sound, Persephone's heart gave a wild thump. "Don't shoot!" she cried, giving the tail of Azriel's bow such a yank that the arrow pierced the heart of the fire instead of the spot between the beast's glittering yellow eyes.

"Let go!" shouted Azriel, jerking the bow out of her hand.

With breathtaking swiftness, he reached for another arrow. Before he could get it nocked, however, the beast in the darkness had launched itself straight at Persephone . . .

The next instant, she was laughing and hugging Cur for all he was worth, while Azriel wheezed and clutched at his chest as though he was having a heart attack.

"Irresponsible . . . irresponsible doesn't even *begin* to describe—"

"Don't be angry," said Persephone as she happily planted a noisy kiss on Cur's smelly wet nose.

"Don't be *angry?*" hiccoughed Azriel, who was still shouting. "What if it hadn't been your infernal dog, Persephone? What if it had been something else—something that wanted to *eat* you and the baby?"

"But it wasn't something that wanted to eat me and the baby," she said, raising her voice to match his. "I knew it wasn't because I recognized the snarl."

At this, Cur snarled again. Then, without warning, he jerked his big, furry head toward Azriel and began barking in such a frenzied manner that the startled Methusian yelped and leapt backward.

The leap caused him to stumble over his pack. He spent several seconds frantically windmilling his arms in an effort to recover his balance before losing the battle and landing with a mighty thump on his backside.

Azriel looked so utterly outraged to find himself sitting in the dirt that it took all of Persephone's considerable willpower not to fall over shrieking with laughter.

"So, um, how is your manly pride?" she finally managed to choke out.

"Wounded!"

"And your backside?"

"Also wounded!"

Biting her lip to keep from smiling, Persephone gently pushed Cur to one side and crawled over to where her scowling husband sat huffing and muttering under his breath. Draping her arms about his neck, she pressed her forehead against his and murmured, "I know that Cur is sorry."

They both looked over at the dog, who silently bared his teeth at Azriel.

"And though I cannot regret having prevented you from killing him, perhaps my actions *were* irresponsible," she continued. "I'm sorry if they frightened you."

"I'm sorry, too," said Azriel. "I should not have shouted at you. But your actions *did* frighten me, Persephone. I have the clan, but you and the baby are the only family I've got. I could not bear to lose you."

"I know," she whispered, wondering how she was ever going to find the courage to tell him about the promise that could cost him everything. "We could not bear to lose you, either."

Twenty-Six

MORDESIUS'S FURY would have known no bounds if he'd had any inkling that the one he called "cockroach" was being transported to dizzying heights of pleasure at the very same instant that he, himself, was being plunged low by a devastating setback.

"It appears that your noble father did not heed your advice to stay where he was and do nothing to raise the suspicions of my general," said Mordesius, without lifting his gaze from the dirty parchment clutched tight in his shiny-pink scarred hands.

"What do you mean?" shrieked Lord Atticus in terror.

Mordesius pursed his lips. The noble ninny had not made such a spectacle of himself since the night he'd been shown what real torture was. Even then, once he'd reconciled himself to betraying his father, received a goblet of wine that did not contain a nose and been assured that he'd henceforth be treated as befitted his noble station, he'd perked up considerably.

Now he was back to being a blubbering worm, and Mordesius was in no mood for his histrionics. For days now, Mordesius had been eagerly awaiting word that Lord Bartok and his insufferable little shrew of a daughter were dead—and with them, any possibility that the nobility of the realm would have the cause or strength to oppose him. That Queen Persephone had slipped through his fingers and eluded his trackers alternately filled Mordesius with rage and twisted his guts into knots. However, he no longer considered the loss of her an impediment to his goal of becoming king. He was done trying to show the world that he did not need to resort to brute force to triumph over his betters. He had the largest standing army in the realm: he would take the throne by force, and all would bend the knee or suffer the consequences.

All that was needed was the swift elimination of the one person in the realm who had the strength, daring and motivation to raise an army strong enough to take on his New Men. Unfortunately, instead of receiving word that Lord Bartok had been killed, Mordesius received this hastily scrawled note informing him that Bartok had taken control of the imperial capital, Murdock had not been seen in days, and that nearly all of the realm's noblemen had abandoned the city and were rumored to be gathering their sworn swords at Bartok Estate.

"I told you my father would not be fooled by that letter we sent!" cried Lord Atticus shrilly, pounding the dining table with his soft fist.

"You told me no such thing," snapped Mordesius, who'd suspected that the letter would not fool Bartok but who'd hoped that it would delay him long enough to give Murdock a chance to murder him.

"Well, I knew he wouldn't be fooled!" amended Atticus wildly, knocking over his goblet in his haste to reach for the wine jug. "My lord father thinks me an utter buffoon and always has. He would never believe me capable of the feats I'd claimed! And now your idiot general has gone and gotten himself killed—"

"It seems likely," muttered Mordesius.

"It is an absolute certainty!" screeched Atticus, clumsily righting his goblet before sloshing more wine into it from the jug that he held in his violently shaking hand. "My father has killed him. Just as he will kill me when he finds me—just as he will kill you when he finds you! Unless . . . unless . . ."

"Unless what?" said Mordesius irritably.

Hope bloomed on the young lord's fleshy face; his whiny voice dripped with it. "Unless the letter is a fake, just like the letter we sent to my father?" he suggested. "Perhaps your general yet holds my father captive—"

"No," said Mordesius flatly. "Even if the words did not have the unmistakable ring of truth to them, the fact is that if the city gates were yet sealed no one but my general would have been able to get a letter to me. That I received a letter at all tells me that Murdock has lost control of the city. That he has lost control of the city tells me that he is probably dead, for he is the kind who'd sooner fight to the death than fail in his duty."

At these words, Lord Atticus's face crumpled with a disappointment so profound that he looked to be, in very truth, on the verge of blubbering. Mordesius regarded him with abject disgust. As he did so, it occurred to him that Lord Atticus was sitting in the very same chair that Queen Persephone would have occupied if they'd gotten as far as dinner on their last night together. Without warning, Mordesius's heart swelled at the memory of her standing still as a portrait at the threshold of the dining hall—her creamy skin aglow, her ripe young body all but spilling out of her gown, the intoxicating scent of her wafting through the air toward him. Then, just as suddenly, he recalled the horrified expression on her face when he'd informed her that they were to be married. At this bitter memory, his heart shriveled. For the thousandth time, he told himself that the only reason he was unhappy that she'd vanished into thin air was because his hope of finding the healing pool had vanished with her. He reminded himself that the queen had ever been a meddling complication and that he was well rid of her. He assured himself that when he became king in his own right, he'd have his choice of women and that he'd not need to settle for some gutter-reared broodmare who was about as much of a queen as he was a—

"Are you even listening to me?" demanded Lord Atticus, who occasionally seemed to forget that he was in the custody of a man who thought nothing of forcing people to cut off their own noses.

"No, I was not listening to you," said Mordesius, taking a sip of his wine.

Lord Atticus pursed his lips. "I was asking what you intended to do now that your little scheme has failed and my father will be coming for us the very instant he finds out where we're hiding."

Instead of answering, Mordesius let his gaze drift toward the threshold of the dining hall. What the addlebrained young lord clearly failed to grasp was that it wouldn't just be Lord Bartok coming for them. It would be Bartok and every able-bodied man that he and the other great lords were able to rally—legions and legions and legions of able-bodied men. Given that this was so, the slaughter of the clans would clearly have to wait. Bartok's army would have to be defeated first, and since no New Man in the realm had a tenth of the battle sense that Murdock had possessed, there was really only one man who could possibly lead them to victory. The question was whether Mordesius, who could hardly sit upon a horse without his brutally damaged body screaming in protest, dared to step into General Murdock's empty boots.

He . . . did.

His cold heart thumping hard at his momentous decision, Mordesius bellowed for his private secretary and kept bellowing until the man hobbled into the dining hall a scant few moments later.

"Send a letter to every New Man camp and outpost in the kingdom," barked Mordesius. "Order the commanders to send as many armed men as they can spare to the training camp north of Syon, and order them to do so at once. Tell them that I will not tolerate delays."

Still breathless from his hasty hobble, the secretary nodded vigorously, took a hesitant step backward, then stopped.

"Well?" barked Mordesius. "What are you waiting for? Get to it. Now!"

The secretary, who'd been nervously awaiting a formal dismissal, nearly tripped over his only foot in his haste to remove himself from sight.

Mordesius glowered after him, then turned to Lord Atticus and said, "Prepare yourself, my lord, for within the week, we shall set out on a journey."

Lord Atticus groaned loudly to show that the prospect of travel pleased him not at all. Then he took a long draught of his wine, wiped his small, pouting mouth with the back of his hand and sighed, "Where are we going?"

Suddenly exhilarated by the prospect of destroying the worm's noble father in a true blood-and-guts battle, Mordesius straightened his twisted back, lifted his heavy head and breathed,

"We are going to war."

Twenty-Seven

THE NOBLEMAN destined to face Mordesius on the battlefield strode briskly across the cobblestone courtyard of the imperial palace. His blue cape flapping behind him, he entered the royal stable and made his way down to the large stall at the end. In the stall stood two creatures: the spirited white mare Lord Bartok would soon ride into battle and the lanky, lowborn stable boy who'd been paying regular visits to his daughter's bedchamber for the past fortnight or so.

"I hope she's been ridden hard and often," Lord Bartok informed the stable boy without preamble.

"M'lord?" choked the boy, so startled that he dropped one of the two heavy brushes he'd been using to smooth the last of the tangles from the horse's white-blond mane.

Lord Bartok pursed his lips ever so slightly.

"I hope my new horse has been ridden hard and often, that she will have the stamina to perform as I require in the days to come," he clarified in clipped tones. "I also hope she's been trained not to shy at crowds or loud noises, for I would not have her falter beneath me in battle or panic if we get caught in the thick of it."

"Oh," said the boy, grinning with relief. Hastily retrieving the brush from the straw at his feet, he dropped both brushes into a nearby wooden bucket, lifted the mare's supple leather halter off its nail on the stall wall and slipped it over the horse's pretty head.

"You needn't worry about her shying, faltering or panicking, m'lord, for I trained her myself," said the boy. "She's a good horse, aren't you, girl? You'll not let the great lord down, will you, sweetheart?"

In response to these questions, the horse snorted and tried to jerk her head away from the hands that were deftly moving the bridle into place.

"Finish saddling her at once and bring her to me outside, do you understand?" said Lord Bartok.

"I do, m'lord," said the stable boy, bobbing his head so briskly that his dirty dark hair flopped into his blue eyes.

As he wordlessly turned and strode back the way he'd come, Lord Bartok reflected that Atticus had done rather well in selecting a stud who bore sufficient resemblance to the dead king that the paternity of any child Aurelia might conceive would not be questioned on the basis of looks, anyway.

It is unfortunate that Atticus is not here to see to the second part of his instructions, thought Lord Bartok absently as he stepped out of the stable, *for I cannot afford to delay my departure to personally execute them, and even the most trusted retainer is likely to wonder what a mere stable boy might have done to deserve—*

"Godspeed, my lord!" a deep voice floated to him over the crisp morning air.

Looking up, Lord Bartok saw Lord Belmont leaning heavily against the sill of an open window on the third floor of the palace. He was dressed in an enormous doublet of crimson, and he was flanked by his ever-present companion, the deaf serving girl. The golden crest of his new office dangled from the chain about his thick neck.

Lord Bartok nodded and waved briefly in acknowledgment of the other nobleman's salutation.

It had been his idea to put Belmont in charge of the city following the removal of General Murdock. He'd needed to put someone in charge and Belmont had been the obvious choice. In addition to being the second-greatest lord in the realm, he could barely stand unassisted—he'd have been worse than useless on the battlefield, an invalid they'd have had to worry about protecting *and* feeding. Moreover, it suited Lord Bartok's purposes to have Belmont out of the way. The lumbering lord would not take kindly to any actions he considered ignoble, and he held great sway with the other lords. Safer by far to have Belmont tucked away, beyond the ability to influence anyone. Once he, Lord Bartok, had wedded and bedded the queen, there'd be nothing Belmont or anyone else would be able to do about it.

Turning away from Lord Belmont before Lord Belmont could turn away from him, Lord Bartok gazed out over the beautifully manicured royal garden without really seeing a single exotic bloom, pretty pond or fluttering songbird.

The other noblemen had ridden out to muster their men and gather supplies days ago, but he'd stayed behind to search Mordesius's papers and personal effects for a clue as to where he'd taken the queen. Unfortunately, his efforts had been in vain. He'd have to hope that the looming war would draw the upstart out of his hole, and that he'd drag his royal wife along with him when it did.

A light tap-tap-tapping sound behind Lord Bartok caught his attention. Turning, he saw Aurelia flying toward him, her slippered feet tapping against the cobblestones as she ran, her skirts and petticoats lifted slightly higher than was necessary to keep from tripping on them.

Lord Bartok's eyes flicked from his daughter to the dirty boy who'd just emerged from the stables leading the saddled white mare. He said nothing until Aurelia had come to a flustered halt before him and dipped him an elegant curtsey. Then, his calm tone belying his irritation, he said,

"You are *supposed* to be with child, Aurelia."

"What? Oh! Yes, of course," she panted. Hastily dropping her skirts, she coughed delicately into one hand before pressing it against the small of her back and pushing her nonexistent belly forward. "Is this better, Father?" she whispered hopefully, still gasping slightly in an effort to catch her breath.

Lord Bartok looked down at his daughter with something vaguely resembling distaste. "What do you want?" he asked, ignoring her inane question.

"I want to know why you did not send for me."

"Why would I have sent for you?"

Lady Aurelia flinched. "Because all the other lords sent for their daughters when they departed the city," she said.

"I am not the other lords," said Lord Bartok. "You are not their daughters."

"That is precisely why you ought to have sent for me!" she cried. "The city is yet overrun by armed New Men—"

"Not so well armed as they were, thanks to my clearing out most of their weapons depots," said Lord Bartok with satisfaction.

Out of the corner of his eye, he saw the stable boy halt a respectful distance away.

"Even so," continued Aurelia, "the lowborns grow more unruly by the hour. The market is empty, the merchants have closed up shop and the craftsmen—even the dressmakers!—are refusing to venture out. There are rumors of war. What is to become of me, left here all by myself?"

"You will not be by yourself," said Lord Bartok, impatiently gesturing to the stable boy that he might approach. "You will have dozens of servants to tend to your every need."

"Servants," sneered Aurelia, wrinkling her nose at the stable boy before deliberately averting her face.

Flushing deeply, the boy handed Lord Bartok the reins, hastily bowed to them both and hurried away.

"I despise Atticus for making arrangements for *that* to visit me each night," hissed Aurelia through clenched teeth. "He purposely chose one that smells like horseshit, I know he did. Where is he, anyway?"

"Atticus?"

"Yes."

"Gone."

"Gone?" said Aurelia. "Gone where?"

Though Lord Bartok sincerely doubted that the news of her brother's fate would shock Aurelia into miscarrying in the unlikely event that she was pregnant, he did not think it wise to take chances. So he said, "It is none of your business where your brother has gone, Aurelia. Your business is to get with child."

The girl looked outraged. "I am *trying*—"

"I believe you," interrupted Lord Bartok. "But I also believe that there is every chance you will fail. If that happens, there is something I would have you do."

"What?" muttered Aurelia, screwing up her pinched face and folding her arms tightly across her chest as though in anticipation of more horseshit-scented unpleasantness.

Lord Bartok regarded her coolly until she uncrossed her arms, dipped him a stiff curtsey and said, "What is it you would have me do, Father?"

"I would have you hide from your maids that your monthly courses have begun," he replied. "I would have you begin padding your bodice and skirts."

The scowl on her face vanished upon the instant. "You're going to find me an infant after all, then?" she asked eagerly, her eyes bright with the hope that even if she failed to conceive the stable boy's child, she might yet have all that had been promised to her. "An infant that I can claim to have given birth to, one that I can name as the dead king's son?"

With a fleeting smile at the thought of the sons he hoped to get upon the queen, Lord Bartok said, "All you need to know, Aurelia, is that I intend to keep my options open."

With that, he swung up into the saddle, adjusted his cape about his shoulders, gave a brisk nod to the captain of his escort and galloped away without a backward glance.

Twenty-Eight

THE MORNING AFTER their hasty departure from the destroyed Methusian camp, Persephone was awoken at the crack of dawn by Cur, who only left off nuzzling her once in order to bark in Azriel's face. As she and her grumbling husband stumbled out of the hollow tree trunk, yawning and rubbing sleep from their eyes, Cur ran half a dozen steps deeper in the Great Forest, turned, looked at her and barked again.

Understanding at once that he meant for them to follow him, Persephone snatched a bite to eat while Azriel broke camp, then the two of them hurried after their four-legged guide, who led them unerringly onward at a brisk but steady pace until late afternoon, when he suddenly bolted ahead.

Before Persephone could reassure Azriel that Cur would *never* have left her side if there was anything to worry about, half a dozen masked men dropped out of the trees and surrounded them so fast that even Azriel didn't have time to react. Shrieking like a banshee, the man nearest Persephone was about to plunge the rusty tines of his pitchfork into her belly when he took a second look at her face and his eyes widened in sudden recognition.

Flinging the pitchfork to one side, he snatched off his mask, dropped to one knee and reverently said, "Welcome back to the Great Forest, Your Majesty! May I respectfully request the honor of escorting you and your worthy prince consort to the camp of the most feared bandit in all the realm?"

"Are . . . are you speaking of Robert?" gulped Persephone, who'd not quite recovered from the shock of having almost been stabbed to death.

"I am," said the beaming ruffian, bowing low.

Concerned that the next lookout might not be quite so quick to recognize her, Persephone gladly accepted the man's offer to escort them the rest of the way down the forest trail and into the heart of the bandit camp she remembered so well.

The uproar caused by their arrival was beyond belief. Led by their leader Cairn, Methusians of all ages came running from their make-shift tents. Bandits racing down the hanging ladders outside their tree shelters could not have made it to the ground faster if they'd jumped. The crowd surged around Persephone and Azriel, every-one calling out to them at the same time, then calling again when they realized they hadn't been heard. Dogs barked and chickens squawked; children shouted with excitement. Bandits bellowed and shoved each other good-naturedly until things got out of hand and several fights broke out. Knowing Robert's men and the Methusians as she did, Persephone had expected a boisterous greeting, but this one was boisterous to the point of making it hard for her to breathe and keep her footing, and Azriel was too busy being hugged by Fayla to notice.

Just as she was beginning to think that she might have to throw a few elbows in order to get people to back off, Persephone heard a shrill, horsey squeal.

As though they knew and were thoroughly alarmed by what was coming, every last person in her immediate vicinity scrambled to clear a path. They did so not a minute too soon either, because dear, dear Fleet was already careening toward her as fast as his knobby-kneed legs could carry him. And it was clear from the expression on his horsey face that he would not think twice about trampling to death anyone who got between him and his beloved mistress.

"Oh, Fleet!" cried Persephone, throwing her arms around his neck as he skidded to a halt before her. "I cannot tell you how I've missed you!"

Fleet stamped his hooves and whinnied with heartfelt joy.

"Look, Azriel—it's Fleet!" she said, smiling at him over her shoulder.

"Yes," said Azriel dryly, rolling his eyes as the jealous horse blew a raspberry in his direction, "I see."

Persephone laughed again, then left off hugging Fleet so that she could embrace Rachel, who, along with Zdeno, had darted forward in Fleet's wake.

"Oh, Your Majesty, thank the gods you are safe and well," exclaimed Rachel, who gave Persephone an anxious, searching look before whispering, "You are well, aren't you? You've suffered no illnesses or . . . losses?"

Persephone knew exactly what Rachel was asking. Without thinking, she smiled, took her lookalike friend's hand and pressed it against the swell of her belly so that she could feel the answer for herself.

"Are you with child?" inquired Cairn sharply.

She spoke so loudly that everyone in the clearing heard the question and stopped talking mid-sentence so they could hear Persephone's answer.

Blushing furiously to see everyone but Rachel, Azriel and Zdeno good-naturedly looking her up and down trying to guess the answer for themselves, Persephone folded her arms across her chest and self-consciously replied, "I'm . . . uh . . . yes, I'm with child."

"And Azriel is the father?" pressed Cairn.

"Of course, Azriel is the father," snapped Persephone as Azriel stepped forward to stand on one side of her and, not to be outdone, Fleet hustled forward to stand on the other.

"I did not mean to offend," said Cairn, who didn't sound as though she particularly cared whether or not she'd offended. "It is just that the child could be important."

"The child *will* be important," corrected Azriel coolly.

"He will be our firstborn," added Persephone.

"He?" said Cairn, raising a fine, soot-colored eyebrow.

Blushing again, Persephone shrugged and said, "That is how it feels to me, for I have tried to imagine the baby as a girl and cannot."

"Is that so," murmured Cairn, her eyes gleaming with the fanaticism Persephone remembered so well and liked not at all. Turning the full force of her strangely powerful gaze upon Azriel, Cairn said, "The prophecy foretold the coming of a girl, and the Fates delivered your wife into our hands. Her brother, the Erok king, is dead, and there is no one in the realm with a stronger claim to the throne than she. If she can win and keep the throne, and if the Methusian child she carries is a boy, and if she can be safely delivered of him, upon her death, he shall be a king." She paused for a beat before adding, "A Methusian king."

A soft sigh went up among the Methusians even as Persephone's heart began to pound. Though Cairn's words had come as no surprise to her, they had abruptly flung her toward a moment of truth she was not sure she was ready to face.

"That's a lot of ifs," grunted Big Ben irritably.

"And a long time to wait to see the justice done," added Robert, even more irritably.

"Not necessarily, Robert," said Cairn. "The prophecy does not say that the Methusian king *himself* will unite the five clans and set wrongs to right. It says that his coming will do so. All that is needed to fulfill the prophecy is to know that he will be king someday. And for that to happen, Azriel's wife will need to sit upon the throne that is hers by right of birth."

With these words, Cairn turned to Persephone once more. The air around her crackled with intensity and expectation.

Persephone felt a flare of irritation. She was not "Azriel's wife" to be used by the older woman as she saw fit. Her baby was not a piece in some clever puzzle devised by the Fates. And fighting for her throne was not a destiny that belonged to the Methusians.

It was a destiny that belonged to her—and hopefully, to Azriel.

Fervently wishing she'd told him of her promise to Finn long before this moment, Persephone drew him to one side, took a deep breath and whispered, "I would not undertake such a dangerous fight for her—"

"Nor will you have to," Azriel interrupted in a voice loud enough to be heard by all. "As you, yourself, have seen, Persephone, Cairn can be a great bully when she wants to be. Yet she shall not bully you into this."

"The child is the fulfillment of the prophecy, Azriel," called Cairn.

"The child, if it is, indeed, a boy, will be my *son*," he retorted as he stalked back over to stand before her.

"Azriel—" said Persephone, chasing after him.

"Your son and wife are part of a greater plan," said Cairn serenely.

"We have plans of our own," he snapped.

"Azriel—" Persephone tried again.

"Don't worry, wife," he said in a hard voice. "I'll not let her force you into—"

"Azriel, listen to me!" insisted Persephone as she yanked him around to face her. Seeing that she finally had his undivided attention, she took a deep breath and quietly said, "I would not undertake such a dangerous fight for her but . . . I *would* undertake it for Finn."

For a long, tense moment, Azriel just stared at her. "What are you saying?" he finally asked, his tone inscrutable. "Are you telling me that you *want* to fight for the throne?"

"I'm telling you that I have no choice but to do so because I made a deathbed promise to Finn that I would."

At these words, Azriel fell back as though in shock. "But . . . but the other night when we were talking about the cottage, I thought . . . I mean, I just *assumed*—"

"I know, I know, and I *swear* I wasn't trying to mislead you," said Persephone desperately as she fought against the need to throw herself into his arms. "I just . . . I could not find the words to tell you of the path that lies before me. Not then, not when we'd only just found each other again! There is nothing on this earth I'd like better than to run away and spend the rest of my life playing farmer with you, Azriel, but I can't. I just can't. Like it or not, that is not my destiny."

"Azriel, if it makes you feel any better, know that your wife will not be allowed to expose herself to danger under any circumstances," interrupted Cairn. "Until her throne is secure and she is safely delivered of the child, she will be kept safe at all costs."

The dispassionate way Cairn spoke of the day Persephone *would* become expendable was like a slap. Thinking that Cairn was, in some ways, not so different from her former guard Tutor, Persephone let go of Azriel.

Turning toward the Methusian leader, she squared her shoulders and said, "It is I who made the promise to my brother, Cairn. It is my throne and my fight. I do not intend to hide while others do the fighting for me."

Cairn glanced past Persephone to Azriel, who'd bowed his head—though whether in thought or despair, Persephone could not say.

"You cannot allow your wife to fight, Azriel," said Cairn calmly. "If you will not forbid her to do so for the sake of our people, think on this: you made a solemn vow to be fearless in your protection of her and any children the Fates might see fit to bless you with. Think, Azriel, think how you will feel if your firstborn dies because your wife stubbornly insisted upon putting herself in harm's way."

Outraged that Cairn would dare to try to manipulate Azriel's feelings and terrified that it might work, Persephone opened her mouth to offer protest.

Before she could say a word, however, Azriel slowly lifted his head. For what felt like forever, he just looked at her, his blue eyes utterly unreadable.

Then, in a quiet but clear voice, he said, "I met a girl, wed a princess and now find myself married to a queen. I would be a poor husband, indeed, if I did not stand her most loyal subject."

Mesmerized, Persephone watched as Azriel drew his sword. Resting it across the palms of his outstretched hands, he went down on one knee, raised it up to her and said, "I hereby pledge my sword to you and declare myself yours to command—even into battle, even unto death. You need only name the task, and I shall see it done."

For an endless moment no one moved, no one breathed.

Then, in perfect unison, Zdeno and Robert likewise took a knee and pledged their swords. En masse (though with wildly varying degrees of grace) Robert's men followed suit. With a little squeak that suggested she'd been so caught up in the moment that she'd forgotten herself, Rachel dropped to her knee a heartbeat after them. A heartbeat after her, Fayla slowly went down. As though seeing their kinswomen kneel had given them permission to do the same, Mateo, his brother, Raphael, and the other children all eagerly scrambled to likewise make the time-honored gesture of fealty. After laboriously maneuvering himself onto his grubby knee, Sabian even bowed his tousled head and solemnly raised the upturned palms of his fat little hands, across which quite obviously lay an imaginary sword. For some reason, the sight of the tiny child pledging himself to Persephone with such heartfelt sincerity spurred the rest of the Methusians to do the same.

All except Cairn, that is.

Persephone could have pointed out to the older woman that the reins of power had just been plucked from her hands. She could have informed Cairn that her days of deciding who would walk what path and who was expendable were over. She could have commanded her to bend the knee—or else.

She did not say any of these things, however. Instead, she looked at Cairn.

And waited.

"If you die before the child is born, hope dies with you," warned Cairn, after a long moment of silence.

"Hope will not die," said Persephone as she watched the other woman reluctantly take a knee. "And neither will I."

Twenty-Nine

THE INSTANT CAIRN'S KNEE touched the forest floor Persephone's own knees began to tremble, for it was one thing to carry around the idea that she'd fight for her throne at some point down the road, and quite another to find herself standing alone in a sea of kneeling men, women and children who'd just pledged to serve her unto death.

"Um, rise," she called to her subjects, wishing she sounded more like a queen and less like a girl.

At once, the forest was buzzing with the sounds of people scrambling to their feet, chattering and laughing. Unsettled by the sudden commotion, Fleet whinnied shrilly and cantered off across the camp (no doubt in search of unguarded tubers intended for the stewpot), and the Methusian dogs began to bark again. Cur and Silver, the half-wolf mongrel who'd been Cur's mate for months now, lifted their muzzles to the sky and howled.

Without taking his eyes off Persephone, Azriel rose with the liquid grace of a cat and slid his sword back into his scabbard. She could tell from his expression that he knew exactly what she needed. Unfortunately, before he could draw her into the sheltering strength of his arms and whisper assurances that she was strong and clever enough to walk the path that lay before her, Robert strode forward, planted himself in front of her and shouted, "So! What's the plan, Your Majesty?"

For the second time that day, everyone stopped talking mid-sentence so they could hear her answer. Luckily, although Persephone didn't have anything remotely resembling a plan, she knew what the first step must be.

"To begin with, we must warn the clans that Mordesius is planning to have them all put to the sword," she said.

"What?" exclaimed Fayla, who'd spent weeks living with the Panoraki after poor Tiny's legs had been broken.

"It's true," said Persephone grimly. "Mordesius thinks it suspicious that none of the clans tried to kill us during the quest for the Pool of Genezing—"

"The Panoraki released an avalanche down upon our heads," reminded Rachel in a voice that suggested this was a point in the Panoraki's favor.

"Yes, but—"

"And that little pissant Miter definitely tried to kill us," said Azriel with a scowl.

"Perhaps," said Persephone, shivering as she recalled the night the Gorgishman tried to seal them up in the corpse-strewn mine shaft. "But Miter did not succeed in killing us and neither did the Panoraki or the Marinese, and now Mordesius is so fearful that they'll unite behind me against him that he is going to send his army to slaughter them all."

Since most of the people in the clearing had never even laid eyes on a member of another clan, few appeared to feel more than a detached sense of dismay at the prospect.

But only Cairn saw it as an opportunity.

"With the New Man army occupied elsewhere in the kingdom," she observed, "your fight for the throne would be an easier one by far."

Persephone stared at the Methusian woman in revulsion for a long moment before coldly saying, "You would have me take advantage of the massacres, then?"

"I would have you always consider all of your options," replied Cairn evenly. "I would have you rule with your head and not your heart. I would have you understand that to lead is to never have the luxury of losing sight of the ultimate objective and to ever suffer some thinking you hard and callous and even cruel. I would have you understand that war is *always* death and that as queen, the question you will ever face is not what you can do to save everyone but who and how many shall die by your command so that others of your choosing may be saved."

By the time Cairn had finished speaking, Persephone felt almost contrite. While she still could not say that she liked Cairn, she realized that she'd judged her without having given a single thought to the brutally hard choices she'd ever had to make.

Choices that Persephone, herself, would soon have to make.

"Your Majesty?" said Zdeno, blushing as though embarrassed to find himself speaking. "While you might have an easier time taking your throne if the New Man army is occupied elsewhere, without an army of your own, I fear you will have an extremely difficult time keeping your throne."

"Problem is, you can't just march out of the forest and start knocking on cottage doors," said Robert. "Mordesius would hear of it by the time you'd gotten through the first village, and he'd have you in chains long before you reached the second. Moreover, even if the common people support your claim to the throne—and we cannot say for certain that they do—we *can* say for certain that they'll not risk following you unless it appears that you've a decent chance of defeating Mordesius, for any who throw their lot in with you are doomed if Mordesius should prevail."

"So she can't raise an army until she has an army?" said Rachel in dismay.

Robert shrugged as though this was obvious, then turned to Persephone with an expectant look on his face. As she stared back at him, she suddenly recalled Finn describing how he'd felt the first time he'd stood alone on the Grand Balcony as a small boy king—how his neck had felt as though it would surely snap beneath the weight of the golden crown upon his head.

Persephone was not even wearing the thing yet and already she could feel herself trembling beneath its weight. Fortunately, before she had to admit that she hadn't the first clue how she was going to solve the rather monumental problem of needing an army before she could raise one, Azriel matter-of-factly said, "The issue raised by Robert is precisely why the queen intends not only to warn the other three clans of the danger they face, but also to ask them to stand with us against Mordesius."

Persephone's heart began to pound, not only because Azriel's idea was a brilliant one but also because as she'd listened to him speak, she'd suddenly realized what the second step in her plan must be. Not wanting to make a general announcement until she'd worked out the details and broken the news to Azriel, however, she said nothing, only listened to the murmurs of surprise and apprehension that had greeted his words.

"My prince," protested Robert, "even if the clans send every one of their warriors to swell our ranks, we will yet be far too few to win a battle against the New Men, much less a war."

"True," agreed Azriel, grimacing slightly at the word "prince." "But we may be enough to protect the queen until she can journey to the imperial capital to be crowned and anointed, and to convince the common people that they ought to throw their lot in with her."

"And if we cannot convince them to do so?" asked Fayla in a voice hardened by grief for Tiny.

"I will convince them to do so," said Persephone, whose mind was yet spinning with thoughts of her next step. "I will convince everyone to do so."

It was too late to send anyone to seek out the clans that night, so they spent a companionable evening sitting around the campfires that dotted the clearing—eating hare stew and dark bread, drinking surprisingly fine wine and recounting all that had happened since they'd last seen each other. Persephone could not believe the stroke of luck that had seen the bandits track the soldiers through the forest to the Methusian camp just in time to prevent a massacre; Robert could not believe how much Persephone could eat now that she was pregnant.

Later, as she lay in bed with Azriel's arm encircling her and her cheek resting on his bare chest, Persephone told him about the second step in her plan. His objections were numerous and emphatically stated, but she addressed each of them in turn until, at length, he rather abjectly agreed that it must be done.

"Just remember that you and the baby are the only family I've got," he murmured as he languidly stroked her back. "Remember that I could not bear to lose either of you."

Wishing she could promise him that he'd not lose either of them but knowing that the risks of childbirth alone were such that she could not, Persephone settled for saying the truest and most honest thing she could think to say.

"We could not bear to lose you either, Azriel," she whispered, echoing her words from the previous evening. "So if you will promise to have a care what risks you take in the weeks and months ahead, I will promise to do the same."

"Agreed," said Azriel softly, planting a kiss on the top of her head.

Early the next morning, Persephone asked Cairn, Robert, Rachel and the three messengers that she and Azriel had settled upon to join her and Azriel at one of the breakfast fires.

After they'd all taken a seat on one of the four overturned tree trunks that ringed the fire, Persephone turned to Fayla and said, "I would ask you to carry my message of warning and request for warriors to the Panoraki prince Barka. Remind him that the last time I saw him, he pledged the everlasting friendship of his people and all that implies."

The beautiful Methusian nodded without speaking.

Resisting the urge to warn the unhappy girl to beware of the ravenous appetite of the mother goddess of the mountains, Persephone next turned to Zdeno. "I want you to seek out the Marinese on the Island of Ru," she said. "And before you ask, Rachel, I'm sorry but you cannot accompany him. He'll be able to travel at least twice as fast if he's on his own. Besides, such a journey would require you to risk another channel crossing disguised as a man, and I can tell you from painful personal experience that sailors do not react well at all when they discover a woman aboard their ship."

"I understand," said Rachel tremulously, clinging to Zdeno as though she did not mean to let him leave her no matter how agreeable she might appear.

Smiling slightly, Zdeno said, "I will certainly do as you ask, Your Majesty. However, I fear that my word alone may not be enough to convince the Marinese of anything."

"I fear you are right," said Persephone. Unclasping the silver necklace that Finn had given her for their birthday, she handed it to Zdeno and said, "Show the Marinese elder named Roark this necklace. He will recognize it as mine and will thus know you for my messenger."

"Yes, Your Majesty," murmured Zdeno as he tucked the chain into the pocket of his homespun breeches.

Lastly, Persephone turned to Big Ben. He was sitting at the far end of the tree trunk on which she and Azriel were sitting, busily trimming his fingernails with a dagger and ignoring them all.

"Big Ben?" said Persephone.

"What?" he grunted without looking over at her.

"I'd like you to carry my message to the Gorgish leader, Miter," said Persephone.

Crumpling his face in a manner that suggested he considered this request the very height of foolishness, Big Ben said, "Why me?"

"You are rude, disrespectful and unpleasant to be around," said Persephone bluntly. "In short, you're much like Miter himself, so I'm hoping he'll get on better with you than he would with someone who actually has manners. Moreover, my husband is one of the finest, fastest, fiercest fighters I have ever known, and I once saw you truss him up faster than a three-legged calf. You'll need that kind of skill in the Valley of Gorg, for the Gorgish are an unwelcoming lot and no mistake." Pausing to tug the ruby ring off her finger, she held it up and said, "I gave this ring to Miter when I first met him; it slipped from his finger the night he abandoned Azriel and me in the Mines of Torodania. Show it to him to prove to him that you speak on my behalf, but do not give it to him. He'll receive no further gifts from me until he shows himself a friend and ally."

With a shrug and another grunt, Big Ben jumped to his feet, trotted over and practically shoved Azriel backward off the overturned tree trunk that he might more easily snatch the ring from Persephone. Affecting not to notice the prince consort's huffs of indignation (which were nearly as loud as the ones he'd emitted when his beloved wife had compared him to a three-legged calf), Big Ben jammed the ring onto his pudgy pinkie and trotted back to his spot.

As Big Ben plopped down and resumed trimming his nails, Persephone said, "I would also like to announce that I've decided to establish a royal Council that will henceforth advise me on matters of war and state."

"Pass!" said Big Ben loudly.

"You're not interested in sitting on my Council, Ben? Oh, how very unfortunate," lied Persephone, who'd never had any intention of inviting him to join her Council. "Still, I suppose I'll have to respect your wishes. Will the rest of you agree to sit on my Council and promise to willingly welcome members of all other clans to sit with you?"

After everyone else agreed that they would, Robert said, "Your Majesty, even if the messengers leave within the hour and reach their destinations promptly, it could take weeks for them to convince the clans to join your cause and return with reinforcements. What shall the rest of us do in the meantime? What shall you do in the meantime?"

"Like any good mother, I'm sure the queen will want to use the time to eat, rest and grow strong for the sake of her child," said Cairn quickly.

"I am already strong," said Persephone, lifting her chin. "And since there are some things that none but I can do, food and rest will have to wait."

Thirty

"WHAT DO YOU THINK?" asked Persephone in a hushed voice.

"I think it has long since been deserted," replied Azriel.

As Persephone let her gaze wander over Pembleton Estate, she had to agree. Nothing moved save for the occasional tumbleweed blowing across the deserted courtyard; nothing could be heard except for the wind whistling through the trees of the untended orchard. The walking paths were unkempt, the gardens were choked with weeds, and the water in the decorative pond was covered with a thick layer of scum. No smoke rose from any of the manor chimneys, the roof was missing tiles and half a dozen panes of glass were broken.

Altogether, it painted a stark picture of the hard times poor Lord Pembleton had fallen on since the execution of his son, the death of his infant grandson and the loss of his health.

A fortnight earlier, Persephone had seized upon the idea of approaching him when she'd heard Azriel speak so matter-of-factly of asking the other three clans to stand with her against Mordesius. With a start, she'd realized that there were not three other clans besides the Methusians, there were four: the Panoraki, the Marinese, the Gorgish *and* the Erok. The prophecy of the Methusian king spoke of uniting five clans, and it was easy to understand why, for a monarch who failed to win over the most powerful members of the most populous clan in the kingdom would not be monarch for long. Persephone did not yet know where Lord Bartok's loyalties lay, but she was certain that Lord Pembleton's loyalties would not lie either with the man who'd executed his son or with the powerful lords who'd laughed at the sight. She would be safe with him, and although he was now powerless, perhaps he was not entirely friendless. Perhaps some of the minor lords who'd never benefited from Mordesius's munificence felt a kinship with him yet. Perhaps, sick as he was, Lord Pembleton could be the key to forging some sort of alliance with the nobility of the realm.

Azriel, Cairn, Rachel—well, everybody, really—had tried to convince Persephone to send someone in her stead, but why on earth would Lord Pembleton trust a stranger who claimed to come in the name of a queen in hiding? And how could she ask someone who'd already lost so much to risk even more while she, herself, risked nothing at all?

Still, to show that she was not entirely insensitive to their concerns for her well-being, Persephone had agreed to spend a week recuperating before she and Azriel set out. Fortunately, the journey to Lord Pembleton's estate had been uneventful. Azriel had predicted that a poor man and his wife traveling on foot along back roads would attract almost no attention in a realm on the brink of war, and he'd been right.

Just as Persephone was thinking that she'd far rather have suffered unwanted attention than to have come all this way for nothing, the door of the manor suddenly opened and a woman stepped out. Her dress was drab, her hair was unkempt and she had what looked to be a basket of laundry tucked under one arm. After pausing briefly to look around, she walked across the courtyard and disappeared into one of the dilapidated outer buildings.

"A vagrant taking advantage of a deserted manor?" wondered Azriel.

"I don't think so," said Persephone with a frown. "She acts as if she belongs. I think perhaps she is a maid left behind to care for the place in her master's absence."

"Lord Pembleton is a sick and broken man," said Azriel. "Where would he have gone?"

"I don't know," said Persephone. "Let's find out."

The woman re-emerged from the outer building at almost the exact same moment as Persephone and Azriel stepped out from behind the overgrown topiary dolphin behind which they'd been crouching. Spotting them at once, the woman froze briefly before hitching up her limp skirt, running into the manor and slamming the door behind her. Undeterred, Persephone and Azriel crossed the scraggly lawn, climbed the dirty steps and politely knocked on the door. There was a long delay, during which time Persephone guessed that the woman was probably studying them from some hidden peephole, trying to decide if they posed a danger.

Then, without warning, the door swung halfway open.

"Good day," said Persephone to the woman who might have been pretty once, but who now had the washed-out look of one who was old before her time. "I am—"

"Queen Persephone," interrupted the woman, nervously licking her dry lips. "Yes, I know. I recognize you. From my time in the capital."

Persephone's eyebrows peaked in surprise when she heard the woman's noble accent. "Have we—"

"Met?" said the woman, reaching up to smooth back her tangled hair. "No. But I saw you that day. With the Regent. Before they took my husband's head."

Persephone exhaled softly. "You're the wife of young Lord Pembleton," she said gently.

"Was the wife," corrected the woman mechanically before casting a twitchy glance at Azriel and saying, "Who is this?"

"My husband," said Persephone, watching the woman's eyes widen slightly at the word "husband." "His name is Azriel."

"Mine is Alice," said the woman, after a moment's hesitation. Stepping back, she pushed the door farther open with a work-reddened hand and said, "Would you like me to see if my father-in-law, Lord Pembleton, will receive you?"

"Yes," said Persephone. "That is exactly what we would like."

Lord Pembleton agreed to receive them, though how Alice knew this was a mystery to Persephone, for the apoplexy he'd suffered following the loss of his son and infant grandson had rendered him little better than a corpse. He lay in his rumpled bed unmoving, his head lolling to one side, his hands curled into claws. The once-round face was gaunt, sallow and slack; the mouth, a puckered hole. Only his eyes moved—darting from Persephone to Azriel to his daughter-in-law, shining with the panic of a man trapped alive.

Persephone felt like retching at the sickly smell in the chamber, but she forced herself not to show it as she said, "Alice, I knew from my brother, the king, that your father-in-law had suffered apoplexy, but I was under the impression that he had improved."

"He has improved," said Alice in an oddly expressionless voice as she wiped her hands back and forth against her limp skirts. "He can wait for the bedpan now. Mostly. And he can swallow. Only mush, like what you'd feed a baby. But still."

"That's . . . that's good," said Persephone as she cast a furtive but despairing look at Azriel.

"It is good," agreed Alice before leaning close to Lord Pembleton and loudly saying, "What is that, Father? You wish to know why the queen has come?" Turning to Persephone, she said, "My father-in-law wishes to know why you have come."

"How do you know that he wishes to know this?" asked Persephone, her gaze straying to the bedridden nobleman.

"I have tended him since the apoplexy that felled him," replied Alice. "He speaks to me with his eyes."

"Oh," said Persephone uncertainly, before explaining her and Azriel's purpose in being there.

After listening intently, Alice nodded. "You were right in thinking that my father-in-law despises Mordesius and the more powerful lords, and also that he yet has friends among the lesser nobility. Many friends. None who have suffered as he has, of course, but still." Once more leaning close to Lord Pembleton, she stared into his eyes for a long moment before saying, "He wishes to know if you'd like me to contact these friends, urging them to support you. He says that while we await their replies, you are welcome to avail yourselves of what meager hospitality we are able to offer. Hot water with which to wash. A clean bed. Food."

Though there was something undeniably peculiar about Alice, Persephone was pleased by her offer to contact other noblemen. Moreover, at the word "food" Persephone's mouth had begun to water copiously. Azriel had done a fair job taking down game on the journey to Pembleton Manor, but for a girl four months pregnant, fair was not quite good enough.

Turning to Azriel, she murmured, "What do you think?"

"I think we need to be cautious," he replied as he absently laid his hand against the small of her back. "But I also think . . . you have done well."

Flushing at the compliment, and at the tingling warmth of his hand so close to her skin, Persephone informed Alice that they'd be honored to stay, at least for a night or two. After wrenching her gaze away from Azriel's hand, Alice fetched a large armful of firewood and shovelful of glowing embers from the fireplace in Lord Pembleton's chamber. Then, after declining Azriel's offer to carry both, she led him and Persephone up three flights of stairs to the top floor of the manor.

"This is our finest guest bedroom," said Alice as she came to a halt before a door that looked no different from any other. Peering over the firewood at Azriel, she said, "Would you mind getting the door?"

Azriel swept her a bow, then flung open the chamber door and stepped aside to allow Persephone to enter first. She'd taken half a dozen paces into the shabby chamber when she heard the sound of firewood clattering to the floor. Looking around, Persephone smiled at the sight of her dashing husband on one knee in the hallway, picking up the dropped firewood for their flustered hostess.

Feeling Persephone's eyes upon him, Azriel paused to look her way. As their eyes locked and he started to smile, Alice hit him across the temple with the fireplace shovel so hard that his eyes rolled into the back of his head, and he dropped like a rock.

Persephone stared in horror for one forever instant.

Then she lunged for the open door.

Thirty-One

MANY MILES TO THE EAST, Mordesius and Lord Atticus were, at that very moment, cresting the hill that overlooked the New Man training camp north of Syon.

"Oh, thank the gods we've arrived at last!" brayed Lord Atticus, wiping the back of his dripping nose with the sleeve of his rain-soaked doublet.

As he slumped in his saddle, gazing down upon the sea of gray tents that surrounded the wooden ramparts of the training camp nestled in the valley below, Mordesius did not thank the gods. Mordesius never thanked the gods, for it was the gods that had seen him burned nearly to death, his perfect body reduced to charred ruin by the fire that was only supposed to have roasted his family alive. When he thought of the gods at all, it was usually to curse them.

At this particular moment, however, he thumbed his nose at them.

And that was because he'd done it. He'd actually done it!

He'd traveled all the way from the black stone castle to this place that was to be the gathering point for his great army, and he'd done so riding on horseback alongside his men just as Bartok or Murdock or any other commanding officer would have done. He'd not even brought along a carriage or litter in which he might rest if riding proved too much for him. Indeed, he'd lashed out at the soldier who'd suggested that he do so!

He was now a military commander, after all, not some *woman*.

To be sure, it had been an arduous journey—arduous almost beyond endurance. After just a few hours in the saddle, the rolling gait of the horse had begun to take a toll, as Mordesius had known it would. After a few hours more, the temperature had dropped so low that his gloved fingers had grown stiff, his muscles had seized up and each labored breath had hung in the icy air like mist. Then it had begun to rain, and it had not stopped raining in the six days since.

Admittedly, the journey had taken twice as long as it might otherwise have because galloping had been out of the question and they'd had to make camp early each evening that he might have time to recover, but no matter.

He'd done it.

Most ironically, it had been Lord Atticus who'd given Mordesius the strength to carry on whenever he'd thought he could not bear the rigors of the field a moment longer. From the outset, the perpetually inebriated young lord had complained—of the cold and the rain and the muck, of the size of his tent and the thinness of his mattress, of the poor quality of the food and the ineptitude of his attendants and the absence of women. He'd complained so shrilly and so incessantly, in fact, that under normal circumstances Mordesius would have given in to the urge to have his tongue cut out, both to shut him up and to give him something worthwhile to complain about.

But under these particular circumstances, Mordesius had relished hearing him blubber like a woman almost as much as he'd relished knowing that the men were hearing him do so, for it had surely made Mordesius look all the more stoic and manly by comparison.

For a fleeting moment, Mordesius wondered what Queen Persephone would think if she could see him now. Then, shaking his heavy head to rid himself of all thought of her, he gritted his perfect teeth, straightened his back as best he could and called, "Forward!"

Eagerly, Lord Atticus lashed his riding crop across the dripping flanks of his horse. Rearing up with a startled squeal, the beast lunged forward into a gallop that nearly sent its drunken rider flying headfirst into the muck. Half a second later, the four soldiers who'd been assigned to guard against Lord Atticus's escape or rescue were hurriedly galloping after him.

Mordesius gave a bark of mirthless laughter at the thought that a broken neck caused by a fall of his own making was the far more likely fate of his imbecile captive than escape or rescue. Then, tersely gesturing for the rest of his escort to follow, he slapped the reins against his own horse's neck and started down the hill.

Word of his arrival had evidently spread like wildfire because by the time he reached the valley and caught up with Lord Atticus, the mucky path before him was lined with black-clad soldiers. Many looked excited or awed; some seemed nervous or even fearful. Here and there, however, Mordesius thought he also spotted men who appeared unable to believe that someone like him had made the journey he had.

Instead of being enraged by these furtive, fleeting looks of amazement, as he normally would have been, Mordesius was buoyed by them.

Let them see that in spite of my terrible injuries, I can lead them as Murdock would have led them! he thought jubilantly. *Let them be reminded that doomed kings are not the only ones who can ride out among them like majestic young—*

"You know, I thought there'd be more of them," complained Lord Atticus with a loud sniffle.

"What?" snapped Mordesius.

"Soldiers," said Lord Atticus, flicking his wormy fingers toward the throngs of black-clad New Men. "I thought there'd be more of them."

Jolted by these words, Mordesius took another look at the crowds of soldiers lining his path and at the sea of gray tents behind them, and he realized that there *were* fewer than he'd have expected. He could not say exactly how many fewer, however, because before he could make a proper count, he and his men were being ushered through the gates of the camp and into the central courtyard. A swarm of soldiers immediately tumbled out of the nearby stables and ran over to see to their horses. They did not even have a chance to greet Mordesius before Lord Atticus had flung his reins at one man and grabbed for the outstretched arm of another that he might use it to steady himself as he dismounted.

Mordesius watched with disgust and disdain. Though stiff and so sore he could barely sit upright, he would not have been helped down from his horse for all the diamonds in the Mines of Torodania. Imperiously waving away the soldier who would have done so, he clutched the pommel of the saddle with both gnarled hands and awkwardly dragged his leg over so that it was dangling next to the foot still tucked into the stirrup. Then, even more awkwardly, he dropped down to the muck, grunting and staggering wildly as he did so.

By the time he'd recovered, the commander of the training camp had emerged from the main building of the camp. Flanked by a pair of particularly burly New Men, he strode forward and briskly saluted Mordesius.

"It is an honor to welcome you, Your Grace!" he called over the splash and splatter of the driving rain. "Let me be the first to say how thrilled we all were when we received the letter informing us that you intend to personally lead us into battle against the treacherous, traitorous lords of this realm!"

Immediately despising the man for being at least a head taller than he was, Mordesius called back, "Why were you so thrilled, commander? Did you lack confidence in General Murdock? Did you fear that he would be unable to lead you to victory?"

The commander, who had the General to thank for his new post, insofar as Murdock had sawed off the feet of the man who'd held the post before him, fleetingly looked as though he'd just been informed that he was about to have his own feet sawed off.

"It was a jest, commander," muttered Mordesius, despising the man all the more for his brief but unmanly display of fear. "Now, are you going to invite me inside, or do you intend to make me stand here in this stinking muck all night?"

Thirty-Two

AS PERSEPHONE LUNGED for the open door, Lord Pembleton's widowed daughter-in-law did the same. Unfortunately, a fraction of a second before Persephone's hand closed around the doorknob, Lord Pembleton's widowed daughter-in-law yanked the door shut.

Flinging herself against the locked door, Persephone fought to sound reasonable as she said, "Alice? Alice, I don't know what you're doing or why but . . . but if you release me at once so that I can tend to Azriel, I'm sure we can come to an understanding."

Alice made no reply. Persephone heard her stamp her foot several times—presumably extinguishing the embers that had been scattered when she'd hit Azriel with the fireplace shovel. Then she heard her grunt softly as she began to drag Azriel's body down the hall.

"What are you doing, Alice? Where are you taking him?" called Persephone. Then, unable to contain her exploding panic for Azriel an instant longer, she hammered on the door with her fists and screamed, *"Answer me!"*

But Alice did not answer her. Persephone heard a nearby door open and close, then heard the sound of Alice descending the stairs. Feeling dangerously lightheaded, Persephone staggered over to the bed and sank down onto the lumpy mattress. Squeezing her eyes shut, she pressed her forehead hard against the bedpost and forced herself to calm down for the sake of the baby.

By the time she'd managed to slow her breathing, Alice had returned to stand outside the chamber door. "Well. I have sent my one remaining servant to the nearest New Man outpost," she informed Persephone. "Within the hour, the commander will know that you are here. And the Methusian, too, of course."

At these words, Persephone felt the blood drain from her face. All at once, she remembered Mordesius threatening to offer a thousand gold pieces to whomever brought him Azriel *or* his head.

Bolting to her feet, she flew to the door. "Alice, you cannot mean to do this," she pleaded.

"It is already done," replied Alice with an almost resigned tone.

Suddenly furious, Persephone slapped her hand against the door and shouted, "For gods' sakes, Alice, Mordesius murdered your husband!"

"Yes," replied Alice. "And my child, too, I think."

"Then why are you giving him what he wants?" cried Persephone. "Why are you helping him?"

"You saw what he did to my husband, who was a good and innocent man," replied Alice placidly. "If he were to find out that I gave aid to the queen he'd intended to marry and to the hunted Methusian who married her instead, I cannot think what would become of me."

"Nothing will become of you, Alice, because Mordesius need never know," said Persephone, thinking fast. "Let me and Azriel go. Now, before it is too late! And when I have defeated Mordesius I will return and—"

"Mordesius will never be defeated," interrupted Alice. "I fear him more than I hate him. He will look well upon me once he knows I had a hand in delivering you and the Methusian's head to him. I will be safe then."

"Head?" gasped Persephone, sinking to her knees. "Oh . . . oh, Alice, please, tell me you haven't—"

"Beheaded the Methusian? No, I haven't. Murder is New Men's work, and I am a lady," said Alice primly. "I will collect my reward all the same, though."

Recoiling slightly, Persephone said, "If this is about the gold, I can promise—"

"I have to go now," said Alice.

As Persephone listened to Alice start to walk away, she slapped her hand against the door again and shouted, "Your father-in-law would not want this, Alice!"

At these words, the footsteps halted. "Perhaps not," called Alice. "But there is nothing he can do about it, for he cannot move or even speak. And I lied when I told you that he yet has friends. He has no friends. He has no one but me."

As soon as Alice left, Persephone ran to the wall that separated her chamber from the one into which she believed Alice had dragged Azriel.

"Azriel, wake up," she begged. "Wake up! Please!"

When he did not reply, Persephone pressed her ear against the wall and held her breath, hoping to hear a snore or a groan or anything that would prove that he was at least alive. When she heard nothing but silence, she gritted her teeth and backed away from the wall. Then she turned and ran to the window. Flinging it open, she leaned out, desperately hoping that she'd find hand- and footholds enough to safely climb over to the window of the chamber in which Azriel was lying.

Alas, she did not. Though the window was not ten paces away, even an especially daring and desperate prisoner—even one who was strong, skilled and incredibly lucky—would be hard pressed to make the climb without slipping. And though she was not nearly as high up as she'd been in the turret chamber, she was certainly high enough to plummet to her death.

Closing and latching the window, Persephone slowly walked over and sat back down on the bed. Unsheathing her dagger, she laid it on her lap and stared straight ahead as she formulated a plan. When the New Man commander arrived, she'd call to him. She'd make him come into her chamber first, and then she'd kill him. Next, she'd kill any soldiers he'd brought with him.

She didn't like to think what she might have to do to Alice.

Persephone spent the next hours alternately pleading through the wall for Azriel to wake up and imagining the attack that would see her enemies dead at her feet.

Then, late in the day, she heard the distant sound of a main-floor door opening, and a few seconds later, the sound of booted feet clomping up the stairs.

Clutching her dagger tight in her sweaty hand, Persephone tip-toed over to the door of the chamber. Licking her lips, she was about to call out to the commander when she heard an odd tapping sound behind her.

Glancing over her shoulder, she saw something that caused her to whirl around and scream.

For there, perched outside the right windowpane on the impossibly narrow ledge, his every muscle straining with the effort of clinging to the wall, his eyes bluer than ever in a face streaked with blood, was Azriel.

Thirty-Three

AS SOON AS MORDESIUS ducked into the main building of the New Man training camp, he barked an order to have Lord Atticus escorted to suitable chambers. Then, brusquely declining the commander's offer of a hot bath, a warm meal and clean clothes, he followed the man into his private office.

"How many soldiers do you currently have under your command?" demanded Mordesius the instant the door shut behind them.

"Not as many as I'd hoped for, Your Grace," admitted the commander.

"How many?" barked Mordesius.

"Fewer than eight thousand," replied the commander.

"Fewer than eight thousand!" shouted Mordesius. "How is that possible? My army numbers in the tens of thousands! More than a fortnight ago I sent a letter to the commander of every camp and outpost in the kingdom. I ordered them to send as many armed men as they could spare and to do so at once. I told them that I would not tolerate delays!"

"It is not really a question of delays," said the commander with a calmness that only served to inflame Mordesius further. "In some cases, the troops are coming from such far-flung places that they've not yet arrived. In other cases, it seems the commanders took to heart your words that they send only those men they could spare, and what with the growing discord throughout the realm, they felt that they really couldn't spare—"

"I care *nothing* for what they felt," snarled Mordesius, outraged that the commander should think that he would when he, himself, was hungry, thirsty, dirty, exhausted and in such agony that he could barely hold his head up.

The commander took a deep breath. "Your Grace, with eight thousand men we should be able to engage the army of the great lords as long as it is not too—"

"*I do not want to 'engage' the army of the great lords!*" bellowed Mordesius, slapping the desk between them so hard that his scarred hand sang with pain. "*I want to crush it before it has a chance to form!*"

"I understand, Your Grace," said the commander.

Mordesius glared at him. He did not know what Murdock would have done in the face of such incompetence, but he knew what he was going to do. He was going to brook no excuses; he was going to show that he could be as steely a general as the world had ever known.

"Commander," he said, "what good is a standing army if it is not prepared to go to war at a moment's notice?"

The commander frowned. "Your Grace, no army could possibly be prepared to go to war at a moment's notice."

"Excuses," said Mordesius softly.

"Your Grace?"

"I ask for action and you give me excuses."

The commander spread his large, capable hands wide. "Forgive me, Your Grace, if it appears that way, but we are speaking of undertaking the single greatest military campaign the realm has ever seen and—"

"I know what we are speaking of," snapped Mordesius, thinking how pleasant it would be to smash to pulp every one of the fingers on those large, capable hands.

"I know you do, Your Grace, I know you do . . . just as I know that you know that preparing for such a campaign requires time.

Even for a standing army," said the commander carefully. "Troops that have recently been made to march hard over long distances must be given a chance to recuperate. Blades must be honed, horses re-shod, and given the size of the force we are bringing together, it is absolutely imperative that we establish a supply train for we cannot be assured of being able to find what we need as we go. Moreover, there is the training of the men to consider—"

"You are commander of a training camp," snarled Mordesius, who was getting dangerously tired of hearing excuses. "Are you telling me that the soldiers under your command are not trained?"

"Of course they are trained, Your Grace," said the commander without flinching, "but they are trained for the tasks that have primarily occupied your great army these many years. Slave catching and Methusian hunting, relocating lowborns and putting down minor rebellions. The men need to . . . refine the skills they have learned that they might be as effective as possible in a true battle situation."

"Well, since I'm quite sure that Lord Bartok is not wasting any time gathering his army, they'd better refine them quickly," said Mordesius with a shrug of his uneven shoulders.

"They will, Your Grace," assured the commander, seeming relieved. "You have my word that all will be in readiness within six weeks."

"You have six days."

The commander looked stunned. "Y-Your Grace, I fear—"

"Yes?" interrupted Mordesius, his dark eyes glittering. "Tell me, commander: What is it that you fear?"

Looking as though he could almost hear the sound of the saw being sharpened against the whetstone, the commander said nothing, only swallowed hard.

"Six days, then?"

Hesitantly, the commander nodded.

"Excellent," breathed Mordesius. "Now, what about that hot bath?"

Thirty-Four

IT TOOK PERSEPHONE less than a second to get over the shock of seeing Azriel perched on the narrow ledge outside the chamber window like a broad-shouldered, bloody-faced gargoyle.

Dropping her dagger, she flew to the window and unlatched it with hands that trembled so badly that she could not stop fumbling.

"No . . . no hurry, wife," gasped Azriel, his voice muted by the glass. "By all means, take . . . take your time."

Finally managing to flip the latch, Persephone hastily flung open the left pane of the window.

"You're insane!" she exclaimed as she watched him inch his way toward the opening.

"Thank—"

He slipped so abruptly that Persephone didn't even have time to scream. One minute he was there, and the next minute he was gone.

Gone . . . except for the one hand that had managed to grab onto the sill.

Leaning out of the window so fast and so far that she nearly pitched herself headfirst out of it, Persephone seized the back of Azriel's tunic with both hands and heaved with all her might. She wasn't nearly strong enough to pull him all the way up, of course, but she was strong enough to lift him the few inches that he needed to be able to throw his other hand onto the sill, and thereafter to give them both the illusion that she'd be able to support him if he slipped again.

"Oh, thank the gods you're alive, thank the gods, thank the gods," babbled Persephone as Azriel finally dragged himself through the window and dropped to the floor. Sinking to her knees beside him, she took his head in her hands and kissed him deeply before pulling back and anxiously examining the frighteningly ugly wound at his temple.

"It's nothing," murmured Azriel as he woozily slipped his arms around her. "Less than a scratch."

"It is *not* less than a scratch," said Persephone fiercely. "I still can't believe—"

It wasn't until she heard the chamber door begin to open that Persephone suddenly remembered the sound of booted feet climbing the stairs. Scrambling to her own feet, she saw Alice leading a one-eyed, saber-wielding New Man into the chamber.

"I thought you said the Methusian was dead," said the New Man, flicking his one green eye toward Azriel while absently fingering his black eye patch.

"I thought he was," said Alice, her eyes darting between Azriel and the open window. "Anyway, he's hurt. Shouldn't put up much of a fight."

The New Man nodded, then casually flicked his fingers at Alice and said, "Leave us, Lady Pembleton."

As she scurried out of the chamber and closed the door behind her, Persephone gauged the distance to her dagger. Just as she was about to launch herself at it in the extremely faint hope that she'd be able to grab it and gut the New Man before he had time to react, two things happened.

The first was that Azriel clamped his hand around her ankle in an obvious effort to prevent her from doing anything reckless.

The second was that the New Man went down on one knee, bowed his head and murmured, "Your Majesty, it is an honor."

"It is?" blurted Persephone, who was so amazed that she couldn't think of anything else to say.

"Yes," said the New Man. "It isn't every man who gets two chances to save a queen."

Persephone stared at him, racking her brains to remember when he'd previously saved her and wondering how on earth she could have forgotten such a thing.

It became clear when the soldier finally lifted his head, fixed his green eye upon her and said, "I was the soldier tasked with removing you from the birthing chamber and disposing of you on the night of your birth, Your Majesty. I was the one who defied the Regent and saved your life."

"Do not imagine that I am a good man, Your Majesty, for I would not have risen to my present rank if I was," said Commander Darius. "Unlike many of my fellow soldiers, however, I try to avoid murdering infants—and queens."

"I see," said Persephone, who had to agree that this did not sound like the personal philosophy of a good man.

"The night you were born, the Regent summoned me to the birthing chamber," he explained. "Thrusting you into my arms, he ordered me to murder you and get rid of your body." He paused for a long moment before continuing. "As I left the palace, it was my intention to do exactly as I'd been commanded. I was a new recruit eager to prove myself and thrilled for the opportunity to do so, you see. As I hurried through the streets of Parthania looking for a likely place to do the job, however, I kept feeling you move in my arms, and I kept hearing you make these little noises."

"She was crying?" asked Azriel, who had staggered forward to place himself squarely between Persephone and the New Man who'd supposedly saved her life twice.

"No, not crying," mused Commander Darius. "Gurgling, more like. Cooing. Like a little dove. I tried to follow my orders, Your Majesty,

I really did. I even pressed my hand over top of your mouth and nose for a few seconds. But in the end, I couldn't do it. So when I saw a heavily laden wagon passing by on its way to the city gates, I set you in the back of it and watched it disappear into the night."

By the way Azriel was glaring at Commander Darius, Persephone could tell that he wasn't especially impressed with the man for having only smothered her for a few seconds before dumping her.

Squeezing her husband's hand to remind him that she had, in fact, survived the ordeal, Persephone said, "Commander Darius, there was a servant who saw you come for me that night. She said you had mismatched eyes."

"And so I had," he replied with a faint smile. "As it happens, I was set upon within hours of spiriting you from the palace. I later realized that His Grace must have chosen me for the task because I was an easily forgotten new recruit, and that he must have ordered me killed to prevent me from speaking of what I'd done. In addition to having my nose badly broken and my face slashed, I lost my other eye—the brown one—in the beating. Though left for dead, I obviously survived. By the time I'd recovered, months had gone by, and I looked so different that I was able to change my name and once more join the Regent's army."

With a derisive snort, Azriel said, "Why would you rejoin the army of the man who'd ordered you killed?"

"Soldiering was the only thing I was good at," replied Commander Darius. "And it is a lucky thing for you that it was, for if it had worked out any other way, I would not be standing here now, and neither would you. You would be a headless corpse and your wife would be on her way back to His Grace Mordesius."

Azriel's eyes flashed dangerously at this, but before he could say anything, Persephone said, "It is a lucky thing, indeed, Commander Darius. I only wonder: What will you tell Lord Pembleton's daughter-in-law? She is expecting the outcome you have just described. In fact, she is counting on it."

"I will not tell her anything," replied Commander Darius. "After you are gone from here, I will place her under house arrest."

"On what charge?" asked Azriel, raising an eyebrow.

"On any charge I like," said Commander Darius with a shrug.

"For how long will you keep her under arrest?" asked Persephone, who couldn't help feeling a pang of compassion for the broken woman who would have seen her and Azriel dead.

"For as long as is necessary," replied Commander Darius. "The realm is in an uproar, Your Majesty. His Grace has ordered the bulk of his army to the training camp north of Syon, your brother's widow is said to be pregnant and her noble father is fast gathering an army at his country estate."

"I don't suppose Lord Bartok is gathering an army for the purpose of helping to set me upon the throne?" said Persephone, shivering as she considered what might have happened to her if she'd called out to Lord Atticus that night in the black stone castle.

"No," said Commander Darius. "I don't suppose he is."

Thirty-Five

OWING TO AZRIEL'S grievous head injury, the journey back to the bandit camp took much longer than the journey to Pembleton Estate had done.

A few days after Persephone and Azriel's not-so-triumphant return, Big Ben returned from his journey to the Valley of Gorg. The Gorgishman Miter was trotting along at his heels, twirling his slingshot, loudly complaining that they'd walked almost the entire way and asking if all bandits were too feeble to run or was it just this one?

Persephone immediately left off meeting with her Council to go over and perform the traditional greeting of the Gorgish.

"Greetings, illustrious one," she intoned as she folded her arms across her chest and bowed deeply.

"Miter is here to take back the ring you stole, female," replied the Gorgishman without preamble. "And also to inform you that you and your little war are to stay far away from the Valley of Gorg unless you long for a hideous death. And also to accept a seat on your royal Council, which would otherwise be woefully incomplete—a sacrifice for which Miter assumes he will be exceptionally well compensated."

For the sake of her unborn son, whom she hoped would someday rule over a united realm, instead of telling Miter to shove off, Persephone said, "You are welcome to sit on my Council, Miter, but

I'll not compensate you for doing so, nor will I give you back the ring you lost when you tried to kill me and my husband."

"You must do these things!" Miter shrieked, flapping his arms.

"I'm not going to," said Persephone, pressing her hand against her belly to calm the baby, who apparently didn't like the sound of Miter's voice any more than she did. "Especially since I see that you did not bring any warriors with you."

"When the rude one told Miter of your ridiculous request, Miter laughed and laughed," replied the Gorgishman. "Miter understands a great deal about the ways of war, you see. Miter knows that no warrior worth his salt would ever follow a pregnant female into battle. That is why Miter did not even consider ordering any of his own magnificent warriors to do so."

"Thank the gods for small mercies," muttered Azriel, rolling his eyes.

"You will not be thanking the gods when you and your stinking clansmen are on the brink of annihilation!" screeched Miter, shaking his small fists in sudden rage. "You will be begging Miter to come to your rescue, and Miter will do nothing but laugh! Ah-ha-ha-ha . . . Ah-ha-ha-ha . . ."

As Miter continued to demonstrate how he intended to behave in a crisis situation, Persephone decided that, upon reflection, perhaps the fact that Miter had not brought with him any of his "magnificent warriors" was not such a terrible thing, after all.

Not long after the arrival of Big Ben and Miter, Persephone was in the Council tent getting a feel for the gleaming suit of armor that the camp blacksmith had fashioned for her when she heard Rachel scream, and then scream again.

Heart in her throat, Persephone turned so fast that the metal strips of her armor skirt clacked together. Forgetting that she had a newly sharpened sword in the jeweled scabbard at her waist, she unsheathed her dagger and began to run, dodging children and dogs, shouting for adults to move and elbowing them aside if they didn't move fast enough.

"Rachel!" she shouted as she tried to shove her way through the small crowd that had gathered around the place from which the screams had come. "*Rachel!*"

Breaking through the crowd unexpectedly, Persephone stumbled forward and very nearly buried her dagger into Zdeno's kidney—a mortal wound he probably wouldn't have noticed, given the way that Rachel was kissing him.

Sabian, who was standing nearby with Mateo and Raphael, looked up at Persephone with wide eyes, cupped one pudgy hand around his rosebud mouth and whispered, "They're kithing."

"I can see that," said Persephone as she sheathed her dagger.

At the sound of Persephone's voice, Rachel broke off kissing Zdeno and looked over at her. "Zdeno's returned!" she announced joyfully.

"I can see that, too," said Persephone, smiling in spite of the sinking feeling that dragged at her when she saw that Zdeno was not accompanied by even one Marinese, let alone an army of them.

"Greetings, Your Majesty," said Zdeno, bowing his head toward her without letting go of Rachel. "Apologies for my late return. The journey was . . . eventful."

"Anything I should know about?" asked Persephone, eyeing several half-healed wounds, any one of which looked as though it probably could have killed him.

Zdeno shook his head. "But you should know that the Marinese aren't coming. For the time being, they're not even sending an ambassador," he said soberly. "The Elder named Roark said that I should tell you that as a daughter of the clan you shall ever have a place among them, but that he does not believe Mordesius would attack a reclusive island people who have ever shown themselves willing to yield to the demands of the more powerful. He also said that it is not the Marinese way to get involved in matters that have nothing to do with them."

"Defeating Mordesius has everything to do with everybody," said Persephone grimly.

"That is exactly what I told Roark," said Zdeno as he handed her the silver necklace she'd given him to convince Roark that he was her messenger. "Nothing I said would budge the Marinese Elder from his position, Your Majesty. I'm sorry."

"You've nothing to be sorry for, Zdeno," said Persephone for the benefit of all within hearing, before stepping close to him and Rachel and murmuring, "We'll just have to hope that the Panoraki see things differently than the other two clans, for without an army, I dare not journey to the imperial capital to be crowned. And if I am not crowned soon, I fear it will be too late."

That evening, Persephone informed her Council that the time had come to take the risk of contacting Lord Bartok to find out exactly why he was gathering an army.

"We know why," spat Robert, who disliked noblemen almost as much as he disliked New Men. "His daughter is pregnant by your dead brother, and Bartok means to set this royal grandchild upon the throne."

"The problem with that theory is that Lady Aurelia isn't pregnant," reminded Azriel. "As Persephone has already told us, one of the last things Finn said before he died was that he'd been too sick and weak to ever perform the act with her."

With a derisive snort, Robert said, "All the more reason not to trust Bartok."

"I'm not saying that I do trust him," said Persephone. "I'm saying that since our chances of victory over Mordesius would be vastly improved if we had Lord Bartok's well-armed thousands fighting at our sides, I need to know for a certainty that I *can't* trust him. Besides, though my attempt to contact the noblemen through Lord Pembleton was not a raging success, the fact remains that uniting the realm means uniting everyone. I am fighting to sit upon a throne that has ever been recognized by the Erok—do you expect me to reject the Erok nobility without even giving them a chance to prove their loyalty? Would you have me win my crown only to preside over an empty court?"

"No," said Robert swiftly. "I would have you preside over a court filled with deserving men."

"And women," added Cairn and Rachel.

"And I would have the same thing," said Persephone as Cur and his mate, Silver, nosed their way into the tent and loped over to sit one on either side of her. "That is why I wish to give Lord Bartok and the rest of the great lords a chance to prove themselves."

"How do you propose to do that?" asked Miter with a sneer.

"Not by having the great lords fight your battle with Mordesius for you, I hope," said Robert, sounding alarmed.

"Not exactly—"

"Not by having them come before you and swear fealty, I hope," said Cairn, sounding even more alarmed.

"Of course not," said Persephone. "I will command Lord Bartok to undertake a mission that will require him to take risks, get dirty and serve without the promise of glory or reward beyond the satisfaction of knowing that he has obeyed his rightful queen."

Robert looked dubious. "There may be a few noblemen who would be willing to obey such a command, Your Majesty, but I'd bet my last copper that Lord Bartok is not among them."

"That is exactly why I will issue the command to him before all others," said Persephone, pretending not to notice that Cur and Silver had both begun quietly snarling at Azriel. "Lord Bartok is the most powerful nobleman in the realm. He will either be a tremendous ally or a formidable enemy, and it is time that I knew which. If he obeys and willingly accepts the gift that I have had made for him, we will know where he stands."

"A thing we will know just as well if he does not do those things," grumbled Robert. "And if he does not, in one fell swoop your fight for the throne will have gotten harder, more complicated and infinitely more dangerous."

"Yes," said Persephone, feeling Azriel's gaze upon her. "It will have."

Thirty-Six

LORD BARTOK STOOD in his war room surveying the large map spread out on the table before him. Frowning slightly, he shifted two intricately carved ivory pawns and a single knight to the spot on the map marked "Bartok Estate." In addition to a lone ivory king, this spot already boasted a small crowd of pawns and knights. Each pawn represented five hundred foot soldiers; each knight represented five hundred mounted soldiers.

The king represented one man: Lord Bartok himself.

The addition of troops did not please Lord Bartok as much as one might have expected. For one thing, Lord Tweedsmuir's recently arrived brother-in-law had clearly spent significantly more coin ensuring that he and his close companions looked splendid upon their dazzlingly caparisoned mounts than he had outfitting his actual fighting troops. For another thing, even with the addition of fifteen hundred men, Lord Bartok's force was still not of a size that he could be assured of defeating Mordesius's New Man army in battle. This was especially worrisome given that Lord Bartok's scouts had been reporting large enemy troop movements over the last few weeks. That Mordesius was gathering his army to him at this time could only mean one thing: he'd learned that he'd lost the capital, his general and his influence with the nobility, and that he intended to use force to take back what he could and destroy the rest.

Truly, the game was about to begin in earnest.

His hair ruffling slightly in the breeze that blew through the open window, Lord Bartok picked up the ivory queen that stood alone among the uncomfortably large crowd of ebony pawns and knights that occupied the space on the map north of Syon. As he regarded the tiny queen's intricately carved face, Lord Bartok wondered how the real queen was faring. Mordesius had surely been enraged when he'd learned what he'd lost, and Lord Bartok knew how blood-thirsty the former regent could become when in such a state. Lord Bartok hoped that Queen Persephone had been spared his abuse. Or, if she had not, that she'd not been abused in a way that would leave permanent scars. Even more than this, however, he hoped that the upstart had not managed to impregnate her. With each passing week, the chances that he'd done so increased, for unlike Aurelia, who'd failed to conceive a child by the stable boy and who was now parading her padded belly through the halls of the imperial palace, Queen Persephone had always had the look of a woman as fertile as a field seven years fallow.

As he carefully placed the ivory queen back among the troops of their mutual enemy, there came a knock at the door.

"Come," called Lord Bartok.

The door opened to reveal a middle-aged servant in Bartok livery. In one hand, he held a letter; in the other, a package tied with a string. Briskly, the servant strode across the room and handed both items to Lord Bartok.

"My lord, these were just delivered by a man who was quite as grubby as he was rude," said the servant, pursing his lips in an unconscious imitation of Lord Bartok at his most elegantly dis-dainful. "The ruffian insisted on planting himself in the courtyard. Insisted, mind you! He said he'd been instructed to wait in case you chose to send a reply to the letter. He also said that I was to tell you that you needn't get any ideas about torturing him for information on the whereabouts of the letter writer because the message had changed hands many times and he hadn't the foggiest notion where she might be."

Shaking his head slightly at this bizarre message, Lord Bartok glanced down at the folded letter in his hand and saw something that made him freeze.

Imprinted in the red wax seal was the crest of the Erok royal family.

"Leave the chamber but stay close," ordered Lord Bartok without looking up from the letter.

Wordlessly, the servant did as he'd been bid.

The instant he was gone, Lord Bartok strode over to his desk and sat down. Using a knife, he carefully separated the wax seal from the parchment, unfolded the letter and began to read.

Greetings, My Dear Lord Bartok,

Please accept my sincerest apologies for not having contacted you sooner. As you presumably know, within moments of the death of my brother, the king, who named me his successor, the traitor Mordesius abducted me. I do not wish to dwell upon that which he hoped to accomplish by his treacherous act, but I do wish to express my deep gratitude to you for having sent your son, Lord Atticus, to rescue me. I can truthfully say that if it had not been for him and his men, I do not know exactly how I would have escaped the walled fortress in which Mordesius had imprisoned me. Unfortunately, your son and I did not get the opportunity to speak on the night in question. However, you may rest assured that I look forward to someday having the chance to tell him exactly what I think of him.

You may also rest assured that I have every intention of returning to Parthania to sit upon my throne as soon as it is safe for me to do so. To this end, I require something of you, my lord. Having determined that Mordesius has evil intentions toward many in this kingdom, I have come to the conclusion that until he is stripped of all power and his New Man army is destroyed or disbanded, life in this realm cannot be as it should be. My army is not yet entirely battle ready, but my intelligence network informs me that you and the other noblemen have been gathering your fighting forces to you for some weeks now. To buy me time to more adequately prepare my own fighting forces, I would have you mount a campaign of harassment against Mordesius and his New Men. Your objective will be to cause widespread confusion, destruction, frustration and fear enough to drive his soldiers to desertion. Be advised, however, that under no circumstances are you to engage in a full battle with or kill Mordesius. The people of this realm need to see none but their rightful queen triumph over the traitor, that they may know who truly rules the kingdom.

Lord Bartok, I understand this is an unusual mission to give to a man of your great station. However, if you show yourself to be my true and loyal subject in the weeks and months to come, I promise that when the war has been won, you shall find me as gracious and grateful a queen as you could ever have hoped to kneel before.

Regards,
Queen Persephone

P.S. I would henceforth have you ride beneath the banner that I have provided. Prove yourself, and this banner will be the first of many gifts you shall receive from me.

Lord Bartok let the letter drop from his hands. As it fluttered to the desk, he seized the package and tugged the string so hard that it snapped. Out of the coarse brown packaging slid great handfuls of white silk; spreading it out on the desk before him, Lord Bartok saw that it was, indeed, a banner. He was not surprised to see the red circle that was the symbol of the Erok royal family but he wondered at the addition of the blue teardrop, which could symbolize anything from the queen's grief at the death of her brother to her anguish at having wasted so many years living so far below her own high station.

Smiling faintly at the thought that only a woman would be so sentimental as to add a teardrop to her crest, Lord Bartok pushed the banner aside and picked up the letter once more. If it was genuine, and he saw no reason to believe it wasn't, it meant that Queen Persephone was not in the possession of the upstart, after all. She was free and had been since the night Atticus stormed the walled fortress in which she'd been imprisoned. For the first time since receiving the duplicitous letter from his son—for the first time in many years, truth be told—Lord Bartok felt a flicker of warmth for the boy. Amazingly, although Atticus had obviously gotten himself captured in the process, it appeared as though he'd actually aided in the queen's escape. It was not precisely what he'd been told to do, of course, but it was better than having bungled the mission entirely. This was especially true given that the queen rightfully credited him with having sent Atticus to rescue her.

Letting the letter drop from his hands for a second time, Lord Bartok leaned forward and rested his elbows on the desktop. The letter raised as many questions as it answered. The biggest question it raised was how he ought to react. To say that the mission was an unusual one to give a man of his station was a gross understatement. Great lords did not harass their enemies. They did not scurry about setting fires, pilfering supplies and sabotaging equipment. They met their enemies on the battlefield with sword in hand! It was an insult to have been asked to do otherwise and yet . . . the inexperienced queen upon whom he hoped to get a fresh crop of sons had suddenly become an unknown commodity. One who spoke of armies and intelligence networks almost as though she knew what she was talking about; one who made no bones about her intention to sit upon her throne. If he ignored her letter, it was reasonable to assume that she'd make contact with some lesser nobleman in the hope that the man would show more loyalty. If she did that, the other great lords would learn of *his* disloyalty, and he'd lose their support. Without it, he'd not only lose the game, but for failing to obey a direct command issued by the sovereign to whom he'd publicly pledged himself, he'd run the very real risk of losing his title, his lands and even his head.

The thought of being humbled to a nobody and thereafter being known to a thousand future generations as the man who'd reduced the great Bartok family dynasty to ashes caused a violent shudder to run through Lord Bartok's body. No. It was too great a risk to take at this point in the game. Many things could happen in the weeks to come. The queen could change her mind about seeking the throne and abdicate it to the infant Aurelia was pretending to carry. She could suffer a wound and die. She could contract the Great Sickness and die.

Or . . . she could find herself so impressed with the fervor with which Lord Bartok carried out her first royal command that upon finding herself pressed by her Council to produce an heir, she might ask him to be her consort.

Heart beating fast, Lord Bartok rose to his feet and walked back over to the table with the map. Picking up the ivory king and queen, he held them together in one hand. As he stared down at them, he told himself that it was not impossible that she would choose him to be her husband.

He was the most powerful nobleman in the realm, after all. Who better to give her the sons she would require to see her bloodline carry on?

Very well, then: for the time being, he would prove himself as loyal a subject as the queen could hope for. He would set his dignity aside and order the knights and foot soldiers under his command to split up and go forth like a band of lowborn bandits.

Carefully setting the ivory king back in its place on the map and setting the queen to one side (since he knew not where she was), Lord Bartok called for the servant he'd earlier dismissed.

The man appeared at once.

"You say that the man who delivered these things is still here?" asked Lord Bartok.

"Yes, my lord," replied the servant stiffly. "As I said, he rudely informed me that—"

"Take him to the kitchens and see him well-fed," interrupted Lord Bartok. "Tell him that by the time he has finished eating, I will have a reply for him to carry to his mistress."

Thirty-Seven

PERSEPHONE STARED AT the gift that the camp blacksmith had presented to her earlier that day.

"Well?" said Rachel. "Aren't you going to try it on?"

Persephone shrugged without taking her eyes off the crown in her hands. Unlike the crown that awaited her in Parthania, this one was not heavy with precious metals or inlaid with gemstones. Instead, it was a simple circlet of hammered silver. Each of the five identical peaks that rose up at the front represented one of the five clans of Glyndoria—all of equal importance, all standing together. It was the exact crown that Persephone would have chosen for herself, and yet for some reason she could not seem to bring herself to try it on.

"I'm almost certain that thing is meant to sit on your head," came Azriel's voice from the entrance of the tent.

In unison, both girls turned. Persephone felt her heart quicken at the sight of her handsome husband. Though he'd been dressing like a prince ever since Robert pointed out that it would not serve for the queen's husband to dress like a pirate, somehow his new clothes did not make him look like a prince.

Somehow, they only made him look like an especially *well-dressed* pirate.

"Zdeno is looking for you, Rachel," said Azriel, flashing the girl a knowing smile.

"Oh!" exclaimed Rachel, two spots of pink appearing on her cheeks. "Oh, well, I, uh . . . I'd better go, then."

Hastily dipping Persephone a curtsey, the blushing girl hurried from the tent. After she'd gone, Azriel lingered at the threshold a moment longer. Folding his arms across his chest, he cocked his head to one side and let his admiring gaze wander over Persephone most deliciously. Then, smiling in a way that was only a little bit wicked, he started walking toward her.

As she watched him approach, Persephone was forcibly struck by two thoughts. The first was that if she lived to be a thousand years old, she was quite sure she'd never tire of the feel of his eyes upon her. The second was that she hoped that the baby looked exactly like him.

"Persephone?" murmured Azriel when he was standing just a few inches away from her.

"Yes?" she said breathlessly, staring at his lips.

Instead of answering her, he used the tips of his fingers to brush the hair back from her face and to tuck every last stray strand behind her ears. Then he gently tugged the crown out of her hands and stepped behind her. Ever so slowly, he lowered the crown onto her head, wrapped his arms around her and planted a kiss behind her ear.

"It fits nicely," he murmured.

"The crown?" she asked, leaning back against him.

"No, the suit of armor," he teased, reaching down to give the steel strips of her skirt a twitch. "You look quite delectable in it, not to mention utterly terrifying."

Smiling, Persephone turned in his arms and looked up at him. "And how do I look in the crown?" she asked, more timidly than she'd intended.

At once, Azriel's expression grew serious. "Magnificent," he said. "Like a queen."

Flushing with pleasure, she said, "And . . . you're sure you don't want one? A crown, I mean? Because if you do—if you think you'll not be content being known only as prince consort and not as king—I'm willing to share the throne with you, Azriel."

It was not a lie, for Persephone was willing. Nevertheless, she found herself giving a tiny, inward sigh of relief at Azriel's reply.

"I have already told you that I do not want to be king," he said. "I want to know that you are happy, and that you love and respect me, and that you and the baby and I will be together forever."

"We will," said Persephone, hoping it was true.

"Then I am content that you should rule alone," said Azriel, rocking from side to side with her in his arms. "Indeed, I think it would be a mistake for you not to rule alone, for there are many men who'd prefer a king to a queen, and I think you'd not take kindly to being overlooked, and I *know* I'd not take kindly to seeing the equipment of said men dangling from every chandelier in the palace. Besides all that, the hard seat of a throne would bruise my tender backside and a crown would flatten my beautiful curls, and I could not abide either." He smiled *very* wickedly before continuing. "No, far better that I should simply remain your Master of the Bath. Ever armed with soap and sponge, my entire being devoted to ensuring that in the whole of the realm, there is no woman with a cleaner pair of—"

"Your Majesty!" bellowed Robert, bursting into the tent. Briskly striding forward, he waved a sealed letter over his head and said, "My man has just now returned with a message for you from Lord Bartok!"

At once, Persephone pulled away from Azriel, took the letter and broke the seal:

Most Gracious Majesty,

I cannot express to you how profoundly relieved I was to receive your message. To know that you are safe and beyond the clutches of the former regent does much to assuage my grief and pain that my only son was taken during the rescue mission.

It fills me with great joy to know that you have already raised an army and that you intend to return to the imperial capital to take your throne.

As for the mission that you have set for me, rest assured that the only thing a man of my station need concern himself with is obeying without question the commands of his sovereign. Therefore, you may depend upon me to rally the other noblemen to join me in mercilessly harassing the army of the former regent. And when the day finally comes that you call for me to stand with you in a true battle against our common enemy, that together we might restore proper order to this great realm, know that the gods themselves will not be able to keep me from your side.

With Deepest Affection, Greatest Respect and Kindest Regards,
Your Most Loyal Servant,
Lord Bartok

"I cannot believe that Lord Atticus was kidnapped that night," murmured Persephone.

"I cannot believe that Lord Bartok signed his letter 'Your Most Loyal Servant'," said Azriel in a mock disapproving voice. "Does he not know that *I* am your most loyal servant?"

"No, nor does he know that you've married and fathered a child upon his precious queen," said Robert. "And it is my very, very dearest wish in life to be there when he finds out."

Smiling faintly as she shook her head at him, Persephone said, "At least it sounds as though Lord Bartok intends to do as commanded. If he does, and if New Men continue deserting in the numbers being reported, the coming weeks should see the size and strength of Mordesius's army significantly reduced."

Robert and Azriel nodded, but before either of them could comment further, there came the sudden sound of frenzied barking and faraway shouts of alarm. Together with Persephone, the two men drew their swords and rushed out of the tent. As they did so, a bandit scout came charging out of the forest toward them.

"Your Majesty, it's the Panoraki!" he cried, his eyes as big as trenchers. "They're coming! And they're hairy! And . . . and there are *thousands* of them!"

Breathless with excitement, Persephone watched as the Panoraki slowly began to materialize out of the misty gloom. All were large, all had long, tangled hair poking out from beneath horned helms, all carried waterskins and food pouches, all had battle-axes jammed into their heavy leather belts. Some had great bushy beards; others did not. Some wore long, shaggy coats, some wore animal skins, and some appeared to have stripped off their shirts altogether, though it was hard to say for certain because all of these had arms, bellies and backs that were quite as hairy as their heads and chins.

As the mountain dwellers gathered at the northern edge of the camp, Cur, Silver and the other dogs continued to bark and snarl and strain against the handlers who were holding them back. The Methusians and bandits, meanwhile, began congregating at the southern edge of the camp. A few wore expressions of curiosity, but most looked dangerously nervous.

All stared mutely at the great hairy multitude that was staring back at them.

Robert adjusted his grip on his sword. "My men and I have never seen even one Panoraki before," he said edgily as his eyes flicked from side to side as though trying to assess the magnitude of an approaching threat. "You're quite sure they come in friendship, Your Majesty, even though by your own admission they once tried to kill you?"

"The avalanche wasn't necessarily meant to kill us, Robert," said Azriel lightly as he laid a steadying hand upon the bandit leader's shoulder.

"And even if it was, it happened before my champion won us our lives and the everlasting friendship of the clan," added Persephone as she scanned the horde for Barka and Fayla.

Unable to spot them but knowing that something had to be done quickly to diffuse the escalating tension, Persephone strode into the gap between the two groups and made a deliberate show of sheathing her sword. As Azriel stepped forward to stand beside her, she turned to the Panoraki, spread her hands wide and called, "Welcome, my friends!"

In response to a gruff order barked from somewhere in the middle of the crowd, the Panoraki warriors at the front parted to allow Barka to walk forward. At his side was Fayla, looking well enough in spite of appearing rather battered and bruised. The Panoraki prince grinned broadly at Persephone and Azriel, but before he could do more than this, his attention was caught by something—or rather, by someone—behind them.

"Mateo!" cried Barka in delight. "Mateo, it's me, lad—Barka!" He thumped his chest twice. "I'm the Panoraki prince what taught you to sing so sweetly! Remember? Back in the dungeon in Parthania?"

As if to remind the boy, Barka began to sing, loudly and quite as tunelessly as if he was utterly tone deaf. Smiling slightly, Mateo hesitated for only a few seconds before joining in with the voice of an angel. Together, the hulking Panoraki and the little Methusian sang all three verses of a well-known and much-beloved Glyndorian lullaby. By the time they'd finished, nearly everyone on both sides of the camp was smiling, and the tension that had filled the air earlier had all but vanished.

Persephone took advantage of the moment by swiftly calling for the Methusians and the bandits to make their guests welcome. Once she was satisfied that the various factions were getting along (or, at least, that they were not trying to kill each other), she invited Barka and Fayla to join her, Azriel and the other members of her Council in the Council tent.

After settling himself down onto one of the rough-hewn stools, Barka gruffly introduced himself to Cairn, Robert and Zdeno, and greeted Rachel as an old friend. Then he turned to Azriel and

Persephone and said, "Condolences to you both on the passing of those you've recently lost. May the mother goddess of the mountain grant them afterlives rich in strong drink, beautiful lovers and wonderful woolly sheep."

"Thank you," said Persephone, privately hoping the mother goddess would spare Finn an eternity plagued by the Panoraki's oversensitive, spoiled, high-strung sheep. "I'm so pleased that you and your clansmen have come, Barka."

"Your Majesty, I once promised you the everlasting friendship of my people and all that implied," he reminded. "You ought to have known that would mean that we'd come as soon as we'd dug Fayla out of the snow and—"

"You don't mean to tell me that you brought *another* avalanche down on her head," said Persephone in dismay as she reached up to adjust her crown.

"It was only a little one, triggered before the lookout realized who she was," said Barka defensively, plunging his fingers into his beard to give his chin a vigorous scratch. "The important thing is that other than the handful of women we left behind to watch over the sheep and the children—may the mother goddess keep them safe in their secret hideout—the mighty Panoraki are here in full force and just itching for the chance to bash in the heads of our hated enemies!"

"You may have to keep your battle-axes sheathed for a little longer yet," warned Persephone. "For we have received reports that Mordesius is taking his army west, not north. Moreover, now that you and your warriors have arrived, I intend to do something that will make Mordesius forget all about his plan to slaughter your clan or any other."

"And what is that, Your Majesty?" asked Barka, cracking his hairy knuckles in anticipation.

"I intend to march upon the imperial capital and claim the throne he so badly desires," she said, hoping that her words didn't sound as fantastical to the rest of them as they did to her.

"And after that?" asked Barka.

"My wife the queen shall raise such an army of loyal subjects that Mordesius will never again be able to threaten to slaughter anyone," said Azriel firmly.

"Because his army will be outnumbered?" said Fayla, raising an eyebrow.

"Because his army will be destroyed," said Persephone flatly. "And because he will be dead."

Thirty-Eight

DEEP BENEATH the imperial palace that Persephone hoped to shortly claim as her own, Mordesius's most favored general moved not a muscle as he watched the rat creep forward out of the darkness.

Though he believed he'd been a prisoner in the dungeon for about a month now, General Murdock could not say for certain because he had no way of accurately marking the passage of time. In his close, sweltering cell, the sun did not rise or set; minutes could be minutes or they could be hours. He never knew how long he'd slept, and he suspected that his guards purposely checked on him at random intervals to keep him thusly disoriented.

It was what he'd always done back when he'd been the one holding the dungeon keys.

He'd been in the dungeon for long enough, at any rate, that the injuries he'd sustained on the night of his capture had mostly healed. He'd gotten filthy, but not nearly as filthy as one might have expected, for whenever he'd been given his ration of tepid water, he'd used a small amount to clean himself as best he could. Lord Bartok's men had jeered him each time they'd seen him dip the torn hem of his rags into the water and carefully wipe his face and hands, but General Murdock had paid them no mind at all. He was a military man, and a military man knew that surviving captivity was as much about mental strength as it was about physical strength, and that nothing leeched mental strength faster than failure to perform those small, inconsequential tasks that allowed one to continue to feel like a human being.

Since his arrival in the dungeon, General Murdock had also lost weight, though not nearly as much as one might have expected, for he'd supplemented his meager diet of moldy bread with daily rations of raw rat meat. Another man might have been revolted by the prospect of snatching up a wriggling rodent and ripping it apart with his hands and teeth, but a military man did what he had to in order to survive. Catching the first rat had been a simple matter of sitting still enough to entice the creature to investigate. After that, it had been an even simpler matter of setting the bloody remains of his most recent meal on the floor beside him, because not even the wariest rat could resist creeping forward to investigate *that*.

And when it did, dinner was served.

His mouth watering, General Murdock watched this day's dinner draw closer and closer. Just as he was about to grab it, however, he heard the sound of a key in the padlock of the cell door. Hastily slumping on his bed of filthy straw, the General donned what he hoped was an expression of bleakest despair. Though he was neither physically weakened nor filled with despair, the last dozen or so times his guards had entered the cell to check on him, he'd pretended to be both in hope of lulling them into a false sense of security.

When the heavy door opened to reveal a single guard who was both young and nervous-looking, General Murdock knew that his ruse had worked. Up until now, whenever Lord Bartok's men had come to check on him and feed the fire, they'd always come in pairs, or even threes and fours. One man—even one highly skilled military man—who was weakened, weaponless and chained to a wall could not reasonably hope to be able to overcome multiple guards.

Overcoming a single inexperienced guard was a different matter altogether.

General Murdock waited until the boy had closed the door and taken three steps toward the fireplace to throw his fit. Thrashing and kicking so violently that his dinner gave a startled squeak and fled back into the darkness, the General bit his tongue so hard that blood joined froth upon his thin lips. Gagging wretchedly, he arched his back and slammed his head against the wall several times before abruptly letting his entire body go limp.

After a moment of stunned silence, the lone guard muttered something under his breath before drawing his sword and tentatively starting forward to check on his prisoner.

As soon as he got close enough, General Murdock struck out with the same speed and ferocity with which he would have struck out at the recently spared rat. In the case of the boy, however, the chains that fixed General Murdock's iron wrist cuffs to the wall were too short to allow him to properly attack with his hands, so he kicked the boy's feet out from under him instead. The boy somehow managed to keep hold on his sword, but before he got a chance to use it—indeed, probably before he realized how he'd ended up on the floor—General Murdock had caught the boy's neck between his thighs, given one sharp jerk and snapped it cleanly.

Pleased that his plan had worked exactly as he'd intended, General Murdock disentangled himself from the corpse and maneuvered it closer so that he could reach the ring of keys in the pocket of its doublet. After quickly unlocking his wrist cuffs, he stood and stretched to take the stiffness out of those muscles he'd been unable to properly exercise while he'd been chained to the wall. Then he walked over and opened the trapdoor in the floor through which he used to dispose of the bodies of dead prisoners and the pieces of living ones. He could not see the underground river below, but he could hear the sound of it rushing past.

With the fleeting thought that he hoped Mordesius had not yet found someone to replace him and a red-streaked vision of the things he would do to once more prove himself a competent and trustworthy servant if he had, General Murdock wrapped his arms around his torso, took a deep breath and stepped through the trap-door in the dungeon floor.

Thirty-Nine

IN THE FOUR WEEKS since setting out from the training camp north of Syon, Mordesius had learned two important things.

The first was that he disliked leading the march to war. The second was that he was not very good at it.

"What do you mean 'we've' lost another dozen wagons?" he bellowed now, flinging a half-full goblet of wine at the head of the blood-splattered soldier who stood before him. "I have lost nothing except for my hope that there is a single man under my command who is not utterly incompetent!"

Infuriatingly, the goblet missed the soldier's head by such a wide margin that he did not even have to duck.

Mordesius glared at the fool, despising him almost as much for not having been struck by the flying goblet as for being the bearer of yet more bad news.

The campaign to crush the great lords had been a disaster from the outset and they'd not even fought a proper battle yet. As Mordesius had commanded, the New Man army had moved out just six days after he and Lord Atticus had arrived at the training camp. Thereafter, however, it had moved so slowly that it had taken weeks to make any progress at all. Supply carts and wagons had continually gotten stuck in the mud created by endless days of rain. Horses had lost shoes and gone lame. Soldiers only recently arrived from the farthest corners of the realm had been so worn out that they'd been unable to maintain a quick march through the mud, and there'd been so many of them that instead of being able to execute them all for their infuriating disobedience, Mordesius had been forced to slow the pace considerably.

Their pace had been further slowed by the need to waste time pillaging the land as they went, for although they'd brought along supplies enough to see the men of consequence well-fed, they'd not had time to establish a supply train robust enough to feed the entire army. As such, each time they'd passed by a farm or a village, they'd emptied the larders and grain silos, slaughtered the animals and stripped the fields and orchards. Farmers and villagers who'd protested the pillaging or the soldiers' treatment of their wives and daughters had been slaughtered alongside their animals as a warning to their neighbors to keep their displeasure to themselves.

On top of all this, his soldiers had continued to desert at an alarming rate. Many of the deserters were conscripts who'd been forced into the army, and since Mordesius did not have the time or resources to waste hunting them down, he'd elected to mete out punishment upon a random selection of those conscripts who yet remained behind. Most unfortunately, the sight of their heads jammed onto pikes carried along by their still-breathing comrades had done nothing whatsoever to prevent further desertions.

On the contrary, it had caused the desertion rate to climb higher still.

It had climbed again when the attacks had begun. Nighttime raids had seen sentries' throats slit, men slaughtered in their sleep, tacking sliced to ribbons, horses freed from their tethers and wagons set ablaze. During the day, bands of armed men would appear out of nowhere to hack his soldiers to bits. Or worse, they wouldn't appear, their crossbow bolts would simply rain down. Then, as quickly as they had appeared (or not appeared), the virtually unscathed attackers would be gone, leaving nothing but death, confusion and fear in their wake.

As it happened, the route that Mordesius had insisted upon taking had gone a long way toward leaving his army vulnerable to these attacks. For while it was without question the shortest distance to Bartok Estate, where the great lords were reported to be gathering their army, the route ran between rocky outcrops and through small wooded areas that were perfectly suited to ambushes. Moreover, the road itself was so narrow that Mordesius's army often ended up strung out over several miles, rendering it even more vulnerable.

The taller-by-a-head commander who'd not yet been cut down to size had earlier ridden back to find out the cause of the latest delay. In response to their on-going troubles, he was ever silent, obedient and respectful, but Mordesius knew what the bastard was thinking. He was thinking that if they'd spent a few weeks preparing and then taken the longer route that he'd recommended, they'd almost certainly be farther ahead by now. He was thinking that Mordesius didn't know how to handle the men and that he didn't lead the army half as well as Murdock would have done.

The idea that anyone would dare to think such blasphemy so enraged Mordesius that he abruptly decided to have the commander flogged to death upon his return to camp. As he opened his mouth to bellow the order, however, Mordesius noticed that the soldier who was still standing before him appeared to have more to say.

"What?" snapped Mordesius.

"Y-Your Grace, the commander told me to bring you this," stammered the soldier, hastily holding out a bloody scrap of cloth Mordesius had assumed was a bandage or compress.

"What is it?" demanded Mordesius, making no move to reach for it.

"An armband ripped from the sleeve of one of the attackers," replied the soldier.

Irritably, Mordesius snatched the bloody scrap from the man's hand, spread it flat on his own withered lap and then let out a cry of shock and dismay. It wasn't the sight of the Bartok crest that caused him to cry out thusly, it was the sight of it entwined with a bastard-ized Erok royal crest.

Mordesius fell back in his cushioned chair, his heart clenching so hard that he actually found it difficult to breathe. When the attacks on his army had first begun, he'd assumed they were being perpe-trated by landless, homeless malcontents or by the outraged neigh-bors of some of the farmers and villagers his soldiers had slaughtered along the way. When it became clear that the attacks were impecca-bly planned and executed, however, Mordesius had begun to suspect some nobleman's trained knights. Still, because the attackers had appeared and vanished too swiftly for anyone to get a good look at their armbands, and since his own idiot soldiers had not managed to kill even a single one of them, it had been impossible to know exactly which nobleman had stooped so low as to attack like some lowborn bandit.

Until now, that is.

Now, if the entwined crests were to be believed, it appeared that it was not just that bastard Bartok who'd stooped so low, but Queen Persephone as well! If the entwined crests were to be believed, she'd not vanished into thin air, after all. On the contrary, the gutter-reared broodmare who'd refused him marriage, sons and her knowledge of the healing pool was back causing him trouble and in league with his mortal enemy.

Nervously wiping his grimy hands on his torn black pants, the soldier said, "Is there any order you'd like me to carry back to—"

"Get out," said Mordesius softly.

The soldier was gone before Mordesius had finished speaking the words.

Flinging aside the bloody armband, Mordesius let his back bend and his head droop. That he would soon know the whereabouts of the queen excited him almost as much as the knowledge that she was entwined with Bartok enraged him. While he was brood-ing upon the things he longed to do to each of them—and to the cockroach, too, if he was still scuttling about—he heard the sound of Lord Atticus shouting and pummeling one of the soldiers who'd been assigned to tend to his needs. As Mordesius listened to the drunken nobleman rant that his supper had been ruined because the sauce that had accompanied his roast pheasant had lacked the hint of mint that he'd specifically requested, Mordesius wondered for the thousandth time why he didn't just lop the worm's head off and be done with it. The answer, of course, was that Lord Atticus might yet prove more useful alive than dead, but still. It was exceedingly tiresome listening to him complain.

When he heard the dreary sound of rain beginning to patter on the roof of the tent, it occurred to Mordesius that much about the game of war was tiresome. Suddenly, he was seized by a yearning to be back in the imperial palace, plotting from the comfort of his own chambers. His camp tent was far more sumptuous than anyone else's tent, of course, but it did not come close to rivaling the luxury to which he was accustomed. Being "one of the men" had long since lost its shine and his poor body ached all the time. Running an army was far harder than it looked, and far less glamorous, and he deeply resented the fact that—

"Your Grace?"

"I told you to get out!" screamed Mordesius.

"I know, Your Grace!" cried the soldier, his knees all but knocking together. "But General Murdock is outside and he requests an audience!"

Mordesius was so surprised by these words that he forgot how enraged he was. "Murdock is alive?" he exclaimed. "Murdock is here?"

The soldier bobbed his head. "Yes, Your Grace. He arrived just a few moments ago."

"Send him in," snapped Mordesius.

The soldier departed even quicker than he had the last time.

The next instant, Murdock crept into the room. He was thinner than he had been and dirtier than Mordesius had ever seen him.

He was wearing ill-fitting boots and breeches, and a doublet with a bloodstained knife hole in the lapel that the General had no doubt made himself in an effort to encourage the doublet's previous owner to part with it.

Mordesius eyed his henchman, trying to decide how to greet him. On the one hand, Murdock had lost control of the imperial capital and for that he richly deserved to be punished. On the other hand, his arrival meant that Mordesius could wash his hands of the day-to-day tedium of running the army.

"Took you long enough to get here," he finally muttered.

"Yes," agreed General Murdock, reaching up to carefully smooth back a lock of greasy hair. "But I am here now."

Forty

FOLLOWING THE ARRIVAL of the Panoraki, it took eight days for Persephone and her royal Council to ensure that everyone and everything was prepared for the journey south to the imperial capital.

Late on their last night in the bandit camp, Persephone pulled Azriel aside and asked him if he'd mind giving her one final lesson in battle strategy before they set out. Tired though he was, he smiled and followed her up the ladder into the tree shelter in which they'd been residing. Persephone waited quietly while Azriel lit candles, set the map and game pieces on the desk, and sat down on the bench. Then, instead of taking a seat on the bench next to him, she eased herself onto his lap, wrapped her arms around his neck and gave him a long, hot kiss. Her surprised (and suddenly wide-awake) strategy instructor offered up some extremely feeble protests in the name of the war effort and the standards set forth by the Instructors' Guild, but their sincerity was rather suspect given that he had Persephone halfway out of her dress before he'd finished uttering them.

"By the gods, I find it very difficult to believe that you are about to become somebody's mother," said Azriel much, much later, as he lay sprawled on the mattress trying to catch his breath.

"Believe it," said Persephone, smiling in the darkness as she, too, tried to catch her breath.

In response, Azriel rolled onto his side and laid his hand against her bare belly. He'd been able to feel the baby's movements for some weeks now, and he seemed to never tire of them, just as Persephone never tired of the sight of him silhouetted above her.

"He's getting stronger," murmured Azriel, his hand shifting slightly as the concentration of tiny kicks and punches shifted from one side of her belly to the other.

"In spite of my gut feeling, he might be a she," reminded Persephone, putting her hand over his.

"Impossible," said Azriel. "For I have great faith in your gut feelings, and I've never heard of a girl named Poddrick."

Persephone chuckled throatily. "Azriel, I have told you many times that we are not naming the baby Poddrick," she said.

Azriel chuckled, too. Then he leaned over Persephone, gave her a lingering kiss on the mouth and whispered, "Call the baby what you will, wife, just keep you both safe from harm in the weeks to come."

"I will," she whispered.

If I can, she added to herself.

It didn't take long to get organized the next morning. Everyone's packs had been checked and rechecked the night before, so the only thing left to do was to ready the horses and pack animals. Predictably, Fleet took exception to being saddled even though Persephone stood nearby heaping praise upon him.

As Azriel stalked off in search of another bucket of cut turnips in the hope that this would keep the "infernal bag of horsemeat" occupied for long enough to saddle him, Persephone went to bid a final goodbye to the women and children who were staying behind. She'd just scooped Sabian into her arms when there came from the other side of camp a shrill, horsey squeal followed by a crash and the sound of an irate Methusian bellowing something about horse steaks.

"Well!" said Persephone brightly as she planted a noisy kiss on Sabian's firm little cheek, set him down and looked around at the others. "It sounds as though we are almost ready to go. I shall think of you often, and if all goes well, when next we meet, you will be able to call me queen in very truth."

Instead of heading directly south after emerging from the Great Forest, Persephone and her army spent several days traveling east to avoid Lord Bartok's army. Although reports suggested that the nobleman was doing exactly as Persephone had commanded, she did not yet trust him enough to risk coming face-to-face with his superior fighting force.

During the march east, they saw almost no one. It was sparsely populated land to begin with, and Persephone insisted on giving the few farms and villages they did see a wide berth so as not to frighten the inhabitants. If there were other travelers on the road—and Robert assured them that there were, for the realm was filled with displaced lowborns forced to ever wander in search of a day's work or a scrap of food—they did not show themselves.

At the outset, Persephone rode beside Azriel at the front of the army, beneath the fluttering banner bearing her crest. By the end of the third day, however, her back was so sore that Azriel had to lift her out of the saddle. She tried to assure him (and herself) that she'd be fit to ride the next day, but Azriel was having none of it. After entrusting Persephone into Rachel's care, he and Robert pocketed a purse of bandit gold and galloped back to the nearest village. They returned the next morning with a surprisingly fine litter and a disturbing description of villagers left traumatized and starving by Mordesius's New Men, who'd passed through about a week earlier. Persephone immediately ordered men to return to the village with as much food as they could spare. It was not much—just some strips of dried bear meat and a small sack of hard biscuits. However, no one knew better than Persephone that a mouthful of food today could mean the difference between life and death tomorrow, and that that knowledge alone was often enough to keep hope alive.

From that point on, Persephone rode Fleet only infrequently. Had her pregnancy been common knowledge, they could have left her mount riderless without risking spies and subjects alike questioning her fitness to lead her troops. It was not, however, so Rachel often played decoy by donning her armor and riding the disgruntled Fleet in her stead. Whenever she did, Persephone spent her day fidgeting inside the curtained litter and chatting with Ivan, who frequently left off hunting to perch on the roof of the litter, alternately glaring at those humans who offended him (all of them) and screeching abuse at poor Cur.

When Azriel judged that they were a day outside Parthania, he sent heralds ahead to proclaim the news that Persephone was coming. Around midafternoon, she and Rachel traded outfits and places, and shortly after sunset they crested a hill and saw the great walls of Parthania looming in the distance.

Silhouetted against a sky streaked orange and red with the last light of the dying day, the walls seemed to stretch from one horizon to the other and all the way up to the heavens.

It was still the most awesome sight Persephone had ever seen. Unlike that first time she'd seen it all those months ago, however, this time she did not gape like an ignorant, ill-bred nobody on her first trip to the imperial capital.

This time she gazed upon it like a queen returning home.

Turning to Azriel, who was staring at her as though she was the most awesome sight *he* had ever seen, Persephone took a deep breath, straightened her silver crown and said, "Ready, my love?"

"For anything," he said with a flicker of a smile.

Forty-One

GENERAL MURDOCK slipped into the tent where Mordesius was supping with Lord Atticus.

Affecting not to notice his henchman, Mordesius selected a meaty bone from the nearest platter and tore into it. In the two weeks since Murdock's unexpected arrival, Mordesius's feelings toward the man had not thawed. Indeed, they'd grown considerably icier, for while Murdock's presence had unquestionably freed Mordesius from the day-to-day tedium of running the army, it had also served to call attention to the ineptitude with which Mordesius had performed that same function. That is because Murdock had been able to quickly and efficiently address every single issue that had plagued Mordesius from the outset. After slow-roasting the training camp commander over an open fire, Murdock had established an adequate supply train, begun a brilliant campaign of retaliation against Bartok, slowed the desertion rate and generally reestablished order among the troops. In short, he'd done everything in his power to prove himself a loyal, competent and hardworking servant.

Mordesius despised him for it.

After noisily sucking every last bit of marrow out of the bone and tossing it aside, Mordesius deliberately wiped his greasy fingers on the clean white tablecloth and took a long draught of wine.

Then, and only then, did he cast a brooding look at his general and say, "Well? What is so important that it could not wait until after supper?"

General Murdock, who'd long since found new clothes and regained much of the weight he'd lost during his imprisonment, did not seem the least perturbed to be greeted in such a fashion.

Stepping forward, he said, "Your Grace, I've just received word that Queen Persephone was spotted two days' march from the imperial capital. At the rate she was traveling, she could be at the city gates even as we speak."

Without thinking, Mordesius put his hand over his heart. "And?" he asked breathlessly, half rising out of his cushioned chair.

"And she could not be recaptured because she and the Methusian were riding at the head of an army of several thousand Panoraki warriors," said Murdock.

At these words, Mordesius's mouth dropped open and he fell back into his chair so abruptly that he jarred his already aching back.

Lord Atticus looked incredulous. "Do you mean to say that there are thousands of armed barbarians traipsing around the realm, and you only just found out about it now?" he jeered. Jabbing his dagger into a large piece of juicy rare beef, the young nobleman shoved the meat into his mouth and said, "What kind of a general are you?"

General Murdock said nothing.

As he watched his repulsive henchman's beady-eyed gaze drift from the grease-stained tablecloth to the juice dribbling down Lord Atticus's weak chin, Mordesius's mind whirled. He was furious that the queen and the cockroach had managed to find each other again, but he was deeply gratified to learn that he'd been right to suspect the clans of uniting behind the meddling whore. If only he'd not believed that crushing Bartok was a more pressing priority than slaughtering the clans! As a result of this miscalculation, it now seemed that there were two armies he needed to defeat to clear a path to the throne.

And if the entwined crests on the armbands of Bartok's soldiers were any indication, the two were in league together!

Since the queen's army was nothing but a ragtag collection of brutes barely better than beasts, Mordesius did not think this development would be enough to tip the odds out of his favor, but it would certainly change the game.

"Your Grace, may I suggest that you march upon the imperial capital at once?" said General Murdock.

"March upon the imperial capital?" barked Mordesius. "Don't be stupid, Murdock! They'd slam shut the gates the very instant they saw us coming!"

"Precisely," said General Murdock, reaching up to scratch his long nose. "And after they'd done so, your army would lay siege to the city. Nothing and no one would get in or out. Starvation or surrender would be their only options."

Annoyed though he was for having failed to think this through for himself, Mordesius could not help being captivated by the image of the broken, defeated, empty-bellied, widowed queen staggering toward him, her gown hanging from her wasted frame, her violet eyes huge above her gaunt cheeks. Swaying on her feet before falling to her knees and whispering to him that she'd do *anything* . . .

Lord Atticus belched richly, shattering the image. "A siege sounds like a bore and it wouldn't work, anyway," he announced as he poured himself another goblet of wine. "In case you've forgotten, Murdock, Parthania is a coastal city."

"With respect, my lord, I have not forgotten," said General Murdock politely as his gaze once again drifted to the nobleman's juicy chin. "I've already sent an order to His Grace's fleet to stand ready to burn any ship that tries to leave or enter either the Parthanian common harbor or the royal one. The inhabitants of the city shall have no supplies delivered by sea. It is a good plan."

You mean it is your *good plan*, thought Mordesius, glowering at him.

"Your Grace?" said Murdock after a moment's silence. "Shall I give the order to turn south and defeat the queen before she has a chance to add to her forces?"

"No," snapped Mordesius, straightening his uneven shoulders as best he could. "For there is something you *have* forgotten, Murdock, and that is that there just happens to be another enemy army out there. A far bigger, better-equipped and better-trained army. Would you have us lay siege to Parthania only to have Bartok march on us from the north? In the unlikely event that the cursèd Panoraki were allowed through the gates upon their arrival at the city, how long do you think they'd stay behind them once they saw our rear flank being attacked?"

Lord Atticus's eyes widened in terror at the thought.

"Your Grace, if Lord Bartok had wanted to engage us in a true battle, he'd have ridden out against us in full force weeks ago instead of persisting with his campaign of petty harassment," said General Murdock, so patiently that Mordesius wanted to hit him. "I think there must be some reason he has not done so."

"And I think you are wrong," said Mordesius, who was suddenly sure that it was so. "That is why we are going to follow my plan, Murdock. We are going to defeat Lord Bartok—"

"A difficult thing to accomplish when he refuses to order his men to stand and fight, and does not seem to care how many noble manors we burn and pillage in retaliation for his attacks," pointed out Murdock.

"I am not interested in your excuses, Murdock," hissed Mordesius.

"Neither am I, Murdock!" brayed Lord Atticus. "Just see your bloody job done so that I can become the new Lord Bartok. A Lord Bartok who can actually be depended upon to keep his word," he added pompously as he puffed out his flabby chest and raised his goblet to Mordesius.

Mordesius raised his own goblet in reply even though he intended to dispose of the useless drunkard long before the game was over.

"Only after we have defeated the current Lord Bartok will we proceed onward to Parthania to deal with the queen, the cockroach and their barbarian army," he said. "Do you understand, Murdock?"

The General hesitated for only an instant before nodding.

"Good," said Mordesius, who was already regretting his decision.

Not because he believed it unwise but because now that he knew the whereabouts of the queen, the urge to hunt her down and attend to the unfinished business between the two of them was almost more than he could bear.

Forty-Two

IT WAS WELL PAST DUSK by the time Persephone, Azriel and the others reined up before the great gates of Parthania. Though the flickering light of a dozen torches illuminated the freshly swept roadway before the open outer gates, and though Persephone could see throngs of people in the street just inside the walls, the heavy wrought-iron inner gate had been lowered.

"I warned you that something like this might happen," murmured Cairn, who was riding beside Robert, just behind Persephone and Azriel.

Persephone did not reply or look around. She did not even look at Azriel, for she did not want her subjects inside the city walls to think that she was looking to him to tell her what to do. Instead, she locked eyes with the extremely portly lord who was leaning heavily against the gate. Without taking her eyes off his, she slid down out of the saddle. Azriel immediately dismounted and started toward her but she stopped him with a raised hand, hoping he'd understand how important it was for her to stand alone at this moment. Or at least, alone except for Cur and Silver, who'd padded forward to stand one on either side of her.

Tossing Fleet's reins to Azriel to keep the jealous horse from charging after her, Persephone took a deep breath. Then, with her head held high, her belly sucked in and a trickle of sweat snaking down her back, she walked forward. Not with the graceful, mincing steps of a noblewoman but with the long, practical strides best suited to enslaved girls and warrior queens.

She stopped three paces from the closed gate. For a long moment, she said nothing, only let her gaze drift past the lord to the moon-lit faces of those in the jostling crowd behind him. At length, she lifted her hands in a simple gesture of greeting and said, "People of Parthania, it is good to be home."

Her words were met with an uncertain cheer.

"Welcome, my queen," rumbled the lord at the gate. "I am Lord Belmont, keeper of the keys to the city."

"Finding the gate of my imperial capital shut against me and my army is not much of a welcome, Lord Belmont," said Persephone, loud enough to be heard by all.

"The gate is not shut against *you*, Your Majesty," said Lord Belmont.

Persephone made a great show of examining the gate before leaning toward Lord Belmont and solemnly saying, "Forgive me, my lord, but I could almost swear that the gate *is* shut against me."

A burble of nervous laughter went up from the crowd. Lord Belmont tugged at the collar of his doublet.

"When I heard that you were being followed by a barbarian horde, I took . . . precautions," he explained.

Persephone deliberately looked over one shoulder, then over the other. Then she turned back to Lord Belmont and, in a puzzled voice, said, "I see no barbarian horde, my lord. I see the warriors who heeded my call to arms before all others. I see men and women who've suffered much and are willing to suffer more in order to defeat the despicable traitor Mordesius. I see a people who wish me to take the Erok throne as my brother, the king, ever intended. You did well to take precautions, Lord Belmont, but as you can plainly see they were unnecessary, for I assume that your wishes and the wishes of the mighty Panoraki are as one?"

"Of course, Your Majesty—" spluttered Lord Belmont.

"Excellent," said Persephone, so calmly that she was quite sure no one would have guessed how her knees were trembling at the chance she was about to take. "Then I command you to open the gate at once, for I would have you and the good people of Parthania give proper welcome to me and my brave and loyal companions."

For one horrible, heart-stopping moment, Persephone thought that Lord Belmont was going to refuse and that she was going to be turned away from her own imperial capital, her bid to take the throne ended before it had even begun.

Then, bowing as low as his vast girth would allow, Lord Belmont ordered the guards to raise the gate. As it slowly began to rise and the crowd began to cheer in earnest, Persephone turned and, with Cur and Silver trotting at her heels, she strode back toward Fleet, who appeared torn between trying to bite Azriel and trying to jerk free of him.

"I did it, Azriel!" breathed Persephone, beaming up at him. "I talked Lord Belmont into opening the gate!"

"You did indeed," said Azriel, smiling down at her. "I can hardly believe how far your diplomacy skills have come since the days you'd routinely threaten to slit a man bow to stern for refusing to do your bidding."

"If Lord Belmont hadn't responded to diplomacy, that was next on my list," assured Persephone, patting the scabbard at her thigh.

Azriel laughed aloud. Then he slid his hands around her waist, lifted her into the saddle as easily as if she were made of feathers and said, "Lead on, my queen."

Feeling as triumphant as a conqueror, and reveling in the ever-stronger punches and kicks of the baby, who apparently felt the same way, Persephone rode through the great gates of the imperial capital. Just inside, she reined up in surprise at the sight of Anya, one of the three sisters who'd attended upon her when she'd first resided at the palace in the guise of Lady Bothwell. The shy girl was standing half-hidden behind Lord Belmont. When Persephone called a warm greeting to her and bade her come by the next day for a visit, Anya smiled and dipped an awkward curtsey, Lord Belmont gaped in amazement that the girl was not deaf, after all, and the crowd went wild.

Giving Fleet a nudge with her heels, Persephone continued on through the narrow, crowded streets, through the watchtower passageway of the imperial palace and into the main courtyard. There, she was greeted by a veritable army of liveried servants. After giving orders that her troops should be fed and sheltered and her Council members assigned chambers in the palace, she turned to the solemn-faced palace chamberlain and asked if he could kindly arrange to have a fire lit in the hearth of her old chamber.

"There is no need for that, Your Majesty," he said. "For upon being notified of your pending arrival, I had the royal chambers aired, swept and scrubbed. The mattress stuffing has been changed out, the bedding and curtains have been freshly laundered, the rugs and tapestries have been thoroughly beaten. I can assure you that all is fit for a queen."

"I'm sure it is," said Persephone with a troubled smile. "But the last time I was in those rooms, I watched my brother the king die a terrible death, and I think I need a few days to get used to the idea of sleeping in his bed."

Looking intensely uncomfortable that she'd felt the need to explain her wishes to him, the chamberlain bowed stiffly, turned and hurried away. After he'd done so, Persephone and Azriel climbed the gleaming steps that led to the wide-open front doors of the palace.

They'd not taken half a dozen paces into the imposing main entrance hall when Lady Aurelia suddenly appeared at the top of the grand staircase. Her honey-blond curls were piled atop her head and fixed with crystal hairpins that twinkled in the torchlight. She was dressed in black as befitted a recent widow but the nod to mourning ended there, for the sleeves of her gown were gorgeously puffed and the underskirts looked to be cloth-of-gold. The top of the bodice was cut low and tight in an obvious effort to accentuate her small breasts, while the lower part of the bodice hung in generous gathers intended to accommodate and emphasize the swelling belly that Persephone knew from her final conversation with Finn must be nothing but padding.

With a theatrical sigh, Lady Aurelia placed one hand at the small of her back, thrust her fake belly forward and slowly began to descend the stairs. Everyone in the crowded entrance hall looked avidly from Persephone to Lady Aurelia and back again, eager to see what would happen when the dead king's sister and his pregnant widow came face-to-face. The former had a clear claim to the throne; the latter would be mother to an infant with an arguably better one.

Persephone kept her expression carefully neutral as she watched Lady Aurelia reach the bottom of the stairs and sashay over to where she and Azriel were standing.

"Your Majesty," chirped the little noblewoman, dipping Persephone the barest of curtseys while ignoring Azriel completely.

Noting the lack of courtesy, and also that the noblewoman looked paler and more pinch-faced than ever, Persephone nodded with considerably more graciousness than she felt before saying, "I would speak with you privately, Lady Aurelia."

Turning, Persephone strode back out of the palace without a backward glance. It was another risk, for if Lady Aurelia did not follow, Persephone knew she'd have to treat it as an open challenge to her authority as queen. She did follow, however, and the next moment the two of them were facing each other in the relative privacy of the pillared portico.

"We both know that you are not with child," said Persephone without preamble.

Looking startled, flustered and deeply offended in rapid succession, Lady Aurelia gave a delicate cough and said, "I am quite sure I don't know what you are—"

"But you are my brother's widow," continued Persephone, a little louder than before, "and as far as I'm aware, he never bore you any ill will. Moreover, by all accounts your father is serving me well, and in doing so he is proving his loyalty to me and my cause. Whatever game you are playing at, Lady Aurelia—however it got started— let it be ended. Tomorrow morning, instead of padding your belly, announce that you have lost the child you were carrying. Do this, and though I cannot promise we will ever be friends, I can promise that I will honor you as a sister, now and forever."

Lady Aurelia appeared so unsettled by the news that her father was diligently serving Persephone that for a moment, she seemed to hesitate. Then her bright eyes caught sight of the dazzling rings upon her own fingers and the bracelets upon her own wrists, and her expression hardened.

"As I started to say before, Your Majesty, I don't know what you are talking about," she said, placing her hand upon the swell of her false belly. "I carry my beloved husband's child and, in due course, I shall bring forth a lusty prince for the realm."

With that, Lady Aurelia curtseyed carelessly, turned and sashayed back into the palace. Persephone watched her go, deeply troubled by her insistence on persisting with the charade of pregnancy, which she'd almost certainly begun at the behest of her noble father. Promising herself that she'd think more on this later, Persephone strode back into the entrance hall herself. Seeing that the chamberlain had returned and was waiting to take her to her room, she gestured for Azriel to join her in following him.

Azriel shook his head ever so slightly.

"Why not?" asked Persephone in a hushed voice. "What's wrong?"

Azriel smiled as though he found her question inexpressibly endearing. "My dear wife, most of your subjects believe you to be unmarried," he reminded gently. "If you invite a wanted Methusian rogue such as me to share your bedchamber—again—they will think you a complete and utter strumpet."

"Let them think what they will," she whispered, reaching out to surreptitiously brush her fingers against his. "I want you with me, Azriel, tonight and every night."

Azriel said nothing to this, but the sudden heat in his eyes sent a ripple of desire shooting straight through her. Hastily, Persephone stepped away from him. Then, pretending not to notice that the chamberlain was looking at her in much the same way as the Marinese Elder Roark had looked at her after he'd caught her and Azriel making love on the beach, she commanded the chamberlain to proceed.

Within moments, they were entering her old chamber. As she looked around, it suddenly struck Persephone as bizarre that her life should have changed so dramatically since her first encounter with Mordesius, while the chamber in which she'd stayed on that fateful night had hardly changed at all. The wood floor still gleamed in the firelight; the dark paneled walls were still hung with thickly woven tapestries depicting ancient tales of heroism and love. The canopy bed was not yet made up with sheets and quilts, but it was still hung with plum-colored velvet curtains; the long table was not loaded down with platters of food, but it still stood beneath the shuttered windows. Best of all, the great claw-footed tub still stood by the hearth, although sadly, it looked to be bone-dry.

Persephone was about to ask the chamberlain to address that grievous oversight when the door at the back of the chamber opened to reveal Martha, Neeka and little Reeta. They hurried in one after another, lined up against the wall and curtseyed.

"Seeing as how Your Majesty preferred the same chamber as before, I thought you might prefer the same servants," said the chamberlain.

"You did well in anticipating my wishes," said Persephone with a smile.

The chamberlain nodded his acknowledgment of her praise. "And is there anything else I can do for Your Majesty at this time?" he asked, casting a meaningful look at Azriel.

Though it was clear that he was hoping Persephone would ask him to arrange for the removal and whipping of the rogue whose very presence threatened her precious royal reputation, she dismissed the chamberlain with no further command but that she was not to · be disturbed except in case of emergency. As soon as the door closed behind him, Persephone grinned at the three servants who'd served her so well in the past.

"It is so good to see you again!" she cried.

All three curtseyed a second time—Martha primly, Reeta excitedly and Neeka without even a passing glance at Azriel, the sight of whom had heretofore ever set the girl's bosom heaving.

The instant they rose up again, Neeka started to say something but Martha, who'd always been the most proper of Persephone's servants, quieted her with a sharp look.

Then she turned to Persephone and said, "It is good to see you, too, Your Majesty. I have ordered the cooks to send up your supper at once and have arranged for the delivery of fresh linens with which to make up your bed." Martha paused and cleared her throat before delicately asking, "Shall we, uh, also make up a bed on the floor as in times past?"

Persephone glanced at Azriel, who shrugged as if to say that she could reply any way she liked so long as she remembered that he and his broad shoulders would be joining her in the big bed, come what may. Flushing with anticipation, and knowing that Martha and the sisters would figure out at least part of the truth for themselves anyway the first time they helped her dress, Persephone said, "A bed on the floor will not be necessary, Martha, for as it happens, Azriel and I were married some months ago, and I am with child."

"Oh, congratulations, Your Majesty!" shouted Reeta excitedly.

"Thank you, Reeta," laughed Persephone. "But you mustn't shout because we've not yet officially announced our good news."

"Oh, yes, Your Majesty!" whispered the girl, wide-eyed.

Looking pleased and relieved, Martha said, "We'll only make up the bed, then. In the meantime, shall we prepare a bath for you?"

"Most definitely," said Persephone with a sigh of anticipation.

Martha and Reeta immediately dipped curtseys and headed for the back door to start hauling pails of hot water, but Neeka stopped them in their tracks by saying,

"Your bath will have to wait, Your Majesty."

Martha gave a horrified little scream at her lack of decorum.

"I'm sorry," said Neeka unrepentantly. "But there is something she needs to do. Now."

Forty-Three

"THE DAY BEFORE you left on your quest for the healing pool," said Neeka, "Mordesius kidnapped and imprisoned the king's nursemaid."

"What?" gasped Persephone.

Neeka nodded grimly. "Mordesius locked her in the dungeon, and His Majesty could think of no safe way to rescue her," she explained. "When he realized he was dying, he made me swear I'd see her saved. The only thing I could think to do was to get myself assigned to the task of delivering bread to the dungeon, find Moira and hope you'd return before it was too late."

"And it is not too late?" said Persephone hopefully, clutching the other girl's sleeve.

"Not quite," said Neeka. "But almost."

That was all Persephone needed to hear. Throwing off her hunger, thirst and exhaustion, she sent Martha and Reeta running with orders to ready another chamber, prepare a bath, send up food and summon the court physicians. Then she grabbed a torch and quickly led Azriel and Neeka out of the palace and across the back courtyard to the small outer building that housed the dungeon entrance.

"Persephone—" began Azriel.

"I know I can't go down there," she interrupted, thrusting the torch at him. As fiercely as she wanted to be the one to unlock Moira's fetters, she did not need to be told that to descend the slippery winding staircase to the filthy, rat-infested depths would be to foolishly and needlessly risk the life of the baby.

Seeming immensely relieved that he'd not had to fight her on this, Azriel flashed her a smile that was almost as good as a kiss, then followed Neeka down into hell.

Her folded arms pressed against her belly, Persephone paced back and forth before the open dungeon door. Every few seconds, she paused to anxiously peer into the inky darkness, worried that something was going to go terribly wrong. Finally, just as she was about to go down after them, Neeka's voice floated up from the depths.

A moment later Azriel climbed up out of the darkness with Moira cradled in his arms.

At least, Persephone assumed it was Moira. It was difficult to say for certain because the poor creature wrapped in the blanket Neeka had thought to bring bore no resemblance whatsoever to the sturdy, smiling woman of Persephone's memory. This woman was caked in filth, starving and covered in oozing sores; what hair she had left hung in gray rat tails. Her right eye was nothing but a sunken socket and her once-capable hands were curled into claws, the nails badly torn and one finger missing altogether.

Persephone, who'd known that Moira would be in terrible condition but who'd never imagined anything like this, took a stumbling step backward. Almost immediately, however, she forced herself forward and laid her trembling hand on Moira's arm.

"Moira?" she said softly, trying not to shudder at the grotesque thinness of the arm beneath her hand.

With agonizing slowness, the woman who'd mothered Finn since birth turned her head. When she saw Persephone, a single silvery tear fell from her remaining eye.

Blinking back tears of her own, Persephone swallowed past the lump in her throat and hoarsely said, "Let's get you inside."

*

Even though she had plenty of capable servants she could have assigned to the task, Persephone insisted upon personally assisting Martha and Neeka in tending to poor Moira. She'd been too late to properly care for Finn in his hour of need; she'd be damned if she'd miss the chance to do so for the woman he'd loved like a mother.

And so, after distractedly handing her silver crown to Azriel and telling him not to wait up for her, she helped remove Moira's foul rags, ease her into the tub and sponge the filth from her poor, broken body. She washed and combed Moira's hair as best she could; she trimmed her ragged nails. She helped her into a nightgown of softest cotton and saw her laid gently upon the bed. Then, after categorically refusing to allow the court physicians to bleed Moira, she watched like a hawk while they applied salve to and bandaged her many wounds.

It was very late when the physicians finally departed. After asking Martha and Neeka to do the same, Persephone tucked warmed blankets around Moira and fed her spoonfuls of broth by the light of the single candle set on the bedside table. At length she set the broth aside and ate some bread and cheese herself. Then she sat with Moira through the night, holding her hand and gentling her back to sleep whenever her moans and twitches told of the torment of nightmares.

Shortly after dawn the next morning, Martha slipped back into the chamber and quietly offered to take over watching Moira. Reluctant though she was to accept the offer, Persephone knew that a queen with an army to raise, a coronation to arrange and a battle to plan for could not afford the luxury of devoting herself solely to one woman's convalescence, no matter how beloved that woman might be. So, with a whispered command to Martha that she was to notify her if Moira took even the tiniest turn for the worse, Persephone rose, tiptoed across the chamber and slipped out into the hall.

When she got back to her chamber, she found Azriel wide awake and drumming his fingers on the long table that was now loaded down with platters of meat and cheese, baskets of buns and breads, and bowls of jellies, jams, custards, eggs and fruit. The instant he saw her, he jumped up, bounded over and swept her into his arms. As he did so, Neeka and Reeta jumped up and dashed out the back door.

"Where are they going?" asked Persephone, who suddenly felt inexpressibly weary.

"To fetch more hot water for your bath," replied Azriel.

Persephone sagged in his arms. "You . . . you had them prepare a bath for me?" she asked in a tiny voice, wondering why she felt like she might burst into tears.

"I did indeed," replied Azriel, leading her over to the fire and tenderly settling her into one of the armchairs. "I am your Master of the Bath, after all."

"Oh, Azriel," said Persephone as she watched him sink to his knees before her and begin easing off her boots. "You are so, *so* much more than that."

Azriel proved himself to be a Master of the Bath quite without equal.

As soon as the bathwater was warmed and scented to his satisfaction, he dismissed Neeka and Reeta, stripped down to his breeches and then stripped Persephone so slowly and sensually that she half forgot there was a bath waiting for her. Once he had her undressed, he carried her over to the tub and gently lowered her into the hot, fragrant water. Leaving her to soak for a moment, he fetched her a plateful of food and a goblet of watered wine. Setting them down on a nearby table so that she could eat and drink at her leisure, he then set to work—soaping and massaging her tired limbs, washing and oiling her hair, shaping and buffing her nails. He was so remarkably skilled that aside from the fact that he paid an inordinate amount of attention to certain parts of her anatomy, Persephone would almost have believed that he'd been trained in the art of soap and sponge in very truth.

When he was satisfied that no square inch of her body had escaped his attentions, Azriel helped her from the tub and carefully patted her dry with a warmed sheet.

"Shall I tuck you into bed now, wife?" he asked in a seductive voice, draping a second warmed sheet around her shoulders and drawing her close.

Smiling slightly, Persephone shook her head. "No, husband," she said, giving his bare chest a kiss. "Tired as I am, this is my first day in my imperial capital, and I would not waste a minute of it."

Forty-Four

WITH MARTHA AND ANYA occupied elsewhere and Azriel having confessed that his talent for undressing women far exceeded his talent for dressing them, Persephone called for Neeka and Reeta to help her into a suitable gown. After they'd done so, she sought out Lord Belmont. The nobleman seemed enormously pleased to be invited to join her royal Council, and though he was initially thrown by the news that his fellow councilors included clan folk, lowborn bandits, Methusian outlaws and women, he adjusted with remarkable ease.

"So, we are all in agreement that our first order of business must be to send messengers to every corner of the realm with an urgent call to arms for all subjects loyal to the crown?" he asked.

Everyone nodded but Miter.

Sucking air through his crowded teeth, Miter rolled his eyes and sniffed, "Miter has already informed you that no warrior worth his salt will follow a pregnant female into battle."

"I disagree," said Azriel, glaring at the little Gorgishman, who yawned theatrically and looked away.

"I do, too," chorused Rachel and Cairn.

"As do I," said Lord Belmont as he selected a particularly delectable-looking cream-filled pastry from a nearby platter. "Yet it matters not what anyone thinks, for the messengers shall not be informed of the queen's delicate condition."

Frowning, Persephone said, "My lord, I will not lie to my subjects."

"I would not ask you to," replied Lord Belmont diffidently. Pausing to demurely wipe a small dollop of cream from his lips, he said, "With respect, Your Majesty, there are protocols for announcing news as momentous as royal marriages and pregnancies, and I can assure you that your subjects would be most distressed if you did not follow them."

"Very well," said Persephone, ignoring Miter's derisive snort. "But the messengers must inform people that if they arrive within the fortnight, they'll be treated as honored guests at my coronation. They must also let it be known that I shall spare the lives of any New Men who desert Mordesius's army before we meet on the battlefield."

"*What?*" exclaimed Fayla, leaping to her feet.

Knowing that she must be remembering the New Men who'd murdered poor Tiny, Persephone did her best to explain. "Fayla, some of those New Men were forced into service after having terrible things done to them and their families," she said. "I won't slaughter them without at least giving them a chance to make amends. Besides, the more we can do to weaken Mordesius's army, the smaller the army we will need to defeat it."

Not the least mollified by this explanation, the Methusian girl shot Persephone a scathing look before stalking out of the Council chamber. Gritting her teeth against the urge to shout at Fayla to come back and sit down, Persephone turned to find Robert, Barka and Cairn all looking almost as outraged as Fayla had.

"The deserting New Men will not be granted a full pardon," said Persephone, trying not to sound as exasperated as she felt. "Though their lives shall be spared, they'll be stripped of any property or riches they've obtained during their military service. They'll be forced to confess to their crimes in public. They'll be required to make what amends they can to those to whom they've done injury."

"Many will think that is not enough," warned Robert, who clearly counted himself among the many.

"I know," said Persephone shortly. "But whose head would ever truly be safe around a queen who'd remove thousands of heads simply to appease the many?"

"Not mine?" guessed Robert, after a long moment of silence.

"Probably not," agreed Persephone, who imagined there were many in the realm who'd like to see the infamous bandit's head parted from his body.

"Well, in that case, Your Majesty," said Robert grandly, "I wholeheartedly support your decision to allow the deserters to keep their heads."

"Yes," said Persephone. "I thought you might."

After ending the Council meeting and checking on Moira, Persephone spent the rest of the day receiving the legions of Parthanian citizens who were eager to be among the first to pledge themselves to her. Azriel and the other councilors, meanwhile, rode out beyond the palace walls to assess the supply situation and determine all that must be done to protect the city and ready themselves for war.

That evening, a great feast was held in honor of Persephone's return. Since nearly all of the nobility had long since departed the city, and since Persephone did not intend to favor lords and ladies above all others in any event, she commanded that all manner of subjects be invited to the feast. Therefore members of the royal Council, Panoraki warriors, Methusians, merchants, farmers, lowborns and enslaved persons sat together in the Great Hall eating heartily of the marvelous and exotic dishes that had been presented to and praised by Persephone before being sent onward to be shared by all. The atmosphere was undeniably strained as people from different clans and stations struggled to find common ground. However, this struggle was much eased by the continuous flow of good wine—so much so that by the end of the meal when six kitchen servants carried out the giant confection that had been so cunningly wrought by the royal pastry chefs, the bleary-eyed revelers were as one in their roar of approval. Barka, in particular, was delighted by the edible re-creation of Persephone and her army marching through the city gates, though he later ate so many little almond-paste Panoraki warriors that he gave himself a bellyache.

After supper, the music and dancing lasted until late into the night. Finally, when half the people in the hall were slumped face-first in their platters and Persephone could hardly keep her eyes open, Azriel leaned over and whispered, "Is it finally time to tuck you into bed?"

"N-n-not quite," replied Persephone, yawning enormously. "There is one last thing I would do this day."

Persephone stood silent and still at the threshold of the royal chambers.

She was barely aware of Azriel quietly walking around the room lighting candles; instead, she was smiling slightly as she recalled the first time she'd stood at this same threshold. How nervous she'd been to greet Finn as brother for the first time, how she'd curtseyed so low that her legs had given way beneath her. How, instead of taking Finn's hand when he tried to help her up, she'd scrambled to her feet like a farm girl knocked off her milking stool. If she listened closely, she could almost hear the echo of Finn's beautiful laugh . . . and his terrible cough.

Could she really have known her twin for only a few weeks? She could have sworn that they'd shared a lifetime of memories.

As Azriel continued to light candles and the chamber steadily grew brighter, Persephone's gaze fell upon the desk in the corner.

Tiptoeing across the polished floor, she frowned down at the immaculate desktop that should have been strewn with the untidy evidence of Finn's neglected studies. Absently opening one of the drawers, her breath caught at the sight of a worn deck of playing cards and a pathetically small pile of white beans. Reaching into the drawer, Persephone turned over the top card and was somehow not surprised to see a joker. Sliding the drawer closed, she wandered over to the mahogany table at which Finn used to take his meals in private. The golden fruit bowl in the middle of the table was empty and for some reason it made Persephone vaguely uncomfortable to know that the snap of her fingers would see it filled to over-flowing with the rarest, most perfect fruit in the kingdom. Setting this thought aside, she next let her gaze drift to the bearskin rug by the fire. Though it briefly called to mind the memory of the mother bear that had tried to eat her on the Mountains of Pan, the more vivid memory was that of her and Finn eating supper on the floor by the fire as they might have done when they were children. And later, playing cards by moonlight for so long that her charmingly disgruntled twin had been left with but a single white bean to his name.

"Oh, Finn," whispered Persephone, feeling tears well in her eyes.

Azriel came up behind her then but did not touch her. "Are you all right?" he asked quietly.

When she nodded shakily and started toward the bedchamber door, Azriel did not move to follow. Persephone felt as though her heart might burst with her love for him, this husband of hers who understood her well enough to know when she needed him there and not there, all at the same time.

Upon reaching the bedchamber door, Persephone stood with her forehead pressed against the varnished wood for a long moment, recalling the sights and smells and sounds that had greeted her the last time she'd stepped through it. Then, steeling herself, she abruptly turned the knob and flung open the door.

Persephone held her breath as she waited for Finn's spirit to come to her, to envelop her, to wash over her.

But instead of feeling her twin's palpable presence, as she'd half expected, Persephone felt nothing at all.

The chamber was empty save for the beautifully carved canopy bedstead, the recently restuffed mattress, the freshly laundered bed linens and half a dozen tapestries.

Finn was gone.

With a soft sigh, Persephone turned and looked at Azriel, who was watching her from across the room. Wordlessly, he came and held her in his arms for a moment before leading her over to the door of the outer chamber and out into the corridor beyond.

As they approached the end of the corridor, Persephone heard someone running toward them from the connecting corridor. Before she could jump out of the way—indeed, even before Azriel was able to step in front of her—a figure in green rounded the corner and barreled into her with such force that she'd have fallen backward if Azriel had not been there to catch her.

Heart thumping madly, Persephone scrambled to find her footing.

"Forgive me, Your Majesty!" cried the little page boy, his hands thrown up as though to ward off a blow.

"It's . . . it's all right," gasped Persephone, smiling weakly to show that she was not angry.

With a darting glance at Azriel, whose face was like thunder, the boy bowed awkwardly and bolted down the corridor as fast as his skinny legs could carry him.

"I don't know what I was thinking," muttered Azriel savagely, his blue eyes blazing. "I should have had guards assigned to you the moment we walked through those bloody gates. By the gods, if that had been an assassin—"

"But it wasn't an assassin, Azriel," said Persephone, slipping her arms around him. "It was nothing but a boy."

Azriel looked down at her with something akin to fear but all he said was, "Can I tuck you into bed now, wife? *Please?*"

"Yes," she murmured, going up on tiptoes to brush her lips against his. "Now you can tuck me into bed."

The first thing Persephone did after breaking her fast the next morning was to command the chamberlain to move her and Azriel to the royal chambers.

The second thing she did was pen letters to several key noblemen, including Lord Bartok, inviting them to attend her coronation two weeks hence and also to join her royal Council.

"You would invite Bartok even though his daughter refused to attend your feast and insists upon continuing to pretend to be with child?" asked Azriel incredulously.

"Lady Aurelia's behavior is cause for concern and caution," admitted Persephone as she rubbed her belly, which seemed to have doubled in size overnight. "Yet we cannot say for certain that her father supports or even knows about the charade, and I cannot ignore that he's done everything I asked of him and more. I've only been here a day and already armed men are flocking to the city to pledge their allegiance to me. Lord Bartok bought me time to take control of my capital and swell the ranks of my army, Azriel. It is time to find out why he did so."

Forty-Five

"MAKE WAY!" roared the soldier at the front of the small cavalcade of blue and gold caparisoned horses. "I say, make way and be quick about it, you sorry bastards!"

From high upon his own mount a dozen paces behind the roaring soldier, Lord Bartok looked around him, unable to believe the number of lowborns milling about the streets of Parthania, unable to believe the *stench* of them all. And there had been more of them crowded up against the city walls outside the gates, and more still on the road heading into the capital. Of course they'd all come for tomorrow's coronation. Or, more specifically, for the free wine and meat that were rumored to have been promised to one and all.

Lord Bartok pursed his lips. Crowded streets, wasteful promises to nobodies, not to mention cobbling together a ragtag army consisting primarily of the filthy Panoraki . . . it was well that the queen had sent for him at last, for it was clear that she needed the firm hand of a strong man to guide her.

And if the gods were willing, that man would be him.

To be sure, for a time it had seemed as though the gods would not be willing. After receiving the queen's initial letter commanding him to begin harassing the upstart's army, Lord Bartok had heard nothing more from her. And as the days of silence had stretched into weeks, he'd begun to question the wisdom of his decision to make a show of loyalty. He'd started to believe that the queen either did not understand or did not care about the respect due him, that she'd not see the advantage of selecting him to be her consort and that he'd therefore have to find a different path to the throne, after all.

Then, a little more than a week ago, her second letter had arrived.

Even now, Lord Bartok did not like to admit how relieved he'd been when he'd read it. For although the queen had made passing mention of the need to discuss the potentially awkward matter of Aurelia's "pregnancy," she'd also lavished him with praise for his success wreaking havoc upon the New Man army. More importantly, she'd offered him an honored role in the upcoming coronation and invited him to join her royal Council. Smiling slightly, Lord Bartok reached up and patted the ivory king and queen he'd slipped into the pocket of his doublet after reading her words of praise and favor. Nestled together in the darkness, the chess pieces were a constant reminder that if he played the game right, he would bring his family more land, more riches and, above all, more glory than any Bartok man who'd come before him had done.

Feeling a swell of satisfaction at the thought, Lord Bartok spurred his horse to a canter, giving those in the crowded streets before him the choice of getting out of his way or getting trampled. In short order, he was clattering through the watchtower passageway and into the main courtyard of the imperial palace. Sliding out of the saddle, he tossed the reins to a waiting groom without looking at him or waiting to see if he'd catch them.

As he began to stride toward the palace, one of the trusted servants he'd left behind to protect his interests hurried toward him.

"Greetings, my lord," said the man, bowing almost as low as if Lord Bartok were royalty. "When I was informed that your party had been spotted on the road, I had food and drink ordered up to your chambers, a bath prepared and a fresh set of clothes laid out."

"Not now," said Lord Bartok in clipped tones. "I understand the royal Council meets at two o'clock each afternoon?"

"Yes, my lord," mumbled the servant, flushing as though embarrassed for having suggested that after days of hard travel, the first thing his master might have wanted to do was to refresh himself.

Dismissing the servant with a look that said he ought to have known better, Lord Bartok strode across the courtyard and up the palace steps. Though he knew he stank of horse and sweat, Lord Bartok would not have missed this Council meeting for anything. The coronation was tomorrow, after all, and having had no nobleman but Belmont to help her learn her part in the long, intricate ceremony or to help her make the thousands of decisions relating to the procession and the feast that would follow, the queen could very well be at her wits' end.

And if she is, and if she sees that I am willing and able to ease all her concerns, thought Lord Bartok as he hurried down the corridor toward the chamber where the Council was already in session, *surely she will come to see that life as queen would be infinitely easier with a man like me by her*—

The sudden sound of the queen laughing stopped Lord Bartok and his thoughts in their tracks, for it was not the laugh of a young, inexperienced woman on the verge of hysteria, it was the easy laugh of a queen in complete control of herself and everything around her.

Cautiously, and with a distinct sense of foreboding, Lord Bartok walked the last few steps toward the Council chamber and tersely nodded to the liveried guards. Slowly, they hauled open the great doors to reveal a sight so appalling that Lord Bartok would not have believed it if he'd not seen it with his own eyes.

There, sitting at the very same table at which untold generations of his noble forefathers had sat while giving counsel to the greatest kings Glyndoria had ever known, were not just the queen and Lord Belmont, but also two men whose clean shaves and velvet doublets did exactly nothing to hide the fact of their vile birth, a hulking, bushy-bearded Panoraki dressed in ratty furs, several women of questionable origin and a sneering Gorgishman. Worst of all, seated at the queen's right hand was the Methusian who'd masqueraded as her eunuch slave the first time she'd come to the capital, and one look at the way the two of them were smiling at each other told Lord Bartok that his hope of marrying her was as dust in the wind.

"Lord Bartok!" called the queen when she saw him.

"Your Majesty," he said, tasting dust.

The queen did not seem to notice his lack of enthusiasm. "I'm pleased that you were able to make it here in time for the coronation," she said. "Come, join us."

The thought of sitting at any table with so many people so far beneath his station caused Lord Bartok's flesh to crawl, but since he could not think of a way to graciously refuse, he forced himself to walk over to the chair he'd occupied since the death of his noble father. As he flipped his blue and gold cape over his shoulders and sat down, the Gorgishman, who was seated nearby, slowly reached up and pinched his nostrils shut.

With an audible sigh, the queen said, "Lord Bartok, my Council and I were just discussing—"

"Your *Council*?" he spluttered.

At the incredulity in his voice, the Panoraki glowered and folded his meaty arms across his chest, and the ruffian in the chair next to him slammed his fist down on the table so hard that everyone jumped.

"Yes, my Council," said the queen. "I do not want a Council composed of none but noblemen. Honorable men like you and Lord Belmont"—she smiled briefly at the ponderous nobleman, who beamed back at her—"shall certainly have a place at the table, but so, too, will deserving Erok women and lowborn men, as well as representatives of the other clans of Glyndoria who've pledged friendship to me and mine."

"Miter has not pledged friendship!" reminded the Gorgishman shrilly. "Miter has pledged nothing but his eternal enmity if you take this tiresome war of yours anywhere near his beloved valley!"

"Oh, stop," said the Methusian dryly. "You're making me feel all choked up inside."

At these words, everyone chuckled. The outraged Gorgishman looked around as though in search of something to fling at the Methusian, who smiled so seductively in response to the queen's murmured admonishments that she flushed like a harlot.

Lord Bartok could almost hear his long-dead noble father rolling over in his grave. "With respect, Your Majesty," he said carefully, "while I am sure that the sorts of people you describe have many fine qualities, they simply don't have the . . . breeding required to participate in the running of a kingdom."

"I wasn't bred to scrub out pots, yet I always made a fair job of it when set to the task," said the queen, before anyone else could say anything. "Shall we continue the meeting now, Lord Bartok, or do you feel that this Council is not one that you wish to be a part of?"

While everyone else at the table stared at Lord Bartok, he stared at the queen, wondering why Lord Belmont did not seem to see how utterly unfit she was to rule. "Forgive me, Your Majesty, I meant no disrespect by my comments," he lied smoothly. "Of course I wish to be a part of your Council. Indeed, as I have already demonstrated, I am content to serve in any way you see fit."

"Excellent, my lord!" said Lord Belmont, seeming genuinely pleased. "Then perhaps you could remind us of the precise word-ing that is traditionally used when announcing royal marriages and pregnancies, for I fear I have quite forgotten it."

Feeling sick with foreboding, Lord Bartok turned his eyes upon the queen. "Why do you need to be reminded of that?" he asked, his lips so numb they could barely form the words.

"Because Azriel and I are married, and I am with child, and I feel the time has come for all my subjects to know it," she replied.

A charged silence filled the Council chamber.

"Who is Azriel?" asked Lord Bartok softly, even though he was sure he knew the answer.

"I am Azriel," said the Methusian, just as softly.

Ever so slowly, Lord Bartok's eyes swiveled toward the Methusian nobody who'd planted his worthless seed in the queen's belly.

"Congratulations, my prince," he said, favoring him with a smile. "This is a joyful day indeed."

The Council meeting lasted almost an hour after that. During that hour, Lord Bartok's smile never faltered. On the contrary, he made many useful suggestions regarding the announcement of the marriage and pregnancy, he agreed to everything that was asked of him with respect to the coronation the following day, and he expressed pleasure at the news that the dead king's nursemaid was recovering nicely.

And all the while he privately and repeatedly assured himself that neither the Methusian's bitch nor her brat would ever rule the kingdom.

"I can think of nothing further we need to discuss at present," the queen finally said, "so if the rest of you would kindly take your leave, I'd like a word alone with Lord Bartok."

Everyone pushed back their chairs and headed for the chamber doors, even the Methusian husband, who was apparently content to be commanded by his own wife. Lord Bartok folded his elegant hands together, placed them on the table before him and stared at them while he waited to hear what the queen would say.

"I am glad that news of my marriage and pregnancy pleases you, Lord Bartok," she said as soon as the doors closed behind the last so-called Council member. "There were those who thought it would not."

"The news was unexpected but most blessed," said Lord Bartok, a courtier of such skill that he could have convinced a three-legged hog of its beauty and grace. "I will pray the gods bring you a son."

"Thank you," said the queen, her hand straying to her belly. "And how fares your own son?"

"Atticus?" said Lord Bartok. "As far as I know, the boy remains Mordesius's captive. However, I know nothing of the conditions of his captivity."

"I'm sorry to hear it."

"As am I, Your Majesty," said Lord Bartok. "It is a heavy thing to lose a son—heavier still, an only son."

"I can imagine," said the queen, with feeling. "It is one of the reasons I regret having to broach the subject of your daughter's pregnancy with you."

Lord Bartok held up his hand. "It is I who must express regret, Your Majesty," he said quietly. "For if, as you say, Aurelia is not actually with child then she has behaved monstrously—even treasonously—to pretend to all of us that she is."

The queen appeared most surprised by these words. "You did not know the truth about your daughter's pregnancy?" she said, sounding almost hopeful.

Lord Bartok looked at the queen, his mind filled with visions of three-legged hogs. Then he bowed his head and murmured, "It grieves me beyond words to know that you thought for an instant that I did."

"Grieving you was never my intent," assured the queen. "You will order your daughter to abandon her charade?"

"It will be my first order of business upon taking my leave of you," replied Lord Bartok, who cleared his throat before adding in a faltering voice, "And . . . if it is your desire to see Aurelia punished or . . . or even executed for her behavior as a further demonstration of my absolute loyalty to you, I . . . I volunteer to be the one who—"

"No!" blurted the queen, recoiling in horror as he'd expected her to. "No," she repeated, more calmly. "Just . . . get her to stop pretending."

"I will," said Lord Bartok, heaving a shuddering sigh of relief to show the queen how grateful he was that she'd not commanded him to behead his own daughter. "And after the coronation, if it pleases Your Majesty, may I suggest that I take Aurelia away from Parthania? Not only to ensure that she does not attempt to cause more trouble for you, but also to teach her that such behavior will not be tolerated?"

After readily agreeing to this, the queen rose and bid him good day. With a fleeting glance at her belly, the swell of which was obvious to anyone who knew to look for it, Lord Bartok bid her the same, then quickly departed.

As he strode through the palace corridors toward his daughter's chambers, Lord Bartok made eye contact with no one—partly because there was no one worth making eye contact with, and partly because he was thinking so furiously. He'd lied when he told the queen that he had no knowledge of the conditions of Atticus's captivity. Several of the raiding parties had gotten close enough to the upstart to see that Atticus was with him and was apparently being treated as befitted his noble station.

This pleased Lord Bartok because the new plan he'd formulated worked better if Atticus was in one piece.

Striding up to his daughter's chamber door, he rapped his knuckles sharply against it. As he did so, it suddenly occurred to him that the teardrop on the banner the queen had sent him wasn't a symbol of womanish grief for a brother lost, at all. It was the Mark of the Methusians! Of course he'd known the Methusian mark was a teardrop, but it had never occurred to him that this could *possibly* have been the meaning of the teardrop on her banner. She'd bastardized the symbol of the Erok royal family with the mark of a clan, and she'd tricked him, the greatest of the great lords, into riding beneath it!

The thought was so nauseating that Lord Bartok found himself slumping against the doorframe for support, the back of his hand pressed against his mouth to keep from vomiting.

When Aurelia opened the door and found him thus, she let out a small scream.

"Apologies, Father!" she cried breathlessly, her bony hands fluttering about like small birds searching for perches. "I was just startled to find you . . . is everything all right, Father? You look unwell. Oh, Father, what's wrong?"

Pushing past her without replying, Lord Bartok walked directly over to a table upon which there sat a large bowl of fruit, a small bowl of nuts and a half-full carafe of wine. Withdrawing the ivory queen from his doublet pocket, he calmly crushed it with the nutcracker. Then, after sweeping the ivory dust and bits to the floor, he poured himself a goblet of wine and drank it down without taking a breath.

Finally, he turned to his daughter and said, "We will leave Parthania at dawn the day after tomorrow."

"Oh, thank *goodness*!" exclaimed Aurelia, coughing wetly. "You don't know how I've despised being here all alone, Father, especially since *she* has returned. She is insufferable and do you see the kinds of creatures she surrounds herself with? It is absolutely disgusting. What's more, she's been utterly frigid toward me since I refused to give out that I'd suffered a miscarriage."

"Tomorrow morning, you shall give out exactly that," said Lord Bartok.

"What?" cried his daughter in dismay. "But if I do that, people will expect me to stay abed resting, and I will miss the coronation and the feast that will follow! And I thought you had plans to get me an infant that I could pass off as—"

"I have new plans for you, Aurelia," interrupted Lord Bartok. "Plans that require you to put aside the padding of your false pregnancy and to remind yourself that it is ever your duty to obey me without questioning."

Lord Bartok saw the sudden alarm in his daughter's eyes but did not try to comfort her by elaborating. Mostly this was because he felt no need to do so, but partly it was because he knew that telling her of his new plans for her would have offered her no comfort at all.

In fact, they would almost certainly have caused her to scream with such horror that the gods themselves would have shuddered.

Forty-Six

"YOU LOOK beautiful, Your Majesty," breathed little Reeta as she ran the brush through Persephone's glossy dark hair for the final time before stepping back.

It had been Rachel's idea that Persephone leave her hair down for the coronation, having pointed out, in her practical way, that she might have trouble trying to jam the heavy ceremonial crown down on top of an elaborate updo. As she stared at herself in the looking glass, now, Persephone was glad she'd taken Rachel's advice, for her loose locks made her feel more like herself. Indeed, if she ignored the diamond rings that twinkled upon her fingers, the cloth-of-silver gown that shimmered like liquid sunlight and the snowy ermine cloak that so cunningly hid the swell of her belly, she could almost have believed that she was back on the owner's farm preparing to milk the cows.

She could almost have believed it . . . but not quite.

"How are you feeling, Your Majesty?" asked Martha hesitantly, as though she wasn't sure she should be asking.

"Like I'm going to throw up," said Persephone at once.

As Reeta covered her mouth with her hands to stifle a giggle, Martha said, "There is no need to feel nervous, Your Majesty. This is a great day for you *and* the kingdom."

Persephone nodded, nervously listening to the cheers of the crowds that waited for her on the other side of the palace walls. They'd been lining the procession route since the previous evening, and that morning she'd awoken to the sound of them calling her name.

"They love you already," Azriel had murmured drowsily as he'd tucked his arm around her.

Persephone had trembled at his touch and his words. She'd hoped that her subjects would answer her call to arms, and each day for the last fortnight they'd arrived by the hundreds. Yet as she'd lain there in the predawn gloom, feeling the heat of Azriel's body so close to hers, it had suddenly seemed to Persephone a heavy thing to bear, the love of so many people. It was like being mother to thousands who depended upon her as a child does a mother: with the faith that she knew what she was doing, and the unquestioning belief that she'd ever care for them and keep them safe from harm.

But she was not going to keep them safe from harm. She was going to send hundreds—perhaps thousands—to their deaths. The inevitable battle against Mordesius's New Men was fast approaching, for though the noblemen continued to engage them in petty skirmishes, they would not be able to hold them off forever.

The sudden sound of the Panoraki bodyguards gruffly accosting someone outside the chamber door was followed by the sight of the door opening just enough for Rachel to slip inside.

Persephone smiled at the sight of her lookalike friend hurrying across the chamber toward her, for she looked uncommonly beautiful, dressed as she was like a princess and shining with the glow of a girl in love for the first time.

"Azriel says that it is time to go," said Rachel breathlessly. "He also says to tell you that Lady Aurelia will not be attending the coronation. Less than an hour ago, her noble father announced the sad news that late last night she went into labor and gave birth to a dead son."

Even though she was relieved that Lord Bartok had done as promised, and even though she knew that no baby had actually died, Persephone could not help shuddering inwardly at these words.

Even so, she evinced an outward calm as she rose and followed Rachel out of the royal chambers.

Flanked by her bodyguards, she walked sedately and without speaking through the flagstone corridors, down the grand staircases and into the main entrance hall.

There, she paused to take a deep breath, straighten her back and lift her chin.

Then, with a fleeting thought that it all seemed like a dream, she ordered opened the great doors to the courtyard where Azriel and her golden carriage were waiting, and stepped out into the blinding light of day.

Forty-Seven

"AND HOW DID SHE LOOK?" asked Mordesius, his dark eyes glowing. "The queen, I mean."

The kneeling New Man who'd witnessed the coronation a week earlier clutched his cap tighter in his dirty fingers. Of the half-dozen soldiers who'd been dispatched to Parthania more than a fortnight earlier with orders to bring back news of the queen's war effort, he was the only one to have returned to make a report.

Clearly, the others had either deserted or been killed, the useless bastards.

"She looked beautiful, Your Grace," the soldier admitted nervously. "She was dressed beautifully, of course, in an ermine cloak and a cloth-of-silver gown with a train at least twenty feet long, but it was more than this. It was her, Your Grace. She . . . she was radiant beyond description."

Mordesius felt his thin chest tighten at the thought of the queen glowing as though lit from within. "What about her hair?" he demanded—harshly, to avoid betraying himself with even the slightest hint of yearning. "What about her demeanor?"

"She wore her hair loose about her shoulders, and she smiled easily and waved at everyone," reported the soldier, who started to smile at the memory before hastily remembering himself. "You'd have thought this would've made her appear less of a queen, but somehow, her familiarity had just the opposite effect. It made her seem *more* of a queen and I'm afraid the common people loved her for it. Never have I heard such an outpouring of love. Not even for her brother, the dead king. And then after the coronation . . ."

"Yes, yes?" said Mordesius impatiently.

"When she appeared on the Grand Balcony, and the bells began to toll, and the criers in the streets began shouting the news that the newly crowned and anointed queen was married and with child— well, the people went quite mad for joy."

"And how did they react when they learned that her husband was nothing but a Methusian?" sneered Lord Atticus, who was sprawled on a couch nearby with his shirt untucked and his codpiece askew.

"That is the thing that surprised me most of all, my lord," said the soldier. "For upon learning that the Methusian was her husband, the common folk went even *madder* for joy. It seems that the prince consort—that is to say, the loathsome Methusian—has won the love of the people in his own right."

Lord Atticus twittered derisively—a jarring, high-pitched noise that earned him a look of disgust from Mordesius.

"And what, exactly, has the cockroach done to win the love of those worthless nobodies?" asked Mordesius softly, his gaze sliding back to the kneeling New Man before him.

"It s-seems that since arriving in the imperial capital, he has made it his business to spend hours in the streets each day," stammered the man, whose clutching hands had begun to tremble slightly. "H-he is the general of the royal army and as a consequence, much of his time has been spent training his troops, establishing a supply train in preparation for the day the army moves out and ensuring that the city is properly defended. Yet he has somehow managed to become known to one and all as a man hard enough to earn the respect of men, charming enough to earn the admiration of women and beloved enough to earn the love of children and animals, with the exception of certain dogs and horses. And since the royal Council repealed the law naming Methusians outlaws—"

"When did they do that?" barked Mordesius, his stomach in knots at the thought of the cockroach being respected, admired and beloved, even if it was by nobodies.

Startled by the sharpness of the former regent's tone, the soldier jumped. "Two days after they arrived in Parthania," he blurted. "They also ordered the dungeon emptied and the entrance boarded over."

Mordesius slumped in his chair, glaring at the kneeling man as though it was his fault that things just kept getting worse. It had been bad enough when the queen had ruined his plan to marry and get sons upon her . . . and then when his plan to swiftly descend upon the noblemen's army had failed . . . and then when Bartok's soldiers had begun descending upon his like a pestilence. Now the pregnant queen was crowned and anointed, with a handsome husband who was not just accepted by the people but beloved by them? And by all accounts, her army was growing stronger each day, even as his own continued to weaken through desertion and harassment.

If her fortunes continue to rise while mine continue to decline, thought Mordesius, looking down at the hands clenched tight in his withered lap, *it is actually possible that the unthinkable might happen and—*

"Your Grace?" came a familiar voice.

"What?" snarled Mordesius, so loudly that the kneeling man bleated and Lord Atticus swore. Jerking his head up, Mordesius saw General Murdock standing just inside the tent. "What?" he repeated more quietly, but no less irritably.

"Several of my soldiers apprehended Lord Bartok and his daughter half a mile outside camp," he said.

"*What?*" shrieked Lord Atticus, leaping to his feet only to immediately lose his balance and crash back onto the couch.

General Murdock glanced at him briefly before turning his attention back to Mordesius. "Lord Bartok made no attempt to resist capture," he reported. "In fact, my men said that it was he who approached them."

"Has he gone mad?" murmured Mordesius in a wondering voice, his problems temporarily forgotten.

"I don't think so, Your Grace," said General Murdock. "Lord Bartok told the men that he wanted to see you. He said that he had a proposal for you."

"Did he say anything about me?" whined the worm.

"No," said General Murdock shortly before turning his attention back to his master. "Lord Bartok and his daughter are waiting outside, Your Grace," he said, sending the nobleman's worthless son into an absolute frenzy of panic. "What would you have me do?"

Mordesius was so intrigued that he barely hesitated. "Show him in, but stay close, Murdock," he said. "And if the high-and-mighty bastard so much as looks sideways at me, tear his liver out."

General Murdock said nothing, but his beady eyes gleamed.

Forty-Eight

AS COMMANDED, General Murdock showed Lord Bartok and his daughter into Mordesius's tent.

"Father!" cried Lord Atticus, wringing his soft hands and bouncing from foot to foot as though unable to decide whether he ought to run toward his noble father or run shrieking in the opposite direction.

"Atticus," said Lord Bartok curtly, his cool gaze dropping to the lopsided codpiece before shifting to Mordesius.

"Oh, thank the gods you are here, Father! And safe—thank the gods you are safe, of course," babbled the young nobleman as he anxiously and clumsily tried to adjust his codpiece. "I-I know that you probably have many questions about, you know, some of the things I've done over these last months, and I swear that I can explain everything if you'll just—"

Lord Bartok, who'd not taken his pale eyes off Mordesius's dark ones, silenced his son by raising an elegant hand to his face.

Mordesius smiled faintly. "Can I help you, my lord?" he asked.

"Yes," replied Lord Bartok. "And I think I can help you."

Mordesius leaned forward in his chair. "I'm listening," he said.

"The recently anointed queen may be of royal blood, but by her companions, opinions and manners I know her for a gutter rat unfit to wear the crown," began Lord Bartok.

Mordesius was dumbfounded—and infuriated—by this pompous announcement of a truth that he, himself, had known from the outset. Breathing heavily in an effort to control his rage, he said, "And yet you have spent *months* causing me trouble on her behalf!"

"That was before I knew what I now know," said Lord Bartok calmly. "That was before I'd seen what I've now seen."

An almost imperceptible tremble in the great lord's voice made Mordesius believe that he was speaking from the heart—or whatever it was the cold bastard possessed in place of a heart.

"And knowing what I know and having seen what I've seen," continued Lord Bartok, "I would have us work together to defeat her."

"To what end?" asked Mordesius sharply.

"When the unworthy queen is vanquished, you shall become the greatest of the great lords," explained Lord Bartok. "And I shall become king."

Mordesius let out a bark of laughter. "You would propose such a thing even though you well know that becoming king has ever been my goal?"

"You will never be king," said Lord Bartok bluntly. "The capital is crammed with people intent upon joining the queen's army and more flock there every day. I had thought they were there simply for free meat and wine, but it seems I was wrong. Soon, the queen will have an army that numbers in the thousands upon thousands. With none but your New Men to fight on your behalf, you will not be able to take the throne by force against such an army, and forgive me, Your Grace, but I think you do not inspire the love and loyalty that would cause the unwashed masses to clamor to see you wear the crown."

"If the queen's army is as great as you say, you will not be able to take the throne by force either," snapped Mordesius.

"No," agreed Lord Bartok. "But assuming I come out of this war alive, Your Grace, I will still be the greatest of the great lords. At best, you will be nothing."

Mordesius felt as though he'd been slapped; out of the corner of his eye he saw Murdock lick his thin lips. "You are without a guard in the heart of enemy territory," hissed Mordesius. "Assuming that you and yours will come out of this *meeting* alive is a big assumption indeed, my lord."

Lord Bartok said nothing to this, and Mordesius understood at once that it was because he knew the implied threat was a hollow one. Alone, Mordesius faced the very real risk of utter ruination. Only by joining forces with Lord Bartok did he yet have a chance, and Lord Bartok knew it.

Still.

"You've tricked me before, my lord," said Mordesius coldly. "Why should I believe you now?"

Lord Bartok turned to his daughter, who'd not made a sound beyond the occasional stifled cough. "Because as a gesture of good faith, I am willing that you should marry my daughter."

Mordesius could not help gasping at these astonishing words. Looking past Lord Bartok, he stared at the noblewoman whom he'd despised as an insufferable shrew even before she'd treacherously entered into a secret marriage with the dead king. In spite of her noble features and her hair, which was long, thick and the color of honey, Mordesius did not find her attractive in the least. She was tiny, bony and utterly lacking in breasts. Moreover, at present her pale face was pinched with misery.

"She does not look best pleased by the prospect of taking me as a bridegroom," observed Mordesius, who could not keep his thoughts from drifting to the ripe young queen.

"Aurelia understands her duty," said Lord Bartok shortly. "She will be an obedient wife to you, Your Grace."

Though the girl did not lift her head, she did lift her gaze, but only to shoot daggers into the back of her noble father before abruptly dropping it again.

Faintly amused, and curious to test just how badly Lord Bartok wanted this alliance, Mordesius said, "Of course I am flattered by the offer, my lord, but your daughter . . . well, she is used goods."

He shrugged as though embarrassed at having had to bring up this most awkward detail.

"Aurelia is the widow of a king," said Lord Bartok, not appearing the least insulted. "She is the first daughter of the greatest lord in all the land."

"Hmm," said Mordesius, drumming his fingers on the arm of the chair. "Is she fertile?"

"We cannot know for certain, of course," said Lord Bartok. "But her mother was of a similar build and she bore live children."

"And when would this marriage take place?" asked Mordesius.

"Immediately, if you wish," said Lord Bartok.

"Immediately?" spluttered Mordesius, who'd just assumed that Bartok would try to get him to play some kind of waiting game.

"That's right," said Lord Bartok smoothly. "If you've a chaplain nearby, you could be bedding her within the hour."

At these words, Lady Aurelia cried out as though she'd just been burnt with a hot poker. Skittering forward, she grabbed at the sleeve of her father's doublet and sobbed, "Father, please! I am begging you—"

Lord Bartok shook her off without looking at her. Taking a step toward Mordesius, he spread his hands wide and said, "Your Grace, I no longer have any desire to play games with you. The situation is too grave. My past enmity toward you is nothing compared to that which I feel for the new queen. She would make a mockery of . . . everything. At least you and I have always been more or less on the same page when it came to understanding that there are those who matter and those that don't."

"You're right. We have," said Mordesius in surprise. Cocking his heavy head to one side, he said, "So. If I agree to your proposal, what happens next? We join forces and march on the imperial capital?"

Before Lord Bartok could reply, Murdock quietly cleared his throat.

"What?" said Mordesius, flicking his gaze toward him.

"May I make a suggestion?" asked Murdock as he daintily picked at something caught between his long, yellow front teeth.

Irritably, Mordesius gestured for him to get on with it.

"Why don't you take advantage of both the queen's soft heart and her belief that Lord Bartok is loyal to her and your sworn enemy?" said Murdock placidly. "Let Lord Bartok return to Parthania with his fighting men, and also with a message from you stating that you will consider surrendering without a fight if she comes north to meet with you in person."

Mordesius laughed loudly to show Bartok what he thought of his general's foolish idea. "Even if she were to agree to a parlay, Murdock, she would hardly come alone," he said scornfully. "She would bring her entire army!"

"Yes," said Murdock, unperturbed, "which means that if Lord Bartok were able to secure a flank position or, better yet, a rear position, when the queen came to meet you, she would find her army sandwiched between two enemy fighting forces." He sighed softly before adding, "It would be a bloodbath."

Despising Murdock for making him look the fool in front of Bartok, Mordesius made no comment but that he wanted the queen and the cockroach captured alive that he might question and kill them at his leisure.

"Just so long as they end up dead," said Lord Bartok before turning to Murdock and asking, "What explanation shall I give for having received a message from the queen's mortal enemy?"

Murdock gestured toward Lord Atticus. "Tell her that your son was released with orders to deliver the message."

Lord Bartok stroked his silvery beard. "It is an excellent plan," he said at last.

"Yes," agreed Mordesius grudgingly.

"Does this mean I'm free? Does it? It does, doesn't it? Oh, thank the gods!" brayed Lord Atticus, hurrying over to stand at his father's side.

As he did so, his sister tried to grab at their father's sleeve again.

Again, Lord Bartok shook her off. "Goodbye, Aurelia," he said in a voice that was not unkind. Placing his hand on her back, he gave her a gentle shove toward Mordesius and added, "Try to be grateful that I am giving you another opportunity to do your duty to the family."

With that, he nodded at Mordesius, gestured to his son that he should follow, turned and strode out of the tent.

As he watched the two of them go, Mordesius wondered if it had occurred to Lord Bartok that if his became the new royal family, and if he and his son were both to die, his daughter, the girl Mordesius would shortly take as his bride, would be next in line for the throne.

With a smile of satisfaction, Mordesius gave the girl in question a lingering, speculative look. "So," he said with a deliberate lack of enthusiasm. "I suppose I ought to send for the chaplain."

At these words, Lady Aurelia collapsed to the ground at his feet and began to wail so hysterically that she drove herself to a coughing fit.

Not the most enthusiastic bride I've ever seen, thought Mordesius as he extended his foot and nudged one of Aurelia's honey curls with the toe of his shoe. *But at least she knows her place.*

Forty-Nine

THE THREE WEEKS following Lord Bartok and Lady Aurelia's departure from the imperial capital had seen the size of Persephone's army swell beyond her wildest expectations.

As she sat in the royal garden with Moira and Rachel partaking of a hearty noontime meal at the behest of her royal husband, who felt that for a woman nearly seven months along, she'd lately been working too hard and eating too little, Persephone said, "Azriel says my army is now nearly of a size to rival Mordesius's."

"I'm not the least surprised," said Moira quietly, her remaining eye briefly closing as she reverently bit into a piece of thickly buttered bread.

"I'm not the least surprised either," said Rachel. She paused to thank Neeka for refilling her wine goblet before continuing in a worried voice. "Yet I must confess that the height of the piles on the city death carts is beginning to worry me, Your Majesty. Parthania has become crowded beyond belief and the grounds outside the walls are not much better. Attempts to contain the filth, or at least to keep it from contaminating everything, have met with futility, and the rats are breeding like . . . well, like rats. Conditions are ripe for an outbreak of sickness, and I worry not only for the fighting men but also for the many women and children who accompanied them to the city."

Persephone, who did not need to be told that an outbreak of sickness would have catastrophic consequences for the war effort, was about to command Rachel to begin quarantining the sick when she glanced up to see Azriel striding across the manicured lawn toward her with Lord Bartok and—

"Lord Atticus?" she exclaimed, jumping to her feet so fast that she bumped the table with her big belly and nearly knocked over Rachel's wine goblet.

The nobleman who'd once given Persephone a vicious backhand now gave her a glittering courtier's smile before flinging his arms wide and bowing so ostentatiously that his noble father winced before bowing himself.

As Lord Atticus straightened up again, Persephone saw his watery eyes slide toward Neeka's bosom. Resisting the urge to snatch up the wine carafe and put another dent in his head, Persephone tried to sound civil as she said, "I am most surprised to see you, my lord, for it was my understanding that you were being held captive by Mordesius."

"He was," said Azriel. "Until a week past when he was released that he might deliver a message to you."

"What message?" asked Persephone.

Before Lord Atticus could reply, his noble father said, "The traitor Mordesius says that he is willing to discuss terms of surrender if you are willing to meet with him in a fortnight's time."

"Terms of surrender?" said Persephone blankly. "Whose surrender—his or mine?"

Lord Atticus snickered at the question.

"His, Your Majesty," replied Lord Bartok, giving his son a withering stare. "According to Atticus, the former regent has heard so many disturbing reports of the size and strength of your growing army that he has come to believe that he will never be able to defeat you. He names a bridge in the north as a neutral ground for the parlay. He says that if you do not come, he will fight to the last man, and that he will drag as many of your worthless subjects as he can with him to the afterlife."

Persephone considered these words for a long, silent moment. Then she turned to Lord Atticus and said, "What did Mordesius look like when he gave you this message?"

Appearing startled by the question, the soft-featured young lord snuck a darting glance at his father before hesitantly lifting one shoulder, curling his hands into claws and replying, "Kind of bony and hunched over, with very skinny legs and horridly scarred hands that—"

"I meant, what was his *expression*," interrupted Persephone with exaggerated patience.

Lord Atticus's rather blotchy red face got redder still. "He looked upset," he muttered sulkily.

"Upset?"

"Really upset," he clarified, gesturing expansively. "More upset than I'd ever seen him."

"You saw him often?" asked Persephone in surprise.

"I . . . I wouldn't say that I saw him *often*," replied Lord Atticus, with another darting glance at his father. "I would say . . . I would say that I saw him often *enough*."

As she stared at the young lord, who was looking inordinately pleased with himself, Persephone wondered what her next move ought to be. Lord Atticus was a fool, and by his demeanor and responses, she was sure that he was hiding something, but she had no idea what it was.

Before she could think of a way to find out, Azriel picked up a brimming goblet of wine from the table. "I am sure that seeing Mordesius at all must have been terrible for you," he murmured as he held the wine goblet out to Lord Atticus. "And it grieves me that it is so, for the queen and I are much indebted to you."

"You are?" gasped Lord Atticus, breathless after draining his goblet in a single draught.

"Of course," said Azriel. "Not only for attempting to rescue the queen from the black stone castle, but also for risking your life to bring her this message now."

Lord Atticus said nothing to this, only nodded pompously and held out his goblet for a refill.

Unsure of why Azriel was being so solicitous to a man who'd repeatedly threatened to harm her, Persephone decided to play along for the time being.

Turning to Rachel, she said, "What do you think of Mordesius's message?"

"I cannot imagine he would ever surrender, Your Majesty," she replied as she tucked a lock of dark hair behind her prominent ears. "Therefore I fear this is naught but a trap to lure you and the baby into danger."

"I agree," said Azriel.

"So do I," said Lord Bartok swiftly. "That is why I strongly encourage—nay, I beg—Your Majesty not to do this thing."

Wondering at the baffled look Lord Atticus gave his father when he uttered these words, Persephone looked away from them all. Nearby, just beyond a topiary sea god rising up out of an ocean of blue chrysanthemums, Cur was excitedly bounding after an emerald-green frog. The frog darted this way and that before leaping high into the air and diving headfirst into a fishpond. Caught up in the chase, Cur plunged his whole furry face into the pond in pursuit of the frog only to jerk his face back out again half a heartbeat later. Persephone smiled at the sight of him sneezing and snorting and trying to shake off the lily pad that was plastered to one tattered ear, and then smiled again at the sight of his mate Silver bounding over to lick the water from his dripping face.

Cairn had once said that war was always death and that as queen, the question Persephone would ever face was not what she could do to save everyone but who and how many would die by her command that others of her choosing might be saved.

But if Mordesius's message was to be believed—and that was a mighty big if, to be sure—the Fates were offering Persephone a way to save everyone, after all.

And that is why she said, "I agree with you all that it sounds like a trap, but if there is even a chance that I can end this war without shedding blood, I must take it. But I am not foolhardy enough to take it alone, not when Mordesius will be waiting for me with his entire New Man army at his back. Therefore, Azriel, I would ask you to proclaim the news that we march north as soon as may be. And then send word to Mordesius. Tell him I am coming."

Fifty

THREE DAYS LATER, Lord Bartok left the latest Council meeting and went directly to his son's chambers to break the unfortunate news he'd just learned. When his knocks on the outer chamber door went unanswered by Atticus's servants, Lord Bartok frowned and pushed open the door himself. He felt a flicker of concern when he saw that the servants were gone, but only until he heard muffled noises coming from the bedchamber. Narrowing his eyes slightly as he suddenly understood why the servants had all been dismissed, Lord Bartok strode across the room and flung open the door to the bedchamber so hard that the brass knob left a dent in the wall behind it.

The younger of the two trollops in bed with Atticus screamed and snatched up the sheets to cover herself; the older one tumbled off the bed and dove behind the armoire with the speed of one used to ducking for cover mid-ride.

"Get out," said Lord Bartok without looking at either of them.

"What . . . what are you doing here?" spluttered Atticus as he scrambled for his blue velvet breeches.

Lord Bartok did not reply. Indeed, he said not a word until Atticus had pulled on his breeches and the terrified trollops had scampered out of the chamber and slammed the door behind them. Then he told Atticus the news.

"I'm to be in the *vanguard*?" Atticus shrieked.

"Keep—your—voice—down," said Lord Bartok through his teeth. "Yes, you are to be in the vanguard. The royal Council just met and the others were all in agreement that if the parlay fails and it comes down to a fight, my cavalry should lead the charge."

"B-b-but Murdock said you were supposed to get your fighting men assigned to the rear flank," reminded Atticus shrilly as he clutched a half-full goblet of wine to his naked chest.

"I am aware of that, Atticus," said Lord Bartok in clipped tones. "But given that the others were all in agreement, I could not protest without raising suspicions."

"But if I am in the vanguard I could be killed!" cried Atticus, getting back to the important point. "I, your only son!"

Lord Bartok stared at his wastrel son, wondering for the thousandth time why the Fates had cursed him with an heir who would surely drag the family into utter ruin one day. "Death is, of course, always a possibility in the vanguard," he said coolly. "Even so, no able-bodied son of mine is going to hang back like some lily-livered coward while lesser men steal his battle glory."

Atticus's bleary eyes bulged with sudden outrage. "I am not a *coward*," he declared. Slamming the wine goblet down on the bedside table, he propped his hands on his fleshy hips, thrust his face forward and said, "For your information, Father, there are some who think I'd make a far better Lord Bartok than *you*."

Without warning, the current Lord Bartok drove his fist into the side of his son's outstretched head. Atticus, who was already unsteady with drink, reeled sideways with the force of the blow, tripped over his own feet and went sprawling.

Walking over to where his son lay, writhing and moaning like a commoner utterly lacking in self-control, Lord Bartok looked down. "That was your plan, then, was it?" he said softly. "Join forces with the upstart and see me dead that you might inherit all the sooner?"

Atticus's eyes bulged again, this time with terror—and guilt. "No, of course not!" he blubbered as he skittered away from the kick he obviously assumed was coming. "Indeed, it wounds me that you would even think such a thing!"

"You may be my only son now, Atticus," said Lord Bartok. "But when this war is won and I am king, I intend to take another wife. And you may rest assured that unless you give up your whoring, drinking and carousing, stop behaving like a buffoon and finally start doing your duty to this family by obeying me without question in all things, on the very day my new wife gives birth to a healthy boy, you shall be disinherited, disowned and cut off forever."

Fifty-One

EARLY ON THE DAY she and her royal army were at last ready to begin the march north, Persephone shared a final meal with Martha and the sisters. Then she donned her suit of armor and crown of hammered silver, and bid them goodbye.

"Goodbye, Your Majesty! Good luck!" cried Reeta, smiling hard even as tears streamed down her thin cheeks.

"May the gods keep you safe from harm," said Martha in a strained voice.

"And the prince consort, too," added Neeka, with feeling.

Anya, who'd been given leave by Lord Belmont to come say her goodbyes, gestured to Persephone's belly to let her know that the baby was in their thoughts as well.

Unable to speak for the lump in her throat, Persephone smiled determinedly and then headed down the corridor to see Moira, who'd recently begun teaching herself how to knit with nine fingers.

"I shall have a stack of blankets, booties and bonnets ready for the infant prince upon your triumphant return, Your Majesty," she promised as she eased down onto her cushioned seat by the fire— a heaping basket of wool on the floor at her feet and a goblet of hot mulled wine on the table beside her.

"Don't push yourself," warned Persephone as she tenderly tucked a blanket around Moira's legs. "Nothing matters more than your recovery."

"You, your husband and your son returning to us alive and well matters more," said Moira as she adjusted the eye patch that she was still getting used to wearing.

Persephone said nothing to this, only kissed the older woman on the top of her gray head and murmured goodbye. Then, flanked by her Panoraki bodyguards, she hurried down to the palace courtyard to join Azriel, who'd gone down earlier to ensure that all was in readiness for their procession through the city streets. She found him at the entrance to the watchtower passageway, sternly reminding Fleet that as the queen's own mount, he must comport himself at all times with dignity and self-control. Looking this way and that as if to emphasize to Azriel that he was paying him no attention whatsoever, Fleet happened to notice Persephone walking toward him. Neighing shrilly in Azriel's face, "the queen's own mount" broke away from his place of honor at the head of the waiting procession and joyfully clip-clopped toward her.

"You are very naughty to show the poor prince consort such disrespect," chided Persephone as she led Fleet back to where Azriel stood scowling and huffing.

"You know, it might help if you didn't sound quite so loving when you were chastising him," he complained, looking so handsome in his suit of armor that it was endearing beyond measure to hear him sound like an outraged boy.

As Persephone stood marveling at how very, very much she loved Azriel, the baby suddenly kicked harder than he'd ever done before, so hard that Persephone staggered and clutched at her belly.

"What is it?" asked Azriel, his eyes flashing with alarm as he hastily reached out to steady her. "What's wrong?"

"Nothing is wrong," said Persephone breathlessly as she forced herself to stand up straight and tall. "Your son is just a strong baby."

Careless of the throngs that were watching, Azriel reverently laid his hands upon her belly, leaned his forehead against hers and murmured, "And if the Fates are willing, someday he will be a strong king."

"Yes," whispered Persephone, stamping down a sudden flutter of panic at the thought of all that could go wrong between this day and that. "If the Fates are willing."

Without further delay, Azriel lifted Persephone into the saddle, swung up onto his own horse and held his raised hand out toward her. After she'd lightly taken it, she turned and nodded at the six uniformed buglers who were standing nearby. As one, they lifted their horns to their lips and sounded the call to move out.

From the streets beyond the palace walls there erupted a mighty cheer.

Everyone in Parthania that day agreed that the cavalcade was the most magnificent the realm had ever seen. In front of Persephone and Azriel rode the standard bearer; directly behind them rode the mounted members of the royal guard. Behind the guard were two curtained litters—one occupied by Miter and the bag of loot he'd managed to collect during his stay in the imperial palace, the other intended for Persephone when she grew weary of the saddle. Behind the two litters were Lord Atticus, Cairn and Rachel—she without Zdeno, he having been sent on a mission of great import six days earlier. Lord Bartok, his fellow lords and his foot soldiers came after these three, then Robert and his bandits, Barka and his Panoraki warriors, and Fayla and the archers she'd spent the past weeks training. Behind all these were supply wagons beyond counting and several of the many battalions of lowborn men who'd answered Persephone's call to arms, the rest being camped outside the city walls along with Lord Bartok's cavalry.

The mood in the city streets was an odd mixture of tense and celebratory. Most able-bodied men were in the procession, but the women, the young, the old and the infirm were many, and they lined the streets cheering wildly and calling blessings upon the queen and her army. Persephone sat high in the saddle, smiling and waving to show her confidence and courage to those who cheered her and, more importantly, to those who might very well have to do battle for her in the days and weeks to come. When she eventually rode through the great gates and beyond the safety of the city walls, she smiled at Azriel to show him that she was not afraid to walk the path that lay before her.

He smiled back to show her that he'd never thought she was.

Some time later, after the last of the soldiers had marched out of the city, the gates had been shut to protect those left behind, and Fleet had paused to denude a rather scraggly looking sugarberry bush, Persephone turned around in her saddle. Looking beyond the vast sea of armed men and women, she gazed at the towering walls that had never failed to awe her.

And she wondered what price might have to be paid to lay eyes upon them again someday, and who among them might have to pay it.

Fifty-Two

THE ROYAL ARMY had marched halfway to the bridge Mordesius had named as the meeting place when Zdeno caught up with them.

By the time he'd finished making his report, Persephone was white-faced with anger.

"I'm sorry, Your Majesty," faltered Zdeno, dropping his gaze to the dirt floor of the candlelit tent. "I know you were hoping I would discover that he'd lied about everything."

"You have nothing to be sorry for, Zdeno," assured Persephone before abruptly slapping the table and snapping, "But for gods' sakes, of all the bedfellows this war might have saddled me with, why did it have to be *him?*"

"The Fates and their tricks," muttered Azriel in a tone that suggested he didn't think much of the Fates *or* their tricks.

Looking over at him, Persephone said, "Is this as bad as I think it is, Azriel?"

"Worse," he replied.

Persephone nodded—calmly, for Zdeno's sake. "And is it too late to turn the tables?" she asked.

Azriel considered her question for a long moment. "We are four days away from the parlay," he finally replied. "Much can change in four days."

And much can stay the same, thought Persephone.

But all she said was, "Do what you can."

Fifty-Three

LESS THAN AN HOUR before the parlay that would herald the dawn of a new age for the kingdom, a page darted into Lord Bartok's sumptuous tent and cried, "My lord, Her Majesty, the queen, requests your presence!"

"Tell Her Majesty that I shall attend upon her the very instant I finish shaving," said Lord Bartok without looking at the boy.

The page nodded and bolted out of the camp tent. After he'd gone, Lord Bartok continued carefully scraping his cheek with the straight razor. He resumed pondering if it was truly worth waiting to disinherit Atticus until he had a new son in the cradle. Unbelievably, during the march north, instead of making an effort to behave in a manner more suited to his great station as he'd been told he must if he wished to preserve his inheritance, Atticus had done the exact opposite. He'd picked fights and complained incessantly; he'd guzzled wine and openly caroused with camp followers who didn't look fit to clean out his chamber pot, much less warm his bed.

It is just as well that he's been avoiding me like the Great Sickness, thought Lord Bartok grimly as he set down his razor, wiped his face with a cloth and ran a comb through his hair. *Otherwise, I might very well have ordered him sent to keep company with the stable boy—and the dirt and the worms.*

His ablutions complete, Lord Bartok stood, lifted his cape off the camp bed, shook it out and tied it on. Lastly, he felt for the ivory king in the pocket of the padded blue doublet he wore beneath his gleaming silver chest armor. Reassured that it was yet there, he smiled and stepped out of his tent.

It would not be long now.

They'd made camp the previous evening after marching hard for more than a week. Within an hour of setting up camp, the queen had sent a message to Mordesius suggesting that as a show of good faith, they should attend the parlay accompanied by only a handful of armed retainers. At dawn this morning, Mordesius had replied setting midday today as the time of the meeting and agreeing to her suggestion. Given that the secret plan called for the armies to meet, that hers might be sandwiched and destroyed, Lord Bartok had been somewhat dismayed by this turn of events. However, he'd understood that for Mordesius to have done other than agree to the queen's suggestion would have been to raise her suspicions to the point that she might not have met with him at all.

No matter. The upstart's canny general would find a way to bring the armies together. By sunset tonight—tomorrow at the very latest—the unfit queen and her Methusian husband would be dead, her followers would be dead or captured, and he, Lord Bartok, would be king of Glyndoria, the man that a thousand years of history would remember as the one who'd elevated the great Bartok dynasty from noble to royal.

Wishing his cold father were alive that he might see how far these achievements surpassed his own, Lord Bartok deftly stepped over one of the puddles of filth that had already begun to accumulate around the camp. Striding the last few paces toward the royal tent, he gestured to the guards to stand down, pushed aside the flap and stepped inside.

The first thing Lord Bartok noticed after his eyes adjusted to the dimness was that Atticus was standing beside the pregnant queen.

The second thing he noticed was that half a dozen battle-ax-wielding barbarians, including the very big one that old King Octavio had once called friend, had silently moved to encircle him the instant he'd set foot inside the tent.

Sensing danger the likes of which he'd never known, Lord Bartok nevertheless affected not to notice Atticus or the barbarians. Instead, he graciously bowed to the queen. "You requested my presence, Your Majesty?" he said, pleased to hear that he sounded as cool as ever in spite of his uncomfortably galloping heart.

The queen said nothing, only nodded at Atticus.

Soft hands clenched into fists, Atticus stalked toward Lord Bartok, weaving slightly as he did so. "So, you thought to disinherit and disown me, did you, Father?" he sneered, his breath heavy with wine fumes. "Well, you'll never get the chance, because I told them everything! How you sent me after Mordesius so that you could kidnap and ravish the queen yourself . . . how you ordered your own daughter to lie with a commoner in the hope of begetting a child you could pass off as the dead king's . . . how you had the stable boy murdered . . . how Aurelia's false pregnancy was your idea . . . how you sold her to the upstart to seal the deal that would see the queen's army sandwiched between two enemies." He laughed shrilly. "As I said—everything!"

Lord Bartok was too skilled a courtier to let his exploding panic show. Thinking fast, he gave his still-laughing son a look that suggested that he couldn't decide whether to pity or be angry at him (when in truth he wanted to kill him).

Then he turned toward the queen and murmured, "I knew the drink would addle his wits someday, Your Majesty, but I never imagined that he would dream up—"

"I do not think it is a dream at all, my lord," said the queen flatly. "My men reported that the body of the stable boy was found exactly where Lord Atticus had said it would be."

Desperate to gain control of the situation, Lord Bartok bowed his head and said, "It . . . it grieves me beyond words to know that you thought for an instant that—"

"And where is your daughter?" interrupted the queen.

"At my estate north of Wickendale, where you gave me leave to take her," said Lord Bartok quickly.

"No, she is not," said the lowborn councilor with the port-wine stained face. Sounding almost apologetic, he said, "I made thorough search of your estate, my lord, and spoke with many of your servants. She is not there and has not been seen for some weeks."

The last of the color drained from Lord Bartok's noble face. "W-well . . . then . . . she must have r-run away," he said, appalled to hear that he was stammering and stuttering like some godforsaken dungeon rat. Resisting the urge to wipe the beading sweat from his brow, he babbled, "Aurelia has ever been a most willful child. I can assure Your Majesty that—"

"Lord Bartok, for your most heinous crimes, I hereby strip you of all titles, lands and wealth, and order you imprisoned to await further justice," announced the queen. "You will henceforth be known as Ned Bartok—"

"But my name is Edward!" he blurted in horror and anguish.

"*Ned* Bartok," she repeated in a hard voice. "And you shall doff your cap and bend the knee to your betters, starting with the gentlemen who will be escorting you out of my tent."

Lord Bartok heard the words the queen spoke but could not bring himself to believe them until he felt a heavy hand on his shoulder forcing him downward.

As Ned Bartok, the former greatest of the great lords of Glyndoria, was driven to his knees before the barbarians who were now his declared betters, he had a sudden nightmare vision of his descendants scratching out a living in the dirt.

And when he realized that the vision was no nightmare but that it was real and that a thousand years of history would remember him as the man who'd made it so, Ned Bartok fell face-first to the ground so heavily that the ivory king in his doublet pocket snapped clean in half.

And the last thing he heard before he lost consciousness altogether was a voice saying, "The hour of the parlay fast approaches, Your Majesty. It is time to go."

Fifty-Four

"IT IS TIME TO GO, Your Grace."

At the sound of Murdock's voice at the entrance of his tent, Mordesius jerked his head around. "She has arrived?" he asked.

"Not according to the report given by the scout most recently returned from his post overlooking the bridge," said Murdock. "But it is nearing midday, and I would prefer us to arrive at the meeting place first that we might gain advantage by having our men in position when the queen arrives. That way, if she has decided to break faith and bring her entire army instead of just—"

"She will not break faith, Murdock," interrupted Mordesius, turning back to the looking glass into which he'd been staring when his general had arrived. "She is too soft-hearted to risk unnecessary bloodshed, even if the blood that would be shed is worthless. She and the cockroach will suspect trickery, of course, but thanks to the added strength they believe Lord Bartok's knights have brought to their fighting force, they will be confident of being able to defeat me should it come to that."

Murdock hesitated for just a moment. Then, with a fleeting glance at Lady Aurelia's inert form beneath the covers of the camp bed, he bowed his head and departed the tent.

Mordesius smiled broadly at his beautiful reflection. He knew why Murdock had hesitated. It was because when Mordesius had sent the message to the queen informing her that he'd honor her request that they attend the parlay with only a few armed retainers, Murdock had assumed he was lying and that Mordesius yet intended to arrive with the entire New Man army at his back. Indeed, his repulsive henchman had been quite pleased by the turn of events, since it would allow them to eliminate the queen and her party first before marching onward to assist Lord Bartok in slaughtering the now-leaderless royal army.

But Mordesius had not been lying.

Though he could obviously see the merit of Murdock's strategy, he'd not been able to resist the urge to play with the queen one last time. To make a great show of hemming and hawing and pretending that he was considering whatever she was offering; to watch her pretty face fall when she realized that they could not come to terms. To see her brimming with determination as she rode away to prepare for the battle she believed she could not lose; to hear her whole world come crashing down around her ears when she realized that Lord Bartok was a traitor and that every last hope she had for the future was as doomed as her pathetic army of nobodies.

Yes, the woman who'd played Mordesius for a fool so many times before was about to get played herself.

It took less than an hour for Mordesius, Murdock and their party of soldiers to ride to the meeting place. By the time they arrived, the day that had dawned so bright and clear had clouded over, and a chill wind had kicked up. Digging his spurs into the flanks of the wretched horse that had so jarred him during the ride, Mordesius galloped to the top of a small rise that he might look down on the meeting spot. As he did so, he could not help noting that Murdock had chosen the place well. The wooden bridge that spanned the river was easily defendable from both sides, and the river, though quite shallow, was broad enough to give both parties a sense of security.

That being said, the slightly elevated bank on his side of the river would allow them the advantage of looking down on the queen, and the mostly open field on the queen's side of the river would prevent her from making a stealth approach.

Mordesius did not bother praising his general for a job well done. Instead, he drove his beast down to the water's edge and sat staring across the river with an expression that evidently did not encourage any in his party to approach him because none did until a quarter of an hour past midday, when Murdock finally drew his horse alongside and murmured, "I fear the queen is not coming, Your Grace."

"Your fears are misplaced," snapped Mordesius, who'd begun to fear the same thing.

Even as he spoke the words, however, he spied movement in the copse of trees beyond the field on the far side of the river. The next instant, mounted archers began bursting into the clearing at a full gallop. Upon emerging from the trees, the first turned sharply right, the second left, the third right and so on until they were lined up facing the river, the exact same distance between each horse except for the two in the very middle. For several seconds no one moved and Mordesius could hear nothing but the rising wind whistling through the trees. Then a fierce female voice called out a command. As one, each archer drew an arrow from his or her quiver, nocked it into the bow, drew back and aimed it skyward in Mordesius's direction.

As the archers froze once more, two beautiful caparisoned horses walked through the wider space between the two middle horses.

That's when Mordesius saw her.

His breath caught at the sight of her riding toward him looking like something out of a fairy tale in her simple silver crown and suit of armor. Her glossy dark hair bounced gently with each step the horse took, and there was a look of unmistakable determination on that face that had haunted his dreams since that first night he'd discovered her standing ankle-deep in alley muck all those months ago.

For a fleeting moment, Mordesius wondered if he loved her.

Then she reined up at the water's edge, and he noticed the gross swell of her pregnant belly and the broad shoulders of the cockroach who'd planted the seed.

And Mordesius's insides turned to ice, and all he wondered was why he hadn't allowed his soldier to run a sword through her belly back in the alley when he'd had the chance.

And he vowed to rectify that error as soon as may be.

Fifty-Five

PERSEPHONE STARED ACROSS the river at Mordesius. She recalled their first meeting—he, sitting high upon his black horse staring down at her with his fathomless dark eyes; she, curtseying low on trembling legs, desperately hoping that her lies and her beauty would be enough to save Azriel, Rachel and Cur from discovery and death.

Even from across the river, Persephone could feel that Mordesius lusted for her now as he had back then. Unlike back then, however, now he also hated her with such a passion that it rolled off him in waves.

In the sky overhead, dark clouds roiled, and Ivan circled and screamed. Lightning flashed without thunder sounding. In her heavy belly, the baby shifted restlessly.

Persephone shivered and resisted the urge to look at Azriel.

"You wish to discuss terms of surrender?" she called to Mordesius as the wind whipped her hair.

"I am willing to explore the possibility," he replied, sounding almost coy.

Persephone gritted her teeth. "Very well," she shouted. "Here are my terms: surrender at once and I am willing that you should not immediately be beheaded but shall be granted a fair trial."

Mordesius made a great show of pondering her offer—furrowing his brow, rubbing his chin, conferring with General Murdock. After a few moments, however, he shook his head, as Persephone had known he would.

"I'm afraid I will need better terms than that, Your Majesty," he called.

In spite of his regretful tone, Persephone knew that he was enjoying himself. She also knew that Mordesius would be content to toy with her for a while yet, and that the longer they stood there, the more nervous Azriel was becoming.

So, eager to snuff out Mordesius's enjoyment and be away before Azriel had apoplexy or Fayla gave in to the urge to turn the New Men across the river into bloody pincushions, Persephone cupped one hand around her mouth and called, "I thought you might be interested to learn that Lord Bartok has been arrested."

Mordesius stiffened so abruptly that he could not entirely suppress his grunt of pain.

"His son, Lord Atticus, told us of your plans to sandwich my army between your New Man army and the sworn swords loyal to Lord Bartok—pardon me, *Ned* Bartok," continued Persephone.

Mordesius let out a bark of laughter, presumably at the news that the greatest of the great lords had been reduced to a commoner.

Then his smile vanished.

Sneering, he shouted, "Let me guess: Bartok's soldiers and the other noblemen are now under the command of that insufferable drunken worm he fathered."

"No, they are now under my husband's command and entirely content to be so," replied Persephone as the first fat droplet of rain pinged off her arm guard. "I confess that Lord Atticus was not best pleased when he realized that by stripping his father of his title, land and wealth, I'd also stripped him of his inheritance, but he cheered up remarkably when I told him that he'd be granted a suitable allowance and also be allowed to keep his head."

Mordesius was breathing so hard now that Persephone could see his thin chest heaving.

Lightning flashed again. This time it was followed by a crack of thunder so loud it seemed to shake the earth.

"I'm sure I do not need to tell you that without a second fighting force, you cannot make a sandwich," Persephone shouted over the rising wind. "If we meet on the battlefield now, your army's defeat is a virtual certainty, as is your death. And if there has ever been a man who deserves death for his crimes, it is you, Mordesius. Nay, you deserve a thousand deaths, each more hideous than the last." She paused and pressed her hand against her belly before speaking the words she'd not discussed with her Council, or even with Azriel. "Nevertheless, if you surrender now, I will better my previous offer. Upon my word of honor, even if you are found guilty at your trial, you shall not be beheaded. Though you will be imprisoned for the rest of your days, you will be allowed to keep your head."

Behind her, Fayla hissed angrily.

Beside her, Azriel stiffened and whispered, "What are you doing?"

Persephone didn't look at him because she knew his eyes would be blazing with anger, and she didn't answer him because she knew that he knew exactly what she was doing. She was looking for a way to save everyone, that she might avoid having to answer the question of who and how many would die by her command.

But apparently, Cairn had been right when she'd said that war was always death. Because instead of accepting Persephone's offer, Mordesius threw back his head and laughed like a madman.

Then he leaned forward in his saddle and shrieked, "I would rather die those thousand deaths you mentioned than ever give myself up to a gutter-reared lying whore like you, Your Majesty! I will see you on the battlefield forthwith, and I hope you enjoy the sight and smell of lowborn blood, my queen, because you may depend upon my New Men to spill an ocean of it before they are finally defeated!"

With another insane laugh, Mordesius yanked his horse around and, driving his spurs into the poor creature's flanks, began galloping up the hill. Through the rain that was growing heavier with each passing second, Persephone watched General Murdock and the other soldiers ride after him.

When Mordesius reached the top of the hill, he turned and called to Persephone one last time.

"Did you truly find the healing Pool of Genezing?" his voice drifted to her over the sound of the wind and the thunder and the lashing rain.

Persephone hesitated, the temptation to torment him so powerful that she could almost taste it. But that was not the kind of queen she wanted to be, and not the kind of woman she was.

And so she replied with a simple no.

Mordesius nodded as though he'd ever guessed it was so.

Then he turned, jabbed his spurs into his horse's flanks again and disappeared down the other side of the hill.

Persephone was so staggered by the enormity of what had just happened and what the consequences would be, that for a very long moment, she sat still as a statue, staring straight ahead through the downpour that had grown so heavy that she could no longer see the other side of the river. Then, abruptly realizing that there was not a moment to lose getting back to camp to prepare the troops for battle, she wheeled Fleet around and was about to urge him into a gallop when Fayla said,

"Wait."

Persephone felt a flare of irritation toward the Methusian girl who'd barely been civil toward her since she'd announced her intention to pardon deserting New Men. In no mood to suffer further recriminations now, she jerked her head around and snapped, "What?"

Pushing her dripping hair back from her face, Fayla said, "I'd never have offered to let him keep his head."

"Yes, well, you don't have a kingdom of subjects to protect."

"Which is a very good thing, I think," said Fayla slowly. "All my life, all I've ever wanted was revenge against those who've harmed me and mine. If we'd done it my way, it would have been a bloody battle to the last New Man."

"It is still going to be a bloody battle to the last New Man," pointed out Persephone stiffly.

"Perhaps," agreed Fayla. "But at least you tried to spare our side the horror. One life to spare thousands would have been a good trade, I think, even if it was his life." She paused to flash Persephone a rare smile before adding, "Tiny always said you were going to be a great queen."

"He did?"

"He did," said Fayla.

The Methusian girl's words renewed Persephone in the most extraordinary way. During the long, rainy ride back to camp, she led the others in an animated discussion of battle strategy and even spoke a little of the things she'd like to accomplish after the battle was won.

As she, Azriel, Fayla and the archers rounded the rocky outcrop that edged the vast field in which the royal army was camped, however, they beheld a sight that wiped all other thoughts from their minds.

It was Rachel. She was running toward them with a look of unadulterated panic on her face. She appeared to be shouting something, but Persephone couldn't make out what it was.

Without thinking, she smacked the reins against Fleet's neck. As Fleet coiled to lunge forward, Azriel grabbed his bridle.

Persephone rounded on Azriel. "What are you doing?" she demanded.

Azriel didn't even look at her. "Wait," he ordered tensely.

"I won't wait!" exclaimed Persephone as she watched Rachel slip, fall, jump up and continue to run toward them, this time waving her arms in front of her. "Something is wrong, Azriel. Rachel needs us! Let go of Fleet's bridle this instant, or I swear I'll—"

"*For gods' sakes, Your Majesty, get away from here, now!*" sobbed Rachel as she slipped in the mud and fell again. "*There's been an outbreak of the Great Sickness! And it is the worst I've ever seen!*"

Fifty-Six

IT TOOK THE GREAT SICKNESS less than ten days to decimate the army Persephone and Azriel had spent months building. According to the hastily scrawled reports delivered by Methusian carrier pigeon, it was not only the worst outbreak that Rachel had ever seen, it was the worst outbreak that anyone had ever seen. Lord Atticus was one of the first to die; Big Ben followed a day later. Cairn and the other Methusians saved as many as they could with their potions, but it was scarcely a drop in the bucket. Men healthy at supper were dead by morning, along with every man who'd shared a fire with them. Within days, there were so many dead that it was impossible to honor them all with proper funerals or even to record their names that their loved ones might know what had become of them. Some bodies were burnt but most were thrown into giant pits dug by men still healthy enough to hold a shovel.

Many of these ended up digging their own graves.

At Rachel's harrowing warning, Persephone, Azriel, Fayla and the archers had hastened back to the copse of trees by the river. As they'd trotted along, the lightning had flashed and the thunder had crashed, and Persephone had been unable to think of anything but her hubris in telling Mordesius that the defeat of his army was a virtual certainty. In pushing him to accept that he could not win, she had convinced him that he had nothing left to lose.

Even now, he and his soldiers could be crossing the river, she'd despaired as she'd bent her head against the driving rain and clung to the dripping pommel. *Even now, they could be coming for us.*

These dark thoughts had consumed Persephone right up until she'd reached the copse of trees and discovered that a miracle had occurred. Namely, the river that had been broad but shallow barely an hour earlier had become so swollen from rains that it was now deep and so fast-moving that any man trying to cross it would've been swept to his death.

Using the back of her hand to impatiently wipe away what might have been tears, Persephone had silently reminded herself that while there was breath, there was always hope. Then she'd said this same thing aloud for the sake of the others, and then she'd made them say it, that the words might imprint on their hearts and souls. Finally, she'd commanded Fayla to split the archers into three watches and to shoot down any New Man who tried to cross the bridge.

Only then had Persephone complied with Azriel's request that she sit and rest awhile to ensure that she did not drive herself into early labor, for though her pregnancy was far enough along that the baby stood a good chance of surviving, she was quite unable to imagine anything worse than giving birth beneath a thundering sky in the pouring rain.

None of Mordesius's New Men had tried to cross the bridge on that first day, nor on the second. On the third day, however, several dozen of them had suddenly appeared on the crest of the hill on the other side of the river. Sounding a hoarse battle cry, they'd charged down the hill and rushed the bridge. Fayla and her archers had dispatched them in a single hail of arrows. Every day thereafter it had been the same thing, and if these attacks had kept Persephone and the others on tenterhooks, they'd also given them the comfort of knowing that by keeping Mordesius's army at bay, they were giving those of their comrades who'd not succumbed to sickness a chance to survive.

For nine long days they huddled in the rain without shelter or a fire, eating raw meat and trying to keep their bodies warm, their spirits up and their hope alive. Every few days, a carrier pigeon would arrive with news so grim that it kept Persephone firmly tethered to reality. During the long, cold nights, however, she could not help dreaming about how different things would have been if only she and Azriel had found the mythical healing pool. Finn would be alive, for one thing; for another, legions of her loyal subjects would not be dying hideous deaths while she stood helplessly by.

"D-do you really think it is out there somewhere?" she asked Azriel on the ninth night as she lay shivering in his arms. "Do you think Balthazar really did find it or was he just telling stories?"

"I don't know," replied Azriel. "Maybe he did find it, but it dried up again."

"Again?" asked Persephone through teeth clenched to keep from chattering.

"According to legend, the first pool dried up after a Methusian spilled the blood of a trusted companion at the water's edge," reminded Azriel, hugging her tighter.

"What a fool," murmured Persephone, closing her eyes.

Sometime that night, the rain finally stopped. The next day dawned with sunshine, birdsong and the sound of something crashing through the trees toward them.

"Hold your fire, Fayla!" bellowed Robert. "It's only me!"

"The sickness?" asked Azriel in alarm.

"Abating," reported Robert. "The danger is past."

"Thank the *gods*." Persephone heaved a sigh as the erstwhile bandit leader reined up in front of her.

"Don't thank them just yet, Your Majesty," said Robert grimly. "One of my scouts spotted the New Man army less than a day's march north—on this side of the river."

At these words, Persephone's belly tightened so painfully that she had to bite her lip to keep from gasping aloud.

"There must be some mistake," said Fayla flatly. "My archers have seen to it that not a single one of those black-clad bastards have made it across the bridge."

"I'm sure they have," said Robert. "But while you've been occupied taking care of the decoy, it appears that the main body of the army marched north in search of another place to cross. And by the looks of it, they found one."

Without giving herself time to ponder this new and terrible threat, Persephone brusquely called for the horses to be saddled at once. She was about to hurry over to assist with the ordeal of saddling Fleet when Azriel reached out and grabbed her hand. Turning, she saw the stricken look in his eyes and knew what he was about to say.

"Don't," she said more fiercely than she'd intended. Stepping away from him, she wrapped her arms around her belly. "Don't tell me to flee while I still can, Azriel. Don't remind me that I promised to have a care what risks I would take. Don't say that the baby and I are the only family you've got, and that you could not bear to lose either of us. We could not bear to lose you either, but I cannot run away. I cannot abandon the thousands who rallied when I called, who showed me faith and loyalty and love before I'd done a single thing to earn it. Whatever the consequences, Azriel, I cannot."

For an instant, the pain on Azriel's face was a living thing. Then he flashed Persephone one of his heartbreaking lopsided smiles and said, "Have I ever told you that you can be most infernally persistent when you want to be, wife?"

"Many times," she replied, trying hard for a smile of her own.

Fifty-Seven

IT WASN'T LONG BEFORE Persephone, Azriel and the others were riding into camp.

The place was swimming with muck, and the smell of death hung so heavy in the air that it took all of Persephone's considerable willpower not to start retching. Rachel greeted them with a dirty face and a wan smile. As soon as she'd been lifted down from the saddle, Persephone hugged her friend so tight that she could hear the THUD THUD THUD of their two hearts beating in perfect unison. She was intensely grateful for the courage Rachel had shown in spite of her terror of sickness, and fiercely glad that both she and Zdeno had survived.

Within moments of their reunion, the other royal councilors had been rounded up to discuss options.

"We have no options," said Azriel bluntly as he unrolled a map of the realm and laid it on the table in the meeting tent. "The only thing we can do is to retreat."

"Retreat to where?" asked Cairn, examining the map. "Even if we were to leave the sick and the weak behind—"

"Which we won't," interjected Persephone as she gave her painfully tight belly a soothing rub.

"We'll never be able to outpace Mordesius for long enough to make it back to the protection of the imperial capital," finished Cairn.

Miter clapped vigorously at Cairn's assessment of the situation, earning himself eye rolls from those who'd been in camp during the outbreak and baffled looks from those who hadn't.

"Well," said Robert, "we can't retreat into the Great Forest for the same reason—it's too far away."

"As are the mountains," said Barka, eyeing the map. "And even if they weren't, the march north would take us straight into the arms of the New Man army. And even if it wouldn't, the appetite of the mother goddess is a fearsome thing, indeed."

Rachel shivered and clutched Zdeno's hand.

"Miter sees that you are all on the brink of annihilation," declared the little Gorgishman, sneaking a glance at Cairn to make sure she was watching him. "He knows you fear that he will do nothing but laugh if you beg him to come to your rescue, but he has had a change of heart. He has decided to save you after all."

"Oh?" said Azriel, looking over at him. "And how, exactly, does he plan to do that?"

"He plans to lead you into the Valley of Gorg," replied Miter.

At these words, Azriel's gaze dropped back down to the map and Persephone could tell by the sudden fire in his eyes that this was the answer they'd been looking for.

Ignoring the exclamations of surprise and disbelief of the other councilors, Persephone placed her clasped hands on the table before her and said, "That is a very generous offer, Miter, but I thought you told us to stay away from the valley unless we longed for hideous deaths. I thought you pledged your eternal enmity if we took our war anywhere near your beloved valley."

"Yes, well, things change," replied Miter with a gooey smile at Cairn.

Persephone looked at Rachel in utter bafflement.

"Cairn personally attended him when he fell ill last week," explained Rachel in confidential tones. "He'd have died if it wasn't for her."

At these words, Miter fluttered his lash-less eyelids at Cairn and pressed his hand to his heart. She responded to these displays of devotion with a faint but remarkably tolerant smile.

"Of course," continued Miter, his gaze sliding back to fix on Persephone, "in return for his unprecedented act of generosity"—here, the Gorgishman paused for dramatic effect—"Miter expects that the pregnant female will return the Mines of Torodania to his people."

"Done," said Persephone, who'd ever intended to return the horrid mines to their rightful lords. "The very instant those enslaved within have been released, the mines are all yours."

Instead of looking grateful or even pleased, Miter looked outraged, as though Persephone had somehow cheated him by agreeing to his terms so readily.

Before he could even think about trying to drive a harder bargain, however, Azriel jabbed his finger at the map and said, "The canyon that leads into the valley is barely half a day's march away. We should be able to reach it ahead of Mordesius's army if we hurry, and as it is only wide enough for a dozen horsemen to ride abreast through it, we ought to be able to defend our position there, at least for a while. What say you, Your Majesty?"

Instead of answering him, Persephone looked at the map for a long moment before looking away. She knew she ought to be grateful for this chance, for this *hope*. But all at once, she was tired of being satisfied with hope. She didn't want to avoid defeat for a while.

She wanted victory—for her kingdom, for Finn, for her baby and for herself.

As she stared at the ground beside the table, feeling the desire for victory swell inside of her, Persephone absently watched several dozen ants chase a fat beetle between two discarded sweetmeats.

"Persephone?" murmured Azriel.

Unable to tear her gaze away from the battle unfolding in the dirt beside her, Persephone held up her hand to silence him. And when the battle was finally won, she turned to him with shining eyes and said, "I have an idea."

All agreed that the plan was clever and daring; some even believed that it had a chance of succeeding. Within the hour, those too sick or weak to fight had been given horses, assigned a small guard and been sent galloping to Parthania. After their departure, the rest of the royal army had set off for the valley with all the weapons and the few remaining horses. Though they arrived at the canyon that led into the Valley of Gorg without incident, according to the scout's breathless report, the New Man army was mere hours behind them.

Come what may, tomorrow the two armies would face each other at last.

After commanding Robert and his men to take up their positions and issuing a final warning to them to judge their moment well, Azriel followed Persephone and the others through the canyon and into the field of flowers and butterflies.

Much later that night, after the sun had set and the troops, horses and dogs had been fed, settled and calmed, Persephone and Azriel settled down in front of their own little campfire. It wasn't until then, as Persephone sat leaning against Azriel's warm chest and feeling the strength of his arms around her, that he quietly told her of the role he intended to play in the coming battle.

"You . . . you intend to be in the vanguard?" she exclaimed in horror, twisting in his arms so that she could look up to him.

"No, Persephone," said Azriel gently. "I intend to lead the vanguard."

Fifty-Eight

ON THE OTHER SIDE of the canyon, Mordesius stood outside his camp tent staring at the flickering light of the campfires that dotted the field of flowers and butterflies. He knew that sitting by one of those fires was the woman who'd stolen everything from him—her ripe young body, his chance to be king, his dream of someday seeing his terrible injures healed.

Well, upon the morrow, he would steal back at least two of those things.

And then, at his leisure, he'd destroy one of them, piece by bloody piece.

At the sound of the noble bag of bones he called a wife moaning and coughing wetly from inside his tent, Mordesius scowled darkly. He was already exhausted and aching from the grueling march. The last thing he needed right now was to have to listen to—

"Your Grace?" came Murdock's voice from so nearby that Mordesius started, causing a fresh wave of pain to course through his body.

Casting a malevolent glance at his ever-creeping general, Mordesius muttered, "What?"

"I've given thought to the challenge posed by the narrow canyon," said Murdock. "And I respectfully suggest that when the sun is at its zenith, we send the foot soldiers through the canyon a hundred at a time. The first waves will be slaughtered by the enemy soldiers on the far side, of course, but as the bodies pile up, it will give those who come behind an advantage, for they will be able to climb onto the pile of their dead comrades and fight from a position of strength. And since the queen's army lacks the discipline of our own troops, when they see that we will never stop coming for them and that they are doomed, they will throw down their pitchforks and beg for mercy."

"And will we give it to them, Murdock?" breathed Mordesius, turning his attention back to the firelight on the far side of the canyon.

"No, Your Grace," said Murdock placidly. "We will not."

Murdock woke the men at the crack of dawn the next morning so that he could give them their orders and remind them to behave like the trained professionals they were when the order to attack finally came.

Curious to see how those in the first waves were going to react when they realized that their job was to die, Mordesius had just pushed aside the flap of his tent when a hoarse battle cry sounded on the far side of the canyon. As it echoed through the valley, there came the sound of horses thundering through the canyon toward them.

And just like that, the battle for control of the kingdom had begun.

Telling himself that he was more startled than afraid, Mordesius hurriedly lurched over to the relative safety of his mount. As he laboriously hauled himself up onto the miserable creature's back, he heard Murdock calmly calling for the men to take up arms and fall into formation. Licking his lips, Mordesius yanked his horse around so that he could watch the methodical annihilation of the fatally reckless enemy horsemen.

Then he saw who was leading the charge and he almost stopped breathing. It was the cockroach—the despicable wretch who'd lied to him about having clues that would lead him to the healing pool.

The one who'd ever flaunted his broad shoulders and long, lean legs; the one who'd made himself beloved by the people even though he was nothing but a Methusian.

The one who'd planted his vile seed in the belly of the only woman who'd ever treated Mordesius as a man like any other!

Mordesius felt a surge of hatred the likes of which he'd never known. Even as he did, he saw the cockroach take in the sight of the vast New Man army. Like the coward he was, he faltered and reined in his horse, forcing the men behind him to do the same.

There was a long moment of silence in which nobody moved.

Then, in a voice thick with fear, the cockroach wheeled his horse around and bellowed, *"Retreat!"*

Heart hammering with sudden, uncontrollable excitement, Mordesius stood up in his stirrups and shouted, "After him!"

As one, the New Men uncertainly looked over their shoulders at him.

"Your Grace—" began Murdock in alarm.

"AFTER HIM, YOU BASTARDS!" screamed Mordesius, frantically waving the New Men toward the canyon. "CHARGE!"

Fifty-Nine

"THEY'RE ON THEIR WAY BACK, Your Majesty!" shouted Rachel, looking almost as terrified as Persephone felt. With the hand that wasn't clasped tightly in Persephone's, she pointed toward the canyon. "And by the looks of it, they have the entire New Man army at their heels!"

Looking past the Panoraki bodyguards who'd been ordered not to leave her side under any circumstances, Persephone went cold when she saw that Rachel was right. And though it was precisely what Azriel had hoped would happen, it was harrowing to see him at the rear of the retreat, just a step ahead of hundreds of sword-wielding, screaming New Men.

Persephone held her breath as he, Zdeno and the other horse-men who'd been used as bait burst out of the canyon and ducked. The instant they'd done so, Fayla and her waiting archers loosed their arrows. The New Men at the front of the attack were hit to a man. As they staggered backward, Fayla and her archers readied their bows for a second volley, and the Panoraki and the rest of the fighting force swarmed the mouth of the canyon. Those in the front stabbed, chopped, bashed and kicked bodies aside; those behind cleared the bodies and cut down the few who managed to escape. Persephone could see panic on the faces of the nearest New Men as they were packed tighter and tighter together by their unwitting comrades at the other end of the canyon who continued to rush forward, unaware that there was no escape.

Distant shouts of surprise and alarm from the heart of the New Man camp informed Persephone that Robert and his men had begun dropping out of the trees in which they'd been crouched all night. Though she was unable to see them, she could easily picture them rushing forward to close off the far side of the canyon so that the New Men could not retreat.

Sandwiched between two fighting forces, they were doomed.

Persephone felt no remorse whatsoever. She'd made it known throughout the kingdom that she'd spare any New Man who deserted before the final battle. Any who'd chosen not to do so were her enemy and the enemy of her realm, and for that they deserved to die.

It wasn't long before the carrion birds began to gather overhead. As the intensity of the battle gradually began to abate, the Panoraki Ghengor grinned over his shoulder at her and said, "Easier than shooting fish in a barrel, eh, Your Majesty?"

Cur, who had been sitting at Persephone's side since the beginning of the melee, snarled wetly at Ghengor's words. Persephone said nothing. The gods had cursed her once before for her hubris—she'd not tempt them to do so again by giving voice to her rising confidence that victory was within her grasp and that those she loved best in the world would all survive to enjoy it.

Unfortunately for Persephone, the gods must have been able to hear her thoughts as easily as her words, because the New Men, each of whom had heretofore been desperately attempting to fight his own way clear from one end of the canyon or the other, suddenly began surging forward en masse. As they did so, the fact that they were packed shoulder to shoulder became an advantage, for it gave them the power of a united front.

One hand clasped tight in Rachel's and one hand pressed against her rock-hard belly, Persephone watched Azriel, Zdeno, Barka and the others fall back a step, and then two. A break appeared in the line, and a New Man tried to dart through. He was cut down, but the space he left when he fell gave the man behind him a chance to fully swing his sword. Zdeno, who was fighting beside Azriel, leapt out of range in the nick of time, but as he did so, he stumbled over a body and went down himself.

As the New Man raised his blade, the spear-toting soldier behind him stumbled through the gap and Rachel screamed.

Wrenching her hand free of Rachel's, Persephone planted both hands on Ghengor's back, shoved hard and shouted, "Help them!"

Ghengor and the other Panoraki bodyguards needed no further prompting than this. Hefting their battle-axes into the air, they ran screaming into the fray with Cur hot on their heels.

It was then that the Fates, who'd ever been so fond of playing tricks on Persephone, played their cruelest one yet.

For as she stood there believing that she was about to see the love of Rachel's life cut to pieces, Azriel, in a desperate attempt to save Zdeno, lunged and lost his footing. He managed to twist in midair before falling on top of Zdeno, but that only made the situation worse for him. Because it meant that while Zdeno was now entirely shielded from harm, the well-muscled abdomen that Persephone had, on more than one occasion, threatened to slit bow to stern, was left utterly exposed to the cold steel of the New Man's raised blade.

Sixty

EVER AFTERWARD, whenever Persephone thought about the three seconds that changed her life forever, they replayed in slow motion.

The grin on the face of the gore-splattered New Man as he prepared to plunge the bloody blade of his sword into Azriel's exposed belly.

The sound of her own scream being cut short as her first labor pain slammed into her with the force of a sledgehammer, sucking the air out of her lungs and driving her to her knees.

The sense, rather than the sight, of the spear hurtling toward her.

The fleeting thought that she was too paralyzed by the excruciating pain to move out of the way and that she'd never thought it would end this way.

And then . . . And then . . .

Sixty-One

"YOUR GRACE, we must retreat at once," insisted Murdock.

"Retreat?" Mordesius laughed hollowly. "We cannot retreat, Murdock, you fool!" he snarled. "My entire army is trapped in that godforsaken canyon!"

"I was not suggesting that the men should retreat, Your Grace, for they are not only trapped but doomed," said Murdock, his protuberant eyes flicking toward the canyon from which the screams of his wounded and dying soldiers rose up like a chorus of the damned. "I was speaking of you and me alone."

"Alone? Without my wife?" asked Mordesius, spitting out the word "wife" like it was a bad taste in his mouth.

"She is sick, body and soul, Your Grace," said Murdock. "I fear she would slow us down to the point of capture."

"Aurelia is the only woman in camp," said Mordesius. "To leave her behind would almost certainly see her ravished without mercy when the queen's army comes looking for the spoils of war."

"Yes, it would," agreed Murdock.

Mordesius did not say anything more on the subject of his miserable wife and her fate, choosing instead to return to staring in numb disbelief at the sight of his ambitions being utterly destroyed. Even when he'd lost his power over the dead king, the queen had slipped through his fingers and his alliance with Bartok had come to naught, Mordesius had always been able to comfort himself with the knowledge that he yet had his great army of New Men and that if all else failed, he could crush—or at least inflict severe damage upon—his enemies.

Now he did not even have that.

And since he lacked the position and means to tempt, coerce or conscript new men into a fighting force loyal to none but him, he would never have that again.

Unbelievably, he was back to where he'd started out so many years before: a ruinously scarred nobody in possession of nothing.

He wondered if he was going to vomit.

"Your Grace," pressed Murdock. "By setting fire to our tents and taking certain other measures, I've managed to buy us some time, but if we do not leave now, while the bandits on this side of the canyon are yet occupied slaughtering the men, we will not get the chance to do so at all."

Still, Mordesius just sat upon his horse staring at the end of his dreams.

"It will never be over until you are dead or captured, Your Grace," said Murdock sharply. "As long as there is breath, there is hope, and you may trust me to do everything in my power to keep you breathing. But you must come with me now!"

Hearing Murdock speak in such an uncharacteristic fashion helped to bring Mordesius back to his senses almost as effectively as did the sight of one of the bandits whirling around and fixing his hate-filled gaze upon him. The wretch immediately received a sword thrust in the back for his troubles, but Mordesius did not need to be told that he might not be so lucky next time, and that if the man's comrades were *all* to turn their hate-filled eyes upon him, the end he would suffer at their hands would be a bloody one indeed.

And so, without another word to Murdock or another thought to his bride, Mordesius wheeled his mount around and was about to begin galloping away when he heard the queen scream, and then stop screaming with chilling abruptness.

His cold heart hammering hard, Mordesius wheeled his horse back around, stood up in his stirrups and strained to catch a glimpse of her.

But the only thing he could see at the end of the narrow canyon was a large pile of black-clad bodies and a tiny but beautiful patch of the pink-tinged early morning mists that hung above the distant jungle.

And so, with the fleeting thought that he never thought it would end this way, Mordesius turned and galloped away.

Sixty-Two

SO CONSUMED BY HER labor pain that she was unable to move or even breathe, Persephone could do nothing but watch in horror as the New Man's spear hurtled toward her belly.

Then Rachel lunged and the next instant, Persephone's horror was multiplied by a thousandfold as she heard the soft, squelching sound of the spear that had been intended for her burying itself in Rachel's back.

The force of the impact caused Rachel to grunt and spun her in a complete circle. By the time she'd come all the way back around again, her face was a sickening shade of gray and her hands were clutching the tip of the spear, which had been driven clear through her chest. Blood had begun to trickle out of the corner of her mouth.

Everything else forgotten in the shock and horror of what she was seeing, Persephone fought through the gradually subsiding pain in her belly to force herself to her feet. On legs that were trembling so badly she was afraid she might collapse, she got behind Rachel and managed to slide her hands under Rachel's armpits just as the other girl's knees gave way.

"It's going to be okay, it's going to be okay, you're going to be okay," Persephone babbled, her words tumbling over themselves as she tried to lower Rachel into a sitting position without jostling her too much. Cradling her as best she could given the awkward position of the spear, Persephone frantically scanned the chaotic battleground for someone, anyone, who could help. When she couldn't see anyone, she hugged Rachel closer, trying to quell her panic, trying to think. Once upon a time, an eternity ago, when she'd been a nobody with nothing to lose, she'd drawn a poisoned arrow from Azriel's shoulder without flinching, but this situation was nothing like that one.

There would be no drawing out this spear, and she and Rachel both knew it.

Knowing that she had absolutely no right to cry in front of this girl who'd just sacrificed her life for her, Persephone nevertheless began to cry.

"Oh, Rachel, I . . . I am so, so sorry . . ."

"Don't be sorry," sighed Rachel, sounding very tired. She let her head fall toward Persephone's so that their foreheads touched and they looked not like two girls but like one girl resting her forehead against a looking glass. "And don't be sad, either."

Persephone made a noise halfway between a sob and a laugh. She was vaguely aware that in the distance, the sound of the fighting was subsiding.

"I mean it," continued Rachel, letting one hand fall from the bloody spear tip so that she could give Persephone a clumsy, comforting pat on the knee. "My father always believed that I would do something important with my life, and now I have done so. I have . . . saved the life of the queen who carries the prophesied Methusian king in her belly." The corners of her pale mouth turned up in a little smile. "It . . . does not get much more important than that."

"No, it doesn't," lied Persephone fiercely, even though her heart was crying out that Rachel getting married and having a baby of her own someday would have been a thousand times more important! Forcing herself to smile, she added, "You know, I think maybe you were the girl in the sketch all along."

"I think maybe you are right," wheezed Rachel.

Persephone could see that her friend was fading fast. In an effort to keep from completely losing control, she squeezed her eyes shut and gently pressed her lips against Rachel's temple.

Rachel sighed softly at the kiss. "Tell Zdeno that I love him," she whispered as the trickle of blood at the corner of her mouth became a stream. "Tell him . . . tell him that he is the handsomest man I have ever seen."

"I will," whispered Persephone, biting her lip so hard that it started to bleed.

Rachel closed her eyes for a moment. Then she opened them again and said, "Remember me."

"Until the day I die," promised Persephone tremulously as the tears streamed down her cheeks.

Rachel smiled again, then closed her eyes for the last time. "My mother used to sing me to sleep," she said, the words hardly more than a puff of air. "Sing me to sleep, Persephone."

In all her long years of hardship and toil, Persephone had never been asked to do anything remotely as hard as this. Nevertheless, she cleared her throat, and, in a voice that only trembled a little, she sang all three verses of the Glyndorian lullaby that Barka and Mateo had sung together at their happy reunion all those weeks ago.

By the time she'd finished singing the final verse, Rachel was dead.

As Persephone gently lowered her to the ground and stood up, from the mouth of the canyon came the horribly incongruous sound of cheering. Looking over, Persephone saw Azriel—not slit bow to stern but alive as he could be. Numbly, she watched as he raised his hand toward her in victory.

Then the sledgehammer pain slammed into her belly again, and she fell to her knees once more.

Sixty-Three

"YOU MUST PUSH, Your Majesty," said Cairn.

Persephone lay in the makeshift birthing bed, too exhausted to answer. Her hair was plastered to her forehead; her shift was soaked with sweat and blood. Time had ceased to exist. There was only the last pain and the next pain and the brief space in between.

Fayla squeezed her hand. "Please, Your Majesty," she said. "You are almost there."

Yes, thought Persephone confusedly before she drifted away again. *But I have been almost there for so long now. I begin to think that I shall never get there at all.*

More pains. More space between the pains. And then:

"If this goes on much longer you may have to choose between the life of the mother and the life of the child or risk losing them both," she heard Cairn whisper to someone.

Persephone did not need to ask which life Cairn would choose to sacrifice. And for once, the two of them were in agreement as to who should die that the other might live. Sacrificing herself for the sake of the baby was as Persephone knew it should be—perhaps even as it was meant to be. Perhaps she and Rachel had both been the girl in the sketch made by the long-dead Methusian Seer; perhaps both of them had ever been meant to die that the baby might live.

Though she would very much have liked to have seen and held and known her son, Persephone was at peace knowing that at least he would live. Her heart ached at the thought of leaving Azriel, of course, but she would rather have had their brief time together than to have had a hundred lifetimes with someone else.

For all she had endured, for all she had lost, for all she would miss out on after she was gone, Persephone knew herself to be a woman blessed indeed.

Even as she fuzzily thought that she needed to speak to Azriel to ensure that he understood what must be done, he was there at her side, holding her hand through another wracking pain. When it was over and she'd caught her breath, she licked her parched lips, turned her face toward his and said, "You . . . you must listen to me, Azriel. There is no sense losing me and the baby both. We are the only family you've got, remember? Therefore you must be strong and . . . and choose. And it must be the baby who lives. Do you understand? It . . . it must be him."

Azriel bowed his head and said nothing for a very long moment. Then he looked up and, in a very quiet voice, said, "Persephone?"

"Yes?" she replied faintly.

"After all the times I've listened to you carp at me to get going when I've been on the brink of death, do you truly imagine I'm going to let you give up that easily?"

Persephone felt the dangerously weakened flame of life within her leap at these unexpected words. "Azriel—"

"Moreover," he interrupted, "I would remind you that when we wed, you vowed to obey me in all things."

"I vowed no such thing," she retorted with a gasp, the flare of indignation she felt at his words causing the flame to leap a little higher still.

"Even so, you are exactly right when you say that you and the baby are the only family I've got," concluded Azriel. "And by the gods, I do not intend to lose either of you. So call upon that infernal stubbornness you've so often seen fit to plague me with and push that baby out. Now!"

With the last of her strength—and with the fleeting thought that if she somehow managed to survive her ordeal that she'd give Azriel a goodly pinch to show him what she thought of the way he'd just spoken to her—Persephone laboriously pushed herself up onto her elbows. As the pain began to build, she fought her fear and tried to concentrate on breathing. And when the pain was at its peak, she took a deep breath, held it in and then pushed as hard and for as long as she could. Indeed, she pushed so hard and for so long that her whole mind exploded with a pain far beyond anything she'd thus far endured.

And then, just like that, the pain was gone.

But the effort had cost her dear—so dear that she couldn't have said if the tiny cry she heard just before she lost consciousness was real or if it was a dream.

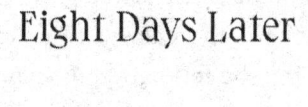

Eight Days Later

Sixty-Four

PERSEPHONE DID NOT awaken as much as she gradually became aware of her surroundings. She did not keep her eyes shut and stay perfectly still because she feared lurking danger, but because she did not seem to have the energy to do otherwise. She half-heartedly wondered why she felt battered beyond belief but was too groggy and disoriented to do more than wonder.

After a time, she became aware of a presence close by. Forcing her eyes open the tiniest of cracks, she beheld Cairn sitting on a stool at her bedside.

"How are you feeling?" asked the Methusian woman.

Persephone muddled over the question for a long moment before finally croaking, "Thirsty."

Cairn smiled, helped Persephone raise her head, and held a goblet to her lips.

It was as Persephone was drinking deeply of the strong wine that she suddenly remembered. Shoving the goblet away with such force that it clattered out of Cairn's hand, she spluttered and gasped, "The baby—"

"A healthy boy, Your Majesty," said Cairn, her joy lighting up her whole face. "Small, of course, on account of his early arrival, but as healthy as any Methusian baby."

Persephone felt a surge of energy she could not have dreamt she possessed an instant earlier. "Where is he?" she demanded breathlessly, wincing as she pushed herself into a sitting position. "Can I see him? Bring him to me—no, wait, have Azriel bring him to me! He should be with me when I meet our son for the first time."

"Of course," smiled Cairn, rising to her feet. "Only, I caution you not to overexert yourself. Your fever broke only a few hours ago, and you've not eaten for more than a week."

"I've been unconscious for more than a *week*?" exclaimed Persephone in shock.

"You have, Your Majesty," said Cairn. "But you are better now. Calm yourself—I will fetch Azriel at once."

Persephone fidgeted with impatience for what seemed a very long time but was probably not more than a few minutes. Then, without warning, Azriel stepped into the tent. In spite of looking as though he hadn't slept in a dog's age, he was as devastatingly handsome as ever. Even so, Persephone barely spared him a glance, so riveted was she by the sight of the tiny, mewling bundle in his arms.

Smiling as though he well understood why he was being so heartlessly ignored by the wife at whose bedside he'd kept vigil for eight long days, Azriel wordlessly walked over and placed the bundle in her arms.

Persephone said nothing, only stared down at her son in amazement.

He was breathtaking.

His head was covered in auburn fuzz, and his eyes held the promise of blue. He was tightly swaddled and did not look best pleased to be so. Persephone stared in fascination at the indignant expression on her son's face and listened to the little grunts he made as he struggled to free his limbs from the constricting wrap. Then she carefully laid him on the bed and unswaddled him that she might undertake a more thorough examination. He had ten perfect fingers, ten tiny toes and skin as soft as kitten fur. Tentatively placing a finger in the palm of his hand, she marveled at his strength when he clutched at it. She tickled his lower lip and laughed when he abruptly latched onto her fingertip. She laughed again when, upon realizing that no milk could be drawn from the fingertip no matter how vigorously he sucked, he spat out the offending thing and bellowed with outrage. Utterly delighted, Persephone reverently planted a kiss on his little naked belly.

Then, with exaggerated care, she rewrapped him, nestled him against her breast and, without looking up at Azriel, said, "Husband, I regret to inform you that I have fallen in love with another."

Azriel's chuckle earned him a glance at last. "You did well, wife," he said, leaning down to give her and the baby a kiss.

"Yes, I did, didn't I?" replied Persephone gloatingly. "What shall we call him? And do not suggest Poddrick."

Azriel chuckled again and sat down on the edge of the bed. "Actually, I was thinking that we might name him after his uncle," he said.

"His uncle?" said Persephone perplexedly. Then her face brightened with sudden understanding. "Oh! You mean Finn!"

"Yes, I mean Finn," agreed Azriel, reaching out to brush a stray lock of hair back from her face. "Your brother was a good and brave man, Persephone. And though I must admit there were moments I could have gladly wrung his neck for having made you promise to fight for your throne, I'd be entirely content to see him remembered in our son."

Persephone crooned the name at the baby several times before looking up at Azriel and saying, "I like it."

"I thought you might," he replied. "Zdeno has asked to be named his sworn protector, and I have agreed. I hope you don't mind."

"Of course I don't mind," said Persephone. Hugging Baby Finn to her a little tighter, she asked, "How is Zdeno doing?"

"He is heartbroken and grief-stricken," said Azriel quietly. "Fayla is trying to help him through it, but there is only so much she can do."

Persephone nodded, the terrible memory of Rachel's final moments coming back to her in a rush. "And how is everyone else? Where do things stand?"

"Your plan to trap the New Men soldiers in the canyon worked better than we could have hoped. Most were killed; the few who put down their weapons and surrendered were taken into custody," said Azriel. "Many on our side were for beheading them on the spot, but I did not think you'd approve."

"You were right," said Persephone, grateful not to have the mass murder of unarmed men on her conscience.

"We suffered only minimal losses," continued Azriel. "Besides Rachel, none of the other council members were killed."

"How on earth did you manage to avoid being skewered after you tripped over Zdeno during the fighting?" asked Persephone, remembering the New Man with the raised sword.

"Cur," said Azriel.

"Cur?"

"He tore out the soldier's throat before he could finish me," explained Azriel. "Either your flea-bitten dog finally decided that he liked me or else he wanted to spare you the loss of your devilishly handsome husband."

"Or else he mistook the New Man for you," offered Persephone mischievously. She smiled at the scowl this suggestion brought to Azriel's face, then her smile faded as she suddenly remembered that according to Lord Atticus, Lady Aurelia had been given to Mordesius. Persephone had never liked the little noblewoman, but she'd never disliked her enough to wish *that* upon her. "What about Lady Aurelia? Did you find her in the enemy camp?"

"Yes," said Azriel. "Fayla got to her before the men did—"

"Thank the gods," said Persephone with a shudder.

"I wouldn't be so quick to do so," said Azriel as the baby began to fuss, "for it appears that Lady Aurelia is afflicted with the same cough that killed your brother, and on top of this, she has gone completely mad. I've ordered her cared for and kindly treated."

Persephone nodded her agreement with his decision. "What of Mordesius and his general?" she asked as she began gently bouncing Baby Finn in her arms to settle him. "Are they dead, or do we have them in custody?"

"Neither, as far as we know," Azriel replied grimly. "We found the charred remains of two bodies in the smoking ruins of their camp tents, but we've no way of knowing if the bodies are those of Mordesius and his general. I would lay odds that they are not."

Persephone felt a stab of alarm. Hugging Baby Finn closer to her, she said, "We should send out tracking parties to—"

"Try to find them? Already done," said Azriel. "We've found no trace of them, Persephone. We'll keep looking, but if I had to guess I'd say that if Murdock and Mordesius are alive, we'll never see them again."

Feeling as though she'd been holding her breath for a very long time without realizing it, Persephone exhaled slowly and steadily. As she did so, the surge of energy that had sustained her suddenly vanished. She yawned at the exact same moment as the baby did.

Looking filled up by his love for them both, Azriel gently took Baby Finn from Persephone's arms and bade her lie back down and get some rest. Protesting through her face-splitting yawns that she did not need any more rest, Persephone laid her head on the pillow and closed her eyes.

"Azriel?" she said drowsily as she felt him drawing the blankets up to her chin.

"Yes?" he said.

"I cannot be certain, but I think I promised myself I'd give you a goodly pinch for the way you spoke to me during my ordeal," she murmured.

"You must be mistaken, wife, for that doesn't sound like you at all," he replied with a smile in his voice. "Now sleep. Your menfolk would see you recovered as soon as may be."

It was more than a week before Persephone was recovered enough even to leave her sickbed, and more than two weeks after that before she was recovered enough to make the arduous journey back to the imperial capital.

Since news of the victory over Mordesius and the birth of the prince had long since spread throughout the kingdom, the progress back to Parthania was like a victory parade. Indeed, when, at last, they passed through the great gates of the city, it seemed to an exhausted but exhilarated Persephone that there was not a single person in the entire realm who was not utterly mad with joy at her triumphant return.

Most unfortunately for her, Azriel and the baby, she was wrong.

Sixty-Five

MORDESIUS WATCHED from the shadows of the narrow, squalid alley as the litter carrying the queen and the little cockroach approached.

After he and Murdock fled the battlefield, Mordesius had thought incessantly about the sound of her scream being cut short so abruptly. He'd imagined her dying a thousand different deaths—each more gruesome than the last, each resulting in the end of the unborn Methusian infant. Over and over, Mordesius had told himself that the twisting pain in his chest whenever he thought of the queen's violet eyes glazed over in death was nothing but the ill effects of common food and hard travel.

Then, a fortnight ago, he and Murdock had learned from a man they'd met on the road that the scream Mordesius had heard had not heralded the death of the queen. According to the man, who'd fought in the battle and was hurrying home to his wife and six children, the queen was alive and safely delivered of a healthy son. Mordesius had first been stunned, then electrified, by the news. The crushing despair that had plagued him since the Valley of Gorg had vanished upon the instant. After absently ordering Murdock to dispatch the lowborn wretch for making the mistake of suddenly recognizing them, Mordesius had decided that perhaps the business between him and the queen wasn't finished, after all. If he couldn't snatch victory from the jaws of defeat, perhaps he could snatch a little well-deserved satisfaction. His position, his wealth, his army and his dreams had been taken from him, but he yet had the ever-resourceful Murdock, and he had something no one would ever be able to take from him: the stomach to do whatever it took to bend those with soft hearts to his absolute will.

Indeed, he had the stomach to do whatever it took to not only bend those with soft hearts, but to break them into a thousand pieces.

Mordesius kept his eyes on the queen as her litter drew closer and closer. Then, just as she was passing by the spot where he stood ankle-deep in muck, a grubby lowborn brat on his side of the cobblestone street darted toward the approaching litter. If it had been Mordesius, he'd have ordered the horsemen to trample the brat and her pathetic posy of wilted wildflowers, but of course the queen did no such thing. On the contrary, she ordered the litter to halt, then she accepted the posy as reverently as if it were some priceless treasure. As she was doing so, the little cockroach in her arms suddenly began to scream like a terror. The queen laughed aloud as the brat in the street clapped her hands over her ears, then she discreetly offered the screaming cockroach her very own breast instead of passing him to a wet nurse for feeding as a proper royal woman would have done.

Deep within the filthy, stinking, homespun hood that hid his all-too-familiar face, Mordesius smiled broadly at this touching display of motherly love.

For it made it very easy to believe that if the little cockroach's life were at stake, the beautiful queen would get down on her knees and do *anything* to save him.

Sixty-Six

PERSEPHONE SHIVERED as she listened to the wind tearing at the shutters as though it would rip them right off the hinges.

"It sounds like the storm is growing worse," she said as she drew her chair closer to the fire.

"Yes, Your Majesty," replied Neeka, looking up from the shift she was mending. "I certainly hope the prince consort is not caught out in this weather."

"I hope not either," said Persephone wryly.

Since learning that Persephone and Azriel were married, Neeka had never again tried to hand-feed Azriel quail's eggs, nor had she gazed at him like he was a giant sweetmeat, but Persephone knew that the girl would ever be enamored of her handsome husband.

Pulling the cozy Panoraki wool blanket tighter around herself, Persephone turned her attention back to the dispatch from the Marinese Elder Roark. It stated that he wished to come to Parthania to act as ambassador for his people. Persephone sighed. She knew that Miter, in particular, was going to make trouble out of this. Since the battle at the Valley of Gorg, he'd been even more insufferable than usual, taking every opportunity to remind anyone who would listen that if it weren't for him, they'd all have been annihilated. He was not going to respond well to the news that the Marinese were to have a voice on the Council when they'd contributed nothing whatsoever to the war effort.

As she pondered how best to break the news to him, Persephone heard a single knock on the door.

Since visitors were normally announced by the royal guards posted outside the chamber, Neeka shared a puzzled look with her mistress before setting aside her mending and going to see who was at the door.

"There is no one there, Your Majesty, not even the guards," said Neeka as she nudged the door closed with her wooden leg and ambled back over to the fire. "There was only this."

Persephone smiled at the sight of the note in the girl's hand. In the six weeks since their triumphant return to Parthania, Azriel had taken to leaving little gifts under her pillow and slipping her love notes when she least expected it. He said he was doing so because he'd never gotten a chance to properly court her, and also because their duties left them so little time together that he feared she would someday forget him altogether.

Smiling again at the notion that she could ever forget the man who slipped into her bed each night to remind her of his presence in such delicious fashion, Persephone took the note from Neeka, eagerly unfolded it . . .

And felt her whole world come crashing down around her ears.

Greetings, Your Majesty,
I have your husband and son. Unless you would like their heads delivered to you within the hour, come alone to the royal harbor at once.

Flinging the note aside, Persephone bolted to her feet and was halfway to the chamber door before the note hit the floor.

"Your Majesty, what is it?" cried Neeka, hurrying after her.

Persephone did not reply. Wrenching open the chamber door, she tore across the ominously deserted corridor to the royal nursery. Seeing that the door was already ajar, she put her shoulder down and slammed full force into it. The door flew open with a bang to reveal the baby gone, Zdeno on his knees with a dagger in his belly and the nursery walls awash with the blood of the three nursemaids who lay dead on the floor. "H-he came through the window, Your Majesty," groaned Zdeno. "I tried to stop him but . . . but h-he had a knife to the baby's belly and—"

A scream behind Persephone cut him off.

Whirling, Persephone grabbed Neeka by the arm, jerked her into the chamber and slammed the door behind her. "After I'm gone, you must bar the door and tend to Zdeno," Persephone commanded tersely, giving Neeka a shake to make sure she was paying attention. "You're to stay here until I've returned, and you're to let no one know what has happened, do you understand? The lives of Azriel and the baby depend upon it!"

When Neeka said nothing, only continued to gaze about the chamber in shock and horror, Persephone slapped her hard across the face. Neeka gasped and her eyes snapped into focus at once.

"Will you do as I've commanded, Neeka?" demanded Persephone harshly. "Can you?"

"I . . . I can, Your Majesty," replied the girl, sounding shaky but sure. "I can and will."

Persephone was gone without another word. Knowing that she'd never be able to make it to the harbor alone if she were to leave the palace through the front door dressed as she was, she returned to the royal chambers, wriggled out of her beautiful gown, threw on the shift that Neeka had been mending and then a simple cloak of black. Pulling forward the hood to hide her face, she fetched her dagger from the desk drawer and took a few seconds to re-familiarize herself with its weight and balance before slipping it into the pocket of the shift and hurrying into the bedchamber. Ducking behind the tapestry on the far wall, she found the door to the secret passageway she'd used to flee the palace after Finn died. She followed the narrow, musty-smelling passageway until she got to a small door.

Pushing it open, she stepped out into the tempest. The instant she did so, she heard a horsey squeal. Glancing over, she saw Fleet standing at the gate of the corral gazing adoringly at her. When he saw that she'd noticed him, he neighed again and then waited expectantly for her to hurry over and lavish him with praise, affection and cut turnips. But, of course, Persephone did none of these things. Instead, she turned, put her hooded head down to help cut the wind and began staggering toward the royal harbor as fast as she could.

By the time she got there, it had begun to rain. Slipping and sliding her way down to the otherwise deserted quay, she found General Murdock sitting in a rowboat that was being battered so mercilessly by the crashing waves of the rising sea that Persephone thought it must surely be swamped at any moment.

"Greetings, Your Majesty," called General Murdock over the wind. "His Grace asks that you join him on yonder ship."

Teeth chattering with cold and fear, Persephone glanced briefly at the small merchant vessel anchored not far away, then she stepped into the rowboat. General Murdock immediately cast off and began rowing hard. The sea was a frothing beast—twice, the rowboat was hit by waves so big that they nearly capsized, and Persephone had to use the rusty pail beneath her seat to bail constantly in an effort to keep them from sinking.

But at last, they pulled alongside.

"After you, Your Majesty," called General Murdock, gesturing to the hanging ladder.

Hands shaking so badly she could hardly hang onto the wet rungs, Persephone forced herself to climb. She was almost at the top of the ladder when, over the sound of the storm, she heard the baby crying. As she scrambled up and over the deck rail, her mind registered the fact that Azriel and Mordesius were there, but her entire being was focused on Baby Finn. He was lying naked on a pile of rags inside an open wooden chest. The chest was sitting on a spindly legged table whose top was even with the starboard deck rail.

Even as she started toward it, a particularly large wave crashed against the ship, causing her to stagger and sending the chest sliding toward the unprotected edge.

"I wouldn't go any nearer if I were you, Your Majesty," sang Mordesius, who was standing at the end of the table. Slipping his hands under the tabletop, he managed to lift it just enough to send the chest sliding a few inches more. Persephone froze. Wrenching her gaze away from Baby Finn, she locked eyes with Azriel, who was standing not far from her with his hands tied behind his back.

Mordesius caught the look they shared. "Ah!" he crooned as General Murdock walked over to stand beside Azriel. "Young love. It warms the heart, it really does."

"What do you want, Mordesius?" shouted Persephone.

"I want many things," he shouted back. "But you have taken them all from me, and so now all I want is to give you a choice."

Guessing what was coming, Persephone began to shake her head.

"Yes, Your Majesty!" said Mordesius in a jolly voice. "The choice involves the lives of your beloved husband and son, though I regret to inform you that it is not a simple matter of choosing one or the other. Rather, it is a matter of choosing one or both."

Another wave hit the ship; the chest slid again. Baby Finn kicked his little legs and cried piteously.

"If you will order the death of the Methusian right here and now, and then watch in silence as your orders are carried out, I shall command General Murdock to row you and the brat back to shore at once," explained Mordesius as Murdock drew a large knife from the scabbard at his belt. "Fail to give the order and you shall still bear witness to the cockroach's well-deserved execution, but thereafter you shall also watch me shut the lid of the chest, and then you shall sit by my side that together we may enjoy the cries of your infant son as he slowly suffocates."

Persephone said nothing, only searched her mind frantically for a way to save Azriel *and* the baby.

Another wave. A few more inches.

Suddenly, Azriel's voice interrupted her thoughts. "Wife, there is no sense losing me and the baby both," he said with that little lop-sided smile she knew so well.

"What he says is exactly so, wife!" cried Mordesius, clapping his shiny-pink scarred hands together.

"Say what you must, Persephone," said Azriel, his gaze steady upon her face. "Say it now."

"Yes!" cried Mordesius, who was fairly shrieking with excitement. "Say it, Persephone! Say it now!"

For the sake of her son, Persephone tried to say it, she really did. Once, twice, three times she opened her mouth and then closed it again without uttering a word. Finally, feeling as though her heart was shattering into a thousand pieces, she shook her head.

She was strong and brave enough to do many things, but she was not strong and brave enough to do this.

Mordesius's happy countenance vanished at once.

And with an expression that said he'd always known that she didn't have what it took to be queen, he nodded at General Murdock who, before Persephone's disbelieving eyes, casually plunged the knife deep into Azriel's belly.

Sixty-Seven

THE INSTANT MURDOCK slid the knife out of Azriel's belly, a rogue wave smashed into the ship. As the ship listed sickeningly, the lid of the wooden chest snapped shut and the chest slid into the sea. Azriel and General Murdock were both flung off their feet, but while the General was able to stop himself at the starboard deck rail, Azriel slammed into Persephone, who'd lunged for the chest and missed. The force of the impact sent both her and Azriel toppling off the ship.

She managed to grab a handful of his shirt as they fell but it was torn from her grasp as they plunged into the raging sea. Water filled Persephone's eyes, her ears, her mouth; blind and choking, she thrashed this way and that in the churning madness in the hope of finding Azriel. Just before the urge to breathe overwhelmed her, her fingers touched hair. Grabbing hold, she kicked hard toward the surface. Rolling onto her back even before she'd taken her first gasping breath, she heaved Azriel's head out of the water and frantically looked around for the wooden chest. She was terrified that she'd see fragments of it floating nearby. Or worse, that she'd see no sign of it at all and she'd know that it had sunk to the bottom of the sea.

By some miracle, however, it had not shattered or sunk but was bobbing toward shore. More miraculously still, from within the chest she could clearly hear the sound of Baby Finn crying.

The fall from the ship had not killed him and the airtight chest that had been intended to suffocate him had saved him from drowning.

He was safe—for the moment.

Turning her attention back to Azriel and her own rapidly diminishing strength, Persephone was chilled to see that the water around them had already turned red with his blood.

"Azriel!" shouted Persephone, her voice sharp with panic.

"I'm . . . here," he said tiredly.

Refusing to acknowledge that this was exactly how Rachel had sounded in her final moments of life, Persephone threw one arm across Azriel's chest and, keeping her ears locked on the sound of the baby's cry, she began kicking as hard as she could. As she struggled desperately to get Azriel to shore, the winds howled, the rains beat down and the salt spray filled her lungs, causing her to splutter and gasp. Mercifully, however, the storm waves that were surging ever more powerfully helped rather than hindered their progress. Indeed, being able to rest and ride these waves forward was the only reason they made it to shallow water before Persephone's strength gave out.

Too breathless and exhausted to speak, she dragged Azriel up onto shore, rolled him onto his side and, using her dagger, sliced the rope that bound his hands behind his back. As he rolled back over, the sight of his deathly pale face and gaping belly wound made Persephone's heart shrivel, but she did not linger. Splashing back into the water, she grabbed the wooden chest inside which Baby Finn was still crying—though not quite so hard. Dragging it up onto shore, she unlatched the lid and saw him lying half-buried in the pile of rags that had almost certainly protected him from being bashed to death by his fall from the ship.

Reaching into the rags, she lifted up her wailing infant son and held him to her chest with a depth of gratitude that only a mother who has lost and found a child could ever understand.

Then she heard the thump of an arrow. Looking up, she saw General Murdock and Mordesius in the rowboat. The General was calmly nocking another arrow in the bow while Mordesius, who was wrapped in the cloak that Murdock had been wearing earlier, was grimacing and awkwardly pulling on one of the rowboat's oars.

Clutching Baby Finn to her, Persephone scrambled back to where Azriel lay unmoving, his legs half covered by the rapidly rising water.

"Get up, Azriel," she pleaded as another arrow whizzed so close to her head that she felt the feathers brush her cheek as it flew past. When Azriel did not answer, she gave him a gentle shake and tried again. When that didn't work, she gave him a vicious pinch on the leg and screamed, *"Get up or I swear to the gods that I am going to—"*

Gasping like a drowned man coming back to life, Azriel clumsily maneuvered himself up onto his hands and knees and staggered to his feet. Casting an anxious glance over her shoulder in the direction of the rowboat, which was now so close to shore that she knew Mordesius and Murdock would be upon them in a moment, Persephone placed her free hand on the small of Azriel's back and was about to give him a shove in the direction of the quay when she saw that it was completely under water. Looking around, she realized that the narrow strip of beach upon which she, Azriel and the baby had landed was totally cut off from the path that would have led them back up to the safety of the palace.

And since they could not possibly scale the cliffs, there was nowhere to go but into the treacherous sea caves.

"Come on!" she shouted, grabbing Azriel's hand and tugging him toward the base of the caves.

His lips white and his blue eyes dimmer than she'd ever seen them, Azriel nodded and wordlessly staggered after her.

"Climb!" she shouted, pointing to the lowest cave and giving him a little shove to get him going.

As best he could, Azriel did as she bid. It wrenched at Persephone's guts to watch him stumble and slip, and to see the rocks in his wake smeared with his blood, but she shoved and prodded and shouted until at last they reached the mouth of the lowest cave. Wishing they could have climbed higher but knowing they were lucky to have made it this far, Persephone pushed Azriel forward into the darkness. As she started in after him, she felt a searing pain in the back of her thigh. Looking around, she saw that she'd taken an arrow in the leg. And judging by the markings, it wasn't just any arrow, it was the kind of arrow New Men used to use when they went hunting Methusians.

It was a poisoned arrow.

Without giving herself time to think about how much it was going to hurt, Persephone grabbed hold of the shaft with her free hand and pulled. The groan she emitted as the arrow came free was horrible even to her own ears, and it was not just caused by the pain of the extraction. It was caused by the burning sensation that had already begun spreading outward from the wound—and by the knowledge of the fate that awaited her when the poison took hold.

The despair that might have overwhelmed her at that moment was only held in check by the sound of Baby Finn's plaintive cry. He breathed, she breathed and Azriel breathed, and as long as there was breath, there was hope.

"Come on, Azriel," said Persephone, trying to sound confident in spite of the fact that she could hear the none-too-distant sound of Mordesius shrieking at Murdock to climb faster. "We won't go so far into the cave that we can't find our way out again. We'll just go far enough to find somewhere to hide."

But like so many things in her short, hard life, things didn't work out the way Persephone had planned or hoped, because they'd hardly taken ten steps into the cave before they were swallowed up by darkness. With the half-hysterical thought that this was probably why they were called the "treacherous" sea caves, Persephone tried to retrace their steps in the hope of finding another, better-lit path. But she could not, and before long she knew that even in the unlikely event that Mordesius and his trusted henchman lost Azriel's blood trail, she and her little family were lost in more ways than one.

During her time in the mines, Persephone's worst nightmare had been that she would die alone, lost in the darkness. She knew now that worse by far would be to die lost in the darkness with those she loved best in the world by her side, and to have the last sounds she heard on this earth be the fading cries of her child and the terrible, rasping breaths of her dying husband.

Trying to ignore the unnatural thirst that was beginning to build in her throat and to remember her old promise to herself that she would never again lie down and wait for Death to claim her, Persephone gave Baby Finn a fierce kiss and then reached up to brush from her face several strands of hair that were being ruffled by the breeze.

Then she froze.

The breeze!

Heart pounding, Persephone gave Azriel a firm push in the direction of the breeze. As he began to stagger forward, Persephone could hear the sounds of their pursuers drawing ever nearer, but she could also feel the breeze growing stronger, and she could see the darkness thinning, and so she found herself beginning to hope against hope that they might actually escape and reach help in time to save them all.

Unfortunately, it was this hope that caused her to drive Azriel onward so relentlessly that when the tunnel curved sharply and ended without warning at the opening of what appeared to be a vast cavern, he was going too fast to stop.

The only thing Persephone heard after she screamed was the thud of his body hitting the ground below.

Far below.

Sixty-Eight

PERSEPHONE WAS HALFWAY down the narrow dirt incline that hugged the cavern wall when she saw Azriel's broken body slowly slide into the glowing tidal pool at the bottom of the cavern. Frantically running over to the pool, she set Baby Finn down on the ground a safe distance away and then dove into the water to save Azriel from drowning.

Just before she hit the water, she noticed the banyan tree growing at the water's edge.

And suddenly she was floating, unmoving, in utter silence, every inch of her tingling as strength and vitality rushed in to fill up the space where weariness and pain had lived mere moments before. And then, after what seemed like a lifetime, an unseen force was gently pushing her to the surface of the pool, and water was streaming down her face, and air was filling her lungs, and she was blinking at Azriel standing before her.

No longer dying and broken but alive and more beautiful than ever.

Before Persephone could even begin to process what this meant, Azriel gave a shout of alarm and lunged for the edge of the pool behind her. He was fast, but General Murdock was faster—so fast that by the time Persephone had turned around, he already had the baby cradled in his arm.

"Move and I will dash his brains out," he said placidly.

Neither Persephone nor Azriel moved. They simply waited and watched as Mordesius grunted and lurched his way down the dirt incline and over to the edge of the pool.

Persephone watched the former regent's expression change from rage to incredulity when he saw that Azriel was standing in the pool looking remarkably well for a man who'd recently been stabbed in the belly with a six-inch blade.

Then he saw the banyan tree.

Without taking his eyes off it, he reached up and clutched the locket that contained the leafy sprig that had never withered. He stood like that, still as a statue, for a very long moment before turning his dark-eyed gaze back toward Persephone and Azriel.

"Out of the water, both of you," he ordered.

Mindful of the General's threat to harm the baby, they wordlessly did as they'd been bid.

"Lift up your shirt, cockroach," commanded Mordesius.

When Azriel lifted up his bloodstained shirt to reveal not a gaping belly wound but the white scar of such a wound long-since healed, Mordesius gasped.

"Of course!" he breathed, his handsome face alight with something close to joy. "Balthazar didn't discover the healing pool after a long sea journey *to* somewhere else. He discovered it after a long sea journey *from* somewhere else. He was returning home! His ship was wrecked and his crew lost in a storm exactly like the one that rages this day! And the sea itself was the frothing monster that chased him into the caves!"

Mordesius threw back his head and laughed like a boy.

Then he quickly removed his cloak and robe and, after taking a last look at the brutally scarred body that had caused him so many years of suffering, he awkwardly slid into the pool.

He stayed submerged for so long that Persephone began to think that he'd drowned. Just as she was about to suggest this possibility to General Murdock in the hope that he'd set Baby Finn down and go investigate, however, Mordesius burst to the surface.

"It worked, Murdock!" he cried, sounding so utterly exhilarated that in spite of everything, Persephone found herself strangely moved. "I am healed so well that it is as though I was never injured at all. I am finally the man I was ever meant to be!"

Wading over to the water's edge, he planted two strong hands on the bank and hoisted himself out of the pool as easily as Azriel might have done.

Persephone could not help staring in amazement. All evidence of the long-ago burns that had nearly killed him was gone. The once skinny, scarred legs were now smooth and powerful; the once sunken chest was exquisitely muscled; the uneven shoulders were broad and straight.

It was a breathtaking demonstration of the power of the pool.

"You like what you see, don't you, Your Majesty?" asked Mordesius slyly, holding his hands wide as though to give her a better look.

When Persephone said nothing, only looked away, Mordesius laughed loudly and wagged his finger at her. Then he briskly strode over, pulled on the billowing black robe he'd been wearing beneath Murdock's cloak, clapped his hands together and said,

"To business!"

"To business?" said Persephone warily.

"For starters, you'll give me that little dagger you're so fond of carrying around," said Mordesius, holding out his hand toward her.

When Persephone hesitated, Mordesius gave a meaningful look in the direction of the baby and the man who'd threatened to dash out his brains.

With a glance at Azriel, who nodded, Persephone handed over the dagger.

"Good choice," commended Mordesius. "Now, Your Majesty, my original plan was to murder you, your husband and your child and then disappear before I could be brought to justice, but that has changed. Indeed, everything has changed! I will still kill you, your husband and your child, of course, but I am not going anywhere." Mordesius paused briefly to stretch and flex and admire his beautiful body. "Now that I've found the Pool of Genezing, there is not a nobleman in Glyndoria who will not prostrate himself at my feet for a single vial of these healing waters. And when I inform the great lords that the royal bloodline has been stamped out for good, they will trample each other in their eagerness to anoint me king, that I might help them stave off disease and death. Noblewomen will flop down on their backs before me—by the gods, I will beget an army of bastard sons!" Clapping General Murdock on the back so hard that the General nearly dropped the baby, Mordesius said, "Don't you think I will make a splendid king, Murdock?"

"I do, Your Grace," said General Murdock, sounding genuinely pleased for his master.

Mordesius briskly nodded the head that no longer seemed to sit so heavy upon his neck. "And I will not just be a king but a *warrior* king, Murdock. I will learn to wield a sword in a manner that shall make those who once mocked me for my injuries tremble with fear." He gasped theatrically as though he'd just been struck by a most marvelous idea. "Do you know what? I think I'll begin practicing right now! Give me your sword!"

With a thin smile, the General obeyed.

"Now, set down the brat," ordered Mordesius, flourishing the sword this way and that.

The very instant Murdock had done as he'd been bid, Persephone and Azriel dove toward Baby Finn. With the speed of a striking snake, Mordesius slit Murdock's throat and set the bloody sword tip against the baby's belly.

"*He's dead if you move another inch!*" Mordesius screamed at Persephone and Azriel, stopping them in their tracks. Pressing the tip of the blade a little harder against the baby's belly to show them that he meant business, Mordesius looked down at the faithful servant to whom he'd entrusted his life so many times and calmly said, "Apologies, Murdock, but of late you've rather annoyed me with your cleverness."

Murdock gurgled and clawed at his slit throat as he tried to drag himself toward the healing pool.

"Moreover," continued Mordesius, "upon reflection, I think I'd prefer to be the only one who knows the location of the pool whose waters, sadly, are never going to heal you."

Mordesius punctuated this statement by placing his bare foot on the General's sloping brow, effectively stopping his progress just inches from the pool. Cocking his head to one side as though listening to beautiful music, Mordesius waited until his general had stopped gurgling and the only sounds to be heard were the distant howl of the storm and the steady drip of the dead henchman's blood splashing into the pool that would have saved him.

At length, Mordesius turned to Azriel and said, "Pick up the body, cockroach. We'll take it with us."

"Where are we going?" asked Azriel as he casually shifted into a fighting stance.

In response to Azriel's words or his change in stance or both, Mordesius applied just enough pressure to the sword that the tip pierced the skin of Baby's Finn's belly, and a tiny trickle of blood appeared.

Eyes blazing with a combination of hatred and helplessness, Azriel stalked over to the edge of the pool and knelt down beside the corpse of the General.

As he did so, Mordesius turned to Persephone and said, "Before he hoists Murdock's body onto those big, broad shoulders of his, go rip half a dozen strips of cloth from the General's shirt and take the pouch of embers from his belt. Put all the cloth strips but one in your pocket. Break a branch off the banyan tree, tie the remaining strip around the end of the branch and light it from the embers.

I am going to need a torch if I'm to follow the blood trail back out of here once I am finished with you."

"You are healed," said Persephone desperately. "Isn't that—"

"Enough?" said Mordesius as he tossed the sword to one side, scooped up Baby Finn and pressed Persephone's own dagger to his little throat. "No, Your Majesty, it is not."

Whistling cheerfully, he watched as she knelt at his feet doing all that he'd ordered. When she finally managed to light the torch, he used the dagger to gesture toward the dirt incline at the back of the cavern. There was nothing Persephone could do but start walking. Torch in hand and Azriel at her heels, she climbed the incline and entered the tunnel. Tormented by the sound of Baby Finn's pitiful cries, she stumbled this way and that in response to Mordesius's commands, marking the tunnel wall with the General's blood whenever Mordesius ordered her to do so until at last he said,

"Stop."

Persephone looked around the smooth-walled, dead-end cave, knowing it would be their tomb.

Pushing down her rising panic, she turned to Mordesius and said, "If you will let them go, I will do—"

"Anything?" he suggested with a broad smile. "Yes, well, the time for that has come and gone, Your Majesty. I confess there was a time when the thought of you tormented—no, plagued—me, but no longer. Set the torch there, by that big, flat rock. Then, once your dear husband has rid himself of his burden and gotten to his knees where he has ever belonged, bind his wrists and ankles. And mind that you bind them well, Your Majesty, or I will slice off your son's tiny feet."

With shaking hands, Persephone jammed the torch between two smaller rocks on the floor and then bound Azriel's wrists and ankles. When she was done, Mordesius walked over to the flat rock, set Baby Finn down upon it and coyly crooked his finger at her. Heart beating very hard at the thought that this might be her chance,

Persephone walked over to him. She was so close to Baby Finn that she could have reached out and run her fingers through his downy hair, but she did not.

"Give me the last of those cloth strips," said Mordesius, holding out his free hand. "Then turn around and put your hands together."

Wordlessly, Persephone handed him the cloth strips and turned around. Then, the instant she heard him set down the dagger to free up his hands, she flung her elbow toward his face. There was an audible crack as it hit him in the cheek—and another one as Mordesius jerked her around and clouted her across the face with all of his considerable might.

"Bitch!" he snarled, throwing her to the ground face-first while she was still reeling from the shock of the blow. Dropping on top of her so heavily that it drove the air from her lungs, he quickly bound her wrists. Then he rolled her onto her back and gave her a hot kiss before standing up and kicking her across the floor. "I've brought you, your husband, your son and the General here because I do not wish to see or smell your rotting corpses every time I visit my new pool, Your Majesty," he panted as he stared down at her. "Using your dagger, I shall inflict a mortal wound upon your son. As he lies dying, I will make the worthless cockroach watch while I ravish you. Then I will make you watch while I slit his throat. Then, and only then, will I grant you the mercy of death."

Mordesius smiled at Persephone and lifted the dagger high so that she could see the blade glinting in the flickering torchlight. Then, without further ado, he turned and strode toward Baby Finn.

Half-wild with terror and nearly choking on her rage, Persephone screamed, *"My Methusian husband and son are worth a thousand of you, you pathetic lowborn nobody!"*

At these words, Mordesius let out a strangled cry and whirled around, his eyes mad with fury. As he did so, his robe billowed out so far that the hem brushed the flame of the flickering torch.

If Murdock's cloak had not been so long and so well-made, Mordesius's robe might have been damp enough to keep it from catching fire.

But alas for him, it was not, and so before Persephone—or, indeed, Mordesius—realized what was happening, his robe, his hair and even his skin were ablaze. Shrieking horribly, the former regent staggered this way and that before falling to the ground and rolling and writhing until the last of the flames had been snuffed out.

Stunned, Persephone stared at the moaning, smoldering, unrecognizable creature that had been her enemy.

"The dagger," said Azriel.

Nodding jerkily, Persephone staggered to her feet, skittered around Mordesius and awkwardly picked up the dagger in her yet-bound hands. In a trice, she'd sliced through the cloth strips that bound Azriel, and he'd done the same for her.

Then she had Baby Finn in her arms, and Azriel had his arms around them both.

"Pleeeeease," came a hoarse whisper from the floor of the cave. "Do not . . . leave me . . . like . . . this . . . take me . . . take me back . . ."

"Let's go," said Azriel in a hard voice.

"Mercy," breathed Mordesius, stretching his burnt claw of a hand out toward Persephone. "*Mercyyyyy.*"

Persephone stared at him, knowing that there was no one in the kingdom who deserved mercy less, but also knowing that her kingdom would be better served by having him publicly tried and executed, that she might demonstrate her intention to be a just queen, come what may. Taking a deep breath, she was about to explain all this to Azriel when she looked up at him and saw that no explanation was necessary.

Her husband knew her better than she knew herself; perhaps he always had.

"You get the wooden torch," he said with a slightly exasperated shake of his head. "I'll get the human one."

They followed the blood smears back to the cavern with all due haste. Even so, they got there too late to save Mordesius.

Not because he had perished before they arrived, but because they arrived to discover that the banyan tree had withered and the hole in the ground that had only a short time before contained miraculous healing waters was as dry as if it had ever been so.

Setting Mordesius down by the edge of the vanished pool, Azriel slowly walked around it as though in search of clues. When he came to the place where the General had fallen, he exhaled with sudden understanding.

"What is it, Azriel?" asked Persephone in a hushed voice. "What happened?"

"Do you remember that night by the river when I told you that according to legend, the pool dried up the first time because someone had tainted it by spilling the blood of a trusted companion at its edge?" he replied. "Well, it would seem that General Murdock was Mordesius's trusted companion."

"So the pool has dried up again?" whispered Persephone, hugging Baby Finn close. "It is gone—forever?"

"Maybe not forever," said Azriel quietly. "But I daresay you and I will never see it again, and neither will Mordesius."

At these words, the burnt creature that had once been the all-powerful Regent of Glyndoria let out a heart-rending wail and fell forward, dead, into the bone-dry bed of the vanished healing pool that might have saved his life.

Epilogue

PERSEPHONE, AZRIEL AND Baby Finn spent two long, cold, hungry days in the sea cave waiting for the storm to abate.

Within an hour of it doing so, Cairn had noticed Ivan circling high above the sea caves, Robert had followed a panicked Fleet to the edge of the cliff leading down to the royal quay, and Barka, Fayla and the royal guard had braved the still-frothing sea to follow Cur into the cave to the very spot where the grateful royal family sat waiting.

The weeks and months that followed were the happiest of Persephone's life. Baby Finn thrived, Moira grew strong and, thanks to Neeka, who tended him ceaselessly and plied him with quail's eggs at every opportunity, Zdeno made a full recovery from the wound he'd taken on the night of the baby's kidnapping. Each day Persephone ruled her realm with the fair and steady hand of a good queen who would someday be known as great; each night, she made love to Azriel as freely, tirelessly and passionately as if she were a nobody who was head over heels in love with a chicken thief.

One sunny afternoon, about six months after the ordeal in the sea caves, Azriel strode into Persephone's sitting room and ordered her to fetch the baby and follow him to the royal garden. Amused, she did as he bid.

"You know, I don't think you're allowed to order me around," she said with a smile as they stepped into the courtyard. "I am the queen, after all."

"Close your eyes," he commanded sternly.

"They are closed," she said.

"Well, you'd better keep them that way," warned Azriel as he began to guide her down a little-used garden path, "or I will be forced to up and give you a good spanking."

At these familiar teasing words, Persephone laughed. Baby Finn gurgled in delight at the sound and reached up to give her hair a yank. As she gave him a tickle in the ribs that made him giggle helplessly, Azriel suddenly stopped walking. Stepping behind Persephone, he slipped his arms around her waist, laid his cheek aside her own and whispered, "Open your eyes, wife."

She opened them at once and then inhaled in amazement.

For there, tucked away into a hidden corner of the royal garden, was a pretty little thatch-roofed cottage. It had a yard full of scratching chickens, an oak tree with a swing hung from a low branch, a neat little garden and a pond that Persephone just knew was stocked with fish.

"A place for you to retreat from your cares, Your Majesty," murmured Azriel. "It is appointed exactly as I ever promised, except that instead of keeping a fat pig and growing our own grain, I thought we'd just order up bacon, beer and bread from the royal kitchens. What do you think?"

Turning in his arms, Persephone kissed him deeply. "Oh, Azriel," she sighed as she pulled away from him. "I think you are perfect."

Looking extremely pleased by her assessment of him, Azriel took her by the hand and led her over to the oak tree. After helping her and Baby Finn settle onto the swing, he gently began to push them. As Persephone listened to the sound of her son's gurgles and felt the warm sun on her face, she reveled in the knowledge that the three of them would be together tomorrow and for a thousand tomorrows thereafter.

She, Azriel and Baby Finn—the Methusian who would be king.

Acknowledgments

Writing may be a solitary endeavor, but bringing books into the world is absolutely a team effort. So I'd like to start by expressing my gratitude to everyone at Tundra Books for doing such a tremendous job with the Fractured Kingdom trilogy. Special thanks to Sophie Paas-Lang for designing beautiful, eye-catching covers, to my publicist Graciela Colin and to the entire editorial team. In addition to working with talented copyeditors, proofreaders, sensitivity readers and cold readers, I was lucky enough to work with two exceptional editors along the way. Margot Blankier's diligence, understanding and unwavering enthusiasm made her a joy to work with, and the incomparable Lynne Missen not only pushed me to make these books the best they could be, but also championed them—twice. My heartfelt gratitude to both of them.

Thanks to my sister Angela Robbie, my brother Steven Gannon and my friends, near and far—Martha Stephens, Sandy Kunkel, Susie Brown, my gifted writer pals Colleen Nelson and Jodi Carmichael, and so many others. Throughout my writing journey, they've always been there for me—celebrating successes, commiserating over disappointments, offering encouragement and gleefully front-facing my books in unsuspecting bookstores and libraries all over the world. I don't know what I'd do without them.

My children, Hannah, Sophie and Sam, have my boundless gratitude for being my brainstormers, my beta readers, my editors, my cheering section. For attending every book launch, for the hugs and high fives, for forgiving me every time I locked them out of my writing room because I was frantically trying to meet a deadline. If there is a mother out there who is as lucky as I am, I haven't met her.

As for my husband Nick, I could spend a thousand lifetimes thanking him and it wouldn't be enough. It was he who first encouraged me to become a writer and he who treated my writing like it mattered long before I ever got published. He has supported me in a hundred big and little ways, had my back through thick and thin and, most of all, encouraged me to dream big and believe that anything is possible. Azriel wishes he was as perfect as Nick.

Last but by no means least, I'd like to extend a heartfelt thanks to every reader who entered the Fractured Kingdom and let themselves get caught up in the adventure.

You are the reason I do what I do.

M.L. FERGUS's many books for young people have been translated into more than a dozen languages, optioned for television, adapted for stage, and won or been shortlisted for numerous prestigious awards. She writes illustrated books for young readers under the name Maureen Fergus. She lives in Winnipeg, Canada with her family.

More information about M.L. Fergus can be found on her website www.maureenfergus.com.